THE HARD WAY IN

A HARRY AND THE HULA GIRL INVESTIGATION

LEIGH ERBE

The Hard Way In

Avondale-Arden Publishing, LLC

Louisville, KY 40220 USA

The best-laid schemes o' mice an' men / Gang aft agley
(Robert Burns, “To a Mouse”)

THE HARD WAY IN

A HARRY AND THE HULA GIRL INVESTIGATION

1

SUMMER SUNSHINE

The little hula girl on my Volvo's dash swished her grass skirt to and fro in rhythm with the road. Seductively, if you could believe her eyes. Or maybe just happy to be rolling through the pines. Plastic-for-brains little bimbo. What the hell did she know.

Last time I'd driven the highway slicing through the woods encasing Kipling was more than fifteen years ago. January of '73, a Friday. But back then, I'd been headed out of town as fast as my cop car could carry me—which wasn't very fast. A winter snowstorm was busy covering the asphalt, slowing my getaway.

The snow was turning the pine trees into cocaine-whitened confections. Wind-whipped birches quivered beside the towering evergreens, the storm's fury stripping bark from trees as thoroughly as the quiet of the grave was busy sloughing skin from the body of the woman I'd killed. Images of sorrow, acid-etched on my brain. But that was then.

This afternoon was different, sort of. The highway still ran straight through miles of trees, but now a summer sun beat down. No snow today. And instead of running from Kipling, a cop in a cop car with my partner beside me, I cruised back toward town, a shamus in a green Volvo with only a little hula girl for backup.

So, only small differences.

Yet some things remained the same. My head still ached with a grief the majesty of trees couldn't dispel. And I drove the highway with the same haunted memories still stoppered in my skull, corked now like soured wine, fermenting, because the golden-haired woman I'd loved all those long years ago was still dead.

"Stop it, Reno," I said out loud. "You didn't really kill her." *Yeah, right.* The silent reproach echoing between my ears. Like always.

Fifteen years of hiding the memory of her death from myself, consciously avoiding the town that got me bounced from my job as a detective on the attorney general's Special Investigations Squad. But alcohol only quenches certain thirsts, and nightmares have a way of pulling drowned thoughts back to the surface. Now I was headed back, but why?

"To find her killer," I heard myself say. Yeah, maybe.

"To find out why she had to die." That, too, perhaps.

Or maybe only headed back to do the job the insurance company had hired me to do: investigate last November's cabin fire; flash my private license around; discover what I could about some redheaded broad who'd crisped herself in her cabin.

I just hadn't decided yet what it was I wanted to do.

The little hula girl didn't know the answer, either. Because if she did, she sure as hell wouldn't still be wearing that shit-eating plastic grin of hers. Not headed back into Kipling, she wouldn't. But she was. Well, good for her.

Up ahead, the old scenic overlook. I pulled off. No reason, just habit. The Volvo jerked to a stop. I rolled her window down, breathed in the pine scent, climbed out to look around.

Kipling still lay spread out below, snug against a long concave arc of lakefront. Dark evergreens standing guard on lakeside cliffs framed the town on the landward side, while silver-blue lake water lapped at brown beaches and weathered docks and gently rocked boats riding at anchor in the harbor.

But the place had expanded. New houses on the outskirts, a hospital complex downtown, construction everywhere. A booming city now instead of the small lakeside town it was last time. But still a North Woods vision of Paradise. Or not.

Back then, the town roared, wide open and fearless: drugs—gambling—prostitution. All illegal and nobody cared. The town fathers wanted things that way—crooked. And I guess the town mothers had liked it, too. Whatever, nobody kicked about it back then. Maybe now they felt differently, but I doubted it.

Today I could see one difference, though: the Wigwam Casino, sitting a ways out of town, hard by the lake. Not there back then, but the billboards on the new four-lane running through the pines wouldn't let you forget it sat here now. Gambling made legal, respectable.

I let my fingers rub the back of my neck, tried kneading some worry from my soul. Didn't work. Legalizing gambling wouldn't have changed anything down there. Still drugs for sale, women turning tricks, and God alone knows what else going on.

"Stop being preachy." Alone, so why not talk out loud?

"What the hell else you gonna do in these woods, Reno, if you can't gamble and whore? You gonna saw logs for fun?"

No answer to offer myself, so I peered into the Volvo, studying the little hula girl. She'd stopped wiggling. Damn. On my own again.

Hey, maybe stop in at the Wigwam Casino. Maybe drop a dollar or two, drink a beer, take in the casino's Vegas-Style Revue, compare showgirl wiggles to hula girl wiggles. The billboards on the highway led you to believe you might even enjoy it, might even see some skin, while the casino skinned you. So yeah, why not?

And out on the lake, something else new. White marble, the roofline of a Greek temple maybe, poking through the pines, lit by the setting sun, on what had been just a rock-strewn wooded island fifteen years ago. What the hell sort of tourist trap could that be?

Sail out. See that, too. Drink some beers, drown some memories.

Tears streaked my cheeks. Maybe only the wind causing my eyes to juice—maybe not, though. God, but I still missed her, missed her most because I'd killed her.

But at least I didn't hear any sobbing. Instead, the tears flowed silently. Then the nose started leaking. Time to blow and go, shamus.

I slammed the Volvo's door shut. Maybe that made her mad. I don't know. Anyhow, I had to ask her twice to get us going again. Old piece of shit. But the little hula girl must have liked the way I closed the door. She was wiggling again.

"Reno," I whispered so Hawaii's hottie wouldn't hear, "just go down there, find what the insurance company wants you to find, what you're paid to find, and get the hell out of Kipling. Just figure out what happened in that damn cabin last November.

"Maybe the redhead really did torch her own place and then hung up on life. Or maybe someone did it for her. I know what the cops say. And I also know an important son of a bitch says it ain't so." Hell, no more whispering. The little hula girl could give a shit. She was too busy gazing at trees to pay attention to me.

So I just yelled the rest of my rant. She could listen or not. Her choice.

"Or nose around and find the truth Iron Mac and the rest of us missed back then. Maybe even sprinkle a little justice around on the filth down there." I banged a fist hard against the steering wheel, an emphasis only my paw noticed.

"But try to make it your choice this time, not theirs." I shook the hurt off, glanced at the little hula girl. No reaction. The wind juicing my eyes must have snatched my words away.

The easy choice or the hard one? The Volvo headed down into town. Harry Reno was never good at taking the easy way out, never smart enough to avoid the hard way in.

Why should it be any different this time?

2

FORTUNATE FINDS

As the Volvo rolled down from the overlook and on into town, I decided it might be good to know what really happened in that cabin last November, even if it had nothing to do with the dead love of my life. Guess I'd ask around. Knock on doors. Uncover whatever I could. Earn my retainer.

Or just say screw it, and head back home to Penelope. Yeah, mind made up, all right.

Shit, first day of this Kipling gig and the ghosts were already spooking me. I just wanted it over with, and fast. Before it churned my insides into . . . Ah, hell. The gnawing jitters in the pit of my stomach weren't bad memories. Just simple hunger pangs from a too-long-ago feeding earlier today.

Around noon, I had stopped for lunch at a Chinese joint—sweet-and-sour chicken, white rice, and an egg roll. Not perfect, but pretty tasty. The waiter brought me a fortune cookie along with the check. When I cracked open the cookie, the fortune read:

ENLIGHTENING EXPERIENCES AWAITS!

Somewhere in China or San Francisco, or wherever the hell they bake fortune cookies, some guy's job is to insert messages for me to find. And I've come to believe it's my job to internalize the wisdom of the fortunes. So I eat the little slips of paper. Yeah, it's goofy, but I usually eat alone and it gives me something other than the restaurant door to look forward to after my meal.

And I tend to pay attention to the fortunes. Even when the grammar or the spelling is off a bit, or the syntax garbled.

Still, I didn't much like what this one promised, because somebody —a female somebody—had pressured me into taking this Kipling shit-work. Nobody likes being told what to do. And if nothing else, at least I qualify as a nobody.

I left my usual 20 percent for a tip on the table, along with the fortune cookie and its message, both uneaten. Enlightening experiences, my ass. By God, I'd show Penny. And so I had, and now I was hungry again. Guess I should have had the cookie.

Since it was almost dinnertime, the Volvo stopped at a diner in Kipling I used to love back then. Only now it'd gone posh—Valet Parking Only. Or so said the sign. The old Volvo already had enough of a Swedish inferiority complex without me inflicting an indignity like that on her.

A couple of blocks into the less-well-heeled side of Kipling, I spotted a bar and grill I thought we both could stomach—the Tam-O'-Shanter. Two neon signs glowed in the windows: a cool-blue *Cold Beer* and a blood-red *Authentic Angus Beef*. The joint had a gravel lot. The Volvo found a spot to her liking, and in I went.

Didn't step on any sawdust on the floor. Didn't see any barroom bloodstains. Nor any drunks passed out in booths. But still, not the Ritz, either—just a neighborhood saloon sporting a spritz of stale beer and testosterone.

Behind the bar stood a powerhouse of a man, polishing glasses. An inch or so taller than my six feet. A few pounds chunkier, too. And a little older. Still, he seemed able to defend the bar's Scotch all on his own without help from me or anyone else. I walked my eyes a little closer.

One of those stupid Scottish hats hung behind the bar. Maybe it had something to do with the bar's name. Maybe it belonged on the bartender's bald head. I decided not to ask. Better get to know him a little better first before I needled him about his choice of headgear—one of his arms made two of mine. They looked to be hard arms, too.

I sat down at the bar instead of taking a booth. The Scottish giant smiled. He seemed sort of familiar. Rust-red whiskers covered his face, like Scottish heather run amuck. I began to detect a theme here. His face glowed a brighter red wherever the whiskers weren't.

A black-and-green tartan apron struggled unsuccessfully to conceal his generous girth. But those arms—well, they were arms you should think twice about, before you decided to say something to their owner you shouldn't. So for once I took my own advice and submarined my smart-ass self deep inside.

"What'll it be, laddie?" the bartender said, no trace of a Scottish burr, none whatsoever.

"How about a beer. You fry steaks in here?"

"Aye," the bartender said. The beer appeared. So did the bar's cook. He nabbed the meal ticket from his boss and scooted back into the kitchen.

His "Gotcha covered" lingered after him for a moment, then that too disappeared.

3

AN ANGUS BEEF

I finished off the rib eye and home fries and glanced up from the beer I'd been nursing while I ate. Down at the end of the bar, the red-whiskered giant looked up from his newspaper and ambled over. "Need another beer, laddie?"

"Yeah, I do."

"Two fifty," he said.

I frowned. "One fifty last time."

"You've been sipping your beer a wee bit too long. Happy hour's come and gone. Two fifty." I put the money on the bar.

"You're not from around here, are you, laddie?" His question held only curiosity, not suspicion.

"Is it that obvious?"

"Still a small enough place. I got my Regulars and my Occasionals."

"Occasionals?" I said.

"Yeah, you know. They come here because they had occasion to get thrown out of the other bars." He laughed. I laughed. Seemed better to laugh with him than at him. Those forearms of his weren't all that funny. Not at all.

"Well, you're right. I'm not from around here."

"You're a cop," he said, more observation than question.

"You like cops?"

"Two local boys over in the back booth," the giant said.

I glanced in the direction he'd pointed, decided either I didn't know them, or maybe just didn't remember them. I'd forced as much of Kipling from my brain as I could and tamped the rest down deep. So no surprise I didn't recognize them. They might know me, though. I still had a name and reputation floating around. Sometimes someone put the two together with my face, said hello—sometimes a friendly hello, most often not.

I turned back to the barkeep. "They like coming in here?"

"Yeah, and I like having them. Keeps the place quiet. I like that. The Occasionals have their fun elsewhere. When they come in here, they gotta behave. Everybody that comes in here's gotta behave, laddie. Cops help people behave."

He shot me a look shading halfway toward friendly. "And as long as cops behave themselves, they're more than welcome in here."

"You don't just work here, do you? The Tam-O'-Shanter's your bar."

"What makes you think so?" he asked.

"The clean mirror. The way you wash and polish the glasses. Way you're careful when you stack them. Help doesn't always do that; an owner always does."

"You're pretty observant," he said. "Like a cop."

He still didn't seem hostile, but not overly friendly, either. A barkeep who keeps his bar as he likes it—buddies in, riffraff out. Guess he was still making up his mind which I was.

"But those local boys don't seem to recognize you," he said, "and those two know everybody. Or else they don't want to know you. I'm not asking. I don't want any trouble in here, laddie. I run a nice quiet little bar."

The bartender glanced around—looking for noise, I suppose.

"If you're nosing after info—well, wrong place. Try the Rowdy Times. Least that's what they called it yesterday. Changes hands a lot."

"Just an ex-cop. That okay?" I asked.

"Yeah, it's okay. And it's a buck fifty. Not being a Regular or an Occasional, you wouldn't know happy hour, would you?"

"No, but two fifty's good. Making a go of a bar isn't always easy," I said.

"You're right about that, friend." One hand scooped up my money, the other paw held itself out. "Gus MacGregor. Short it be for Angus," he said through a red-whiskered grin.

"Harry Reno," I said as we shook.

Over at a booth a hand went up, so Gus headed over, no barmaid in evidence just then. Out from behind the bar where I could see the big man better, I noticed he didn't so much waddle as roll with his weight. Bet he could move fast enough when he needed to. Probably the real reason why his was a quiet little bar.

Gus deposited the empties and took some more beers back to the booth. Settled behind his bar once more, he wiped his forehead with his towel, puffed his cheeks, and let a little whiff of effort escape. Then he rested those massive arms on his bar and leaned forward, poking his eyes into mine. "What brings you to Kipling again, Harry?"

"Insurance," I said, ignoring his *again* for the moment. "Don't worry. I'm not selling. Just checking on a claim."

"The judge's burned-out cabin, laddie?"

"Maybe." Wouldn't stay a secret long. "What makes you think that's where I've been?"

Gus handed me his bar towel. "The wee soot smudge on your forehead." His laugh lingered while he walked down to the end of his bar —squinted—took a photo from a corkboard crowded with pictures.

"The AG's Special Investigations Squad. The Goon Squad, we called 'em. I figure that's you on the left, right above the name *Harry Reno*. 'Bout fifteen-something years ago, right before I started this bar. Not being a deputy anymore, I been collecting these little mementos." Gus waved the photo around.

"Your hair's a wee bit more gray now, laddie. Makes you look like that Indiana Jones guy in the movies."

"Who?" I said.

"Indiana Jones. Harrison Ford? *Raiders of the Lost Ark*? Come on,

Harry. You know who I mean." Gus folded those arms of his across his chest, let muscles bulge like he was working his way into some kind of Scottish hissy fit. "Quit messing with me, Harry."

I tossed his towel onto the bar and slid off my stool to go check out his collection, see if I could calm the Highland palooka down a bit.

"I don't go to movies. Waste of time," I said. "Unless it's Bogart." But I said it with a smile. No need to match my mood to his.

Some of the men I recognized from before—when I'd been a detective in the attorney general's office. I patted the Scottish giant's shoulder, pointed out the cops I remembered.

Then I saw her, like you see your own fresh-dug grave, just waiting there for you to deep-six yourself. I stumbled back to my bar stool. Gus trailed after me, almost as upset as I was.

"Sorry, Harry. I'm . . . oh hell." Gus popped the top on a beer and started to set it down. *On the house,* he was trying to say. I grabbed at the beer, almost knocking the bottle out of his hand, just pouring it inside of me.

"We don't talk about that much anymore around here," the bartender said. "And I just forgot her picture was there. You just surprised me, coming in here, you know, unannounced. No warning. Sorry, Harry." Gus's apology flowed out quick, as quick as the beer sliding down my throat.

I put money on the bar, forced words out. "I got no beef with what you hang on your walls. So forget it, Angus. I have." A fine sheen of tears began to sprout in my green eyes. "I'll be in town for a while. Just so you know."

I found my way out of the bar before the eyes let the tears have it their way. Damn that picture of her, damn it to hell.

The Volvo started on the first try. The little hula girl stayed quiet as the grave. Guess they sensed my foul mood. I headed us toward the motel the insurance company had decided to spring for, my soul as sour as my soul ever gets.

On the way, I stopped and bought some beer—full strength, no lite stuff. I had some heavy thinking still to do tonight. I even let a half-pint of whiskey rub my palm for a moment—my sour mood, remember?

But I put the bottle back on its shelf. I had a job to do tomorrow, a list of people the insurance company wanted me to see. So, no bourbon tonight, just beer. And maybe no hangover in the morning. Wouldn't that be something different.

The motel the company put me up in would be cheap. It always was. But maybe it would be quiet, too. I'd had enough fun for one day.

4
BRAS FROM ABOVE

The motel ice machine growled at me like a pit bull guarding a crack house. So I kicked it. It calmed down and filled my ice bucket. As I headed back to my first-floor room, sounds of partying floated down from above. Beers clanking, country music twanging, off-key voices singing along. Big pickups and muddy Jeeps filled the motel parking lot. Construction cowboys easing their way toward the end of the day.

A beer bottle thrown from somewhere overhead shattered out in the parking lot behind me. A black bra floated down from the party above and landed in front of me, followed by a red chest harness. One bra's owner draped herself over the railing and waved, her newly liberated assets bouncing and jiggling.

I saluted back and chuckled. A free Las Vegas–style floor show, no cover charge. The bean counter at the insurance company I was working for would love the *free* part. But as to how and why bras slip off babes, well, he wouldn't have any idea how to account for that. None at all.

I stepped over the bras and opened the door to my cheap-ass, company-approved room. I iced down the beers in the sink, nabbed one, and settled into the only halfway decent thing in the room: a worn-out recliner. Looked and smelled like it'd been filched from some other motel's Dumpster.

As I downed the beer, I tried keeping my mind blank, letting memories of the golden-haired love of a lifetime sink deep inside. Wasn't working.

Why'd that fucking barkeep put that fucking picture of her right where I fucking couldn't miss it? Just too damn hard now to forget I'd killed her.

Hell, not Gus's fault. Not really. *She'd* drawn me tonight. I knew she had, just like she did so long ago—me a moth to her flame, as the trite phrase goes. I only ended up singed by the candle; she finished snuffed out. But even cold in the grave, she still had a hold on me. All she had to do was let me see her. And she had tonight.

———

Yesterday, I'd been a reasonably happy, if somewhat underemployed shamus, sitting in my own one-man two-room private investigation bureau. On the outer office door, gold letters proclaimed who and what awaited you within:

HARRY RENO—CONFIDENTIAL INVESTIGATIONS

No secretary prowled the premises. But if you pushed the buzzer by the inner door—the one lettered PRIVATE—you might hear "It's open," if I was there. And if you were admitted to my inner sanctum, there I would be—waiting. Waiting for a client, waiting for the phone to ring, the door to open, the next page of the newspaper to splash something of interest across itself. Just waiting.

And now, sitting in my cheap-ass motel room, I wished nothing had happened yesterday. But it had. The telephone had rung.

"Mr. Harry Reno, please," a superior-sounding female voice had said. No, not said, but intoned. Yeah, that's the word: *intoned*. And *superior-sounding* because she spoke with a British accent. Not Boston snobby, just pure Brit and sexy as hell. But still, she intoned rather than said. I hate when she pulls that shit on me.

"Whom shall I say is calling?" I said, trying to imitate her Brit speak. No go. Mine sucks. Plus, I never can get *who* and *whom* working right. But the voice on the phone always does.

"Cut it out, Harry. You want work or don't you?" The superiority faded somewhat. The accent stayed. It was real. And the bite to it unmistakable. I wasn't intimidated, though. Not yet, anyway.

"Want or need?" I said. "Sometimes they're one and the same, sometimes not."

"Thank you. I shall connect you with Mr. Dillingham." Her voice superior once more. Well, hell. Stuart Dillingham III, the bane of my existence, the benefactor of my bank account. Sometimes they're one and the same, too.

"Reno? Dillingham here. I have an assignment for you." His voice direct. Precise. Superior in a bad way. I hated it.

"I'm listening."

"There has been a claim made which the company has denied."

"Nothing unusual in that." My sneer audible. Dillingham's a pompous asshole.

"Really, Reno, your attitude is a puzzlement at times." A numbskull asshole to boot.

"So you denied a claim. So what?"

"Apparently it bears a trifle more looking into. The company would like you to oblige." Wow.

"Who's putting the squeeze on? Which one of those big-city, billboard-advertising attorneys has you by the balls now?" Needling Stuart Dillingham III just comes naturally. He invites it.

"Really, Reno, you must seek to control that attitude you too often manifest. Perhaps I shall employ one of our brighter, younger investigators instead."

"Suit yourself." I hung up.

After a minute, my phone rang again.

"Mr. Harry Reno, please," the British-to-the-core female voice intoned once more.

"Who's calling?" My snarl too angry to worry over *who* or *whom*.

"Don't piss him off, Harry. You need this one," Penelope Phair said. "You may not want it, but you need it."

"Same question, Penny. Want or need? Sometimes they're one and the same. Sometimes not."

"It's *Kipling*, Harry. Thank you. I'll connect you with Mr. Dillingham again."

I sat there frozen, my ass stuck to the chair, the rest of me Popsicle-cold too, waiting for Dillingham's voice, dreading a Kipling assignment.

"Harry. So sorry about the connection problem."

So it's Harry now. And my hang-up merely a connection problem? You must need me bad for this one, Stu. But then again, it's Kipling—who the hell else you gonna call?

My ass could move a little. It'd come unstuck. But dread still sat cold and hard in my gut, like a swallowed snowball.

"An insured has become deceased and the beneficiary has presented a claim on the life insurance. And, also, a related demand on a homeowners policy," Dillingham said.

Deceased, huh. Insureds do that sometimes. Big deal. I kept all of that inside, though, and tried listening to Dillingham a little more closely. He still hadn't said anything about Kipling.

"The beneficiary on the life insurance is also the company's insured on the homeowners policy. The company has decided more information should be garnered before we finalize the company's position as to the claims."

"Once again, who's putting the squeeze on, and why? And incidentally, who's the deceased, who's the beneficiary, and where did the tragic events transpire, Stu?" He hates Stu. I love it.

"Really, Reno."

So it's Reno again. All right, I'd had my fun, and I did need to pay the office rent. Even a modern-day shamus needs a place to call his own. Clients expect it.

"How about some facts before I say yea or nay?" Penelope's *Kipling* still gnawing at me.

"The position is easily stated," he said. "A young lady is the deceased. The police and coroner conclude suicide. The police and fire department also reach the conclusion the fire was deliberately set, perhaps by the deceased. And the life insurance policy was only recently underwritten. Suspicious, Reno. Hence, our denial of the life insurance claim—standard suicide clause, you know—and perhaps a hesitation as to the homeowner's demand."

"Who's the deceased's unhappy beneficiary?" I asked.

"Her uncle, Judge Arthur Walker-Doer." An icy wind blew out of the phone and into my ear.

"The judge maintains that his niece, Mallory Mordred, did not commit suicide. Nor did she set fire to his cabin." The chill from the phone seeped into my head and crept down my back.

"The judge states unequivocally that she was murdered. He has not, however, divulged by whom." Now my ass was Popsicle-cold again. Kipling and Walker-Doer and murder. A less than salubrious combination, as the judge would probably phrase it—fucking old fraud.

"Go on" was all I could manage. Hope to God the cold of the grave wrapping icy fingers around my soul wasn't frosting the phone lines, too.

"Are you still there, Reno? The connection seems poor."

"I'm here. So, Walker-Doer says you owe him some money, and you said no." There. I'd said the devil's name. The ice cracked a bit. "So what?"

"You make it appear personal on my part, Reno. It is merely the company's present position. I myself have never had the pleasure of meeting the esteemed judge, the Honorable Arthur Walker-Doer."

Stuart Dillingham III didn't have to work at sounding pompous. He was a natural, remember?

"You'll never have that pleasure, Stu."

"And why might that be, my good sir?" Dillingham just couldn't turn it off.

"Because nobody's ever pleased to meet the judge—not never, Stu."

Dillingham ignored my wisecrack. He didn't even wait for me to say yes or no to the assignment.

Instead, he told me he'd have "Our Mistress Phair" send over the "Company File" by "Courier" along with my "Retainer." Stu adores pontificating in capitals, but he had said the magic word—*retainer*.

And while I like money as well as the next guy, Kipling was something I had thought I could do without forever. But apparently Penelope Phair didn't share that feeling. Maybe she was tired of my nightmares waking us up in the middle of the night.

I had hoped Penny would come over with the company file and my check, playing the courier part herself, wearing something revealing. She didn't.

Arnold, the office runner, showed up instead. Fully clothed, thank God.

5
A COWBOY AND COP COTILLION

But that was yesterday. Tonight, I was pacing the carpet, measuring the room, slugging down beer, trying to avoid thinking about the woman I'd killed back then. Wasn't working.

I grabbed another beer, made myself sit in the big recliner again, quiet like, to do some thinking.

Fifteen years ago, I was a detective in the attorney general's Special Investigations Squad. Detectives traveled in a four-cop squad back then. Most times, Mac McCabe and I bunked together. The other pair varied. And most nights, after we'd had dinner, we'd all sit in one motel room and review what we'd done that day. Then Iron Mac, the squad commander, would line out the day ahead.

After that, the TV came on and the sports bullshit began—basketball, football, baseball, even golf. Sometimes fucking bowling. The hell with that. I'd sit with a chess book and my travel chess set—the sort where the chess pieces wear little pegs on their bottoms and the fold-out board is drilled full of holes—replaying a grand master's greatest victory or defeat.

But none of that tonight. I sat alone, my little electronic ChessWiz untouched while I tried drowning sorrow in suds. Then, over on the nightstand, the telephone decided I'd had enough of alone.

"Yeah?" My tough-guy hello—sounding pissed because I was. The telephone's squawk had screeched my train of thought right off the tracks. Plus, my beer was empty.

So who the hell was this bothering me? And why?

"Mr. Reno?" Sweet, female, inquiring. Not Penny, that was for sure. I softened a little.

"Yeah. Who's this?"

"My name's Gwen Poole," the voice said.

"Okay." My throat tightened while something in my stomach decided to do somersaults.

"I think you knew my mother. And I kind of remember you. At least, I think I do, Mr. Reno."

"Okay." My repartee simply scintillating tonight.

"Is this a bad time? I could call tomorrow." Still sweet, still female.

"No, tonight's good." Gruff. I couldn't turn it off.

"If it's not a good time, I can call tomorrow. Really I can." Jesus, grow some balls, kid.

"Quit apologizing." I wasn't sure I could do this. "What do you want?"

"Well—" Sweet hesitation, like her mother. Gruff took a hike. I was hooked.

"Gus said you were here in Kipling. After I finally got to work. He told me, 'Take off, go see him,' I mean you. I guess I just want to talk to you. I'm not making much sense, am I?"

"You're doing fine, kid. Just fine." God, but she sounded beautiful.

"I just wanted to see if you could help me. Maybe help me think through some things. From back then. Before Mom . . . died. I know you're here working now. I can pay you for your time."

Pay me for my time? I thought it, but didn't say it. Don't you remember when I pushed you in the swing at the park? When I walked with you and your mother by the lake? How I helped your mother get herself killed in that double-wide pigsty of a trailer? Don't you remember how you and I tossed a last yellow daffodil on your mother's coffin together—your sweet little hand in my big rough paw?

God, I hope you don't remember that part. But pay me for my time? Never. I owe you a lifetime of whatever you want. I've just been waiting for you to ask, only waiting. None of that came out, either.

What I did say was, "Okay, I've got time to see you, and tonight's fine, kid. Where?"

"Well, actually, I'm at the front desk. Karl the night clerk let me use the phone."

"Get Karl to tell you my room number, then. And watch out for flying bras."

"What?" True puzzlement. Good—back on my game.

"Just come on over," I said. "I'll watch out for the bras."

I hung up, stepped out of my room, brushed a moth away, and looked in the direction of the motel's office for Gwen Poole.

Down the sidewalk—a tall woman walking toward me. Young, early twenties, long blond hair, and a sweet, fresh-faced look. I raised a hand.

Her mother had had those same long-limbed movements—not a swivel, not a glide, just a bewitching stride as she strolled one beautiful leg after another my way.

And her mother hadn't been quite so tall, hadn't worn her blond hair quite so long. Gwen didn't dress like her mother had either, not demure at all. Her blouse—no need to guess what it was trying to hide. And the short flouncing skirt Gwen had on reminded me of a barmaid's uniform. Oh, right. Gus's missing server tonight. Some detective you are, Reno.

But the closer Gwen came, the more I realized she and her mother would sure as hell have tied on who was the most beautiful.

Gwen saw me standing there and raised her hand to wave just as a beefy construction cowboy bounded down from above and grabbed her around the waist.

"Time to party," he shouted.

Gwen shrieked, tried to pull away.

"She's with me, buddy," I said.

"Like hell she is. Come on, let's party, baby." He pulled her toward the steps, and she tried pulling away as three more nail pounders appeared from above.

Then Gwen did the unexpected. She kicked the asshole's shin—hard. Must have hurt. He yelped and let go. I moved in—fast.

Joe Construction quit hollering about his leg and swung a drunken punch my way. I let it breeze by, stepped inside, landed a fast uppercut. He hit the concrete and stayed there.

His three buddies didn't much like the result. I showed them my .38 Smith & Wesson. Only a two-inch barrel. Still, they hesitated, unsure of their next move. But our little cotillion didn't get to decide if there would be a next dance on the card, or, if so, who my partner would be. Or is it *whom*? Three other somebodies had decided to crash the dance.

One, two, then a third cop car screeched into the motel parking lot, lights swirling, sirens cutting the night air like the wails of Irish banshees on steroids.

They slammed to a collective stop, their headlights plastering our group in harsh white beams. A big cop with an even bigger voice jumped out, commanded obedience, and got it. Not a cowboy moved.

I took my hand off the butt of my .38 and stood still, too. Gwen huddled next to me, not quite so calm. I put my arm around her. She didn't pull away and she stopped shaking so hard. God, but she felt soft. And smelled even softer. Like lilacs.

The big cop with the big voice told us to stay where we were. Nobody argued. The other two cops circled each side of our little dance group. They were big men, too. Maybe that was all they bred up here in the North Woods: big men.

"Private license. Gun on my left hip. Permit." The cop beside me told me to shut up.

The other cop walked up to Gwen, asked her, "You okay, Gwen?"

Smooth, just like me, same excellent vocabulary. But then again, he did know her well enough to call her by name. And he stood tall and handsome in his uniform—a head taller than my six feet, and, well . . . maybe a bit more handsome, maybe not.

The patch on his sleeve said *Kipling Police Department*. At least now I knew where the posse had ridden in from.

Gwen turned toward the big cop who knew her name; I suppose to tell him, *Harry Reno just saved my life.* Only she didn't get the chance. Beautiful, but not as tough as her mother. Gwen fainted right back into my arms. I held on so she didn't hit the sidewalk. Not that she would have, quick as the cop who knew her name moved.

"Give her here," he growled as he grabbed her. He pulled her to him with not so much as a thank-you kiss for me either, the bastard.

The cop with the big voice, a sergeant, had backed the three construction cowboys who were still upright over against the motel wall. Their buddy was stirring now, rubbing his jaw. I glanced at Gwen and saw her sitting on the curb now, with the cop who knew her name parked there beside her—towering over her even sitting.

"Okay if I see how Gwen is?" I asked the cop who'd told me to shut up.

"Lance, okay for him to step over?"

"Yeah," Mr. Personality said.

"Name's Harry Reno, Officer. Glad you fellows showed up." I held out my hand. Lance ignored it—one paw stayed clamped around Gwen's shoulder, the other caressed his gun.

"What the hell was Gwen doing here with you?" he asked.

Lance had hard blue eyes. He used them to hold my green ones in a frigid cop stare. I let him. It just seemed the polite thing to do, given the circumstances.

But polite didn't help. His close-cropped blond hair almost stood up and bristled. It wanted to—it was just too short to pull it off. Lance wasn't happy with Gwen. That was obvious. And the way he tilted his head didn't convey approval of me, either.

"Lance," Gwen said, "I asked myself over. He knew Mom." She brushed a blond strand back into place. "Hello, Mr. Reno."

Oh God, blue eyes that smiled like her mother's. Pastel, gentle, but soft and bright at the same time. Not frost-bright like Lance's, just beautiful, even in the harsh yellow-orange glow of parking lot lights. Blue eyes fixed right on me, right now.

Watch yourself, Reno. She's only a kid.

"Hi, Gwen," I said. "You okay?" Hey, I'd added *hi* to my okay vocabulary.

Lance the Cop ignored me. I could have been a man from Mars, and he wouldn't have shown any additional interest. He yanked Gwen up, and not so much suggested as told her, "I'm taking you home. You can talk to this Reno character tomorrow."

He turned his cop eyes on me again, his glare a prowl car's searchlight nailing an alley peeper in its beam. "After he talks to me." Hard stare. "But not before." Harder stare still—a genuine North Woods tough guy. "I want to be there when you two talk. Okay?"

Maybe Gwen just encouraged the okay in guys, but this Lance character was getting madder at her and me the longer we stood there, so I didn't argue the *okay* point for her. I did try to divert Lance's anger, though.

"Okay by me. Okay bayou?" I offered.

The hand that wasn't locked around Gwen's arm balled tight, ready to pop me. Lance had finally gotten it, figured out I was just another wise guy. But his sergeant continued to eyeball me, like he'd seen my act before.

"Easy, Lance," his sergeant said.

"Taking Gwen home then, Sarge."

Sarge didn't disagree. Lance put Gwen in his cruiser, ducking his buzzed head as he got in, and squeezed behind the wheel. It was a tight fit.

I walked over to the big-voiced sergeant. In his blue uniform he could have been any other cop I'd ever danced with. Sarge was about my size, about my age. He wore the same build, had the same world-weary face. He'd seen it all, like me. And like me, he'd realized it too late.

"Harry Reno," I said, and stuck out my hand.

Unlike Lance, he took it. A vise like the ones they use to crush cars in junkyards wrapped itself around my outstretched mitt. I crushed back. Our eyes met: two men sizing each other up. We figured it out and both let go at the same time.

"Yeah, I know," the big-voiced sergeant said. "Watch yourself, Reno. Lots of construction up here in Kipling. Stop by the PD tomorrow, early. I'll need a statement."

Sarge turned, walked away, then fired a parting shot over his shoulder. "And leave your lame-ass jokes in your suitcase. That one only works if you read it. Same old Reno." Yeah, he'd seen my act before, for sure. Wonder when?

The construction cowboys shuffled back upstairs—their party over.

6

VICTORIA'S HOUSE—ROUND ONE

Back in my motel room once again, I sank into the recliner, turned off the light, let my eyes have a rest. Didn't work.

The eyes popped open, stung by dots of parking lot light filtering into the room through holes in the curtains—ragged holes, the sort bullets would make, if someone needed a curtain to die. Reminders of the puncture the gun made in Gwen's mom all those years ago. A bullet hole I should have prevented, but didn't.

Shit, no sleep for Harry Reno, not now. I turned the nightstand light back on, nabbed a beer, and tackled what really was gnawing at my gut—my meeting earlier in the day with the retired judge I hated most in this world, the Honorable Arthur Walker-Doer.

I'd stopped there first, before I gobbled my Chinese lunch and passed on the fortune cookie, before I toured the emptiness of the judge's burned-out cabin, before I found Gus and that damn picture of Gwen's mother on his wall. Before Gwen found me.

At the judge's gated entrance, two massive pillars flanked the drive. Spotlights bored through the morning's fog soup and lit each stone shaft. Veins of red ran through gray granite, marbling the stone as if blood had seeped from the earth's core into the living rock and then run rampant when it was quarried.

From the top of one granite shaft, the head of a bull with the body of a man stared down, snarling fury to all and sundry below. On the other pillar, a goat man cavorted about, ecstatic, in an icy-cold, sculpted sort of prancing.

"Hey, boys," I said. "The old bastard home this morning?" If they worked for the judge, they'd know who I meant. A crow cawed in the distance, but that was all I got.

Since neither the bull nor the goat seemed the talkative sort, I didn't press them on why their gate was open, or what they were up to, atop their perches. The hell with those two—let them keep their petrified imaginings to themselves. I had enough stony thoughts of my own. Fucking judge.

It sure as hell wasn't a cold call I'd made on the old boy this morning. I knew Walker-Doer from the company's file: uncle of the deceased; owner of the burned cabin; the company's insured. But I also knew the son of a bitch from when I'd investigated the mess that put me where I was today: a low-rent shamus instead of a gung-ho state detective.

As the Volvo sailed along the arrow-straight private drive into the judge's estate, the accolades piled on him over the years jostled around in my head: A former prosecutor respected for his ability to size up a case and do the right thing. A retired judge with years behind him of dispensing North Woods justice from the bench with fairness to all. A silvered-haired, soft-spoken, genteel lawyer of impeccable standing.

In other words, a devious son of a bitch nobody wanted to get sideways with if they could help it—then or now—unless the nobody's name was Harry Reno.

We both knew how I felt about him, and he about me.

The oak-lined drive ended in a circle of concrete with a bubbly fountain smack in the middle. I parked the Volvo off to the side, away from the spray. "No skinny-dipping," I warned the little hula girl. All I got in return was her island smile.

The old fraud's Victorian mansion towered above me, departing lake fog kissing its upper story. The house's exterior wore a mustard yellow coat with green trim around the windows and on the gingerbread of the second-story widow's walk. The widow's walk formed the roof of the porch running across the front of the judge's hobo shack.

Wherever the mansion's walls formed angles, the house painter had slapped a blood-red hue to highlight said intersections. How appropriate.

Stacked one on top of the other, three rounded turret rooms rose on the left side of the house. The uppermost in the stack was a glassed-in lookout post, its floor-to-ceiling windows commanding the grounds and capped by a red conical roof like a rocket's nose cone.

If the old boy was up there peering out, he'd better hang on. The stacked rooms looked ready for lift-off. A crescent of green fir trees on the hill behind the house framed and completed the scene. Stone steps rose toward the porch. Not as many steps as Mr. Lincoln has at his memorial, but close enough.

Fifteen years ago, on my way out of town, I'd made up my mind to put a bullet in Walker-Doer the next time I saw him. So over the intervening years, I planned dozens of scenarios to punch the crooked bastard's ticket.

But now I know life's a little more complicated, calls for subtler solutions. Maybe I could think of one. In case I couldn't, I left my gun in the car.

Still, I wasn't particularly angry that the judge had engineered our meeting. I knew this assignment could give me the chance I needed to exorcise Kipling's demons and maybe find the solution to Gwen's mother's death. I knew Penelope wanted that. Maybe I did, too.

But standing there in the judge's driveway, about to see him for the first time in years—morning light cutting through fog, the scent of pine crisp in the air—I wasn't all that upset at the prospect. But I wasn't so happy, either. There were a hell of a lot of those damn stone steps to scramble up first.

I swallowed my pride, hobbled my honor, and climbed.

I searched for a doorbell to jab, but didn't see one. Before I could puzzle out whether to knock or yodel, the etched-glass doors swung in and their wrought-iron partners swung out. A tall, gray figure appeared in the opening.

"You are expected, Mr. Reno," the man said, his oh-so-proper delivery rubbing me an oh-so-wrong way, his condescending voice just plain pissing me off. But I stepped inside nonetheless and tried to be polite myself.

Even in the dim light of the entrance hall, I could see what the gray figure was supposed to be. Still, I walked my eyes a little closer and gave him the once-over, nose to nose, so to speak. Somebody had decked him out like an English butler, properly attired for his duties in a black-suited, traditional manner—except for a gray ponytail.

"Yeah, I'm Reno," I growled in my best tough-guy style. "What do you go by?"

"I shall go by this way, sir. The judge awaits. Mind the stairs." Damn. No name, plus a quick, butler-discreet put-down.

He pivoted gracefully on one foot, but not a swishy ballet move. It had another quality, something more akin to the easy move to the basket you see in pro basketball, if you watch pro basketball. I don't. But I still know it when I see it.

As he turned, his ponytail swung and nearly brushed my nose, and I almost took a poke at him. Gotta keep a close eye on this ponytailed clown, I said to myself—at least I think I kept it to myself. Off we went across the judge's football field of an entrance hall.

Weak sunlight filtered in through ancient stained glass. Scenes of damsels and dragons, saints and sinners, boiling fires and bloody crucifixes glowed dimly, leaving the rest of the entrance hall indistinct, ill-defined. We kept walking. If a knight was lurking anywhere in the shadows this morning, I couldn't spot him.

I followed the butler toward the staircase dominating the rear of the hall, the stairs' polished wood likely imported from some long-lost colonial empire, sawed and crafted by long-dead hands, and only to be trod on in a properly reverential manner by the feet of today.

Hell, Walker-Doer must be receiving important callers like me in his upstairs, private quarters this morning. Or not. The gray ponytail ignored the staircase and instead headed toward the back of the house, the butler leading it on its way. So much for important.

"The judge will entertain you in the Norway, Mr. Reno." The ponytail beckoned me on, and on I followed.

The butler led me down a long hall running off the central entrance. A straight shot for a hop, skip, and a jump, but then the wood-paneled hall began to angle this way and that, seemingly at random, creating a mazelike effect.

Rooms opened off the labyrinth on both sides. To the left a Victorian parlor appeared, dimly lit. I slowed and poked my head inside. The ponytail stopped and waited without so much as a backward glance. I started up again and so did the ponytail—eyes in the back of his damn head, I guess. Hard to guess his age. Midfifties? Hell, he could be pushing seventy, for all I could tell.

"Please mind the steps, sir," the butler said. Every so often, for no apparent reason, three little steps took you down and then three little steps took you back up—again for no apparent reason. The whimsy of the house's builder, I suppose.

However old the butler was, he looked damned dangerous. His way of moving the kind practiced in the quieter, deadlier martial arts —not the sort they teach kids on Saturdays in shopping mall dojos. Wherever the judge bought this butler, he'd gotten his money's worth. I hung back a couple of extra steps before I resumed my silent march along the ponytail trail.

At the far end of the hallway we entered a dining room. Or maybe the kind of barn where embassies hold their receptions. I'm sure there's a difference, but I don't know what it would be.

The ceiling disappeared above me; the chandeliers weren't lit this morning. Guess Harry Reno didn't rate diplomatic status—so what. The walls were covered in a gold foil wallpaper that glowed as morning sunlight peeked through the French doors forming the entire far wall of the dining room. Mirrors divided the other walls into discrete golden sections and magnified the effect of the sunlight. I blinked hard and focused on the butler.

The ponytail stopped swinging, and the butler turned and faced me. "Still with us, Mr. Reno? So good, so very good. The Norway is this way, sir." Condescending bastard.

The butler led me through the center set of French doors. Outside, a stone patio gave way to broad steps leading down to a flagstone path crossing the dew-sprinkled grass toward a remarkable building.

"The Norway, Mr. Reno. The judge suggested that you be given a moment to *take it all in*, as he likes to phrase it. So please, indulge yourself, sir."

7
NORWEGIAN INTERLUDE

The French doors closed. Maybe Ponytail had stayed outside, maybe he'd scooted back in to buttle some more. I didn't much care. I just stood there taking it all in. Ponytail and the judge were right. It was that sort of moment.

In front of me rose the judge's Norway, a two-story wooden confection topped by a cupola whose blood-red spike was busy piercing a puff of lingering fog like a heroin needle cuddling cotton—still bloody from the last jab. Fortunately, the morning breeze quickly separated fog and spike, and I moved on to a somewhat less-colorful assessment of the judge's backyard ornament.

The building itself sat well back from the main house. The evergreens I'd seen from the driveway down below stood sentinel on the hill behind it, accenting the weathered wooden exterior without smothering it—the secretary at the travel agency across the hall from my office lets me have their old *Architectural Digest* issues. Gives my clients something to read. And the ones who can't read can look at the pictures and dream.

Sometimes I peruse the pictures, too. And dream about the secretary.

At the peak of each of the building's layered roofs, a blood-red barbed arrow shot out of the gaping mouth of a fierce-looking green dragon. Or maybe it was the dragon's tongue flicking out. Or the green dragon breathing red fire into the sky.

I didn't know then and I still don't know. I never had the chance to ask any of them. Right then, I was just hoping I wasn't standing there slack-jawed—a yokel overawed by all the judge possessed: first Queen V's mansion, then this Scandinavian funhouse in his backyard.

Well, if I was, so what. I shook it off and went back into observation mode.

The Norway's layered wooden roof should have been covered in green moss. Instead, the shingles sparkled with dew, like a dragon's silvered scales. More green dragons slithered up and down the walls and carved posts of the building. I kept rubbernecking, but with my mouth clamped shut now for sure.

The whole structure sat on a raised stone platform with steps leading up to an arched entrance. Off to the side of the Norway was what I guessed was the Walker-Doer family cemetery. A low iron fence enclosed weathered tombstones and a fresh pile of dirt next to a hole in the ground. Maybe the butler was digging the judge's grave. Or the other way around. I could only hope.

A tall, silver-haired, wraithlike figure appeared in the doorway. Judge Arthur Walker-Doer smiled and waved a claw around in greeting. "Harry, Harry, my lad!"

The old ghost still had his booming courtroom voice, even if his frame had shrunk over the years. He beckoned me forward, and forward I went.

The judge's bony hand was still waving itself around in the morning air as I reached the Norway's front steps. Maybe I could make the hand stop if I shook it. A shiver ran across my shoulders. I climbed the steps, anyway.

The judge grabbed my hand in one blue-veined claw and gave it a squeeze—a surprisingly firm squeeze. "A cool morning, is it not, Harry? You are shivering. Come in, my boy, come in. Willem has prepared a fire. I may call you Harry, still, may I not?"

I told him Reno would do just fine.

"Well, well. Harry it is, then." He'd allowed no dissent in his courtroom, nor did he now. "I trust Willem has treated you properly."

"If Willem has a gray ponytail, then yes."

"Excellent, Harry, excellent. I only inquire because Willem does have a mind of his own at times."

"Is that a good or bad butler feature, Judge?"

"Ah," he said with a smile, "still the same old Harry."

The judge laid an arm across my back—his bones caressing my bones—and squeezed my shoulder with a skeletal claw, herding me along. Even old, shrunken, and obviously ill, Walker-Doer couldn't be resisted.

Once inside, he gestured toward a curved-back wooden barrister's chair by the fireplace. I sat. He lowered himself gingerly into its twin—its fraternal twin. His had pads for his seat and his back. Mine was the bare-assed, bare-backed model. A vintage Walker-Doer reminder of who he was and who you were not.

The judge told me that I had come as a response to his questioned claims. I told him I knew that. "But why me, Judge? Any company errand boy could look into this." Maybe even Arnold.

"Harry, my lad. We both know the why. And worry not about the how. I need an honest man for this. I need you."

"Judge, I'm the company's man on this job. You're not my client." He couldn't have agreed less.

"Now, now, this is a fluid situation, Harry. We must navigate in changing currents." One hand wrung its mate.

"I want you to view the facts with your practiced, professional eye. And give our course and heading a fair appraisal." Gnarled, rope-rough hands. Probably bloodstained, too. A little dim in here to be certain.

"You, Harry, will know right from wrong. You will discern what justice requires." The hands stopped kneading each other and clasped themselves together in prayer instead. "I trust you, my boy. I sincerely do." Bullshit, just bullshit. I stood up.

"Judge, I'm here because the company questioned your insurance claims. It wants to deny them. Because your niece's death was a suicide. Because she set fire to your cabin."

I crossed my arms and glared down at the old bastard.

"I'd say the company's right on the suicide—too new a policy. You're right on the homeowners. She burned your cabin. Not your fault. Let's call it even and call it a day. But I know you won't. I just don't know why." God, but I hated the man.

"Sit down, Harry." His goddamned courtroom voice. I sat, but I didn't like it.

"I say this with certitude, my boy. Mallory did not kill herself. That is fact. It is not within the realm of the possible that hers was a suicide. Someone murdered my niece."

The hands were still now, intertwined across his stomach. "Someone tried to make it appear a suicide. And said someone then covered the tracks, tampered with the evidence in a rather thorough and convincing manner."

The hands steepled themselves in prayer once more, fingertips brushing his nose. "I have my suspicions as to the malefactor's identity."

"Who, Judge?"

"Oh, Harry, my boy. Do not let me taint your investigation with an old man's conjectures." His hands couldn't stay still. Now they were clasping each other in a deadly, fratricidal twinning. "Do your own sleuthing, Harry. I trust you."

The hands pulled apart, found a knee apiece, while the old judge leaned in and delivered his closing. "I trust your nose for justice to lead you down the path of righteousness to the malefactor." Said sleuthing nose wrinkled. Listening to Walker-Doer pontificate stunk. Plus, the old bastard smelled like he'd slept under a bedspread trimmed in mothballs.

I blew air out and pressed on. "You say it couldn't have been suicide. I've read the company's file. The coroner swore it was. The sheriff thought so, too."

I waited a beat for the judge to contradict me. He stayed silent.

"But now you tell me whatever evidence there was has been

covered up, tampered with, faked. And all I have to do is play the shamus-by-the-lake, and it'll all float to the surface, like a week-old sturgeon, dead and stinking and obvious."

My jaws tightened, holding words at bay. Then a quick twitch let 'em out. "You know I hate you, Judge. Always have. Always will."

The old man's face hardened, his lips a compressed blue line under his nose. Then the skull showed its teeth and grinned. He patted my knee. We were friends again.

"Harry, you're right. I told the company to send you. Told, not asked. I know this homecoming cannot be a pleasant occurrence for you, my boy. However, remembrance of things past may well propel you forward to the proper present conclusions.

"What I need, Harry, what my niece Mallory deserves, is sleuthing with a mind, sleuthing with a heart and soul. Feet rooted solidly in the past, nose sniffing eagerly forward into the morrow. A beagle on the hunt, on the scent. Uncovering the how, the why, the who of her murder."

Walker-Doer leaned back in his chair, rested a moment, let his rheumy eyes wander a bit, then fastened them back on me. "Do you know where we are, Harry? What this building is?"

My head twitched a *no* in his direction, and I waited for the judge to enlighten me. Unfortunately, he did—and at great length.

When he had finished, I knew we sat in a replica of a Norwegian stave church—*Oh boy*. I knew that it was built for the 1893 World's Columbian Exposition in Chicago—*Just great, Judge*. The Chicago World's Fair—*You don't say*.

Then he told me how his great-grandfather had visited the fair, gone to Norway's exhibit, and met a blond Norwegian girl working there. He married her. I perked up.

Great-granddad had tons of mining and timber money, the judge said. He bought the Norway after the World's Fair closed and moved it up here to Kipling, piece by piece, boxcars of it, just to keep the Norwegian chick happy—*Wow*.

"Judge, you have a picture of this blond goddess?" Walker-Doer cocked his head to the side, pursed his lips as if ready to say something; he didn't.

It had been a long tale the judge told me; not exactly boring, but close. What it had to do with Mallory's death, I didn't know, but I trotted out a quick summary nonetheless.

"Judge, I think I've figured some of this out. Your great-granddad wooed the blond babe, won her, and somehow this Norway trinket ended up here in your backyard. Right next to your family cemetery. The one with the open grave. Good—damn good. End of story—good-bye."

I stood up again. The judge sighed. His breath reeked of damp moss in a bog. But a nice complement to the mothballs.

"Harry, my boy. The tale's important to our purpose. Otherwise you know I would not bore you with it." Yeah, right.

"Okay, Judge, I'm sorry. I shouldn't try to speed you up. Your great-grandmother Marta enchanted your great-grandfather Jasper. They got married, moved here, brought Norway with them. So, what happened next?"

"I dug her up." His death-head's grin searchlight-bright now, illuminating each gloomy corner of his Norway. "Had her disinterred, Harry."

My poker face split apart. What the hell? Dug up Marta, his great-grandmother?

"Oh, Harry. Not Marta. I had my niece Mallory exhumed," the old judge said. "You don't play cards, do you? You really shouldn't, you know."

I let the slight slide. Not because Walker-Doer was right. But because he had more to tell me.

"Exhumed and sent off for a proper autopsy. By the state medical examiner's people. That is not in your company's file, is it?" No, it wasn't. Wonder why?

"I still have power, Harry. Connections. Do not doubt that. When I have the autopsy results, I shall share them with you first. I promise." A Walker-Doer promise. Good luck cashing that marker. "Ah, here is Willem," the judge said.

Willem indeed. I didn't say it, but words scrolled before my eyes like print on a teleprompter. Why me? Why not just use the butler? He looks damned capable, and he was already on the payroll.

Later, I found out the *why not* part. It just took me a while.

8
PONYTAIL TRUST

"Harry, I shall trust Willem to show you on your way. You too, Harry, may trust Willem." Off we went.

"Mind your step, Mr. Reno," the ponytailed butler said once again, his voice even and measured—deferential modulation, just like they teach 'em in Jolly Olde England. Maybe.

"I've been walking just fine without help now for, oh, forty-something years, thank you, Willem." I stumbled over the next flagstone in the path.

"Indeed, sir. An impressive statistic, to be sure." Ponytail mounted the patio's stone steps and stopped at the dining room's French doors, swung them open, and beckoned me to enter with a sweep of his arm.

"You first, Willem."

"As you wish, sir." He stepped through, and I followed. A hand squeezed my shoulder, a foot hooked my ankle, sweeping my legs out from under me. The hand on my shoulder pushed me back and down—then made sure my head didn't bounce on the dining room's polished floor.

At least, thinking back, that must have been what happened—he was just so damn quick. No sooner than I had stepped into the room through those French doors, I found myself flat on my back, gazing up at that high embassy ceiling instead of admiring the room's golden wallpaper.

Then Willem's impassive butler's face intruded on my view, but with a sardonic smile beginning to play at the edges of his thin lips. It had to be the gentlest takedown I'd ever suffered. The only thing bruised was my ego.

"The judge suggested you trust me, Mr. Reno. Trust on your part should, I venture to suggest, be evidenced by proper etiquette. Reciprocal feeling would then ensue."

Willem held out his hand. I trusted, and like that, he had me back on my feet.

The butler turned and marched toward the entrance hall. I followed his ponytail, but at a respectful, Miss Manners–correct distance. At the front doors of the judge's homage to Queen Victoria, Willem stopped, opened the doors, and stood aside. "Trust, Mr. Reno."

I looked out and down. Down all those damn stone steps. Could be a bouncy exit, especially if someone offered you a respectful shove to start you on your way. What the hell. I walked through the doors onto the porch. Nothing happened.

"So good, so very good, Mr. Reno. You see, trust breeds confidence."

"Where'd they breed you, Willem?"

"Ah, Mr. Reno. Still the same old Harry. A pleasant day to you, sir. Please stray not so far that I should have difficulty locating you, should the judge require it." And with that admonition hanging between us, he less than gracefully slammed the doors in my face.

I trudged back down the steps and slipped behind the Volvo's wheel. To hell with Norway, I'd take Sweden any day.

I drove back out along the judge's immaculate concrete driveway —a ride too smooth to excite the little hula girl. At the gated entrance, I paused.

The two monstrosities perched there uninhibited by fog now, in all their sensual, mythic glory. Man, this place could get to a guy. Who the hell guards his home with weird shit like this? And why would you figure a goat guy and a bull man would scare anyone off? Creepy, but . . .?

"Hey, boys," I said. "I didn't shoot him. Maybe next time." The Volvo wheeled out of the drive, and I headed away.

What the hell did all this mean? Why the personal audience with the great man himself? The judge could have picked up the phone, told me Mallory was aboveground once more—or had Willem do it.

What I did know was this: Judge Arthur Walker-Doer had a purpose in bringing me here. Beyond that I didn't have a clue.

And most of all, I didn't know why he had (or needed) a lethal, ponytailed butler named Willem. And why did Willem act like we knew each other, why the *same old Harry* routine, like the judge?

So much for my late-night motel room reminiscences. Somehow I put myself to bed, because that was where I woke up the next morning—alone. No Gwen; no cops; no judge; and, sure as hell, no butler.

Just me and my hangover. Yet again.

9

RYE TOAST

Sunlight bled through my motel room's bullet-riddled curtains and splashed in my eyes. I ignored the intrusion by rolling to the other side of the bed. Then the alarm clock shrilled inside my aching skull. I hit the snooze and pulled a pillow over my head for protection. When my front desk wake-up call bleated in my ear a minute later, I gave up and got up.

Showered and dressed, I levered myself with care into the Volvo and headed out to begin a day investigating something I didn't give a damn about in a town where I didn't want to be.

I made it as far as the motel office. I shut the Volvo's door softly and went inside slowly. A perky blonde had replaced Karl the night clerk. She sure seemed built for more than manning a cheap motel's front desk. I perked up, too.

As I stood there leering at Karl's replacement, I realized I needed a lot of joe and something to eat. Soon, real soon.

"Hey, babe. Got any coffee?" Maybe I should have introduced myself before I called her *babe*. Maybe I would, after some coffee. God, but I felt rough.

The perky blonde made her big boobs jiggle, said her name was something or other Swedish sounding, and said she already knew I was Mr. Reno. And then she giggled.

I said, "Call me Harry. You know, like 'Call me Ishmael.'"

More giggling. Maybe I made her nervous, me being such a well-known PI and all. Or maybe she'd read *Moby-Dick*. Or maybe that's just what she did best—giggle and jiggle. Yeah, that had to be it.

But this morning I had to get beyond that nonsense. I needed food; I wanted coffee. So, undeterred by her mirth and her figure, I asked her for a breakfast recommendation. I half expected her to say *Me*, but she didn't, thank God. I wouldn't have been up to it.

"The Hash House is around the corner and up a block, Mr. Reno. I mean, Harry."

"They got a morning special?"

"The best corned beef hash and eggs in town," she said.

"Corned beef hash for breakfast? A whole city block away? You got any coffee here, babe? I'll never make it that far." She did, and after two paper cups full of something approximating coffee and some more scintillating conversation—and accompanying jiggling and giggling—I managed to find my way to the Hash House.

I slid into the first empty booth and waited for coffee to appear. Instead, a woman, thin as six o'clock and with a tired face, showed up and peered down at me. "Harry Reno," the tired face said.

I glanced up. I couldn't place her. "Coffee," I replied.

"Harry Reno," the tired face said, louder this time.

"Black coffee," I said, trying something different. I wasn't giving up. I needed more coffee, and soon.

"Same old Harry," the woman said, softer this time. She went away.

When she came back, she held a steaming mug clutched in a blue-veined hand. The coffee and the waitress both sat down.

"Alice, Harry. Alice Vaughn. Remember? I heard you were in town. Drink your coffee. I'll be back with your breakfast." She patted my leg and slipped out of the booth with that quick movement thin women sometimes have, like snow showers blowing across asphalt. Here one moment, just a memory the next.

Back with my breakfast? What the hell, I hadn't even ordered.

I sipped a little coffee and—Alice Vaughn, oh no. I did know Alice. Of course I did. What the hell was wrong with my memory up here? I slurped more coffee and waited for whatever I hadn't ordered to appear.

"Corned beef hash and a fried egg, Harry. Want something else to go with it?" I knew the plate behind her back held the answer. And now I knew what it was.

"Rye toast with grape jelly, please. Christ, Alice, it's been fifteen years. How do you remember this stuff?"

"Same old Harry. So wrapped up in himself he can't recognize a beautiful woman when he sees one. Or remember why he loved her so once." At least she was smiling as she delivered her lines.

Alice Vaughn, bony and thin in all the places she'd been soft and, well, filled out. One of the best-looking women in Kipling. Best-feeling, too. But that was long ago. What the hell had happened to her?

"I can read your face, Harry. It's just me and Sam the cook this morning. Just me and Sam last night. We got help, only the help likes to party up at the casino too often. And too late. At least she isn't working there yet."

"Alice, I'm gonna play detective. Help equals daughter?"

"Harry, I'll cry. Eat your breakfast. We'll talk later." Her grin fled and Alice followed. But the hurt in her face stayed.

I finished my breakfast and went to the register to pay. I asked Alice if I came back in for a late lunch, could we talk. She just nodded a tight-lipped *yes,* like the hurt was ready to spill out, and she didn't want it to. But a little hint of relief danced in her eyes.

I smiled, she smiled, and we left it at that.

When I hit the sidewalk, I scoped the scene. Coffee and corned beef hash had cleared my head somewhat. That and the rye toast and grape jelly. The cool morning air was finishing the job. Alice had gotten my brain working again, had it remembering where I was and who I was. And why I was back here in Kipling.

My fifteen-year blackout was beginning to clear. Pretty soon I'd be an eagle-eyed detective again. Maybe Penny did know what she was talking about after all. I did need to come back to Kipling, to end all the nightmares.

I knew the way to the police department. Remembered how to stumble into the sheriff's office, too. And I figured I'd just get the same info I already had in the company's file. Maybe receive a gruff reminder from the cops that gumshoes weren't particularly welcome in Kipling. Especially Harry Reno.

But it's always good procedure to say hello officially to the local gendarmes, even if they only spit in your eye.

As I crossed the street, I kicked at a pebble. It sailed true, hit the storm sewer opening across the street dead center, and—with a reassuring plunk—sunk into the crud below. That's where I needed to go —down into Kipling's filth. And now, finally, I wanted to.

So I really was back. And that felt good, damned good.

10

KUSTER'S MORNING AFTER

Gwen's Lance wasn't home at the Kipling PD when I strolled in. He'd called in after taking Gwen home; no double shift for him. The big-voiced sergeant wasn't around, either. At least the blue posse that was there seemed somewhat hospitable.

Not so at the sheriff's office. Nobody jumped up to shake my hand. A collective stink eye met my cheerful "Howdy do." I handed the deputy at the desk my card. He handed it back in little pieces. So I wished the deputies a pleasant good-bye and stepped out the door before they threw me through it.

With no particular place to go, I wandered toward the docks, inhaling scents of charter boats and trawlers: floating fish, diesel fumes, stale beer. I didn't linger.

Farther along the harbor road, I came upon a two-story clapboard building busy shedding its coat of faded paint. Faint gold letters on its plate-glass windows proclaimed it the home of *The Kipling Pioneer*, the local contribution to that cornerstone of our Republic, Freedom of the Press.

Some half-forgotten memory had steered me to the newspaper's front door.

When Mac McCabe and I tried scouring evil out of Kipling fifteen years ago, *The Pioneer* and its editor publicized our efforts. All I knew about the newspaper now was that the judge's niece, Mallory Mordred, was working there when she died.

What the hell. Worth a try, shamus. The door was unlocked. Nobody home in the newsroom, though, just empty whiskey bottles scattered about. And the lingering scent of weed. Still the same editor. Had to be.

"Tom Kuster!" My roar a wife's waking of a husband who'd come home too late the night before. "News flash. Harry Reno's back in town! Get up, you old newshound." It worked.

A tall, stooped-shouldered man made his way gingerly down the stairs, one hand gripping the rail. His trademark mop of Mark Twain white hair floated down with him.

"Christ, Harry, not so loud. I'm hung over." The editor stopped in front of me, swaying slightly. "It's good to see you, dude."

I put a hand on his shoulder, steadying his wobbly frame. Waves of last night's alcohol washed over me, mingling with Tom's ever-present oily herb aroma.

"I heard you were back in town," he said.

Tom hugged me, staggered over to a desk, collapsed into its boss-man chair, pulled a drawer open. "How 'bout one, Harry?" A fresh bottle of rye appeared. "It'll warm us both up."

"Gotta pass, Tom. Long day in front of me, long night behind me. But you go ahead."

Tom sipped, said, "*The Pioneer*'s a weekly now, Harry. I'm slowing down." More rye slid inside. "Yesterday was print day. The run's probably sold out by now." The editor hacked out a sour laugh in counterpoint to his newsroom optimism.

"And since the paper's put to bed, I need a day off. Running this rag of mine requires a lot more inspiration juice these days." A sweep of his hand, the one that wasn't clutching the rye, indicated the empty whiskey bottles. "Especially since Mallory went away," he said.

Wow, talk about an opening. I ran straight at it, a fullback with the goal line only a quick stride away.

"That's why I'm here, Tom. I know it's tough, but I need to know some things about her. Something to help me figure out why she died." Reno, the subtle-as-hell gumshoe.

Tom shook his head, telegraphing a whole lot of nothing my way.

"What was she working on?" I asked. Wrong approach. Too direct. His eyes focused now on amber memories swirling in his glass along with the rye. I needed those eyes back with me. So I tried a gentler prodding. "I need to get a feel for her." Soft. Harry's voice, not Reno's. "I can't solve a case if I'm tracking a phantom." That did it.

Tom's head whipped up. Suspicion filmed his eyes, my words an unexpected typo. His words fast, precise. "What do you mean by that, Harry? Tracking a phantom? She's dead. Buried, too. Until Walker-Doer dug her up."

Whiskey wet his lips; a good-sized gulp coasted inside.

"There's nobody to track. She's dead, Harry." His glass back on his desk. "Dead and gone." Arms folded tight across his chest, lips compressed and silent now.

My chance phrase had struck a nerve, and now the editor had clammed up. Maybe I ought to avoid rousting drunks so early in the day. Maybe I ought to stay in bed myself.

I gave it another shot, my voice barely above a whisper.

"Sorry, Tom. Just trying to picture Mallory in my mind. All I really know is, she was a redhead. Right?" That's about as sensitive as Harry can do. Wasn't working. So Reno went right for the jugular. "She killed herself, didn't she?"

Tom cradled his head in his hands. Then his white mane began shaking back and forth, powered by the rhythmic beat of "A Hard Day's Night" pulsating through the newsroom from above. "My morning alarm. An all-Beatles station. I love 'em, man."

Tom raised his glass, focusing attention on the last of the whiskey instead of on me. "But I don't know what to think about Mallory. And that's the truth," he said, and let the dregs of his salvation slide inside. "Sure you don't want that drink? I'm having another."

He'd either talk or drink until he couldn't. Just like before. He kept talking—for now, the empty glass forgotten in his hand, the whiskey still wearing its cap.

"I might have been in love with her, Harry. You remember how I get." Yeah, horny for every female in sight back then. Probably no different today.

"Mallory didn't have to work here. She could have handled the state capital beat, national stuff, investigative journalism."

"What was she working on?" I asked again.

"Didn't give her assignments. Didn't have to. Mallory just kept me and Jayne—you remember Jayne Rask, don't you, Harry?" Oh, no. Still around. Not good. Really not good.

Tom poured, whiskey spilled. He drank, two-handed. Both shaking. Drops of amber dotted his jeans. "Mallory just kept us up on what she was working on, when it could go to press. She even went to Florida investigating."

"Where in Florida, Tom?" What the hell was he babbling about now? But he ignored my question, began to talk about something else.

"She was so pretty, guys just couldn't help but answer her questions. Tell her what she wanted to know. Women loved her, too." Yeah, I bet. Especially Jayne.

Tom's words were running together now, a seek-and-find jumble. He was wandering away from me, using the rye to get there. That tracking-a-phantom shit.

Tom picked up the bottle, started to pour himself another shot.

"Thomas Kuster, you okay in here?" A booming cop voice, one I knew, right here inside the newsroom. Then the cop himself. "This clown bothering you?"

"Huh? Oh, no, John, it's just Harry. We're having a drink. Leastways I am. It's okay. Go away."

The front door banged shut, and John the Big-Voiced Sergeant from last night headed off down the sidewalk. At least I knew Sarge's first name now. I pressed on.

"Tom." His shaggy head swiveled from the front door to my voice. "I told you why I'm here. It's simple. The insurance company. They sent me to investigate the judge's claims. Mallory's death. The fire at the cabin." My voice dropped a couple of notches. "That's all."

Nice and gentle—simple. Even sounded like the truth, the whole truth, and nothing but the truth. "That's the only reason I'm here."

Tom puffed his cheeks, let a sigh escape. "Ah, hell, Harry. Sorry. Let's get out of here. Grab some coffee. Go for a drive. Walls closing in, know what I mean, man?"

11

RUSTY MEMORIES

We locked up *The Pioneer*, and the Volvo found us some Golden Arches java, while the little hula girl tried out her island charms on Tom. "She's cute. Where did you find her, Harry?"

"Not Hawaii."

"Pity. Hey, drive on out the lake road," Tom said. "Not toward all those rich shits. The other direction, man. I'll show you what's not left of Mallory's cabin."

I'd been there yesterday, rubbed some soot on myself poking around, peering at a whole lot of nothing. But if I could see the cabin-that-wasn't-there through Tom's eyes, maybe cajole him into bringing the place to life again, I might come up with something I could use to pry information loose from somebody somewhere here in Kipling. Maybe.

The road ran beside Great Cold Lake, tracing its shoreline, moving up and down, snaking past jutting cliffs. The Volvo almost kissed the guardrail a couple of times. Not a short drive; not quick, either.

"It's up there, dude. Next driveway. See that dirt road? That's the cabin. Watch you don't bog down. Looks kind of muddy."

The Volvo swung off asphalt and onto something in between dirt and mud. Mountain climbing in slippery conditions wasn't the Volvo's forte. The little hula girl, however, was really digging the topography. She wiggled her hips madly the whole way to the top, dancing to a tune only she could hear—just like yesterday.

The Volvo stopped in the same bare clearing, and we got out.

"This it?" I said. Same as yesterday—rustic nothingness. Hope to hell yesterday's fucking snake was still rustic dead nothingness. God, but I hate 'em.

"Yeah, man. The cabin sat over there. You want the *Welcome to Paradise* guidebook description?"

"If you think I need it," I said.

Tom stood, put his hand on his heart, started reciting some puerile nonsense.

"It sat as if rough-hewn from the surrounding forest, its logs seemingly as ancient as the trees themselves. A rude shingled porch ran across the cabin's front. Two Adirondack chairs and a small table huddled together near the cabin door. A clutter of discarded hunting and fishing gear lay piled nearby."

Tom stopped, made sure I was listening. Unfortunately, I was. But I couldn't complain. I wanted to see the cabin through Tom's eyes. And now I was.

"In a patch of tilled earth beside the cabin's front steps, sunflower stalks drooped, the last remnants of a summer garden, their seed heads long since picked clean by scavenging crows. From the chimney, a thin curl of smoke struggled upward, only to find itself held down, defeated by the autumn dampness." Tom paused, glanced my way.

Always be careful what you ask for, Reno. Yeah, thanks, Harry. Tom started up again.

"Mallory's mud-splattered Jeep sat beside the desiccated sunflowers—the sinking wood smoke wreathing both the dead stalks and the Jeep's canvas top, mingling with the rising fog."

I couldn't take any more. "I'm good, Tom. Burned in my brain."

"Sorry, Harry. I never get to write shit like that for the paper, dude. No travel section anymore." Tom sighed, wandered away.

I went to sit on a flat rock closer to the pine trees. Tom scuffled around, kicked at this and that, mostly stuff I guess only he could see. After a while he ended up beside me and sat down.

"This used to be a happy place," he said. "Paradise. I'd sit on the porch in an Adirondack, drink whiskey. In the sunshine. Let Mallory kiss me now and then. Not much left, is there?"

No, there wasn't. Yet something was here. I could sense it.

"Maybe you're seeing something I don't see," I said. "Because today all I see is a deserted clearing. A big empty space." I didn't say anything about faint voices I thought I'd heard yesterday, or ghosts stomping around in my head this morning. That could wait. Probably just hang-over residue.

"Help me out some here," I said instead.

"A big empty space," he repeated, and sighed again. "Yeah, you're right, Harry. Let's go back to town." Tom's detachment from the place's echoes was puzzling. Hell, his lover died here. That ought to make a guy feel something. Anger, maybe? Would me.

But Tom didn't head for the car. Instead, he stood up, stretched, started to wander about again. He'd gone ten feet, or maybe ten yards. I don't remember. Didn't matter then and doesn't matter now—not the physical distance. It was his mind that had slipped away.

"Tom." Not exactly a shout. But he turned toward me nevertheless, a smile quickening.

"What, Harry?" His words hung there, like the faraway hoot of an owl, almost too faint to be real.

"The cabin sat here, didn't it, Tom?" I tried matching my voice to his. "Then it burned. Nothing's here now. Where did it all go?"

Tom's eyes wandered over the nothingness. "Guess Mr. Peabody's coal train hauled it away," he said, his grin tracking ear to ear.

Shit. He was giving me John Prine—not the answers I'd wanted to hear. Then Tom's memory ticked over and fired.

"It's bare up here because they wiped the crime scene clean, Harry. Clean off the face of the earth. Health Department, building inspector, whoever, came out here after the fire." Tom's words tumbling out now, no longer foggy, alcohol-fueled remembrances.

"Said it was a health hazard. Safety hazard. Kids would play in it. Damn it." Tom slammed one fist into the other—the pop the sound the first fastball of spring makes as it smacks the catcher's freshly oiled mitt. Surprised me, too. "You see any kids, Harry? Up here?"

I shook a *no* his way.

"The sheriff kept the state boys out," he said. "The town cops didn't even bother to drive by. The sheriff controls the coroner. Always has. No state medical examiner needed. Verdict: suicide. Coroner certified by Doc Decker. Fire clowns said arson. End of story."

Tom snatched a rock, zinged it hard and far. Probably trying for the departing coal train.

"But what about Walker-Doer?" I said. "How did they get him to go along? His own niece? No questions asked? I don't believe it. It just doesn't figure." My words matching his, tumble for tumble.

Tom wandered back over, spent once again. We sat together on the rock. He put his arm around me. Old white-haired editor lecturing cub reporter. "The judge did not give the enterprise his blessing." Tom's words slow to form, deliberate.

"He could not. Walker-Doer had a heart attack the night of the fire. He spent weeks in the hospital, completely out of it most of the time. No other next of kin around to make decisions." Tom's memory train was picking up speed again.

"The sheriff, the coroner, whoever, wanted Mallory, or her remains, cremated some more and buried. But our circuit judge, the one who inherited his esteemed place on the bench from old Walker-Doer, finally grew a backbone, said, 'No way, Jose!' Said to bury Mallory in Walker-Doer's family cemetery. Made it a court order, Harry."

Tom began fading again. Up—down, up—down. Damn odd.

"I don't know who asked for the order. Willem, maybe. They buried her in the family plot, right there beside the Norway." A faraway look in Tom's eyes now. "You ever seen it, Harry? Norway? I have."

Clouds his focus now. My hand on his shoulder—just a friendly squeeze.

Tom took the hint. "Sorry, Harry. When Walker-Doer got out of the hospital, figured out what had happened, he had her dug up. Disinterred. Sent the remains away.

"But I expect you know all that. Working for the insurance company. Being a first-rate detective and all." Tom's shaggy Mark Twain head shook from side to side.

He stood up, swatted a fly away. "Harry, sometimes I think my skull's filled up with rusty red rocks. You know, like those ore boats out on the lake." Tom brushed at the fly again.

"Rusty memories rattling around in my head like forgotten ore in a ship's hold. I just wish the rattling would stop. Know what I mean, man?" Yeah, I knew that feeling.

"Let's go get some lunch," Tom said. "I'm hungry."

12

SPEED TRAP

The Volvo rolled down the cabin driveway and back toward Kipling. Tom dozed beside me. I let him. I had my own thoughts to deal with. Why had he brought me to the cabin site? Did he know I'd already been there yesterday? Gus the bartender knew. Did he tell Tom? Did that even matter?

A cop car's snout was poking out from a dirt road up ahead, the rest of the cruiser shielded by trees. But my mind was on Tom and the cabin. The Volvo didn't exactly roar past the law, but he lit me up just the same.

I nudged Tom, told him to wake up. "Hope you're buddies with all the law up here."

"Huh?" Shit, no help there.

I pulled over, opposite the guardrail that was supposed to keep you from visiting the scenic sights at the bottom of Great Cold Lake. Sure enough, the cruiser pulled in behind us, and the cop pried himself out from behind the wheel. Great, Gwen's Officer Lance.

Last night he'd told me he wanted to see me today. But he wasn't at the Kipling PD when I went calling, so I guess he'd come looking for me. Staked me out—whatever. He and I were together now.

Lance filled up the Volvo's window and then some. "How you

doing, Mr. Reno?" Lance poked a paw into the Volvo, and I shook it. Not exactly proper police procedure. And a sea change from last night's chilliness.

"I missed you this morning at the PD, Mr. Reno. Sorry. How you doing, Mr. Kuster?"

"Okay," Tom said.

I groaned. Penny hates it when I say *okay*. Now everybody in Kipling was busy making sure I had it locked in my head again. And I'd pay her price when she heard me mouth it back in Ithaca. I always did.

Lance's attention swiveled back from Tom to me. "You okay, Mr. Reno?"

"Yeah, Officer, I'm okay. How about you this afternoon? You okay, too?" See what I mean? Lance didn't answer. Cop eyes swept the Volvo's interior. We must have passed. No weed, no booze, no guns in sight. And no Gwen.

"Mr. Reno and me are going to walk over there and talk a minute. Okay, Mr. Kuster." It wasn't a question.

The big cop took the lead and headed into the pine trees. Good, no easy bullet in the back of the head this afternoon for Harry Reno. Probably a more nuanced demise being planned.

Lance walked a little farther into the woods. Pine straw crunched underfoot. Somewhere overhead, a hawk was keening, searching for prey. Routine North Woods noises.

The big cop stopped, turned. I waited. A bullet or a punch? Wrong on both counts. "Gwen's gonna, gonna . . . quit her job at Gus's place."

"Ah, Lance, that doesn't sound like a good thing." My voice was more commiserating purr than jab to the gut, but Lance clutched his stomach and winced like I'd socked him hard.

"No, it ain't, Mr. Reno." More stammering. "She . . . she . . . she got a job at the casino. One of the show-your-tits jobs. I ain't happy." More stomach clutching.

"Her mother wouldn't be either, if she were still alive." Now mine knotted up on me, too.

Yeah, that's the way to win me over to your side, boy. Remind me about the woman I killed. I thought it, I just didn't let it out to roam. Not the time. And sure as hell not the place. Fucking dark woods.

"You've got to help me, Mr. Reno." One hand still clutching his gut. The other gripping my shoulder. "You got to."

I gestured toward a flat rock. They seemed to be standard equipment around here. *Have a seat,* my hand said. So we did.

"The casino's a bad place, Mr. Reno. Lots of girls, pretty girls, go up there. They . . . they ain't the same after a while. It ain't good, whatever it is that goes on in there." Were those cop tears in his cold blue eyes? Hard to tell. Too gloomy here under the trees.

"I don't want Gwen working there. Pouring drinks, dancing, show . . . showing guys all the shit she's got." Lance let out an animal moan, a low wail of pain contorting his face. Something deep in the woods answered him. I shivered. I couldn't help it. You would have, too. The big cop did it again. The whatever-it-was moaned back louder still. And closer.

I had to do something, but what? A pat on the shoulder. Maybe that'd calm his dumb ass down before the whatever-I-hoped-it-wasn't crept out and ate us both.

There, there, my boy. It'll all be okay. Uncle Harry will take care of you. Yes, he will. And little Gwenny, too. I didn't say that, of course. But what the hell was I going to say to the big lug? I wasn't sure, but I gave it a try.

"Lance. This sounds complicated. What you're telling me about Gwen. The casino." More shoulder assurances. "I thought it was just a harmless little gambling joint, with a Vegas floor show thrown in."

His eyes narrowed. He stood up, stepped away, took off his hat, ran a hand across his bristle of hair. "You really think that, Mr. Reno?" Eyes frost blue, hostile. The hat back on. Squared up.

"No, Lance, you know I don't. And yes, I'll help you. Let's get together tonight at the Tam." Maybe Gus could help me with the big ox. "About seven?"

"Okay, but no Tom." I didn't ask why. We walked back to our cars.

Tom was nudging the little hula girl's grass skirt, trying to coax a wiggle. No use. She had other interests. She swiveled toward Lance, little floozy.

"Watch yourself, Mr. Reno," Lance said. "Not all the cops around here like you." Yeah, no shit. Lance motioned for me to pull out, and he headed off in the opposite direction.

As we cruised back toward town, Tom fixed a bleary eye or two on me. "You get out of the ticket, Harry?"

"No, Tom, I don't think I did."

13
A LATE LUNCH

The Volvo found the curb by the Hash House, and we went inside. Empty booths, plenty of choices. Tom already stumbling toward one in particular, menu in hand. Homing instinct. His usual spot. He won the race, if that's what it was. I nabbed a menu and followed his lead.

Alice didn't exactly rush over, but when I raised my head, there she was. Looking worse than she had this morning. "Hey, Alice. I did say a late lunch. And I brought a date. Good, huh?"

"Whatever, Harry. You don't have to haul Tom in here. He practically lives here." Alice swiped her towel across our tabletop, knocking toast crumbs into Tom's lap. He never noticed.

"Right here," she said. "This booth. Unless he's at Gus's doing 'research.' Or slurping whiskey at the office, editing that news rag of his." Her voice had an edge to it, but when she fixed her eyes on the editor, she smiled; sort of like she was sucking on a lemon, though.

"Gimme that menu, Tom," Alice said. "I'm gonna bring you something special, and you're gonna eat it. Every bite. You two can hit Gus's later and drink your dinner, if that's what you wanna do." That lemonade smile again. "Harry, what do you want for lunch?"

She snatched my menu, too. Didn't wait for an answer. So I

figured whatever Sam the cook made back there in the kitchen, I'd eat.

Tom watched Alice's rear disappear along with the rest of her, then swiveled bleary eyes my way. "What'd you do to piss her off, Harry?"

"I don't think she's mad. She just wants you to eat something and tell her you like it."

"Mission impossible," he mumbled, his head in his arms now, searching for comfort on Hash House Formica. The head stayed down. Its mouth might even have started snoring a little. Great, just great.

Alice came back with a bowl of beef stew and set it in front of Tom. He raised his head, sniffed at her offering, grabbed a spoon.

"Harry, Sam'll have yours ready in a minute," she said. "Today's special."

"Pasties, I hope," I said, licking my lips. I love those meat pies.

Alice slapped me hard, called me a son of a bitch, dropped down beside me in the booth, and let out a wail of a sob—all at once. I didn't even have a chance to duck and cover. What the hell?

Tom glanced over, said, "Good soup, Alice."

"Screw you, you drunken bastard. It's stew." Her second moan sounded a lot like whatever had answered Lance in the forest this afternoon. "Harry, you've got to help me."

I resisted the urge to shove her bony ass onto the linoleum while I made for the door. Instead, I put an arm around her. "Alice." She kept sobbing uncontrollably. "Alice. I don't have to have a pasty for lunch. Honest I don't." This time she went for my throat.

Tom scooted out of the booth and pulled her off of me, while I tried massaging my windpipe all on my own. No other customers. And Sam the cook nowhere to be seen. A sensible man.

Tom was hugging Alice, kissing her head, smoothing her hair. Probably not for the first time, either. "Don't worry, Alice," he said, and shot me the look. "Harry'll make it all better."

Yeah, right. Better me than him, he meant. Tom sat Alice back down beside me.

"What the hell, Alice? What's wrong?" And yes, I know you're never supposed to ask a woman what's wrong. You're supposed to know why she's upset. Be intuitive.

On the plus side, she didn't try to throttle me again. Only a softly delivered chin chuck.

"It's Brynn. That damn daughter of mine. She called right after you left this morning and told me she got a job at the casino. She starts tonight. Gwen's getting a job there, too."

Alice pressed her elbows tight against her thin frame, jamming her hands deep into her armpits. She sat as close to me as she could. Shaking as though her bones might burst apart.

"I don't even want to think what they'll be doing up there, half-naked," she said. Now her shivers were my shivers, too.

Sam crept out of the kitchen with my lunch, eyes wary, fixed on his boss. He sat the Welsh pasty down in front of me and headed back to his kitchen. Sam the cook, a very sensible man.

"Okay if I eat?" I said. "Then I'll save Brynn." And Gwen, too, maybe.

"Harry, I'm sorry. I'm just worried. Girls up at the casino wear pasties—when they wear anything at all. You said it, and I blew. I'm just worried. About Brynn and Gwen. That's all." She patted my hand. "Eat your lunch. And thank you." Guess I had agreed to save them both.

Alice struggled out of the booth, still hugging herself, head down, watching her own two feet shuffling across her own spotless linoleum toward the kitchen.

My eyes swung back to Tom. Still spooning in soup. Or stew. Still looking wasted. Maybe the food would help.

"Finish your lunch," I said. "Go back to *The Pioneer,* have a drink maybe, get some rest, and for God's sake, take a shower and change your clothes."

He shook his head, his white mop of hair flopping around. Might have been a Samuel Clemens *yes,* or maybe a Mark Twain *no*. Hard to tell with Tom, but I took it for agreement and pressed on.

"Because tonight, Mr. Kuster, you are going to escort one Harry Reno to the casino and initiate him into the pleasures contained therein. Do you think you can pull yourself together enough to do that, Tom? Point out Brynn for me?"

"Yeah, I will." His head came up, a smile creasing his face. "I know the proprietor. And I'll guide you through the labyrinth, too." He wiggled fingers in front of my face, like you would if you were scaring a five-year-old. "I might even lead you back out." Idiot.

"Meet me at the Tam tonight," I said. "Eight o'clock. That'll give me time to talk to Lance. Then you can tell me why he didn't want you around. And Tom." He tried focusing bleary eyes my way again. "I don't need you completely sober tonight—just do not be wasted."

Five wasted words, but I said them without hesitation. Maybe they were for my ears as much as for Tom's. I slapped a twenty on the Formica and got the hell out of the Hash House before Alice and her lemon-sour mood put the squeeze on me yet again.

The Volvo's tan leather felt good after Alice's tender caresses. And since the little hula girl didn't feel like going back to the motel, I let the Volvo whisk us away, told the hula girl, *Your choice.*

She directed the green love of my life to a beer joint beside the water, where we cruised to a stop under a shade tree. The little hula girl seemed to be enjoying the lake breeze. She was wiggling a lot. The Volvo sat without complaint, just happy for cool shadows, I suppose. In I went.

I drank a couple of beers, ate some stale pretzels, picked around in the peanuts. Asked the barkeep a few aimless questions. But when he switched the TV to bowling, I hit the door.

14

THE NIGHT CLERK

Back in my motel room once again, I checked for signs someone had been nosing around. Nothing touched, not even the dirty towels. I crashed in the recliner and dialed the front desk. Karl, the night clerk, instead of this morning's Swedish giggler, answered.

"You got room service here, Karl?"

"Certainly, Mr. Reno."

"Beer, Karl? That on the menu?" Karl said beers were four fifty each—plus tip. Wow, who knew I was staying at the Ritz. Not the company's bean counter, I bet.

"Bring a six-pack and some ice. And put a good tip for yourself on the bill while you're at it. Oh, and some clean towels. And hurry. I'm thirsty."

Almost before I could hang up, Karl rapped on the door.

The beers and ice went in the sink, minus one apiece for the detective and his mark. I motioned for Karl to take the recliner. I perched on the corner of the bed, sucked some suds, and launched into one of my expert interrogations.

"Where's the towels?"

"You asked for clean ones, Mr. Reno. We had none." Yeah, go ahead, smirk. You'll wish you hadn't. I fired off another question.

"What's the name of that Swedish girl who works mornings?"

"You mean my sister?"

"Yeah, right, and you're a fucking comedian. Wait a minute." Karl did have a certain gleam in his eye. "Your sister? Really?"

"You sure you're a detective?" Little shit. How the hell had Karl shifted roles, ended up doing the questioning? Not good. Really not good.

I swallowed more of my beer. So did Karl—his, not mine.

"Yeah, Karl, I am a detective. A private investigator for an insurance company. With an expense account. And acquiring information is a legit expenditure."

Karl's face lit up, a lighthouse beacon flashing the homing signal to a lifeboat full of *Playboy* centerfolds. "Mr. Reno, how can I help you, sir?"

Good old avarice, man's motivator. I had control of the interrogation again.

"I'm interested in your vast knowledge of the local nightlife. A night clerk always knows about the sort of nightlife I'm asking about. Right?"

Karl nodded, eager to please.

"Tell me about the casino and the girls up there." The little man squirmed a bit in the recliner, not so comfortable as a moment ago.

"My parents are watching the front desk while I run room service. They own the motel. They're probably ready to call it a day." But his words came accompanied by a greasy grin.

I didn't offer any sunshine in return. Instead, I pulled a Jackson from my wallet, and let Old Hickory do the smiling for me. "Sure you don't have a little leeway in getting back on the desk, Karl?"

"I might know something about the casino." He nabbed the twenty. "Then again, I might not." Karl obviously knew how to play the game.

I slapped a Hamilton in the wet spot left by the beer currently at the night clerk's mouth. "It's an expense account, Karl. It ain't the vault at Fort Knox. Now give."

"Okay," he said. The good old Kipling *okay.* I could have punched him. But that would have ruined the ambiance of the moment.

Instead, a swallow of beer helped me achieve optimum interrogation mode. "First off, when's the last time you were up there?"

"Up where?"

"The casino, moron."

"You do not have to be nasty," he said.

"Yeah, and you don't have to play stupid."

"Two days ago, Mr. Reno."

"How do you like to part with your money when you visit Paradise, Karl?"

"I work there." The little shit sounded offended. "I do not gamble."

"Sorry. I didn't know. Tell me about the babes. They do let women work there, don't they?"

"Of course they do, Mr. Reno. The girls do not wear a lot, though. Just skimpy Indian maiden costumes." A smirk peeked out from behind his beer. "That is the theme for the casino, an Indian motif." Smug-ass little creep.

Karl was pissing me off. I was paying for info, not smirking and smug grins. I took a stroll, fished a couple more beers out of the sink, passed one to Karl.

Then pushed him a little harder. "When you aren't staring at boobs, what do you do up there, stupid? At the casino."

"You do not have to be offensive, Mr. Reno. Hey, I like a good ass, too." I let him laugh alone. Karl probably did a lot alone. Night clerk at a hot-sheets motel. Probably had peepholes bored all over the place.

My silence started him talking again.

"But I have bigger plans. I do not intend to remain a night clerk, as you put it. I have studied electronics. And I am enrolled in mortuary school." Smug as sin again.

"I intend to become a preeminent embalmer and funeral director." Self-important, too.

"There is a great need here in Kipling for such services." Electronics and funerals? Bullshit, just weird-ass bullshit. Karl was sitting up straighter, though, staring off into space, imagining his future, I suppose.

I needed him back here with me.

"Karl." He jerked, spilled beer. Maybe I had said his name a trifle too loud—and a little too close to his ear. So what. I was the one paying him to pay attention. "The casino. What do you do there, besides touch the babes with your eyes?"

"I have achieved a very important position. Very trusted, I am. By Mr. S himself, no less."

"Well, Karl. That's good. I'm impressed. Tell me about your important position." This ought to be good. Maybe this Mr. S character lets him clean the ladies' restrooms. That sounded like the little peeper's idea of an important position.

"I serve at the temple." Karl self-inflating, fit to burst. "The Temple of the Labyrinth. On the island. Out on the lake," he added, in case I didn't know where islands floated. "When the need arises." I wanted to slap the little shit.

"What need?" I asked instead. Thirty Judas bucks, and all I was getting was adolescent nonsense.

"It is sexual, and I am sworn by the highest and most frightful oaths not to speak of it. But not sordid sex, as I imagine private detectives engage in. The fulfillment of a holy need. In the temple. Out on the island." His eyes sought the heavens. Or the island.

My hand found his shoulder, fingers kneading some sense into his garbled tale, just friendly like. But maybe it hurt.

Karl yelped.

"Don't. Please. I can tell you more about the casino." He was whining now, squirming around, searching for the exit sign. "But I cannot talk about the temple. I cannot. I will not." That last declaration a little too independent for Reno's liking.

"Ow, ow. That hurts. Please don't. Owww. Okay, the temple." Talkative now. Good. "I know a girl. A girl who serves at the temple. And she tells me about it." Karl's face said, *Is that enough?* It wasn't. I didn't leave him wondering about it, either.

"Ow. Oh, please don't hurt me again. Oh, please, please don't."

Man, but he was getting good at it—very convincing. The tears were a nice touch, too.

"Now Karl, why would she do that? I mean, why tell you?" He tried to get out of the recliner. I discouraged him.

"Because I do stuff at the temple, too." Karl, lachrymose to a fault now. "For Mr. S, himself."

"You already said that." My fingers reached down, caressed his shoulder. He yelped some more. I let him. "Now tell Uncle Harry why this nice young girl spills her guts to a greasy little slob like you."

My fingers eased up on the shoulder and gave his ear a vicious twist instead. His moan was reminiscent of Lance in the forest this afternoon. Or Alice in the diner.

Got him back on track, though.

"I get her things—please stop—things she needs. Things the bosses give and then withhold. That's their power over the girls." Bimbos. Bosses. Drugs. How inventive.

"So," I said, "when she can't get the things she craves on her own, you get this girl of yours, what . . . a line of coke, a syringe full of the stuff she likes, maybe a little something to smoke to calm her nerves. A pill to pop." Uncle Harry, all sympathy now.

"Then she tells you what goes on out at that temple. Things you haven't seen. She's naked when she tells you this. Right, Karl?" He nodded his head, but stared at my hand.

Hey, I'm not a sadist. I don't get a grin hurting people, unless they're trying to put the ouch on me. Or lying to my face. Even then I don't enjoy it. Just part of the job.

"Karl, what's this girl's name?" He shook his head. My hand flexed. That's all it took.

"Elke," he moaned.

"Elke what, Karl?"

"Elke Sorrenson."

"And this Elke babe really knows what goes on out at the temple?"

"Yes."

"I need to talk to her," I said. Why, I hadn't a clue. But anything important enough for a little weirdo like Karl to absorb all the grief I was handing around had to be worth looking into.

"I . . . I . . . I don't know if I can do that. You hurt people, Mr. Reno." Without any warning, Karl banged the recliner upright. I let him. He walked to the door, turned the knob, pulled the door open. I let him do all of that, too.

"One last thing, Karl." He stared at me the way an antelope eyeballs the lion about to spring and tear its throat out. "You left one of my questions unanswered.

"What's the name of the Swedish giggler on the front desk in the mornings? The one with the big boobs."

A sob escaped, hovering in the room as Karl scooted through the open door.

"Elke Sorrenson" floated back inside, drifting on the sound the wind makes when it touches your cheek. "And she's Norwegian," the wind whispered, "not Swedish, you bastard."

Damn. And her giggling and jiggling had seemed so pretty and pure this morning.

15

BEER ON THE MOON

I'd originally come back to my motel room to call Penelope Phair down in Ithaca, but my yak session with Karl had put that on hold. New thoughts in my head now.

Maybe drugs and casino babes and sex-crazed temple broads played into Mallory's death. Have to knock on a few doors and see. Hey, might make this trip's legwork a bit more exciting. Plus, if Karl peeped into rooms, he probably bugged phone calls, too. So I decided to call Penny from the Tam-O'-Shanter.

On the way, I caught all the lights, or they caught me. Not that I was in any hurry. Still, sort of pissed me off. "Damn it. I really need to talk to Penny," I shouted at one of the red eyes. Fat lot it cared.

But the little hula girl heard my lament. And she did care. Boy, did she ever. My mention of Penny froze her gyrations in mid-swish, and she sulked the rest of the way to the bar.

Just so you know, she hates competition.

Strolling into the Tam, the first thing that caught my eye was Gwen.

Likely the first thing to catch any guy's eye stumbling into Gus's bar, unless you happen to groove on fake-Scottish bartenders.

Gwen was as easy on the eye tonight as she had been when I rescued her from the construction cowboys. *Careful, Reno, watch yourself* swirled in my head. And for once, I paid attention. I went to the bar and ordered my beer from Gus.

"Good to see you, friend Harry. You missed happy hour."

"Not exactly. I had a private happy hour with Karl the night clerk. Know him?"

"Yeah, a little piece of shit. What'd you do, buy some of his room-service beer?" Gus chuckled and wiped at my beer ring while I took a swig.

"Like you said, a little shit. Can I trust what he tells me?"

Before Gus could answer, Gwen was beside me, catching all my attention with a playful bump from one of those distracting hips of hers. "Hi, Mr. Reno."

"It's Harry, Gwen, just plain old Harry."

"Well. Hi then, Plain Old Harry." Golden hair brushed across my hand as she leaned over the bar to get rid of her empties, her touch sending chills racing from hand to heart to head.

Oh God, just like her mother.

"I need three Buds and a Moon Girl," she said to Gus. Then she turned and smiled, mouth parted just enough to show off her glacier-bright teeth. "Gus taught me all about the Moon Girl. Look, Plain Old Harry, there she is up on the wall."

I swiveled the way Gwen was pointing and on the far wall saw a metal beer sign—round and blue and inviting. A young girl sat on a crescent moon, holding a glass of beer aloft in a toast. In her other hand, trailing over the edge of the moon, she held a clear beer bottle. Stars sparkled in the sky, clouds drifted by reflecting the moonlight. Oh, man.

The Moon Girl wore leather boots, a flared skirt, and a low-cut corset top. Hum, not such a young girl at that. Certainly old enough for a beer. And her cascade of red hair, well . . .

Perched on her head was what looked like a witch's hat. Later, much later, Gwen told me not to think such thoughts. The Moon Girl was a good girl, just like her.

Whatever, the bar sign sure drew you in.

I must have stared too long, because when I came back to Earth, Gwen had slipped away. Now all I had to interest me was my own beer. Oh, yeah. Phone call. That's why I'd stopped in. Supposed to call Penelope down in Ithaca.

I asked Gus if he had a private line I could use.

"No," he chuckled and pointed to the other end of the bar, away from the witch on her moon. "It's not private, but you can use it. Plus you don't have to drop a dime. It's free. But I'll listen to what you say, if I can." He pointed to his ear, just to be sure I understood.

"It's long distance, Gus. Put it on my tab—double it if you want to —we'll let the insurance company eat it." He gave me a thumbs-up, as pleased as he could be with me and with himself.

I tried Penny at home. No answer, so I dialed her direct number at work. A bit late, but . . . she picked up on the first ring. Not good. Still there, waiting for me to call.

"Big Bad Insurance Company, Limited. May I direct your call to the Black Pit of Hell?" Not her friendly voice, no sir, not at all. But one I'd been hearing all too often.

"No, thank you, ma'am. If you would, please connect me one level lower. I'd like to speak with a Penelope Phair. Satan works for her, I believe."

She hung up. I dialed again. Again she answered on the first ring.

"Damn your eyes, Harry Reno. It's been two days, you bloody stupid man. Check in like you're told to." She sounded pissed, but caring, too.

"Penny, I love you."

"Show it once in a while, Harry."

"Penny, I do love you. And you're pretty, too."

"Bollocks, Reno."

"All right, but I need a couple of things handled. Things I can't do from here. Plus, the motel line isn't secure. Don't tell Karl the desk clerk your address. The little shit's a peeper."

"Then I am quite sure you and the diminutive Mr. Karl will get along famously. Because you too, Mr. Harry Reno, are a little shit. An impure little shit. Now tell me what you need, where you are, and why you haven't called."

My mouth opened, but she was too quick for me.

"Wait. I know where you are. Kipling. In a pub. And I know why you have not called. You are presently chasing some fantasy of your perfect woman. Some young goddess your fevered imagination has conjured into your next true love." Yeah, she'd just about nailed it, all right. "Now tell me what you need me to do, you bloody awful excuse for a man."

I swallowed a slug of beer. Penny's good, right?

"Yeah, you got it. I am in Kipling, it is a bar, and yes, I am gazing at the most beautiful woman I have ever seen, almost. Her name's Gwen. I mention her mother from time to time, don't I?" That was mean, but she'd pissed me off with her *check in like you're told to* jab.

"I still wake you up at night, don't I? Dreaming and screaming about Gwen's mother. Remember, you told me I had to go to Kipling. Wasn't my damn idea." Still mad she'd set me up for the assignment. So let her complain about what I did here. The deafening silence from her end spooked me, though.

So I filled it with good old Harry speak. "Hey. Penny. I'm sorry. That was mean. But I really do need you to do a couple of things. I'll be home in a day or so. Then I'll show you how sorry I really am." Wait, that didn't come out right at all.

"Ah, Penny, just forget that. Gus the bartender is here at my elbow. He won't let me get out of line, will you, Gus?"

Gus hooted a Highland "Hullo, lassie" in the general direction of the phone. Gwen and the rest of the bar turned our way. Gus shot them the old cop stare. They all looked away, including Gwen.

"That's a fact," Gus boomed. He pulled my hand and the phone it held toward his mouth and whispered, "I'll watch over Harry. Just like before." Huh? What before? Why tell her that?

"Harry Reno . . ." She left it at that.

"Penny, a couple of things." I pushed Gus away and tried talking on my own. He grinned, but didn't go far. "One, see what you can dig up on the Wigwam Casino. Who owns it, who runs it. And two, find out why the hell there's a Greek temple out in the lake."

Gus's face soured for a second, then his publican's smile was back in place. It was quick, but I'd noticed. Harry Reno, the always-on-the-job shamus.

"And Penny, I need you to call the medical examiner's office. Ask for—"

"I bloody well know her name, Henry." Uh-oh. Henry. Really not good. "Barbara Nolan, the assistant state medical examiner. Your somewhat ex-girlfriend."

"Penny, please. I need to know the autopsy results before the judge does. Oh, he dug up his niece. Did I tell you that? Just call Barb. Please?"

"Very well, Henry." *Click.*

16

MEMORIES ON THE WALL

I eased the phone back onto its cradle. "I love her, Gus. I swear I do."

"She sounds a bonny lass—Henry." Now we both were laughing.

"Gus, you'd love her, too. She is most definitely the real deal. Not fake like you." He shrugged as if to say *So what.*

"I met her the day after she stepped off a jet from London. I walked into Stuart Dillingham III's office. He's the character who tells me what the insurance company wants me to do next."

Gus set another beer in front of me, and I partook.

"So I walk into his office because there's a new assignment for me. Only Stu's secretary has a new face and a new body. No more old Miss Matilda.

"Instead, there's Penelope Phair of St. John's Wood, London, bent over doing some filing. I said, 'Howdy do.' She straightened up. Tall, leggy, with chestnut hair piled up on top of the most beautiful, intelligent face you could ever imagine.

"She studied me, circled me slowly. Looked me over carefully, from my wild hair down to my scuffed loafers, and the worn-out braided belt in between. She stopped in front of me, hooked a finger in my waistband, and tugged. We kissed.

"Then she touched her finger to my nose, said, 'Sit, Sir Harry.' So I sat. It was lust at first sight, for both of us. Love came later. And stayed —most of the time. Be ten years in September."

Gus nodded his head in a knowing way, and escaped back to the kitchen.

I sat at the bar nursing my beer, musing about Penny. I went to set the beer down and, as if by magic, Gwen glided onto the stool next to me.

Her finger touched my shirt cuff. Then slowly, ever so slowly, she let her fingernail slice my soul in two on its way down to the tip of my finger. I shivered. I shook. I couldn't help it.

"Plain Old Harry, did you love my mother?"

"Of course I did, Gwen." What the hell?

"How did she die?" A tear slipped from her eye, started down her cheek. "She didn't kill herself, did she?" Oh, shit.

My mouth hanging open as I tried to form words, tell her, *No, your mother didn't kill herself. I screwed up, and she died. I killed her.* Thank God I never had the chance.

"Gwen!" Lance's cop voice, a jet's sonic boom, breaking the sound barrier, rattling bar glasses, wobbling beer bottles.

Where the hell had he come from? Oh, yeah. We had a date tonight. And now here I was, caught snuggling with his girlfriend instead of with him.

Lance stormed across the barroom floor, shoving chairs and tables and then bar stools out of his way. "You ain't gonna take that casino job," he said. He wasn't talking to me.

"Take it easy, Lance," I managed before he shoved my stool, and me with it. I hit the floor hard, but not too hard. I've learned to handle such transitions.

I swung my leg in a quick arc, knocking his feet out from under him, and rolled away from the toppling ox. Not a classic Ranger trick, but one I've perfected on my own out of necessity. I seem to fall off bar stools a lot.

Lance landed on the floor beside me—and that was the end of it. He and I never had the chance to continue a reasoned discussion on how best to counsel Gwen on forgoing employment at the casino, because Gus the bartender had a foot on my chest and a billy club shoved hard against Lance's throat.

"I'll let you live, Lance. But you'll crawl on your hands and knees to the door and be gone." Hard to believe, but the big ox did as Gus said.

Once Lance's rear and the rest of him disappeared through the Tam's front door, Gus reached down and pulled me to my feet. Gwen was nowhere to be seen.

We put the bar stools back in place, and I sat back down and kept the front door in view in the bar's mirror. "Will he come back in, Gus? Guns blazing?"

"No, Harry, he won't. Lance is a hothead, but he's no killer. He's just mad about Gwen going to work up there at the casino. He's in love, remember, like you."

In the mirror, I saw Gwen come out of the restroom, a tissue still busy wiping eyes. She walked up to Gus, threw her apron down. "Shift's over. I'm going home." And then, like Lance, Gwen too was gone.

Maybe I was getting too old to rumble. I tried shaking the cobwebs and the barmaid out of my head, tried sipping beer instead of gulping it. Barroom floors seemed harder of late.

"You okay, Harry?" A hand planted itself on my shoulder. I followed the hand to a face, told the face, yeah, I was okay.

"What did Lance do to piss Gus off?" Tom asked.

"Lance raised his voice," the barkeep said. "Spoke in an unseemly fashion to a young lady of his acquaintance. That's what he did, Thomas Kuster.

"Oh, and he knocked Plain Old Harry here onto my barroom floor." Angus MacGregor, comedian and commentator on the human condition—funny, real funny. Tom sure thought so.

The hell with both of them. I hit the restroom.

On the way back to the bar, I detoured to scope out Gus's memory wall again. Gwen's touch and her questions had triggered a need to see her mother's picture again.

I walked over to confront my demons and stepped back in time.

Fifteen years ago, I told Tom Kuster, the editor of *The Kipling Pioneer*, I was close to solving the murder of Rusty Neel, the drug dealer someone had blown away with a shotgun blast to the head in his own driveway.

I'd told Tom I thought Kipling's DA had engineered the hit, maybe pulled the trigger himself, or had his brother blow Rusty apart to protect their own dope-running op. Either way, I was ready to nail that too-cool district attorney for it.

Tom Kuster printed the story on his paper's front page. Only he left out the part about who I thought murdered Rusty. One more interview, the article said, one more witness to question, and the case would be solved by State Detective Harry Reno.

Tom didn't print the name of my witness either, but he knew who she was.

I was young, brash, full of myself. And I was stirring the pot. I didn't really know if I could prove it or not.

The same morning the above-the-fold story came out, I went to interview that final witness at her home, a double-wide trailer outside of town. And I took Gwen's mother with me. I wanted the woman I loved right next to me when I cracked the dirty DA's murder-and-dope ring wide open. She was a cop, too, and a damn good one. She deserved to be beside me that afternoon to share in the glory.

Plus, she knew the witness, and I didn't.

Then, when my star witness bolted off the front porch and ran back into her trailer under the force of my questioning, Gwen's mother told me to chill. And I said, "Okay." Of course I did.

Gwen's mother opened the screen door and slid in on a whisper. I chilled like she said, tried listening to what was being said inside.

Wasn't easy. The woman's radio was playing—Carly Simon bitching about some guy she knew being too vain. Big surprise.

All I heard our witness say was "Okay" a couple of times.

A minute or two passed. I should have gone in, but I didn't. I stood on that ramshackle porch like I'd been nailed to its warped boards, my feet crucified by indecision. I left Gwen's mother in there alone with a woman we both knew was unstable and I just stood there. Because the woman held the key to my case, and Gwen's mother was going to hand it to me.

I violated procedure. Gwen's mother paid the price.

When the first shot exploded, I drove my shoulder hard into the screen door. Didn't even try to pull it open—just went through it like it wasn't there.

As I burst into the living room, a second shot boomed inside my head.

Gun drawn, I swung in a crouch into the bedroom doorway and saw the two women lying there—just the two women, nobody else. And just the one gun—Gwen's mother's service revolver, on the floor between them.

I knelt to check Gwen's mother. Other officers poured into the trailer; we'd had local backup. Somebody, a couple of somebodies, took my gun away, dragged me out of the house. The somebodies wouldn't let me back in.

The ambulances took forever to arrive. One of my squad got me into a cruiser. Forced me to sit. Maybe it was Mac McCabe. I still can't remember.

Then, months later in court, the special prosecutor the state brought in to handle Rusty Neel's murder case, the Honorable Arthur Walker-Doer, told the judge back then that the state had to dismiss the case against the cool DA.

"For lack of evidence, Your Honor. I cannot prove it," Walker-Doer had said. Bullshit. It was a cover-up. Walker-Doer engineered it. And yours truly got railroaded.

When it was all over, I was bounced off the attorney general's cop squad. And the honorable prosecutor quickly took the honorable judge's place.

And the only thing that got nailed down in my investigation of corruption and murder and drugs beside that cold lake was the lid on the coffin of the woman I loved.

That's why I hate Kipling. Why I scream in my sleep. Why I want Walker-Doer dead. I headed back to the bar. Drank some more beer. Talked to Tom. Waited for my dinner.

All without anyone knocking me off a damn bar stool yet again.

17

NORTHERN LIGHTS

Gus was taking his time getting dinner out to us. Finally, he appeared with a steak apiece and fries enough for the whole bar. I poured Heinz 57 over the fries and the steak. Gus pulled a face.

"What? I like 57. You got a problem with that?" Harry Reno, All-American tough guy again. "If you don't like it, why'd you give me the bottle?" Gus shook his head and left us alone.

We finished our meal and our beers, and I checked my watch. "Who's driving?" I knew the answer.

"Green Volvos agree with me, Harry. Comfy seats," Tom said. "And I like your little hula girl—she's hot."

"Okay," I said in surrender, and off we went. Some tough guy, huh?

The Wigwam Casino sat outside the city limits. I'd only seen it in the daylight, from the heights of the overlook. A North Woods hunting lodge, only bigger—two stories of faux-timbered pleasure, acres of parking for the soon-to-be-poorer.

But at night—lit to attract that money—it pulsed with an otherworldly luminescence. Contrasting orange and red neon outlined the casino's roof. Dead center in the middle of said roof sat a giant glass wigwam. Green and purple spotlights shot out from inside it, illuminating the sky in a lame rendition of the Northern Lights.

We rolled on in, and for once I bit on the valet parking scam. The green love of my life didn't seem to mind. Lots of worse looking clunkers in the we-park-it corral.

As we walked up the steps toward the casino's entrance, you sure as hell couldn't miss the totem poles flanking the doors. Both carved poles had half-naked Indian maidens riding the backs of enormous lake sturgeon. The Indian maidens had enormous parts, too. Both the fishes and the young ladies seemed pretty happy with the whole idea.

So all right, Indian stuff. We were in the North Woods, after all.

But as my eyes worked their way up the poles, studying each pairing, I caught a glimpse of something up top that caused me to hurry my analysis along. A couple of somethings.

On top of one totem pole, a bull man reared up, horns and angry snout surmounting a Schwarzenegger body. Atop the other totem pole, a goat man beamed a greasy smile my way, frozen in mid-prance, holding a pan flute in one hand and a wine goblet in the other —leering like a perverted Harpo Marx, minus the harp.

I grabbed Tom's arm. "Hey, what the hell does Greek mythology have to do with Indians and fish?"

"It's just fun stuff, Harry. That's all." If he couldn't convince himself, he sure as hell couldn't convince me—so I prodded ever so gently.

"I saw these same two guys out at the judge's place. You going to tell me the connection?"

"No, Harry." His sudden firmness startled me. I let it go for now.

Tom said, "Hi, Sven," to the doorman, and walked on into the casino. I tailed along behind. The doorman pulled a hard stare routine, hand up, palm out—universal sign language even I could interpret. I stopped. Maybe Sven wanted to pat me down. Maybe he liked boys, not girls.

Sven asked, "He with you, Mr. Kuster?"

"Tonight he is," Tom said.

The doorman's hand flicked itself toward the casino, indicating I was free to enter.

Hot damn. "Hello, Sven," I said, adding a string of *O*'s to the greeting and emphasizing his name as if it were printed in capitals. "Nice to meet one of the native-born."

His muttered "wise guy" floated around behind me. The doorman's appraisal of my character a bit unfair, though. Hey, I'm sensitive to the plight of America's Indians. I've made it all the way through *Bury My Heart at Wounded Knee,* for God's sake. Just bullshitting the casino's doorman, that's all. No offense, Dee Brown.

Left a grin on my face, though, as I headed on into the gambling den. I'd made a new friend. A Scandinavian-monikered, steroid-bulked body builder with red-bronze skin and a nose Crazy Horse would have been proud to call his own.

Only this chump sported a dyed-blond Mohawk punctuated by electric blue eyes: a Cigar Store Indian, Viking Punk Rocker look.

Weird place, this Kipling casino.

Inside, however, that's all it was—no different than a roadhouse gambling joint. Slot machines and blackjack, poker and craps. Roulette tables attracting both gamblers and sightseers. And all of the casino's denizens smoking, drinking, losing, wishing. Maybe even a few without their hopes and dreams beaten out of them yet.

Hell, you can always be a winner at the buffet. I hate casinos.

"Why fight it tonight," I said in surrender, and searched around for a beer, an open slot machine, and Tom Kuster, sort of in that order. What stopped my swiveling eyes was something else entirely.

A quick flash of eye-popping female splendor amidst the Wigwam Casino's chandeliered materialism brought me up short, like a bolt of summer lightning searing across the night sky, startling your unsuspecting peepers.

I blinked, stood still—frozen in place. Good Lord.

She sported the abbreviated Indian maiden costume, which covered damn little of her spectacular anatomy. That alone would have been enough to bring a man to his knees. But when the babe said, “Hi, Plain Old Harry,” I was hooked. Who the hell was this?

Tom strolled over, said, “Hi, Brynn. How ’bout some brewskies?” Wow, Alice’s daughter. Some shamus you are, Reno.

Brynn’s hazel eyes laughed and her voice sparkled. Or maybe it was the other way around. I can’t remember. Her big eyes drew me in, that I do know. Brown, flecked with green, and rimmed in blue.

I blinked again, and her eyes seemed to morph into drowning pools of desire. Brynn’s boobs were hard to miss, too. Damn lightning bolt. Where’d she go?

Poufed hair—jet black, red highlights luminescent under casino chandeliers—grabbed my attention. Brynn caught my green eyes scoping her out, and held them a moment.

“I’ll be right back with your beers, Plain Old Harry,” she said, a lighthearted merriment jingling her words. “Don’t wander off.”

Wander off? I wasn’t about to go anywhere, ever. Three inebriated gents stumbled across my field of view, and by the time they’d begged my pardon two or twenty times, Brynn really had vanished.

“Damn it, Tom, is that Alice’s daughter? Is that really Brynn? You didn’t warn me she looked like that.”

“What, Harry? I could have said she has hair like Farrah Fawcett? Only black? And that would have helped you how?” Tom’s head suggested I scan the casino crowd.

So I did. At least ten Farrah wannabes were wandering the casino floor. In every shade Clairol could imagine. Even one or two with similarly arresting breasts.

Tom shrugged, and we left it at that.

Brynn brought our beers, wiggling and shaking what needed to be wiggled and shook, and disappeared back into the casino, her “See you later, Plain Old Harry” tingling my ears.

Tom and I found a row of slots nobody else considered lucky and sat down. Tom took a swig of beer, brushing ineffectually at the golden stream rolling down his chin. “Mistimed the opening, Harry. Getting old and drunk all at once is a bummer.”

"Tom—besides the costume—why is Alice so worried about Brynn working here? Just looks like a gambling joint to me."

"Dunno, man." His eyes drifted away.

"Not an answer. You do know," I said. The eyes swerved back.

"I don't know the answer. Not here, not now. Catch my drift, dude? Later, maybe. Not healthy to talk shop in here." Tom's eyes roamed the casino. "Let's go watch the floor show. Then I'll take you to meet Perry."

"Who's this Perry, again?" I asked.

"Pericles Stavros. Runs this casino. Head honcho at the Lodge. Big-time lawyer, too. You remember him, don't you? The Greek? His wife's the DA now." Nah, wasn't ringing the bell that it should. "When you meet him, none of your wise guy stuff, either."

Tom slurped some more beer. I raised an eyebrow.

"Yeah, I heard you and Sven back there. He's not nice, Harry. Doesn't like being reminded he's a Scandinavian Injun. So behave, brave." Tom belched, wiped a hand across his mouth. "Let's go enjoy the floor show," he said.

The casino's Live Vegas Revue didn't do much to jack me up. Standard stuff, lots of skin, just not showing anything real important. The girls were pretty enough, the musicians worked the material with some flair, and the audience was eating it up. But my mind wandered elsewhere, and not just with Brynn and Gwen for company.

Who the hell was this Perry? The name rang the bell at the door to Kipling I'd slammed shut and locked years ago, the key long gone.

But now certain someones wanted me to pick that lock and put all the puzzle pieces back together. Why now and why me? Made no sense.

Maybe if I knew what the crazy broad had been going to tell Gwen's mother that afternoon so long ago at that double-wide shit-hole of a trailer, I could figure it out.

But it could have been nothing, just wacko bullshit like Karl had been spouting. Nothing that would have helped me nail the cool DA back then, nothing to help me with Mallory's death now. Maybe the trailer broad had been just that—batshit crazy.

And maybe Walker-Doer's Mallory had been nutso, too. His niece just crazy enough to set fire to the cabin and then kill herself for whatever wacky reason—or no reason at all. Just something to help the day on its way.

I couldn't make sense of it tonight, not with all those boobs bouncing in front of me, all those rear ends passing in review. I punched Tom's shoulder. "The casino's hootchy-kootchy show's too highbrow for me. Let's go."

Tom shook his head, gazed wistfully at the G-stringed babes strutting onstage, and led me back into the casino. "I mean it, Harry. None of your wise guy stuff with Perry. Guys who hire guys like Sven aren't nice, either."

"Hey, you know me, Tom. Prince Charming. Anytime I need to be. Come on, let's go see this Perry character." Maybe a visual would jingle my jangled memory. Ya never know.

18

CASINO HOSPITALITY

We strolled away from the floor show and headed toward a staircase that led up to—hell, I didn't know then and I still don't. Better times, I guess. Didn't matter. Tom's destination wasn't steps but a door just past the roulette tables.

"Here to see the Boss, Mr. Kuster?" A hood in a tux sat on guard in a red velvet chair outside the black door.

Tom nodded, the gorilla opened the door, and in we went. Expected, perhaps?

A zigzagging, red-lit corridor ended at another door. No attendant gorilla, just the door itself, with a brass knocker the size of a dinner plate and shaped like Medusa's head smack in the middle of it, snakes and all. Greek stuff again. Snakes, though. Ugh.

Before I had to bang the hell out of the snake lady, the door opened, and Tom stepped into what I took to be Perry's lair. I held back, let my eyes wander around a bit first.

A good-sized executive office with tasteful decorations and wood-paneled walls. An expensive Mediterranean-blue carpet covered the floor. I followed my eyes and put a foot on the carpet—expensive and soft, a good combination.

The door snicked shut. All on its own.

Torchiere floor lamps glowed dimly in corners. The lamps could have been columns cut from the Acropolis, their naked caryatids far sexier frozen in faux marble than the floor show's live tits-and-ass girls were, prancing about out there on their stage.

A white marble desk dominated the back of the room. A crystal chandelier hung over the desk, unlit. Probably filched from the casino. Since the room was so dim, I edged closer to the marble extravaganza to get a better view.

On one corner of the desk stood a bronze lamp fashioned in the image of a Minotaur. The bull man's ever-present companion Pan had his own lamp on another corner. Carvings on the desk's sides showcased Greek warriors spearing and slicing, gutting and stabbing their enemies. Or maybe their friends. It was hard to tell.

The man sitting behind the desk stood as I finished my tour, and touched a button. The chandelier blazed to life. He came out from behind the desk.

He was a pound or twenty past being overweight. Armani suited, slicked-back black hair. A white streak angling through said hair, like he'd been careless painting the bathroom yesterday.

A grin spread across my face, and he grinned back—two wolves baring their teeth before the fight. He held out a paw. I kept mine to myself.

Hell, I did know the son of a bitch.

"Well, hello just the same, Harry," said the Greek, his voice slimy, like he oiled his tongue along with his hair.

"Pericles Stavros. Son of a bitch."

"Same old Harry. Still the tough guy. What brings you back to Kipling?"

"Tom here tells me you run the place now. Town, casino, something called the Lodge. Oh, and the DA's office, too. Or your wife does.

"So why don't you tell me what brings me back, Mr. Big." The hell with me telling him.

Tom tugged at my sleeve, stage-whispered my name. Maybe I was scaring him. Maybe I didn't care.

Stavros glanced over at Tom, made his fingers and thumb a gun, said, "Get out, Kuster," and pulled the trigger. Tom got—and quickly. *Snick-snick* went the door.

"You look like shit, Harry. The years haven't been kind to you."

"Pericles Stavros," I said again, a shake of my head imitating his counterfeit worry. "The shiftiest lawyer I ever did meet."

"Now, Harry, I know you do not mean that." His courtroom voice —deep, confident. "You are simply frustrated by your own failure. Because I caught you in the spotlight of Truth, exposed you for what you were—a lazy underachiever trying to pin crimes on innocent souls." Stavros paused, smiled.

I had no comment.

"Yours was and still is a fantasy world, dear man." At least he didn't point his make-believe gun at me. As Stavros finished his critique, his eyebrows, twin caterpillars hovering above his peepers, raised up and wiggled their agreement. Somehow that made juries love him. Didn't work on me.

I told him so. I also might have said, "Get your barber to shave those creepy critters. And dye that white streak in your hair. Looks stupid, fatty."

That sure changed the mood there in the office.

"You were a shit-ass cop back then, and tonight you're just a motherfucking bottom-feeding shamus." The caterpillars let me know they thought their boss had nailed it.

But his little temper tantrum left me wondering why his courtroom courtliness had evaporated so easily. "Yeah, well, you're just a cocksucking Greek bastard." Wow. Stavros didn't seem to like that. Not at all.

His voice sank, growled. "There's guys—and gals—out there in that cold lake who're there for even thinking such a thing, much less saying it." Then his voice clambered back up into the friendly range. "At least I hear there are. I wouldn't know, myself, you understand. But surely you don't mean it." He smiled. I didn't feel any warmth.

"Oh, but I do mean it, Perry Boy. Who are you supposed to be?" My head twitch led his eyes to his bull lamp. "The Minotaur lurking back here in your labyrinth, waiting for the next sacrificial babe to drop by and party with you?"

Man, that hit a nerve. Stavros's face reddened, clouded over. I punched harder.

"Yeah, I saw your macho bull man and his flea-bitten goat pal out front. And I see them prancing there on your desk. Wooly bully, you fucking shamster."

Stavros grinned, let his eyebrows wiggle some more. Guess my *fucking shamster* wasn't much of an insult. Just schoolyard name-calling like the rest of it.

And now Stavros was laughing. At me.

"Well, Harry, I see you still have the ability to add two plus two and come up with three. Four facts and a less-than-perfect understanding of what you have seen, just like before."

Stavros walked over to his liquor cabinet, showed me a bottle of Scotch, splashed two fingers' worth into a crystal tumbler, took a sip. He didn't offer me any.

"Poor benighted Harry. Perry understands your plight. No friends up here by the lake." He beamed his jury smile my way again—cold white teeth, devoid of any genuine affection.

"Just go away, loser, before I squash you," he said. "Oh, and tell Penelope I asked about her, hope to see her soon." Huh?

"Now beat it, dirtbag. And take Kuster with you, before he drinks himself to death in my casino."

A goon, as opposed to a gorilla, appeared at my elbow, gave me the tough-guy stare. Only a goon though, because he hadn't earned a gorilla suit yet. Still working his way up in the tribe.

As I turned toward the office door, I spotted a guy sporting an iron gray crew cut and black jeans and a black silk shirt. He was leaning against the wall, one hand keeping a caryatid company. Rangy and hard-looking, but relaxed, as if he and not Perry were in charge. I think he winked at me. Or maybe it was just the white-bright lighting—hard to tell. My God, that chandelier. The door opened on its own again, and I walked back into the red-lit corridor.

19

NIGHT SHAKES

I followed the twists and turns back to the entrance, stepped out, tapped the door gorilla's shoulder. "Your boss said, 'Tell King Kong to get his monkey ass back here now.'"

The hood sprang up, fists balled, ready to rumble.

"Hey, can't help it. That's what Stavros said. Better hurry, King." The gorilla snarled and raced into the red-light district. I went to find Tom.

He was at a roulette wheel, hanging on to the table, clutching a drink, drooling over the low-cut view of the woman next to him. Probably boring her to death with newspaper gossip. But then again, she did seem somewhat interested.

I laid an arm across Tom's shoulders, winked at the lady, if that really was what she was.

"Time for us to depart, Mr. Kuster. That's his real name, ma'am. I'm not going to ask you who he's been claiming to be."

She gave me a professional smile, said, "In my business, I never ask real names. If you need to tell me yours, though, that's okay." I didn't, and she sashayed away, hoping to hook some other poor John. And I bet she would. It was a lot of woman in one hell of a dress.

We headed for the entrance, the majority of Tom's steps sideways.

I did my best to keep him upright. "You didn't piss Perry off, did you?" Tom sounded a little fearful, but with all the alcohol inside him, it was a tough call.

"No, I didn't. We got along super. Just reminiscing about old times. And putting my classical education to use. Along with a bit of archaic rock and roll."

"Harry, tell me the truth. You shouldn't mess with Perry. You didn't, did you?" Scared to death, that's how he sounded. Wonder why?

"Nah, not at all. I merely tried enlightening him concerning Greek mythology. Oh, and I told him about some things I saw." Tom broke the grip I had on his arm.

"You didn't. Not the Minotaur. Not Pan out front. Not at the judge's, too. Tell me you didn't."

"All right, I didn't." And that was close to the truth. I hadn't mentioned the judge's pair to Stavros. Still, Tom didn't believe me. And why should he? I can't bluff. No poker face, remember?

"Oh, shit, Harry. We're dead men."

"Take it easy." Still holding him up, a wobbling kid out on the ice—fearful the skates would betray him. "Oh, and Perry called me a motherfucker, and I returned the compliment by assuring him he was a cocksucker, of the bastard, Greek strain."

"Oh, God. We're dead." Beads of sweat popped on his forehead.

Tom almost made me think the casino trip had been a mistake. But all I was doing was checking up on the place for Alice, right? And nosing around just enough into Mallory's death to justify putting tonight's adventure on the insurance company's tab.

Why should that concern Stavros? Or make trouble for me? And I'd met Brynn. So, all in all, not a bad night. Time to blow and go.

Sven held the door, gave me his best scalp-'em stare.

I beamed an angelic smile his way, said, "Your boss said to get your Red Injun ass back to his office."

The doorman seemed unsure if I was messing with him or not. Maybe his boss did talk to him like that. The door gorilla had sure swallowed his dose as if it were gospel.

"Stavros told me to tell you, 'Like pronto, Tonto.'" And like the gorilla, Sven snarled and raced off to find his boss. "Hey, his words, not mine."

"Harry," Tom started to say, but as we stepped outside, the Volvo glided to a halt in front of the steps. The flunky held the passenger door for Tom and then his hand out to me for his tip.

"Your boss said he comped everything tonight, including gratuities. See him if you've got a beef. Nighty-night."

The valet didn't snarl like some other casino employees I knew. He just stood there, hand out, confused, unsure if I was screwing with his head or his palm.

I left him standing under the porte cochere, unenlightened.

On the way back to town, while Tom snored, I told the little hula girl about his lady friend at the roulette wheel. The little hula girl jiggled giddily, elated perhaps to leave casino competition behind. Or maybe just gyrating in rhythm with the road.

Either way, I pushed the Volvo hard, like the Hordes of Hades were after us. Because maybe they were.

The Volvo rolled up and over a hill on the road back to Kipling—and we were headlights to headlights with a pickup truck in our lane. I cut hard.

The pickup nipped the Volvo's mirror.

While I waited for my heart to creep back down from up in my throat, I checked to be sure Tom hadn't bailed on me. Still there, but busy holding his head in his hands, trying to stop the shaking.

"Damn it, you drunk, Harry? Watch the road. It drops off. Straight down, into the lake."

Brakes screeched truck tires to a halt behind us. A roaring V8 spun rubber in the night, and the pickup kissed the Volvo's bumper the way a hammer pecks delicately at a nail.

"He's back!" I said, and floored it. But in a Volvo sedan, that's not very exciting or very fast. Nor very evasive.

The pickup closed quickly once more, and we were playing bumper cars again. For keeps this time. The Swedish love of my life scraped her way down the guardrail but avoided a swim in Great Cold Lake.

Whoever was behind the pickup's wheel was serious. Well, so was I.

"Glove box. Hand me my gun." Voice calm, heart pounding, expecting Tom to drop my piece, blow his foot off. But he didn't.

Hard brake. The pickup backed off. Foot stomping the Volvo's accelerator, putting a little distance between us. But just like that, the pickup closed and was dead on our bumper again.

Left hand wrapped tight on the steering wheel, right arm extended straight back, I kept the little snub-nosed .38 in my hand pointing the pickup's way.

"Duck," I said. Maybe Tom did, maybe he didn't. At least he didn't quack. The shot shattered the Volvo's rear window and convinced the pickup's pilot the rules of the game had changed.

The truck braked hard, screeching and fishtailing sideways to a stop.

The four of us kept going: Tom, the Volvo, the little hula girl, and Harry, the hot rod crack shot. At least the little hula girl seemed to be enjoying herself, the lake breeze swirling through the car, reminding her of the islands, perhaps.

We didn't see any more of the truck. Guess it went back to wherever it lived. Or better yet, was just sitting there beside the road, waiting patiently while the driver's blood leaked all over its glass-sprinkled front seat. I really didn't give a damn.

An eye on Tom as we raced along. The peaceful drive along the lake shore had sure upset him. He was still shaking. Not me. I felt great.

I'd stirred the pot tonight, created some local interest in one Harry Reno, shamus-by-the-lake. My kind of PI work up there at the casino, bearding the lion, or the bull, or the goat, or whoever Stavros pretended to be, right there in his own den. Then a snappy leave-taking with a quick dash for home and a drink.

Or should I say, whomever he pretended he was? The hell with that nonsense. I wanted a drink. Needed a couple of stiff ones. Coming down off an adrenaline high. A son of a bitch in a pickup had tried to kill us.

On toward town we rolled. Only now I had the night shakes like Tom.

20

NEWSROOM INTERROGATIONS

The Volvo nosed into the curb outside *The Kipling Pioneer*. I helped Tom stagger in. He was in no shape to return the favor. The nearest chair sat beside his desk, but I dropped him off on the couch instead and went in search of whiskey.

"You gonna report that, Harry? To the police?" The burn from rye sliding inside was bringing the newspaper's editor back from the edge of wherever he'd been on our way back to Kipling. It wasn't necessarily an improvement.

"Report what, Tom?"

"Damn it. That guy tried to kill us. Call somebody."

"How do you know it was a guy?" I asked.

"That guy tried to kill us. Do something."

"I did. I persuaded him to leave us alone."

"Shit, Harry. You probably killed him. They're gonna come and arrest us. I mean it. Report it, man." Tom working himself up, getting loud. At least he'd stopped shaking.

I poured him another shot of rye. He gulped it down and held out his glass for more, like a kid begging Kool-Aid. "I mean it, Harry. Call —the—cops."

"And who do I tell them it was? Stavros? Try to convince them he keeps thugs in pickups circling his casino, in case some gumshoe insults him? I don't think so, Tom."

"Might've been Lance." Tom slugged down the rest of his whiskey. "You decked him at the Tam, and he thinks Gwen and I, well—you know . . ."

Huh? Gwen and you what? I let it slide for now. Shouldn't have, but I did.

"Slow down, big guy. I'm not calling anybody. Especially not to say a cop just tried to kill us." Now my whiskey was gone, too. "Anyway, the somebodies I would call probably already knew about the hit before it went down. If Stavros and his wife run this town like you say they do."

Tom made a face like Gus in the bar. Maybe I was onto something —Stavros and his missus, the casino, the Lodge and its temple. The judge's dead redheaded niece.

"So, if the somebodies were pissed about the outcome," I said, "they'd already be here."

The knock on the newspaper's front door made us both jump. My hand caressed my .38. That and the rye gave me the courage to check out the knocking. It wasn't letting up.

Outside, in the pool of light at *The Pioneer*'s front door, Lance the cop was leaning against the newspaper's plate-glass window, as if he couldn't stand up without its fragile support. His free hand, the one not attached to the leaning arm, kept beating its staccato tattoo.

I opened the door, let Lance see the snub nose held close alongside my leg.

"You can put it away, Mr. Reno. I'm friendly again. Sorry about earlier." Which earlier? The woods, the bar, or the lake road? I didn't pursue the topic. No use. Lance was too taken with drink, as they say.

Since he was still leaning his ox body on plate glass despite the opened door, I pulled him in before he broke in. But I kept a grip on my gun. Tom was right, we hadn't parted on the best of terms earlier.

Lance staggered to the recliner beside the couch. I slipped the .38 into my coat pocket.

"What happened to your car's window, Harry?" Not that Lance enunciated his words that clearly. Something more akin to *Wha hap u car win?* spilled out of his mouth. But I knew what he meant. I speak and understand drunk. I've had a lot of practice. I favored Lance with a shrug.

The cop swiveled bleary eyes toward Tom, the Volvo's window momentarily forgotten. "Hi, Mr. Kuster. How you doing? Need some help with that bottle?"

I answered for Tom by pouring a shot apiece for the three of us.

Then I tackled Lance's window question. "Tom got overheated, up at the casino," I said. "Too much booze. Too much floor show. He needed a little night lake air on the way back to cool himself off."

Lance scowled at the mention of the casino and its floor show. "Did you talk to Gwen like I asked?" So much for Lance the Forgetful Drunk.

"Well, you sort of ruined the mood back there at the Tam. So no, I didn't, but I will."

"I don't want her working there. I'm gonna tell that Stav . . . Stav . . . that shithead so, too," Lance said. "Don't want her working no casino." Aha. An opening.

"Hey, Lance. Tell Uncle Harry about the bull man and goat guy. I saw them lurking around the casino tonight. Maybe they were waiting for Gwen."

Lance stared, not comprehending the change in the conversation. His "Huh?" eased out on the tail of a belch. Tom scrunched around on the couch, let a grunt of displeasure drift my way. The hell with that.

"Come on, Lance. Right beside the entrance. A goat guy and a bull man. Prancing around at the top of totem poles. What gives?"

Tom came alive, latched onto my forearm. The shuffling drunk had a pretty good grip all of a sudden. "Harry . . . don't." His knuckles white, the fingers digging into my hide.

I jerked my arm away. "Easy, Tom. No harm in asking. Have

another drink." I needed some Kipling answers, and maybe Lance had them.

Tom rubbed the rim of his glass with his finger, looked thoughtful, shrugged his shoulders. "Your funeral, Harry. Just don't drag me along in the hearse next time." He grinned and sipped more rye.

I swung back to Lance. "So, what gives with those two, the bull and the goat?"

"Ah . . . Harry, that's just the Lodge's, uh . . . you know . . . uh . . ." Lance had been at the alcohol all night and it showed, but I knew what he was trying to say.

"Symbols?" Lance nodded. Now we both knew what I was talking about.

"The Lodge, Lance. Do you belong?"

"Course not. Rich guys belong. Not working stiffs like me. You belong, Harry?"

"No. I'm so poor, I can't even afford a car with a rear window." Laughter times three—alcohol turning detective into comedian.

"The Lodge is just something rich guys get to belong to, Harry. That's all," Lance said.

He wasn't exactly following my skillful questioning. No surprise there. He was drunk. And rapidly approaching dead-drunk. I could tell. I wasn't far behind.

"What if you pull a Lodge brother over," I said. "How do you know he's a Lodge brother? And if he is, do you give him a ticket, or just say 'Sorry, Brother Goat—Sorry, Brother Bull.'"

Laughs all around. Maybe it was my wry way of speaking—or my rye delivery. That was it. I'd poured three more shots before I said it.

"You know 'em," the cop said, "because they wear these funny rings. They tell you that when you get your badge. 'Don't you be haulin' no goats or bulls in here, boy.' That's what Sarge said." We laughed harder and let some more rye slip inside to celebrate. "So that's what I do. Or don't do," Lance said.

"But what if it's something serious. Like arson and murder, what then?" I asked.

"Huh?" Too complicated. Stick to simple.

"Murder, Lance. You investigate that? Bull or no bull?"

"Shit, I don't investigate no murder. Get real. The lieut or a detective does that."

This was going nowhere. All I was accomplishing was getting us drunk. Or drunker. Still, I gave it another shot. "What about DUIs? Do bulls and goats skate on those?"

"Well, yeah, sometimes. Most times, yeah they do. If it's bad, they just hire that shithead Stav, Stav . . ."

"Stavros?" I offered.

"Yeah, him. The Big Goat."

"Sure you don't mean the Big Bull?" Tom said.

Peals of laughter. I spilled my whiskey. In the midst of it all, Tom shot me a look that said, *Stop*. The hell with that. "Lance," I said, but that was as far as my interrogation made it.

"Gentles all," Tom said, "tomorrow's an early rising for me. Lance, you stay in the recliner. You're half-asleep anyway. Harry, you take the couch, if you don't mind clearing away my, uh, research."

Tom's research consisted of two empty wine bottles. I held them aloft, waggled them back and forth. "A man does not live by rye alone, Harry."

The laughter from Tom's nugget of truth did us all in. Lance laid the recliner back, and Tom headed upstairs. I turned out the light, tried one last shot at Lance. "You still awake?"

"Kinda, Harry."

"Who would cover up murder, Lance? Who?"

"Don't know . . . Don't . . ." He was fading on me.

"Who, Lance? Who?" No answer. *Goodnight,* said the rye.

21

DEWY-EYED REUNIONS

Sunshine. The newsroom. The casino trip. Last night still scratchy grit in my eyes. Searching for coffee, aspirin. Head hurting. Stomach a mess. Stale crackers. In Tom's desk.

Finally, drinking coffee, but still fumbling around in drawers for aspirin. Then *The Pioneer*'s front door banged open loud enough to make me reach for my gun. Where the hell was it? No idea.

So I stood there, empty-handed, facing the flailing blond fury that was Jayne Rask thundering into her newsroom. Jayne and I had a bit of a history. She'd helped Tom run the paper back then. And helped Harry Reno some, too. Yesterday Tom told me she was still around.

And so, here she was. Watch out, Reno. Good advice, Harry.

The blond tempest drew closer. A still-youthful face floating above a fully equipped body. A bitch who left heartache in her wake. Jayne's fury crashed ashore.

"Damn you to hell, Harry Reno. And that drunken lowlife over there, too." Jayne reached down, yanked at Lance's recliner, shot him bolt upright.

"Get up and get out. Go oppress Kipling's citizenry, you worthless bastard." She kicked at the cop, hit the recliner instead.

To his credit, a still-drink-befuddled Lance complied peaceably.

"See you, Mr. Reno. Tell Mr. Kuster thanks." He tried out a smile. "Good-bye, Ms. Rask. You look very nice today." And then he was gone.

"Where the hell's Tom, Harry?" Her periwinkle blue eyes screamed *I'll kill the bastard.*

My silvery tongue purred, "Easy, Jayne. He's upstairs. Let him sleep." I touched her shoulder, stroked her hair. She calmed a bit. I considered kissing her. Kept talking instead.

"Blame me, Jayne. I let him drink too much last night." Wasn't true. I said it anyway. "Know why I'm here?" Not really a question. Bet she knew the answer, though. "Tom knew why. That's what pushed him off the cliff last night. My fault. Sorry."

Jayne pushed me away. Gently. I let her.

"Yeah, I get it, Harry. Mallory Mordred—Mallory Mordred—Mallory Mordred." A little girl's singsong voice. Then the grown-up woman stepped in again, growled, "Fuck her." Spit dappled my cheek. "I'm glad she's gone." Jayne, snarling mad again. I wiped the spit away.

"What happened to the Volvo's window, Harry?" Jayne abruptly softer—and drier. Her fingertips tickled their way across the top of my hand, tracing a pattern only she could fathom.

"Somebody tried to kill us last night," I said, like it happened every day. "After we'd been to the casino. And met Stavros." Green eyes found blue ones, made them soul mates.

"I don't believe in coincidence, don't know why I'm suddenly such a threat to him. Do you?" A little edge to my voice. "Is Stavros mixed up in Mallory's death?"

I waited to see if that set her off. It didn't. Whatever fierce wind had blown her into the newsroom this morning had played itself out. Jayne Rask, queen of mood swings. Same way back then, too.

Now she wouldn't look at me at all. Her head hung down, her too-sharp chin pointing the way to her chest. Yeah, she'd had a little boob tune-up for sure.

I took her chin in my fingers and ever so gently raised her face until she had to look at me. Her blond hair sported frosted highlights—perky, like her renewed breasts.

"Will you tell me the truth about Mallory and what she was working on? Please? Tom sure as hell won't. Or can't." The PI in the room pleading, not punching.

Jayne shuffled away, slumped on the couch, thought that over for a while. I sat with her and waited. Rubbed her some, too, like you do with a cat, just hoping it won't claw you.

Finally, her thousand yard stare focused back on me. "Maybe I will, Harry. When I know what you're up to, when I know if it'll hurt Tom or help him. But not today I won't—now, beat it."

But while her last words sounded harsh, she'd parted her knees so her skirt rode up, showing off her still trim legs—encased in sheer black stockings, not the pantyhose kind, not at all. Jayne's typical technique, just her usual way of maintaining control over the men in her life.

It still worked. So I said, "Me Cheetah." Our old routine.

"Me Jayne. See ya, Harry Reno. Don't stay away from the jungle so long. I love Tom, just not all the time. I still have spare moments to pet the other animals."

I got the hell out of there. With my jacket and my gun. And my life.

The Volvo stopped at an auto glass place. Even this early, I was second in line. An immense, grubby-looking character was leaning on the fender of an older pickup. A pickup with a busted windshield. Hmm.

I rolled out of the car and headed into the shop's office. "Think you could tape some plastic on my Volvo?" I pointed out the obvious.

"I got a guy ahead of you," the fellow behind the counter said.

I slapped a Jackson down in front of him. "I'm sorta in a hurry."

"I'll still have to ask him if it's okay." He pointed to the grubby giant by the pickup again. A second twenty magically appeared on the counter. Investigation expenses. Out the door we went.

"Hey, Dewey, gotta take care of this fellow first. I forgot, he had an appointment." What the hell, I wasn't paying for the truth, just fast service.

The Dewey character said, "Dewey no mind." Good thing. Son of a bitch was the size of a grizzly.

The counter dude and his glass guy taped plastic where the Volvo's rear window used to reside. "Lucky Dewey's in a good mood today," the counter guy said.

"Yeah, lucky," the glass guy agreed.

"Lucky for who?" I asked. They didn't know. Or at least, they didn't say. Maybe I should have said *whom*.

"All done," the counter guy said.

"Yeah, done," the glass guy agreed.

I shot a gunman's salute Dewey's way. He didn't wave back.

As the Volvo pulled out, I swear I heard the little hula girl say, "My, but Dewey's a big bear, isn't he?" No argument there.

22
BLACK LACE PANTIES

A little later the Volvo cruised into the motel parking lot. Karl was slinking into the office, still on duty. Guess Mom and Pops were sleeping in, letting the little creep keep an eye on the place, literally. The Volvo ignored the desk clerk, found our room instead. The little hula girl wiggled her approval.

Nobody had been in to tidy up. The bed hadn't been made; no fresh towels, either. But it was something else altogether that caught my eye.

Right in the middle of the bed's white pillow—dead center—lay the prettiest pair of black lace panties a man could ever hope to see, on or off of a woman. Panties trimmed with little red bows on the sides. Pull the bows and the panties would slip right off whoever had been nice enough to put them on in the first place. Or did I mean whomever? Not that I really cared.

Pinned to the pillow was a note—*Sorry I missed you, Plain Old Harry*. That was all. No name. What the hell? Who the hell? Brynn, Gwen? Elke the Giggler? Karl, maybe? I shuddered.

So while the panties had multiple ways of arriving on my pillow, they had only one way of leaving. I nabbed the panties and the note and stuffed them both into my suitcase.

Evidence of trouble afoot in Kipling? Dunno, Harry. But too exciting to just throw away, right, Mr. Reno? Maybe Penny would help with the black panties inquiry, model them while Harry and Reno considered the implications, the possibilities. I could always hope.

I drove up front to check out.

Inside, Karl glanced up from his magazine. Probably *Teens You Would Love to . . .* Fill in the blank. And the girls in it wouldn't be the eighteen or nineteen variety. The night clerk was a creep. A disgusting creep. Karl seemed surprised I was there. Guess he hadn't seen me cruising back in.

"Checking out, Karl. I appreciate all that you did to make my stay here feel like home."

He didn't know what to say, so he fell back on, "Thank you, Mr. Reno."

I paid my bill and let my eyes wander a bit. The coffeepot was nearly empty, so I asked Karl if he would mind brewing a fresh pot, fill my travel mug for the road. All said so friendly like.

Karl said, "Certainly, Mr. Reno," and walked back into the storeroom to get some coffee packs.

I walked around the desk, took a gander at his reading material. I was right, sort of. *Preteen Dreams,* complete with pictures. Not a little girl over twelve in the whole filthy mess. I followed him into the storeroom.

He turned when he heard me behind him, his face white, pulsating with fear. Good.

A hard shove into the wall next to the motel's industrial washer and dryer setup. Karl banged his head. Suddenly he seemed crossed-eyed. My hand wrapped around his skinny throat, kept him pinned to the wall. *Preteen Dreams,* my ass.

"Who's been in my room?" A punch to the stomach, the fist twisting a bit while it was there. Let him dream about that.

"Nobody," Karl groaned, when he could talk again.

"Think about last night, this morning. Who?" I heel-stomped his foot.

"Nobody," he said again, voice cracking. "Nobody." Maybe those were real tears in his eyes. Maybe I didn't care.

"No points for consistency, Karl. I don't believe you." Another tummy tickle.

Karl doubled over like it actually hurt. Guess it did. I'm not really the soft sort of shamus, not at all. Especially not if you're a preteen-loving pervert.

"Tell Mom and Pops to hire some better help, get somebody to keep an eye on you. See you around." A step toward the door. "Hey, Karl—" A quicker step back to the night clerk.

"I know this motel is a franchise deal. Real private eyes know that kind of stuff." A shoulder squeeze, a Reno specialty. "Bet they wouldn't like to hear about your little peepholes--or your choice of reading material." Another bust to the gut—he deserved it, little deviant.

"No need to mention our conversation here this morning to anyone. Because I'll be back. And soon." He was crying and moaning, clutching his stomach as I walked out, minus my coffee.

Damn. Oh well, there's always Mickey D's.

On the way out of town, I stopped at the overlook. I sat in the car, sipped some clown java, let the bitter and sweet mix in my head—the people I'd met, the meager intel I'd gathered, the shit stink I'd have to inhale if I came back. *If?*

Hell, I'd have to come back to earn the company's retainer—to unravel the fire and Mallory's death. Once Barb finished her autopsy for Walker-Doer.

And the black lace panties. I both needed and wanted the answer to that silky conundrum. Who wouldn't? But for today, good-bye to all that. Time to get back to Ithaca and Penelope Phair. I mashed down on the accelerator, and the Volvo got us the hell away from Kipling, the little hula girl wiggling her approval.

Stupid whistle bait. What the hell did she know. Her panties had polka dots.

23

PENELOPE'S PILLOW TALK

"Wake up, Harry. Blower's ringing."

"Huh? What?"

"The telephone, you wally. Answer it," Penelope Phair said.

"Your home, your phone." I rolled onto my stomach, pulled the pillow over my head. Sunday morning. Still dark. Didn't need or want to talk to anyone right now. What I did have and didn't want was half a hangover. Last night had been a late one. Memorable, but late. And boozy. For me. Never Penny, though. Too perfect for that.

"Bloody hell," Penny said, and made a point of digging her elbows into me as she crawled across to answer her phone.

No complaints from Harry or Reno, though. Felt good, the way a massage sometimes does. Hey, maybe it was Brynn or Gwen on the line. Or Elke. Half-asleep thoughts aren't always the most rational.

"Bloody hell," she said again. I squashed the pillow tighter over my ears. "It's your girlfriend, Reno."

Damn, my girlfriend? Wasn't I in bed with my girlfriend, wasn't she lying across me naked, talking to someone on the phone? God, but my head felt fuzzy.

Penny rolled off, and I asked, "Which one is it?"

Silence. Then, "Ya-ouch." The hand that wasn't holding the phone reminding me to behave myself—a Penny reminder, a unique sensation, like a bee that both pinches and stings at the same time, but in a good way. I rolled over, sat up. Wide awake now.

Penny smacked the telephone into my waiting palm. I grouched, "Yeah, who's this?" and waited for the phone to say something back.

I get my telephone manners from the cheap detective novels I'm always reading. Probably why I don't have a lot of clients, or earn a lot of money, or make many friends. You got a problem with that? Well, do you?

"Oh. Hi, Barb. You're looking good, I mean, you sound good, I mean it's good to hear your voice." Damn bleary brain this morning. "Yeah, I'm okay." Penny took a pinch of flesh and twisted. I yelped again.

"No, I'm awake, Barb. What's up?"

Penny grabbed my anatomy's most vital part, started helping me answer my *What's up* question. Guess that meant she wasn't too concerned that Barbara Nolan, assistant state medical examiner, was the ex-girlfriend who was on the other end of her blower.

"Now? Okay." Penny stopped trying to find the answer to *What's up* and pinched me instead—right there.

"Cut it out, Penny. No, really, Barb, I'm all right." There, I'd stopped with the *okays*. They had to be the cause of Penny's reminders, not Barb on the blower.

"Be there in a half hour or so. Yeah, yeah, yeah, I'll hurry." I hung up, ran my eyes over the naked woman beside me, then switched on my murder-one face. "Gotta go sleuth, babe."

"Let me venture a guess, Mr. Reno. The cadaver's autopsy completed?" Penny's hand was wandering my cadaver. And it wasn't pinching anymore. No sir, it surely wasn't.

"Your girlfriend, the medical examiner, desires you in her surgery, so as to impart to you her opinions regarding the female anatomy, how the various parts function and interact with the world at large, and with the two of you in particular?"

I tried holding Penny's eyes with mine. I couldn't. She was laughing too hard.

"Gotta go, sweetheart." I rolled out of bed and started for the bathroom.

"Really, Reno. Love 'em and leave 'em, as you Yanks are wont to say and do." But Penny was sitting up now, smiling as she delivered her chastisement, chestnut hair swinging as she shook her head to and fro. Then she wiggle-waggled her shoulders, and her two major chassis parts took to swaying as well.

I blew her a kiss. God, what a woman. The shower was hot, too.

Traffic this early was sparse. Still, just from habit, I checked for a tail. A silver Ford fell in behind me. I watched it for a couple of blocks. Then it stopped at a donut shop, and I lost interest—lucky Taurus, stopping for crullers. I was hungry. Stomach growling. Head still fuzzy.

Forget about donuts and coffee, Reno. Think about what Barb has to tell you, what's so important she wouldn't just say it over the phone. Barb knows how Reno feels about Sunday mornings. Sundays had been our bedroom mornings, too.

By the time I stopped thinking about donuts and coffee and lost Sundays, the drizzle had turned steady, a chilly-for-summer drumbeat of a rain. The windshield wipers shoved drops away, and the sign pointing the way to Barb and her body appeared. *State Medical Examiner's Office Next Right.* I took it.

The Volvo eased herself into a parking space marked *Staff Only* while my mind was idling along on its own, resurrecting half-forgotten memories of Sunday mornings with Barb.

I shook the fog from my head, glanced up at the former hospital. The medical examiner's bailiwick occupied the third floor. The rest of the place had state offices of one stripe or another, all dark this morning. On the third floor, only one window was lit. Barb's office.

I slid out of the Volvo and headed for the front entrance.

A weather conspiracy tried forcing me to linger outside. A hurricane wind, full in my face, doing its damnedest to shove me back to the shelter of the Volvo. Raindrops pelting hard, stinging like Penny's reminders, but in a bad way. Wind and rain squalling together, as if sent by some malevolent weather god to keep me from reaching Barb and her body.

I finally made the entrance and pushed on the doors. The red-lettered sign explained why I couldn't get in: *Front Entrance Closed on Weekends—Please Use Morgue Entrance*. Malevolent weather god, my ass. The wind and the rain had been trying to save me wasted effort. I turned around and trudged back to the Volvo.

Damn it, I knew better. How many times had I driven Barb down here to her morgue? Driven her down here to cut up cold meat on a Sunday morning? A rainy Sunday, just like today. Because some cop she knew had to have the corpse spill its guts—right away, Reno's Sunday fun be damned.

And that was why we weren't a couple anymore. Too damn many interruptions of my Sacred Sunday Rituals. And maybe, just maybe, some other stuff.

I'd said, "I'm splitting." Barb had spit out, "Good. Get out now!"

And that's how we ended. How and why we still tolerated each other was a memory to resurrect another day. And since now I was back at the Volvo, I climbed in and tried sloughing off raindrops along with reminders of ruined Sundays.

As the green love of my life headed around to the morgue entrance, I noticed a silver Ford Taurus parked out on the street. Maybe it was the same one. Maybe it *was* a tail job.

Hey, if it was still there when I came back out, I could walk over and punch its driver in the nose. Kick the car, break its antenna, tear a mirror off, or some other tough-guy shit.

Yeah, just maybe I would. All for adding yet another layer of ruination to Reno's Sacred Sunday Ritual.

I parked the Volvo on my own this time and went in to see Barb and her body.

24
DOC NOLAN

The red arrow on the wall said *Medical Examiner's Office Third Floor,* and I'd always believed it. Today was no different. I strolled toward the elevator, down the same puke-green corridor with the same scuffed black-and-white floor that had always begun the journey to Barbara Nolan and her bodies. Damned place smelled of cheap bleach. Like always.

The same balky elevator lifted upward, slowly. The doors refused to open. So I kicked 'em right where it hurts elevator doors the most. Magic. The doors opened. Just like always.

The medical examiner's office sat at the end of a corridor, this one antiseptic white, immaculately clean, smelling of quality disinfectant. I guess because the cleaning lady was there, on a Sunday morning, cleaning.

"Sorry," I said, apologizing for stepping on her freshly mopped floor.

She smiled, assured me it was all right. "Least there ain't no blood today."

What a cheerful thought. Have to wonder, though. Would that hold true for the whole day, here in the morgue?

Repetitive *Entrance Forbidden* portals, pleasure palaces reserved only for gods and doctors, pockmarked the hallway. At the end of the corridor, black lettering on frosted glass proclaimed:

BARBARA A. NOLAN, M.D.

CHIEF ASSISTANT STATE MEDICAL EXAMINER

FORENSICS DIVISION

PLEASE KNOCK BEFORE ENTERING

I turned the doorknob and went in.

"You never did absorb directions well, did you, Reno?"

"I still don't, Barb. Hey, good to see you, too. You look great." Only she didn't.

Her once flouncing mane of auburn hair had been shortened. Ugly short, chopped and cropped. Barb's face looked lousy, too. Haggard, pasty white.

"What's the matter, Reno? Don't like the hair?" Damn my poker face.

"No, Barb, I don't. Except for the better neck access. That looks inviting."

"Well, Penelope's inviting, too. Inviting me to call her if you misbehave. So don't."

"Okay." Her office still cluttered as hell. No room for a picture of me. No surprise there.

"You want to see the body, read my report, have a cup of coffee? You want to try and remember why you came here?" What the hell was wrong with her?

"I came here, Barbara Ann, because I guess you don't like me surfing in bed with Penelope on a Sunday morning." A twitch of her lip, not quite a smile, but almost. "But a cup of coffee and the report would be good." Good old Beach Boys, always a Barbara Ann favorite.

"But no viewing the body, huh?" Barb snickered, turned, headed toward the back room.

"Somewhere to sit would be good, too," I said. No answer—she'd disappeared.

Coffee sounds and smells drifted out while I scrounged for a seat. Masses of files piled everywhere. Her stupid monkey skull paperweight atop one stack, mocking me.

"Same old Harry," she said as she handed me a mug of her always-too-strong coffee. Her other hand held a donut.

"Looks stale."

"Eat it anyway, Harry. Maybe it'll quiet your stomach." Gruff, but Harry instead of Reno. Always better for me, better for us.

I took a bite of the donut, tried paying attention to what she was telling me.

"Are you listening, Harry? I said, the fire didn't leave me a lot to work with." Whatever her perfume was, it smelled a hell of a lot better than her hair looked.

"Oh, I had the reports from the sheriff and coroner to fill out the details. There is even a write-up by some illiterate assistant Lake County fire chief." I wondered: had she put the perfume on just for me?

"All three are either botched jobs or outright lies." The snarl in her voice curled her lip, hiking it high. Just like always.

Barb didn't think much of police and coroners out in the state. So, back in my cop days, I'd learned to listen to Barbara A. Nolan, Assistant State Medical Examiner, and do what she told me I needed to do with bodies. Especially what she said we needed to do with hers.

I'd listened and followed orders back then. Up to a point—the point of me leaving.

"Reno. Honest to God. Where are you this morning? Pay attention, will you?"

I ate the rest of the donut. I was right. Stale as hell. Barb's office seemed stale, too. Like she'd been here all weekend without opening the door. Could be. She had her own bathroom.

"I said, the detective and his crystal ball conclude that her intent was to set the place on fire and then hang herself. A Viking funeral with her uncle's cabin for her longship. That's me talking, not the detective, Reno. No poetry in his report, only lies."

Her eyes flashed, narrowed, stared at me—crow's-feet perching at corners, nostrils scrunching in. What the hell. I didn't write the damn report.

"But a Viking funeral is not what happened. Yes, Mallory remained in the cabin until all she was, was remains. And that is the only part of the report that rings true," Barb said.

"The detective *surmises* that Mallory splashed kerosene on herself trying to douse a pile of furniture by the fireplace, and lit both the furniture and herself on fire. Then lay down on her couch with a noose around her pretty little neck and, like a Buddhist monk, waited peacefully for the flames to do their job."

I took a last sip of coffee. Maybe she'd get me a refill. And another donut. The last one wasn't all that stale. Maybe *I* could find where the rest were hiding.

"You still with me, Reno? Reno!"

"Yeah, I'm right there in the cabin. I read the reports. Can I have some more coffee?" She ignored me.

"They scooped up what was left of their Mallory, dumped it in a body bag that night, took it to a funeral home, and wrote it up that way. Only sketchy details of the fire scene. No autopsy of the body. No interviews with Mallory's friends or coworkers at the paper to establish her state of mind leading up to her so-called suicide. Not even, and this is crucial, Reno— Hey, you awake?"

"I'm awake, Barb." And I was, sort of. Never expected to be up this early. Not on a Sunday. Could have planned for it, if I'd known.

"I said this is crucial. Put your eyes back on me." I did, but I still wanted more coffee. Needed some aspirin. Fucking headache.

"No basis," Barb said, "to conclude the body in the cabin was Mallory Mordred. Except for the uncontroverted facts that it was Mallory's cabin, the one her uncle the judge let her live in, that her Jeep was parked outside, and that what was left of the body was most definitely a female with fire-singed red hair."

A snort instead of a snarl. Maybe an improvement; maybe not.

"And based on that in-depth poking around, everybody agreed the crispy bacon on the couch was in fact Mallory Mordred." Barb's hands on her hips. Better if mine were there instead.

"A total bullshit investigation, Reno." Hands on her desk now, eyes leaning in on me. No use asking Doc for aspirin. No use at all.

"All right then. I get a body in a bag. I'm told it's the remains of one Mallory Mordred, late of Kipling up by Great Cold Lake. She's not much to look at anymore.

"So I try dental records. Takes a while. Finally, bingo! I had her dentist and maybe an orthodontist." Barb on a roll. I kept quiet, except for my stomach.

"I struck out with the crooked-teeth doc," she said. "Dead and gone. But with the dentist, I hit gold. Records, X-rays, charts. Her old dentist still had them."

She caught me snooping around again. I hadn't given up on donuts. Or aspirin.

"You want some more coffee, Harry?" Her voice softer, at least for now.

"Yeah."

She went and filled my mug, shoved it my way, slopping java all over my cuff. I don't think she even noticed.

"Now pay close attention, Harry. Get whatever is causing you to look like that out of your head. I'm only going to tell you this twice. It wasn't Mallory Mordred they scooped into a body bag at the cabin that night." Huh? What the hell?

25

BARB'S BODY

And, true to her promise, Barb repeated her Mallory news yet again. "Stunned, Reno?" Twice now she'd told me it wasn't Mallory. You would have thought it would have sunk in. Well, you would have thought wrong.

"Are you sure it's not Mallory?" I asked.

Thunder and lightning—fire and brimstone—Harry and Reno damned to Hell. Then as quick as it blew in, the storm sailed away. Never will understand women, just never will.

"Hey, I like that, Reno. Good idea. Let's call her Not-Mallory." She reached over, patted my hand. Ah, the softer, gentler Barbara Nolan. The Barb who played Reno's Sunday games and invented some of her own, back when her hair was long and playful, too.

I was drifting again; she sensed it.

"Come on, Harry. Stay with me. Focus. You know this. Four specific things an autopsy is supposed to establish. One: cause of death. The instrument or physical means. Two: mechanism of death. The pathological condition that results in death."

Yeah, yeah, yeah. I didn't say it, but I sure as hell thought it. I'd heard her lectures before.

"Three," Doc Nolan said. "Manner of death. You know the possibilities: natural, accident, suicide, homicide. Choose one, and it excludes the others. And four: time of death."

I hate autopsies. I hate burned bodies. Like old girlfriends, they throw me off my game.

"The first question I ask myself when a cop or some other idiot dumps a crisped corpse in my morgue is, did the fire kill her or was she already dead?

"Not-Mallory was already dead. And yes, I can read your poker face, Reno. Remember? So I am sure, damn you." What the hell was wrong with her? Why the mood swings?

"Trauma to the neck by powerful hands. Not-Mallory's neck showed fractures of the hyoid bone and the thyroid cartilage." Okay.

"A big, mean bear of a man wrapped his hairy hands around poor little Not-Mallory's throat and gave her a not-so-gentle tickle." Huh?

"Hairy hands? You don't really know that, do you, Barb?" She ignored me.

"Might have tickled her between her legs, too. A little too scorched to be sure, but I'd say he did. And I do mean 'butt' with two *t*'s, Reno. Bear man nailed both her holes. Am I somewhat too graphic for you this morning, Detective?"

Barb waited for me to say something. I didn't. But she was right. Too graphic. This early in the day, anyway. And too reminiscent of our own bedroom games.

"I swear, Reno. What did I ever see in you? What potential? God knows."

If she'd had that long hair of hers still, she'd have shaken it, let it emphasize her disgust. But the hair wasn't hanging around anymore, so I had to make do with her scowl.

She was lecturing again.

"And no, she couldn't have done that to herself, so don't ask me that. Hanging wouldn't result in those injuries, and a person can't do damage like that with their own hands.

"So it's a homicide. Death by hairy hands. Still with me, Reno?"

"Yeah . . ." My assent partially drowned out by a prolonged stomach gurgle. Mine, not hers.

"That leaves number four—time of death. No help from the reports. Not enough physical body. I did talk to a Thomas Kuster at the newspaper in Kipling. You know him, Harry?"

Another "Yeah" from me, and Barb went on with her dissection of the crime.

"Kuster told me Mallory worked for him. She was out of the office all that day. Maybe had a source she needed to meet with. Kuster wasn't too clear on that point. Talking to him was a lot like talking to you. How come, Harry?"

Shoulder shrug. It wasn't any kind of an answer, really, but it seemed enough right then.

"Kuster did remember the day had been rainy. Heavy downpours during the night. Could have smothered the blaze, kept it from consuming all of Not-Mallory." Okay.

"That would account for the clue I discovered when I examined her." Clue? I sat up straighter. "Any questions on your mind, Detective? Anything you'd like to know about Not-Mallory?"

I gave it a shot, but I was ready to duck and cover, too. "Yeah, Barb. There is. Who was she then, if she wasn't Mallory?"

"I don't know that yet. Doc Adams will peer review my work tomorrow morning. Then we'll call Walker-Doer right after that. By about noon tomorrow, he'll know it wasn't Mallory who died in the fire. So will everybody."

An odd look played around on her face. One eye twitching, both lips quivering, except when her teeth tried holding one of them still. She seemed ready to cry. Why, I hadn't a clue.

"Then I'll call Penny, tell her company to keep the life insurance proceeds out of Uncle Artie's bony old hands. Because while it's a dead body, it's not Mallory's corpse." Barb's voice broke. I glanced up from my coffee. "Yeah, Harry. I know the judge too."

What the hell? Barb was definitely crying now. Maybe I should have tried to comfort her. Maybe I should have jumped out the window. I sipped coffee instead.

"That animal who raped Not-Mallory damn near chewed her breast off," Barb said.

I didn't know what to say, so I kept quiet.

"Sorry, Harry. I stayed up all night on this one. Stayed up to get it done for you. And for her." Which *her*? Mallory? Not-Mallory? Penelope? I didn't ask.

"So, the official autopsy line will be: not Mallory Mordred, but an as-yet-unidentified female who suffered death by strangulation. Please ask the cops whodunit. Partial Amen. The Mass is ended. Go in peace, Harry Reno." She dried her last tears with a tissue and stared down at me.

I just sat there. Which was pretty much all I had done the whole time. Had to say something, though, so I did.

"You said you found a clue when you examined her. What did you find?"

Barb walked around her desk, handed me a photograph. "Officially, Reno, I will never know how you saw this." A blowup of forceps retracting a corpse's lower lip—a scorched lower lip. Something etched inside the lip.

I scratched my neck. "What the hell is this, Barb?"

"It, Detective, is the clue you seek. Turn the photo around, genius. Tell me what's tattooed inside Not-Mallory's lower lip."

I peered at the photo again. Definitely a tattoo—I SCREW DO U. I said as much out loud.

"Good boy. You got it. *I Screw Do U*. Now get your sorry ass up to Kipling today—today, Reno—and find out which delightful young lady up there sported such a delicate inscription."

Doc Nolan turned, walked toward the back door of her office. "Oh, and you might try to find Mallory, too. While you're at it." I knew she had a couch back there. I'd been on it. With her. But that was centuries ago.

"Turn the lights off," Doc Nolan said. "Then get the hell out of here, Harry."

As I stepped into the hall, I almost knocked the cleaning lady over again. Again I told her I was sorry. Again she said, "Least there ain't no blood today," and laughed.

Helps to keep a positive outlook, I suppose, if you have to get up on a Sunday morning and mop the morgue.

Outside the old hospital, gray drizzle met me. I glanced up at the solitary light still burning in the ME's office. Damn, forgot to flip the switch. Just another Reno screw-up for Barb to add to her list.

But at least now I had a real mystery to solve. An *I Screw Do U* conundrum. And maybe a still-alive Mallory to find. The Volvo eased out of its parking space. Across from the entrance and down a little sat the silver Ford Taurus. Too far to ID anyone inside.

Rattle the windows or not? If the tail stuck, *then* play the big bad wolf, and huff and puff until answers blew out. Otherwise, haul ass back north. That's what I was being paid to do, for a little while longer, anyway.

The Volvo pulled out. The Ford stayed put. Good. I was anxious to pack and get back to Kipling by tonight. Imagine that.

On the way back to Penny's, I told the little hula girl about the I-Screw-Do-U chick. Her hips began swaying wickedly, as if flicking hot sinful sand from her grass skirt. Maybe she wanted and needed the same tattoo. To entice the beach bums.

Or maybe it was just the pothole I hit. I didn't ask. She didn't say.

26

DEWEY'S AUTUMN REVERIE

Sven unlocked the casino's back door, and Dewey shuffled in. Sven shoved the door shut, but not before Dewey's goat stink slipped through, too.

"Why Boss want see Dewey?" the big man said. "It Sunday morning."

"Your guess is my guess," Sven said. "You fuck something up again?"

"Dewey not like talk like that." The big man stepped close, glared, then let his eyes fall to the floor. "Why you say me fuck up? Why, Sven?"

"Come on, Dewey. Let's go." Sven made for the staircase sweeping down into the casino, and Dewey fell in behind him.

"Stay here," Sven said, pointing to the red velvet chair beside the black door. "I'll be back to get you. Just sit. Might be a while. Got it, goat man?"

Dewey sat and waited. And worried. Why'd the Boss want to see him? Then he let his mind slip off to a happier place: last fall in the woods. Something he'd done, and done right.

The big man closed his eyes, let it play like a TV show in his head

—the place where the words always came out right. Where Dewey was always the leading man, the star.

Dewey crouched under the trees in the damp pine straw and watched the redhead moving around inside the cabin. "You're still there—alone—still gonna be my date . . . and still gonna die."

He'd watched her for hours, either squatting at the edge of the forest or sitting farther back under the evergreens on a flat rock, whittling sticks to pass the time.

Dewey sighed—still not dark enough.

The Boss wanted the redhead killed. But the Dutchman and the Pilot had both said no—right there in the Boss's office. The one under the stairs. The Boss hadn't liked that. He'd cussed them all real hard.

Dewey struggled to keep still under the trees. But thoughts of the redhead kept stumbling through his brain, images of what tonight's lovemaking would be like causing his legs to twitch and jump, a competing hardness swelling between his thighs.

But what if he fouled this up? His hardness limped away.

Dewey tried letting his plan roll through his head. When the redhead answers the door, I'll tell her something so she'll ask me in. But what? His mind lunged for words, but they slipped by, unformed. No big deal, he'd think of something.

"But I do know what to do inside—pull the old chloroform trick. Then string her up. Make it look like suicide. Ha! I am smart."

He waited until he could wait no longer. He broke his watch to relieve himself.

When he crept back to his rock, he saw a silver car parked next to the Jeep. Snakes writhed in his stomach. Hairy hands smacked his head while his feet danced a frustration jig under the trees. "No, no, no. Ruins my plan. What'll I do? What'll I do?"

"Dewey. Dewey. Calm down, will ya? See that couple staring at you? You're scaring the shit out of 'em," Sven whispered. "What the hell are you doing? Having a bad dream?"

"Me sorry, Sven. Dewey be quiet."

Sven walked away, free buffet passes in his hand to placate the upset couple still pointing at Dewey, still shuddering at the sight of a dirty bear inside their favorite casino. Well, fuck them too. "Here you are sir. Madam. Let me apologize on behalf of the management. Please enjoy the buffet, compliments of the casino. And please do not worry," Sven assured them. "He's really quite harmless."

Dewey leaned back, hit Play, got back to his TV dream. Back to the cabin.

But then the silver car's engine started up, and whoever was behind the wheel headed down the driveway and drove away. The snakes gripping his stomach slithered away, too. He'd caught a glimpse of red hair through a cabin window.

"She's still there, still gonna die. Dark enough. That car might come back." He shivered and licked his lips. "Time for my date."

Dewey inched up the cabin steps and stepped onto the porch, his bearlike body causing the weathered wood to sigh. He tried the door's thumb latch. It made a clicking noise.

"Back already?" the woman called out. Dewey froze. Damn, he'd forgotten to knock, to say he had something to tell her. He heard her footsteps approaching the door. Was someone coming back after all?

As she opened the door, he drove his shoulder into it, bursting into the cabin, grabbing the redhead by the throat, squeezing her hard—harder even than the fear coiling in his guts. The redhead wasn't big or strong, but she had fight in her.

He liked that. He kept squeezing.

When it was over, he laid her gently on the couch and began removing her plaid shirt and tight jeans. He felt himself growing hard.

"She's sure pretty." But she had soiled herself. "Guess I choked the shit out

of her." His chuckle floated by itself inside the cabin. He wiped up the mess with the woman's shirt. "Smells pretty, too." The redhead's face betrayed no embarrassment, only wide-eyed death.

Dewey pulled off his pants, ready for his date. Drool leaked from the corner of his mouth where the knife scar met his lips. He wiped at the wetness, let the drool coat his rigid desire.

He was quick with the redhead. Too quick, some women complained—the live ones, anyway. But this one voiced no words of reproach, not even when he bit her. The big man wiped the blood from his mouth, pulled his pants back up, and got on with what the Boss had wanted the Dutchman or the Pilot to do. What they had refused to do.

Dewey took the noose from his backpack. He'd meant to use chloroform, knock her out, then strangle her with the noose, but he'd forgotten that part in the excitement and fear at the cabin door. He'd used his hands instead. He stared at the noose.

He'd forgotten the plan. Dewey smacked his forehead—hard. He was stupid.

That got him moving again. The plan. Just do the rest of it, like the Boss had wanted it done. Dewey placed the noose gently around the redhead's neck. His hands trembled as he touched her. "Pretty, real pretty."

He stood on a chair, threw the other end of the rope over a roof beam, began hoisting the redhead upright. But other thoughts still swirled in his head, tingling his loins. He let the naked redhead back down and laid her on the couch again. He sat beside her, stroking her hair.

Dewey couldn't resist a second time together with the woman. "So pretty," he said, drool muffling his words. He rolled her over on her stomach on the couch. Grasping her hips, lifting her to him, he entered her from behind, right in that spot he liked so much.

It didn't take long. He pulled free.

Dewey kept staring down at the woman, his eyes wrapping themselves around her body. The redhead, the naked redhead, the naked redhead with the bruised and crushed neck, her breast with the deep bite marks put there by his lovemaking.

"Owl shit. That ain't how a suicide looks. Got the noose on her. Done that

right. Got to fix this. And quick. Before that silver car comes back." The redhead didn't disagree.

A kerosene can sat by the back door. He snatched it up, shook it—kerosene sloshed. He carried the can into the living room, then rushed out onto the porch, grabbed an Adirondack chair in each hand, and squeezed himself back through the cabin door, like a bear dragging its kill.

He ran out again, scooped up some old hunting and fishing gear, threw that on the chairs by the fireplace. He smashed a wooden table into kindling and piled that on, too.

The big man dribbled a trail of kerosene from the cabin door to the pile by the fireplace, emptied the rest of the can onto the pile. "This'll work. I know it will."

Dewey stood by the cabin door, fumbled a box of matches from his pocket, lit one, and touched the trail of kerosene. He lumbered out and across the clearing into the night-dark woods. The whomp of the kerosene exploding made Dewey feel complete. "Yeah, I like fire. She'll like it, too."

Rain sprinkled Dewey's head. Doubts sprouted inside. Was he supposed to string the redhead up inside her cabin or outside on the porch? The choice nagged at him.

Dewey chewed his lip, locked his eyes on his feet, like in the office when the Boss cussed all of them so hard, when the Boss said, "So you two won't do this? Maybe I'll get Dewey to kill her."

The Dutchman and the Pilot had laughed. Then even the Boss himself chuckled and said, "Stupid bastard," just like he wasn't even there. Dewey's stomach flipped, churned, hurt. Then the snakes quit slithering and started squeezing instead.

Outside. The Boss had said outside. String her up on the porch. Leave the suicide note inside. For the cops to find.

"Owl shit. Too late now." Dewey took the note from his pocket, tore his childish scrawl into little pieces and ate them. He stared at the empty porch.

Down at the bottom of the hill, where the long dirt driveway met the lake road, headlights flickered through the trees, coming up the driveway. Fear clenched his guts. The car came up the hill a little farther, then backed down the driveway and sped away.

The snakes relaxed. "Going for the fire boys." The hurt slithered away. Flames licked at a cabin window. "Won't do no good."

The rain turned harder. The cold drops tickled his neck, slid down inside his muddy field jacket, but Dewey didn't care. "Got laid. Twice." A lopsided smile crinkled the bone-white knife scar. "I tickled that redhead, tickled her good."

He took his time circling back to where he'd left his pickup, the rain churning the forest paths into rivers of mud. Sirens wailed, far away.

"Too late, let her burn." Then the Boss wouldn't know how much of the plan he'd screwed up and wouldn't know all that he and the redhead had done together.

The cold November rain pounded harder on the truck's roof. Dewey hit the wipers and drove away into the night, his urges satisfied—for now.

Sven poked Dewey's shoulder. "Come on, goat man. Wake up. Boss'll see you now." Dewey shuffled after Sven, images of the redhead and their date still swirling happily in his head.

27

A SUNDAY MORNING CASINO SQUALL

"You goddamned slobbering screw-up. Did I tell you to kill anybody—anybody at all? Well, did I?" Pericles Stavros poked a finger hard into Dewey's chest, rocking the big man back on his heels.

"You . . . You . . . kinda did . . . Boss."

"You hairy cocksucker. I kinda did not. And even if I had, you killed the wrong redhead, you corpse-fucking degenerate." Stavros banged a fist on his marble desk, swept papers aside. The Pan lamp jumped for the safety of the carpet and stayed there. The white streak in the Greek's hair flashed in the chandelier's harsh brightness—a bolt of lightning in a black storm cloud.

The Greek stabbed a finger into Dewey's chest again. "Quit slobbering, you slack-mouthed crackbrain. You're soaking my carpet, damn you."

The big man shrank back, stammering, "Sorry, Boss . . . Dewey sorry," until the office wall stopped his retreat.

"The wrong damn redhead." Stavros stomped toward Dewey. "And now we don't even know where Mallory really is." The Greek's hands flew to Dewey's throat. Stavros twisted the big man's head, fingers digging deep into flesh.

Dewey let him. Stavros was Boss.

"Just because the Dutchman wouldn't kill her, you thought you'd do it." Stavros slapped Dewey hard across the face. "Thought I'd want you to do what the Pilot wouldn't. That it? I said, that it, jackleg?"

As quick as the Greek's storm broke, it ebbed. Cunning replaced curses. "Just sit down and shut up. And quit slobbering." Stavros motioned for the Pilot to join him back at the desk.

The Pilot stayed where he was, leaning against the wall next to one of the floor lamps, his hand caressing a caryatid's marble rump. "Break your hand, Papa P?"

"Watch your mouth, you son of a bitch. Be careful I don't break your fucking head." Stavros kicked at the Pan lamp on the floor, missed. "Shit-ass goat."

He jerked a thumb at Dewey. "Get screw-up and his goat stink out of here, Sven. Then get your Injun ass back in here. I got an idea you'll like. It involves Reno."

Dewey shuffled out, and Sven slipped back in.

A half smile floated across the Pilot's face. "Hey, the way you just chatted with Dewey, that how you talk to your juries, Papa P?" A small laugh spilled out. "They like those fancy curses of yours?"

Splotches of anger flared on Stavros's face—white islands flecking a sea of red. His hands balled into fists, his eyes bulged, white froth bubbled at the corners of his mouth.

The Pilot strolled over, patted the Greek's shoulder. "Hey, don't stroke out on me, old man." His chuckle softening the confrontation.

"What the hell have you got to laugh at," Stavros said. "Mallory could send us all to prison if she connects the dots. You, me, Sven. That son of a bitch the judge, and his butler. And Ariadne, too." Stavros sat down behind his desk again. "You want that to happen, because it still might." The Pilot said *No way*—with his eyes.

"You want to find Mallory for me, kill her?" Stavros asked. The Pilot shrugged.

"Yeah, I didn't think so. You get soft once you screw 'em. Well, I'm the brains, so I do have an idea how to solve all our problems, how to change Dewey's fuckup into gold for us."

Stavros leaned forward, beefy arms supporting his bulk. The marble held firm. "Reno's on his way back up here today."

"Is that a good or bad thing, Papa P?"

"Shut the hell up with that Papa P shit—okay?" The Pilot just grinned.

"Like I said, Reno's on his way back to Kipling. We're going to use him to run a scam that'll get rid of him, and neutralize that goddamn McCabe."

"Ambitious plan—Pericles."

Stavros glared. One day . . . He let it slide. "Reno's a drunk. He'll never realize it's us using him. Here's how I got it figured. We get Reno worried about those two broads . . . uh . . ."

"Gwen and Brynn, Papa P," the Pilot said.

"Stop calling me that." Stavros turned and vented his anger where he could—on Sven. "Come here, you fuckin' Injun." Stavros grabbed Sven's ear and twisted.

"Ow, Boss, you don't gotta do that. I'm paying attention. Reno's a drunk. I heard ya."

"Well, be sure you keep listening. Got it, red man? Take a couple of the boys with you tonight. Rough him up. He'll be at the Tam. I got that on good authority."

The Pilot shook his head in feigned disbelief.

"You got a better idea?" The Greek's eyes flared. "Well, do you?" He took two steps toward the Pilot.

The Pilot didn't flinch. "Yeah, I just might." His smile a sneer now. "Plus a way to solve our Mallory problem. But I'm going to run it by your wife first. The Mistress of the Labyrinth. The real brains of this outfit. Remember her?"

The Pilot opened the office door. "But hassling Reno is a good place to start." He stepped into the red-lit corridor. "So go for it. And spray some air freshener around in there, why don't you, Papa P."

Snick-snick said the door.

28

A KIPLING SUNDAY NIGHT—PARKING LOT FUN

Sunday night at the Tam-O'-Shanter seemed unusually slow. Easy to find a bar stool. Gus held out his hand. We shook—man, what a grip. I pulled loose, said, "How ya doing, big guy?"

"Bonny, Harry Reno. Bonny," Gus said, loud enough for everyone inside and outside to know I was there.

"You old fraud. Your accent's as phony as ever. But it's good to see you again. It'd be even better if I could see a steak and a beer."

"Aye, friend Harry," Gus said. A true Scot he wasn't. A true friend—maybe.

Gus hit the bell, the cook scuttled out, said, "Good to see ya, Harry," grabbed the scribbled order, and skittered back to his kitchen. The guy was always in a hurry; a short-order cook short on time.

Gus put a beer in front of me as I asked who his new barmaid was.

"She's a sweet one, right, Harry?"

"Spot her some hair dye money, Gus. She'll look better, and you'll sell more beer."

"I shall, oh ye of the discerning eye. All shit aside, it's good to see you." Then he was gone, headed out with some beers. His relief hovered behind, though.

Why? I'd only been gone a week or so. Stuart Dillingham the

Third, Pompous Ass Supreme, had handed me a quick insurance job when I hit Ithaca. Knocked it out in a couple of days.

After that, Penelope and I laughed and played a bit, until Barbara Nolan finished her sawing and interrupted Reno's Sacred Sunday Ritual this morning to enlighten me concerning Not-Mallory's crispy corpse.

Now I was back in Kipling drinking beer and searching for an *I Screw Do U* sort of clue. Great way to spend Sunday night, huh?

Gus came back from wherever he'd been and motioned his new barmaid over. "Lassie, this be Plain Old Harry. Laddie, this be Molly."

The introductions completed, Molly beamed a smile my way. "Gus just told me his barmaids get free hairstyling. Isn't he terrific?"

"That he is," I said.

Molly smiled some more and waved a little good-bye with her fingers while a tooth or two bit lightly at her lower lip. Oh, Lord. Plus, she already knew how to swirl that kilt of hers. She'd move a lot of beer here at the Tam. No doubt about that, no doubt at all.

I caught Gus's eye. "You old fraud."

"I do what I can, Plain Old Harry. I do what I can."

"And who you can," I suggested.

"Aye, that I do," Gus said and winked.

When the kitchen bell finally rang, Gus served my steak himself. I sawed some beef and ventured a question. "Gus, do you know a girl with a lip tattoo? A tattoo that says 'I screw do you'?" I gnawed at the Angus while Gus chewed on my question.

"Maybe . . . maybe I do. Haven't seen her in a while, though. A long while. I'll have to think a little on that."

"It's important," I said. "Real important."

Out of the corner of my eye, I noticed a shifty-looking dude sit down at the end of the bar. Shifty because he wore a black sports coat over black slacks. A black T-shirt showed itself under the black coat. His hair was black, too—black and slicked back. Polished shoes dangled down at the ends of his legs, one shoe swinging rhythmically as he said, "Beer." The shoes were black. So were the tassels.

A caricature of a Mafia hit man straight out of a low-budget *Godfather* knockoff. Low-budget because his socks were white.

Gus came back, said, "If you're finished, Harry, it's on the house tonight."

I figured he meant I was, so I said, "Okay," my voice soft and low, matching his.

He tore a guest check off his pad—wrote something on it—pushed the scribbling toward me: *Come back at closing—watch yourself.*

I nodded and slipped off my stool. As I headed out the front door, Molly made sure to smile and say, "See you soon, Plain Old Harry."

Gus sure did know how to pick 'em. No doubts about that. But I should have been wondering why Gus wanted me out of there rather than musing on barmaids.

But I wasn't. Molly and her kilt had triggered lustful visions of Gwen and Brynn, Elke and Penny. All romping together with Harry and Molly.

Like I said, should have been paying attention to reality instead.

The parking lot was darker than it had been when the Volvo cruised in. The pole light had burned out. From the shadows at the rear of the parking lot, a man came at me fast. Another dude popped up behind me, blocking any escape in that direction.

It was a crude but effective plan. A rusher from the front, a blocker to the rear, and my own car making the third side of the box. Only one way to go, if I was inclined to run. And I wasn't, because there stood my old bar-stool buddy, the ersatz Mafia hit man.

The character from the shadows reached me first. As he closed, I saw he had a sap in one hand and brass knuckles caressing his other paw.

I pivoted like a matador on Sunday in the bullring, death only inches away. But this guy was no prize bull. A neck chop as he blew by, and he went down and stayed down—just a wannabe toreador.

His buddy barreled toward me. So did my bar-stool wise guy.

Waltzing with them both at once seemed poor etiquette, so I turned and ran hard at the imitation Mafia dude, flailing my arms and shrieking like Bruce Lee risen from the grave.

The Mafia hood tried pulling up short, but he couldn't stop in time. My Bruce Lee kung fu wasn't imitation like his Mafia good looks. He went down and stayed down. Along with his white socks.

The other apache was a different matter.

I caught a glimpse of the familiar, then took a shot to my face, felt a foot connect with my leg. I'd have gone for the groin, but that's just me.

I managed to stay upright and moved in close.

A palm shot to his chin with my left, the heel of my hand snapping his head back. Then my right gave him all I had. His head flew back a second time and the rest of him followed. He lay still.

The guy wasn't bad at what he'd tried to do—both his buddies down, yet he kept on coming instead of running away. So I made sure his head had something soft to rest on.

My heel ground his ear into the parking lot's surface—gray gravel—red blood—yellow hair. Such a fetching combination. Hey, the son of a bitch sort of resembled that Scandinavian Indian up at the casino. Sven, the bodybuilder with the blond Mohawk.

But only sort of, because their ears didn't match anymore. But neither did my eyes. Sven's lucky punch had sliced open an eyebrow. I'd need patching.

I left the three thugs to sleep it off, and let the Volvo take me back to the motel. On the way, the little hula girl just stared at me—no swaying.

Awestruck, I suppose.

29

A KIPLING SUNDAY NIGHT—MOTEL MUSINGS

Earlier, I'd checked back in at Karl's motel before hitting the Tam. Pops had said my old room was available, so I took it and dumped my luggage inside, iced some beer, then went in search of Gus and food. And now that I'd done that, plus made some new friends in the Tam's parking lot, here I was back in my room. My travel bag was just as I'd left it. No inquisitive hands had fumbled through it. Nor left any clean towels. Didn't spot a fresh pair of black lace panties lying around, either.

I patched up my eye, put the first-aid kit back, and zipped the bag. A beer from the sink felt good in my hand. Still cold. I pressed the can to my forehead and sank back in the recliner to let the cobwebs clear.

So much for an easy Sunday in bed with Penelope Phair.

Penny had shooed me out the door this morning after I told her about Barb's Not-Mallory carcass. But not so quickly that we didn't say good-bye, a most impressive and proper Sunday Ritual good-bye.

And now here I sat in my same shitty motel room again, leaking blood, drinking beer, trying to figure out Kipling and its mysteries. Alone. Except for the beer.

Who the hell had tried to kill Mallory Mordred, only to screw up and kill the wrong redhead?

Arthur Walker-Doer? Why not start there? I had to see him tomorrow. Grieving uncle or scheming judge? And what about his sidekick, Willem? Professional hit man or just a decent imitation butler who happens to sport a ponytail and live up in the North Woods?

But why would either of them have killed Not-Mallory? Don't know.

Pericles Stavros. Did he kill Not-Mallory? Fat fucker. He had the means. The crew-cut guy in the corner, feeling up that statue. Glad he wasn't in the parking lot tonight. Might have been one too many, even for Harry and Reno.

But why would Stavros need Mallory snuffed? Dunno.

Hey, Jayne Rask, maybe she tried to kill the competition. But would she have mistaken Not-Mallory for Mallory? Of course not.

Damn, but my eye hurt. I downed some more alcohol-based anesthetic.

Mallory Mordred, could she have been the killer? Strangled Not-Mallory, burned the cabin? Yeah, possible. If she were strong enough.

But what about the double whammy to the redhead's privates? So no, not Mallory. Or not Mallory by herself.

Need to find out why Not-Mallory was there at the cabin. Barbara Nolan said Tom Kuster told her he thought Mallory was meeting a source, someone who would help her along with her investigation into back then. Was that Not-Mallory?

Hey, could be Not-Mallory was the target all along. So where's Mallory, if it's not her in Barb's morgue? Man, talk about missing babes.

Gotta keep my eyes on Gwen and Brynn. Two beautiful young women maybe conspiring to drive Plain Old Harry bonkers with a black lace panties conundrum. If only I could remember what I'd done with the damn panties.

Not good. Mind drifting, thoughts off-target.

Okay, focus on Not-Mallory instead of dreaming about babes modeling black panties. Black panties with little red —

A knock on the door interrupted my lack of concentration.

I opened the door, and Gwen's Lance grabbed me by the throat, shoving his way into the room, kicking the door shut behind us. I'd forgotten to eyeball the peephole.

Funny how you remember the little things after the fact.

"Where you been, asshole?" Lance sounded somewhat pissed off. "Where you been?" He spun me around, braced me against the wall. I let him. It seemed the wisest course until I figured out why he was here.

Plus, so far he hadn't really hurt much of anything, except my private investigator's pride. And that was a consistently self-depleting commodity, anyway.

As a change of pace, Lance quit calling me an asshole. Now I was a son of a bitch—over and over and over again. I detected a more than faint smell of sour beer and vomit—his, not mine.

Finally, after a couple of years, Lance forgot about keeping me butterflied to the wall. The big cop sank to his knees, crying. What the hell was it with this guy? No wonder Gwen had ditched him. I wanted him gone, too. Didn't happen.

"You got to help me, Mr. Reno. I'm in over my head." Man, a tall order indeed.

I helped him to his feet, guided him and said head generally in the direction of the room's ratty-ass recliner. God, but he was big. Lance flopped down—the recliner emitted a sickening scrunch, protesting his unwanted attention the only way it knew how.

I fetched Sir Lancelot a beer from my dwindling sink supply and told him to drink. He did. One prolonged gulp. While Lance nursed another one, I grabbed my gun, just in case. The cop never noticed.

"Okay, Lance," I said, armed and ready, "now tell Uncle Harry all about it."

Lance stared up through red-rimmed, watery eyes—the sort cops always say drunks have when they pull them over. "I figured you were an okay guy, Mr. Reno. That you'd help me."

I assured him I really was an okay guy. And just to prove it, I asked again why he'd stopped by to see me.

"I tried to score at roulette, up at the casino. Now Mr. Stavros says I got to do some things, some stuff I don't want to do." What stuff?

Did it really matter? Not right now, it didn't. And here I thought he busted in to tell me Gwen had put the black lace panties on my bed last trip, and therefore, I was a dead man. But that wasn't it at all, was it?

"I didn't know what to do," Lance said, "and then I heard you were back in town. You being a PI and an ex-cop, and, well, I guess, a man of the world and all. You'd help me."

Honest to God, that's what he said: *a man of the world and all*. Yeah, I sure was all of that and more.

"I just wanted some dough so I could buy pretty things." Lance retched, hocked, but didn't puke. Reno's luck holding for now. Except for the additional slime on the carpet. "It's Gwen, Mr. Reno. She loves pretty things. That's why I need help. Gwen."

I wanted to tell him, *No shit, Lance. It's always going to be Gwen with you.* But I didn't. No death wish. Not tonight.

30

A KIPLING SUNDAY NIGHT—BACK TO THE TAM

Lance drank too much. I wanted him out of my room; nobody loves a drunk forever. Maybe Harry should remind Reno about that, before Penelope runs across that nugget of truth all on her own.

"Let's go, big boy." Lance stared up at me, a big dumb ox, dressed all in blue—Babe the Blue Ox Cop.

"Where we going, Harry?" At least that's what the blue ox might have said. He'd guzzled a lot of beer to help numb his Gwen-pain.

"Go see Gus. Get some more beer. Okay?" That registered. Out the door we went, me guiding, the Blue Ox Cop stumbling along beside me.

"Let me drive, Harry." He belched. "I'll hit the siren, get us to the Tam fast." Get us to the slaughterhouse, you mean.

"Okay, Lance, but lie down in my backseat first, while we go for more beer." You don't need logic with a drunk, just the promise of more beer. I know, trust me.

Off we went. The little hula girl dozing on the dash. Sleeping off a bender of her own? You never know with that little floozy.

The Volvo pulled up close to the Tam's back door. Gus waiting for my return, the lights inside his bar dim. No Molly, no kitchen help. No goons lurking in shadows, either.

A crescent moon floated high up. Soft wind fingers tickled my skin. The bar's garbage can lids snug. No rotten odors assaulting my nose. Ah, such a pleasant finish to such a busy summer day and night. Except for the snoozing bovine in my backseat.

Somehow Gus and I levered Lance out of the Volvo and into the bar. We dumped the ox in a booth and left him there, snoring away.

Gus fished two beers out of the cold box. I shook a *no* his way. He shrugged, put one back, stayed behind his bar—drinking his beer, guarding his Scotch.

"I'm glad you came back, friend Harry. Wasn't safe to talk earlier. Occasionals who had no occasion to be here." He winked. "What happened to your eye?"

"Just a little problem I occasionally have." But I said it with a grin. "Who were they?"

"Three mugs who work for Stavros."

"But you didn't warn me about them, did you?" I said.

"I told you to watch yourself. Remember? Even wrote it down." We left it at that.

Gus nursed his beer, pausing between sips to study me. "The autopsy results. They've brought you back to Kipling. Right, Harry?"

He was going for the throat—no softening me up. Direct interrogation. The hell with playing that game.

"Being a bartender is a lot like being a detective, isn't it?" I said. Throw questions at him, break his flow.

"Yeah, I listen to a lot of bullshit before a newfound friend pours out his troubles, asks for my help." Gus put the beer to his lips again. Just a small sip, though.

"Sometimes it's an interesting job, sometimes not," he said. The bottle back on the bar, a frown turning down the corners of his mouth. "Like when I was a cop."

I was leading him off track. He'd sensed it.

"Now, Harry, about the autopsy. The results will be out tomorrow." He didn't ask me to confirm it. Just stated fact and went on, letting me know he already had all the answers.

"These results. Somehow a girl with a lip tattoo is involved," he said. Facts still. No questions yet.

I stayed quiet.

"And it was the tattoo girl who died in the cabin, not Mallory," he said. Gus walking me through it, seeing if I agreed with his analysis. I'd used the same method when I was an investigator in the AG's office. Wonder where he'd gotten his intel. But why fight it. I nodded, said he was right.

"And Ms. Tattoo didn't die by her own hand."

"Right again. So where's Mallory, Gus?"

"Hell, Harry. Girls, women, they slip off all the time. Shuck off one life for a new one. No big deal one more's done that, huh?"

I didn't agree or disagree. "So who was the tattooed charmer?" I asked. He ignored my question, kept talking.

"That's how Stavros and the other sin sellers get their girls. You know that, don't you, Harry? They find the ones who shuck and then fuck, or the ones who fuck and then shuck. Or girls who just suck and then fuck." Gus, pleased as hell with his own insight. Some philosophy, huh?

"And now your company doesn't owe the judge any life insurance money. No dead niece, just a disappeared female." Gus finished his beer, twisted the top off another.

Screwing up his courage? Hard to say.

"What'd you call it, Harry? Big Bad Insurance Company? You got that right. Never had an insurance company that did right by me."

He was drifting now, remembering his own problems, losing interest in his subject. A fatal interrogation error. Good. Maybe I could do the questioning. That'd be a change.

So I sympathized with him, said I didn't like working for the lousy company any more than he liked paying premiums for crappy coverage.

Gus nodding his head—up and down, agreeing. Mine nodding the same way, too.

I had it wrong. Still Gus's interrogation. The ex-deputy pulling the old nodding horse routine. My head bobbing up and down, like a colt frisky to be off and running. Agreeing with whatever he said. I wasn't in control here, not at all.

"You're out of a job now, aren't you?" he said. He nodded *yes* my way. I nodded *yes* back.

"But you're not about to let go of this case, right?" His head nodded my *yes*.

My head miming his movements—up and down—telegraphing my assent to whatever he was wiring my way.

"You've sniffed out a connection. Between now and back then. Back to Gwen's mother. Right, Harry?" Yeah, I had. He nodded. I nodded. Damn him. At least I didn't whinny.

"She was a throwaway, Harry."

"Like hell she was." My hand grabbed his apron, pulling his face close to mine across the bar. "Like hell she was," I said again, my other hand balling itself into a fist, floating around under the bartender's nose.

Gus's words came fast.

"Not Gwen's mother, Harry. I meant the girl with the tattoo. She was the throwaway. That's who I meant." The shamus in the dark, wrong again. I turned loose of his apron, let the fist relax.

"Sorry, Harry. You want a beer?"

"No."

"Coffee, then," he said, and went off to make a pot for both of us.

While Gus was gone, I walked down to the end of the bar where the old photos hung. Gwen's mother—all smiles. The hurt stabbed, and I shoved my eyes elsewhere. A younger Gus in a deputy's uniform—long time since he'd been that size.

Then a photo I hadn't noticed before. Three people standing together, hugging each other, laughing for the camera. A girl in the middle, a guy on either side, tugging on her, like one didn't want the other to have her.

Shit. Stavros, Jayne Rask, and Walker-Doer. Triple shit.

The connection Gus thought I'd sniffed out. No need tonight for the shamus nose to do its Toby the Bloodhound imitation. The Sherlock Holmes of Ithaca's eyes had pegged this clue all on their own.

The Kipling dots connecting now—motes from back then coalescing into a darkening cloud. Stavros, Jayne Rask, and Walker-Doer. An old photo, from before my time here fifteen years ago. Hugging back then.

Why hadn't I noticed this picture last trip? Maybe it wasn't there. Didn't matter. In my head now. I was still standing there when Gus came out with our coffee.

"She was a beauty. Inside and out. A beauty and a damn good cop," he said. Guess he thought I was staring at Gwen's mom. He checked on Lance—out and going to stay that way.

We took ourselves and our coffees over to a booth. The nodding horse ambled off in search of clover. I was asking the questions now.

"Okay, Gus. What about the girl with the 'I screw do you' invitation inside her lip?"

"Her name's Lacie Doyle." One shoulder rose, shrugged, went back to where it'd been. "Or was." A tight-lipped grimace floated on his face for a second, then faded.

"How'd you know her?" I asked.

"She danced at the local titty bars. Worked here at the Tam when she wasn't into dancing and hustling. When she had herself together. Then she moved on to the casino. Moving and shaking herself for money—for cocaine, for kicks, for whatever."

Gus swallowed some coffee, let his bar towel float across his lips—just tidying up a bit.

"Sven—you know Sven, right, Harry." Not a question. No answer needed. The bar towel back on his shoulder again.

"He took a liking to her. Her and her red hair. Called her Racy Red Lacie. Sven's an Indian, a Scandinavian Red Man. You know that too, right, Harry?"

He shrugged again, like he wanted to say sorry about the parking lot, but couldn't. I let it slide. Gus kept his eyes fixed on his coffee as he started up his story again.

"Racy Red Lacie, always racing to show that tattoo and deliver on it. Trouble with Lacie, she liked to run with more than just Sven. I'm not surprised it was her in the cabin."

Now he was looking at me again. "She knew stuff. Things Mallory would want to know," he said. "For her newspaper stories. Her big break."

"You think there's a connection—Lacie, Mallory, Stavros? The casino, the temple, the Lodge?" I left out Walker-Doer and Jayne. Why give it all away?

"Yeah, I do." A tightening of lips amidst all that bristling Scottish heather he called a beard. "How much do you know about the Lodge of the Labyrinth and its temple, Harry?"

"You mean that big boys' sauna club downtown? The fake Greek temple out on the island? Not much, Gus," I said. "I guess not much at all."

31

TWISTS, TURNS, DEAD ENDS

Gus refilled our mugs, took a sip, winced. "Coffee's hot. Be careful." I blew on mine. He was right. We stared at each other—waiting. Gus broke first.

"You sure you want to know what I'm about to tell you?" he asked.

"How the hell do I know? I told you I don't know shit about the Lodge or its temple."

"Some detective you are," he said. But he laughed when he said it, so I laughed, too, even if I didn't feel real friendly right then. My eye hurt. All because of Sven. And Gus.

"When you were here before—not last trip, but fifteen years ago—was the casino here?"

"You know it wasn't," I said.

"What about the Greek temple out in the lake?"

"Wasn't there, either. I do remember the island." I'd sat on a bench by the lake with Gwen's mom all those years ago. Watched as a setting sun backlit the island's trees, turning them orange and red-tinged yellow. Our first kiss. Gus didn't need to know that. Not at all.

"What about—what did you call it? The big boys' sauna club downtown," Gus said. "What do you remember about it?"

"I never went in. No cops welcome, I guess. What's all of that got to do with my troubles?"

Gus seemed tired. I was tired, too—the coffee wasn't kicking in. Gus rubbed a hand across his forehead, puffed out a sigh.

"Harry, I'm about to impart wisdom to you. How you use it is up to you. However it unsettles your life or brings you some peace, well, that'll be your doing, too. Fair enough?"

"Fair enough," I said. Maybe I even meant it.

I started to drink, didn't. But my eyes stayed with the joe. Gus seemed a bit nervous. So why stare?

"Back in '73," he said, "the Lodge was already more than just a big boys' sauna club. It had control over Kipling and tentacles reaching into Ithaca, too.

"And its power kept growing, seeping into more places it shouldn't have—if people are honest, if people aren't greedy."

I heard him sigh. Didn't look up, though. Harry Reno, too busy watching coffee cool.

"But you and I know they aren't and they are, Harry, so its influence spread. Anyway . . .

"The Lodge of the Labyrinth started out as just another weird fraternal bunch back around the turn of the century. The 1890s. I belonged to it."

I stopped staring into java and stared at Gus instead.

"No, Harry—that's some poker face you've got—I didn't belong to it back then. I'm not a Scottish vampire, some Highlander ghoul."

Whew, what a relief. Body of famed PI not found sucked bloodless in a bar. No news at eleven.

"Later's when I joined." He flicked at a crumb on the table. "I'm not making much sense, am I? Just rambling along. Sorry. It's late and I feel old tonight."

He tugged at his whiskers, then went on with his story.

"But that's how the Lodge grew. It just rambled along. Men in funny costumes parading down Kipling streets, raising money for the poor, helping build a hospital. Having fun at the Lodge with fellow Lodge brothers. Maybe even indulging in a little gambling, a little drinking. A little Lodge fun with women who liked that kind of fun.

"Prohibition came and went. The Lodge stayed. Even grew some, already protected in the corridors of power down in Ithaca."

Gus stretched, grabbed a handful of peanuts from the bowl on the table.

"Breakfast of champions, Harry." He crunched away for a minute, took a pull at his coffee, made a face. "Cold." He wiped his mouth with his bar towel and went back to his history lesson.

"A Greek guy moved up here after Hitler and Tojo lost their jobs. A businessman and lawyer named Aristotle Stavros. Perry's old man. Wasn't long, Ari was running our Lodge."

Penny had mined all this and more on her own, down in Ithaca. No need to tell Gus that.

"Ari built a maze inside the old Lodge building downtown. A maze you had to navigate to join. With the Minotaur and Pan. The Labyrinth, Ari called it. Full of twists and turns, spooky stuff. Naked broads to look at, maybe even touch. Maybe even do a little more than just touch. Lots of naked broads, Harry. Lots." His sigh made me wistful for naked broads, too.

Gus stopped, made sure I was listening. "This is important. It holds the key to your troubles." I perked up—now even cold coffee and peanuts tasted good.

"Pericles Stavros transformed the Lodge of the Labyrinth into an honest-to-god criminal enterprise. And the Minotaur and Pan helped him do it."

What? The key to my troubles? That bull stud and his mangy pal the goat? I tried listening a little harder.

"Perry turned Kipling into a transit point for money, drugs, women, guns, whatever. All protected in those corridors of power." Gus snorted.

"Perry found ways to do good deeds, too. Never hurts to do good deeds. Helps cover up evil in the world, salves the collective consciousness."

"I didn't know you were such a philosopher," I said.

"Hell, gotta be. I'm a barkeep. Remember?"

He grinned. I grinned. It had already been a long night. Why fight it? Peanuts found their way into my mouth again.

"And Perry turned the Minotaur and Pan into something else altogether." Gus scanned his darkened bar—searching for Greeks? "Something his dad wouldn't even recognize."

"You still a member, Gus?"

"No. I got out. Perry let me. He had to. I knew too much. And I'd stashed that knowledge where he couldn't get at it.

"So he let me go. Then he made sure I had to retire. Bad heart, Doc Decker said. Can't run after criminals no more. A medical liability, the county judge agreed. Me driving a cop car with a bad heart and all. No more Detective Angus." Another snort; more bad memories.

I had plenty myself. And now I had his, too.

"So I walked out of his Lodge, and Perry waltzed me out of my job. But Stavros is shrewd. He knew I had the goods on him.

"So what does he do? He sets me up here at the Tam. Free and clear. Everything in my name. His money, my name. Go figure."

"What do you have on him?" I asked.

"Oh no. That's a dead end. If I told you, if I told anybody, then I wouldn't have it to myself anymore, would I? And Stavros wouldn't have any reason to keep taking care of me. "So that's a dead end—a labyrinth of dead ends."

He eyeballed me like that last bit meant something. If it did, I'd missed it.

"And maybe that's why I didn't keep you on your bar stool tonight. But I did look out the back door after Marty Mafia followed you out. And I told you to be careful, remember?"

Yeah—careful. Well, thanks a hell of a lot, you old fraud.

"You didn't need any help though, did you? Three of them, and you didn't need Gus at all. You're still a dangerous man, Harry Reno," he said. "That you are."

He had that much right. At least when it's forced on me.

"Now," Gus said, "you've got more to work with than you had when you came in here tonight. I'm going to bed—upstairs.

"Lance can sleep where he is; he's done it before. There's a cot back in the storeroom. I'll get you up in time for breakfast, if you're still here."

Gus put a foot on the steps leading up to the apartment over his bar, a setup like Tom Kuster's at *The Pioneer*. "You shouldn't be out on Kipling streets tonight, Harry. Too many goons. Too many goons." His laughter fading as he climbed.

Lance, the snoring Blue Ox Cop, and Harry Reno, the exhausted Man of the World, left to fend for themselves until daylight. I left the cop in his booth. I took the cot.

32

MONDAY MORNING RAIN

I slept for a couple of hours, my sleep peopled with Mafia hit men trying to pierce my brain with ice picks. I'd wake up, shake off the nightmare scare, go back to sleep, only to find the goons waiting to resume their efforts at eradicating Harry Reno.

Finally, I gave up and got up—time to blow and go.

Outside, the sun still hadn't lit the Monday morning sky. The Volvo headed back to the motel. Maybe I could catch a couple more hours of shut-eye.

A light rain trickled from desultory clouds—just enough to mist the windshield. Out over the lake, thunder rumbled. A donut shop appeared. I stopped, grabbed a sack of crullers and the biggest coffee they sold. To hell with motel sleep. The Mafia goons would probably catch me the next time for sure.

As I walked out, cradling my coffee and crullers, I had to step around a guy mopping the floor. At least I said, "Excuse me."

Rain dotted the windshield while I sat in the Volvo, munching and sipping. At least this wasn't yesterday morning's cold Ithaca rain. At least it wasn't a downpour. At least I hadn't slipped on the donut shop's wet floor.

"Least there ain't no blood today." Where the hell had that come from? Oh yeah. The cleaning lady back at Barb's morgue, that's where. Bingo.

Stavros must have known Walker-Doer had dug up his niece, sent the body to the state medical examiner's office. So, to know the results quickly, Perry needed an inside source. Bribing Barb was out of the question. Wouldn't work, not even if it was me dangling the prospect of wild sex in front of her. Especially not then.

But the cleaning lady, who the hell ever notices the cleaning lady? Even if you almost fall over her—twice. Me, that's who. Harry Reno, the Sam Spade of slippery floors.

But only because the cleaning lady had said, "Least there ain't no blood today." Memorable—sort of.

Sorry, Stavros. Now I know you know it wasn't Mallory who died in the fire. The cleaning lady, your cleaning lady, listening at Barb's door. Clever.

But why care about autopsy results? Why the need to know before anyone else? Worried Barbara Nolan would call it murder—the girl dead, strangled before she turned crispy?

Yeah, maybe he was. And still is. Stavros probably ordered the hit on Mallory. Had he suspected it wasn't Mallory who died? Hard to say.

But for sure he'd be sore as hell with his hit man. Wrong redhead dead. And sore at me for leaving his little welcoming committee leaking blood all over the Tam-O'-Shanter's soft gravel. So what.

The little hula girl was beaming an island smile my way, wiggling in sync with the wipers. Proud of her Harry Reno, I suppose. Well, me, too.

I headed for the motel, and a shower out of the rain.

Church bells were chiming eight o'clock as I strolled into the Hash House, crullers in the rain not enough on their own to fuel Harry Reno for a morning of sleuthing. Especially not a showered and shaved Harry Reno.

Tom's booth was empty, so I took it. Then I saw the proprietress, and what I saw, I didn't like. Alice Vaughn looked like hell, like she'd been up all night. And not up having a good time, like me. Still, she managed to pour me some coffee.

"Harry." That's all she said, just *Harry*, like before. Not *Good morning*; not *What are you doing back in Kipling*; not *What do you want for breakfast?* Just *Harry*.

"What, Alice?"

"Have you seen Brynn?"

"No, not in a week or so. I've been in Ithaca. Remember?" Alice sounded worried. Now I was, too. I sort of liked Brynn. And her buddy Gwen. And Elke, too. Who wouldn't?

"Why, is she missing or something?" I asked. Images of the beautiful trio tied up and in peril began swirling in my head, bobbing along in my ever-present current of lust. Tied tight together, struggling to break free. Half-naked. Then all that nonsense stopped abruptly—my scalp tingling where Alice had smacked it.

"I *said*, she didn't come home last night. Are you listening?"

"I am now, Alice."

"Brynn said she had a special job up at that shitty casino." Tears were leaking from her eyes, dripping, endangering my coffee. "Or at the temple. I can't remember what she said."

She wiped at the tears—coffee safe, for now. "I'm worried, Harry." Alice kept dabbing. "Worried they'll turn Brynn into a hooker and a whore."

I put my coffee down, almost said I was only half as worried, because *hooker* and *whore* were functionally one and the same. But the Hash House's door chime tinkled and saved my still-tingling scalp from such a god-awful mistake.

We both turned and watched as Brynn herself bounced in—all five foot buxom five of her. Careful, Reno, careful.

"Hi, Mom. Oh! Hi, Plain Old Harry. You're back." Her smile was for real and I think for me. Yeah, careful, Plain Old Harry, be real careful.

Alice shot me her trademark lemon-sour look and took Brynn by the elbow, moving her daughter back toward the kitchen.

"Hey, Brynn." She turned, smiled. "It's good to see you again," I said. And then she was gone. Mom, too. Tugging her along. Alice's "Come on, I need some damn help in here" floated back my way, along with the smell of bacon frying..

Maybe that's what I'd have for breakfast—with some rye toast and grape jelly. And OJ and more coffee—and Brynn. And Gwen. And a side order of Elke, please.

Stop it, Reno. Penelope's voice, but only in my head, thank God. I drank coffee, waited for food to appear.

It didn't.

33

HASH FOR BREAKFAST—YET AGAIN

After four or five minutes, the rest of the breakfast crowd, all three of them, threw in their napkins and headed out the door—toward the Golden Arches, no doubt. Maybe sounds of crying, screaming, and plates breaking back in the kitchen propelled them on their way. Couldn't make me run scared, though. I'd enlisted for the duration.

I kept my head down, slurped coffee.

Finally, the kitchen noises subsided. Brynn came out clad in an apron, said garment doing its best to temper her figure and my lust. Wasn't working. God, she looked good. No food, however. But no complaints, either. She had coffee.

"Sorry about that, Harry. I guess Mom, well, I guess I upset her. Not coming home last night and all."

"Want to tell me where you were and who you were with last night? If it would make you feel better, that is." Oh, Reno, how incredibly lame. Some detective you are. "Ah, that way I won't have to ask."

"You're too funny, Harry. Are you coming up to the casino tonight?"

"Yeah, now I am. Sven still holding the doors open?"

She flashed me a questioning frown, like I must be stupid not to know Sven was the doorman. Or maybe that face because Sven wasn't there last night. Or if he was, his ear looked funny.

I pushed on with my investigation. "What time will you be there? And where?"

"About eight, Harry. I'm working the Big Room."

The Big Room. What the hell was the Big Room? I didn't ask her, though. I was trying to impress her with my detective act. "I mean, what time do you get off?" Smooth, Reno. Real smooth.

"Midnight, Plain Old Harry." Damn it, she was laughing at me. Go with it.

"I'll be in a green Volvo," I said. "You know, a Swedish car. Just not Scandinavian like Sven."

"Poor Plain Old Harry." She giggled, touched my shoulder. "Maybe Mom won't be mad if I stay with you tonight, you know, after work."

I shivered. Stay with me tonight? Is that what Brynn had just said? Stay with me tonight in my motel room? I swallowed hard, something I'd been doing a lot of up here in Kipling.

"It's a chance we'll just have to take, kid. I'll be there at midnight. Plain Old Harry'll get nervous if his little princess doesn't appear on the palace steps at the stroke of twelve." I flashed her my best smile. "Nervous. Just so you know."

"I'll be there. She said I'd like you. You're cute, like Indiana Jones." She finger-bopped my nose. "Only older."

I didn't ask who *she* was or who the Jones character was, either. Instead, I asked about breakfast. And then she was gone.

Indiana Jones, huh? I hear that a lot. Maybe I ought to track him down, find out who the hell he is. *Only older?* Well, shit.

"Sorry, Harry." Alice, from the kitchen door—guess she'd been watching my shamus-in-the-diner act. "The bacon got burned and the toast got broke, or something like that. You can have hash for breakfast. Corned beef hash. Same as before. I'm famous for it."

At least she was smiling when she said all of that.

"And he needs some more coffee, Brynn. Harry in the morning

always needs more coffee. Wants it, too. Even if you just topped him up."

She kept on smiling—Alice, not Brynn. Brynn was back in the kitchen now, helping Sam, fetching my food and coffee. But the smile on Alice's face couldn't disguise the worry percolating inside her.

Alice came out from the doorway, trudged my way, tired feet clomping across the diner's spic-and-span linoleum. She stopped beside the booth, gave me the once-over.

"Looks like somebody tried to knock some sense into you last night, Harry." Alice, ever observant. "Good for them. Wouldn't want that job. No sir, I wouldn't. Too much like real work." She sat down in the booth.

"Your face does look wonderful, though. Very masculine. Still avoiding trouble, huh?" I didn't answer her. "Are you really going up to the casino and pick up Brynn tonight?"

She poked my bandaged eyebrow. I winced.

"I get it, Alice. I'll pick her up and I'll behave. I'll keep her safe tonight, too. I swear I will. And I'll try to find some more info about what goes on up there." And some answers for me, too.

"Yeah, right, Harry. I can remember a couple of times you kept me safe at night. Just don't start me any grandkids. You got that, *Plain Old Harry*?"

With that, Alice slid out of the booth, and Brynn set a plate full of hash in front of me, along with rye toast and grape jelly. Guess not all the bread got broke.

I blew Brynn a kiss. She blew one back—behind her mother's back, of course.

Corned beef hash for breakfast had never tasted so good. God, but midnight seemed a long way away. I stuffed breakfast inside as fast as I could, and got the hell out of there before I did or said something really stupid, even for Harry Reno.

Across the street, the phone booth on the corner beckoned. I had some catching up to do. So over I strolled, slotted some change, dialed Penelope's work number.

"Mr. Dillingham's office." Clipped, precise. No doubts about who had answered. Only doubts about if I should be thinking *whom*.

"Hi, sweetheart. I made it back to Kipling. Can you talk? Are you alone?"

"Quite alone, Mr. Reno."

Uh-oh. Why that voice? We'd parted on good terms yesterday. Loving terms, to be precise. What the hell had happened?

"What's the matter, Penny?"

"How is Brynn, Harry? Or is it Elke or Gwen keeping you warm up there?"

"Ah, it's Brynn. She's fine. She just made me breakfast." *Click.*

Damn it. Why had I even mentioned Brynn to Penny when I went back to Ithaca? Or blabbered about Gwen? Or gushed about Elke? That had to be it. Penny had spent the rest of Sunday stewing about me being back in Kipling with the three witches—her words as I left, not mine.

I didn't call Penny back and beg forgiveness. That left my version of macho manhood intact for a while. What I needed and wanted from Penny could wait. She'd cool off after a bit, maybe.

Instead, I dialed the judge's. Willem the ponytailed butler answered. When I asked to speak to his boss, he informed me Judge Walker-Doer was indisposed. That's what he said—*indisposed.* Who the hell really talks like that? Not a genuine English butler, I bet. A fake one, yeah, a fake one would say *indisposed.* Maybe.

But since Willem made it obvious he wasn't going to put his boss on the horn, I asked the ponytailed nuisance, "How about a teatime get-together."

Willem said three thirty would suit His Honor. "And be prompt, Mr. Reno," he admonished. "Be prompt."

"I'll be there with bells on, you limey bastard," I said, and quickly hung up. That evened out my telephone score so far this morning. Penny one—Reno one.

I dropped the dime and dialed *The Kipling Pioneer*. Jayne Rask answered. I told her I was back in town and that she sure looked pretty this morning, along with some other nonsense.

"Come on by and see how I really look," Jayne said. She sure as hell didn't sound very pretty.

I said, "Okay," and we both hung up at the same time. A tie—my score stagnant at 1-1-1.

34

NEWSROOM REVELATIONS

The Volvo found a spot in front of *The Pioneer,* and I reminded the little hula girl to sit tight while I went in to see Jayne. She pulled her pout face. So what. Nothing new. She could always try out her Waikiki wiggles on whoever happened to wander by.

The newspaper's front door yielded to my gentle touch. However, my "Hey babe!" elicited a big zero. The door clicked shut.

The only light on in the newsroom was the green-shaded lamp on Jayne's desk. And there she was, head nestled in her arms, sobbing little sobs, just enough to keep tears flowing, enough to let me know she was alive.

I walked my eyes a little closer. Tears dripping onto her desk calendar, turning white days gray. Not good. Really not good.

The rest of the newsroom resembled the rubble left by a tornado. Books and magazines littered the room, shredded by the force of whatever had passed through. The same twister had styled Jayne's hair.

Doc Reno decided he'd better prescribe something to break the sob cycle—coffee juiced with a little whiskey seemed the right cure. But where to find it.

Back in the newspaper's morgue, the old bound editions, big as poster boards and telephone-book thick, had been flung from their shelves, as if giants had decided to play Frisbee with the newspaper's archives. I cut my way through and reached the kitchen. The coffee maker had survived.

I found two mugs, loaded them with some of Tom Kuster's ubiquitous rye, then topped them up with the coffee I'd made. Wouldn't want Jayne drinking alone.

"Here," I said.

Jayne raised her head, grunted, snatched at the mug, spilling more than a lot. The calendar's days alternating now between coffee-brown and sob-gray. A couple days the color of mud.

"Try two hands," I said. She did, and I sat down and followed my own advice.

Eventually, the coffee-drinking ritual brought some order back into her life. The sobbing stopped and her shaking tapered off.

"What in the hell happened in here?" I said. And when? And why? And who made this incredible mess? And how I questioned her that morning was no smoother than that. I got my answers, though.

"Tom got mad, Harry. That's what happened. Mad at me. And I got mad at him. Or maybe it started the other way around. Or all at once. All at once, I imagine, Harry, all at once."

I tried patting her shoulder; she shrugged me away.

"You want to know when? Last night, late. Or early this morning, to be reporter-precise. What the hell difference does it make? He came in from being up at the casino, or his Lodge. I forget. The lousy bastard."

She ran a hand through her hair—didn't help.

"And why? I'll tell you why. Because Tom Kuster always wants to bed any female in sight, especially me. And last night, I wanted no part of him. He'd drunk himself twice as shit-faced as usual up at the casino. Or his Lodge. Or wherever the son of a bitch had been doing his whoring."

All of Jayne's answers were rushing out at once, bobbing along together. I had to listen hard not to drown in the flow.

"And he smelled like that's what he had been up to—whoring. You can't hide that, not from a woman you have, that you had . . . Oh hell, Harry, not from the woman you screw. Or did screw, or did love. Once. You can't hide it." Tears again. Lots of them. "Oh, Harry—I'm sorry."

I handed her a tissue. Jayne tried drying her eyes. Like the hand through her hair, the tissue wasn't much help.

"You want to know who made this mess? I did, and Tom Kuster did, the two of us together." I gave her another tissue. "And Mallory was just the last straw, just the tip of the iceberg of Tom's whoring." I passed the whole box over.

"And last night, we stuck our straws into that frozen concoction of nothingness and sucked on it for all we were worth." Jayne blew her nose.

"And that, Detective Harry Reno, comprises the who and the why and the when of my iceberg-like sundae. Only it's Monday, right, Harry?" Jayne drained her mug, held it out for more—just like Tom, last trip. "I'm mixing metaphors or something, aren't I, Harry?"

Jayne couldn't stop saying my name, throwing a *Harry* in every five words or so. Maybe I was a metaphor, too. Or the absolution she sought. "Jayne—where's Tom? Where is he?"

She ignored me, kept staring into her empty coffee mug.

"Where's Tom?" I was shouting now. "Where is he?"

She glanced up, a smile spreading across her face. Smug-looking. I didn't like it.

"Upstairs, Harry. I shot him. He's dead."

35

KUSTER'S RECRUDESCENCE

I raced through the newsroom rubble, dodging broken furniture, leaping over the tombstone-sized newspaper archives Tom and Jayne had somehow flung at each other in their mutual fury.

I cleared the rear stairs two at a time—adrenaline pumping. Tom's upstairs bedroom door stood open. I shot into the room, braked to a stop—heart pounding.

Tom Kuster was lying on the bed, his Mark Twain head of white hair plastered against the pillow. No blood there. My eyes passed over his face to the sheet pulled up to his chin, a fairly clean sheet; clean by Tom's standards, anyway.

No blood pooling in his mouth, running out, staining his fairly clean sheet. No blackened bullet holes leaking red, dyeing the sheet and Tom. And no burbling sounds, either, no red froth speckling his lips.

I walked my eyes a little closer.

Tom Kuster was alive, no doubt about that. His snores, soft though they were, confirmed that much. I sniffed the air. A gun had been fired, and somewhat recently. A searching once-over again of Tom as he slept.

Beside his head on the pillow, a bullet hole, a little bullet hole, the sort a .22 makes. Jayne had missed Tom's head by inches. On purpose? Maybe.

Tom grunted, turned on his side. His snoring drawn out, heavy. Soft no longer. Music to my ears, though. Yeah, definitely alive and unhurt.

And since Tom was a hippie, peace, live-and-let-live, forgiving sort of dude, he wouldn't hold a little thing like attempted murder against Jayne—right, man?

No answer, just the quietude of the sawmill.

I went back down the stairs a lot slower than I had raced up them. Jayne still sat at her desk, not quite so dazed-looking now. The whiskey-laced coffee was working. I stared down at her; she stared back up at me. "I heard him snoring, Harry. I didn't kill him, did I?"

"No, you didn't," I said. "Where's your gun?"

"I love him, Harry. I do. Why else would I want to kill him?" A goofy, adolescent smile plastered her face. Lots of different looks in Jayne's arsenal. Lots of different heartaches, too.

I had to ask her twice more where the gun was.

"In my purse. I put it back, like a good little girl." A good little girl. The vulnerable sort. Bullshit. I went searching for the purse.

Yeah, a .22 revolver. If Jayne had been packing an automatic, she'd have emptied the clip at Tom. Then he wouldn't be up there sawing timber right now, and I would be calling the cops. As it was, I decided not to call anybody at all. I stuffed her gun in my pocket.

"Let's get out of here, Jayne. Tom needs to sleep it off. Go clean up, and we'll go for a drive. I'll buy you breakfast, get you some more coffee."

Jayne walked slowly toward the paper's restroom. When she finally came back, her hair was brushed, along with her teeth, and her panties were pulled up. At least that's how she put it.

I didn't check to see if she was telling the truth.

She'd put on some scent, smoothed out her rumpled dress, too. Even after a night like she'd had, Jayne Rask remained a remarkable-looking woman—tall, still slender, moving with a jungle cat's grace, hips gliding, frosted hair flouncing, tuned-up breasts more than entrancing.

I told her she looked gorgeous.

She smiled, said, "Go to hell, Harry."

I told her I had a story for her, ready-made for her typewriter's clickety-clack. "Just need some background stuff from you first, before I dump it in your lap, let you run with it."

She smiled at me again when I said *story*, and picked up her purse. She followed me out, locked *The Pioneer*'s front door. "I doubt we'll get it out on time this week, Harry. The paper, I mean."

"We'll see. Maybe my story will inspire the two of you."

I opened the Volvo's door, and she slipped in and her skirt rode up —up to the top of her thighs. She didn't bother to pull it back down. Oh, brother, whatever would the little hula girl think? I climbed in and started the car.

Jayne glanced at my little friend on the dash, then let her eyes find mine. "Can we put her in the glove box, Harry? I don't like competition." Two of a kind, huh? Takes one to know one.

Jayne touched my arm—ever so lightly—sighed and opened her mouth, ran her tongue over her teeth, around her lips, waiting to see if I'd kiss her.

"Me Jayne, you Tarzan," she said. No Cheetah this morning—her old submissive *take me* signal floating between us.

I passed on the kiss and all that would go with it, but I did put my little hula girl away, like she'd asked.

Sometimes I do get some things right.

36
ICE MELT

The Volvo passed up the Hash House and ended up at the Golden Arches instead. I bought us both some coffee and Jayne some food. Then we headed out the lake road, all the way to the burned-out cabin. Or rather, to the spot where the cabin had been before they bulldozed it and hauled Tom's paradise away.

Maybe the cabin site would thaw that iceberg Jayne had been babbling about, get her to spill some info about my Mallory problem, maybe even something about Gwen's mother's death.

Jayne had partaken of the whole enchilada back then, and kept it to herself all these years. And since Mallory Mordred's investigative journalism caper focused on back then, Harry Reno, ace detective, figured the two might be connected.

The Volvo bumped her way up the dirt driveway and settled down for a Swedish snooze under the trees. Man, what a setting, even with the cabin on the lam. I could almost imagine the ghost of Not-Mallory, the for-sure-dead redhead, lingering under the trees, reluctant to leave.

We sat on the flat rock in the cabin clearing. No rain here last night. A soft breeze wafted floral scents around to mingle with whatever Jayne had put on back at *The Pioneer*.

"Harry," she said, and laid her head on my shoulder. "I let Tom fall in love with Mallory. I just did. I could have stopped it, but I didn't." Her voice soft, like the breeze. "I told myself she'd grow tired of him. His drinking would wear on her, his damn snoring . . . But I was wrong."

Jayne's hair smelled of citrus. I said as much, but she was only listening to herself. "A young woman less than half his age and as hopelessly in love with him as he was with her. I hated them both. And most of all, I still hate myself for letting it happen."

She reached down, picked a wildflower, plucked at the petals, let the pieces trickle through her fingers. She tossed the stem away.

"The little tramp fell for him," she said, her words quickening. "And it wasn't an act. She thought he walked on water. And he did straighten up—a little. He quit drinking so hard." Jayne's nose twitched along with her lip. "I guess he had to stay sober to keep it hard enough for her."

Jayne's spit splattered my cheek, carrying the threat of more storms approaching. I dried my face on my sleeve. Damn her mood swings.

"I was jealous, Harry—still am. She was all Tom talked about or thought about. Once Mallory showed up at *The Pioneer*, I ceased to exist."

Her hands were scratching at each other now, one hand's fingernails afflicting the other hand's palm—frantic bitch scouring.

"I decided to fix my mistake by putting a bug in Mallory's ear, a wicked, brain-destroying weevil. So I gave the luscious Ms. Mordred all she needed and more to investigate and expose the exalted Lodge of the Labyrinth." Jayne glanced over at me, a question in her eyes.

"You know all about the Lodge and its temple, don't you, Harry?"

I said I didn't, but she wasn't listening.

"My weevil told Mallory all about Perry's own personal perversions. And his wife's."

Jayne didn't seem so cuddly right now. My arm found its way off her shoulders. She jumped up and paced in circles around our rock.

"A front-page story to make her career. Maybe a Pulitzer. That's what I told Mallory. Little bitch couldn't write worth a damn. I just wanted to destroy that damn temple, pull it down on Perry's oily Greek head." Jayne was rolling now.

"God, but I fired her up, fed her full. And she swallowed it all, just like she swallowed whatever Tom wanted her to swallow. Bitch, fucking bitch, fucking little granola bitch."

I ducked. I covered. But after that jab, she seemed spent. Her head came down, arms hugging her body, tears flowing like meltwater off the dissolving iceberg of Tom's whoring.

I pulled her back onto the rock. At least she dried her own tears. But on my shirt, rubbing her face back and forth like a puppy. Now the shirt front matched the sleeve—both sodden.

"I was playing with fire. I knew Perry wouldn't allow Mallory to probe his Lodge, hurt his precious temple. He's ruthless. I hate him. He dumped me, back then, even before you showed up and left." Periwinkle eyes glared, blond eyebrows frowned, a crease rising between her eyes. Oh hell. Was I on her shit list, too?

Then she whirled her fury back on Perry, not Harry.

"We were together forever. The three of us. Me, Perry, and his precious Lodge. Then that bitch Ariadne showed up, and I was history. I hope all of them fucking fry in Hell."

"Who's Ariadne, Jayne?"

"The bitch who took Perry away from me. His wifey-poo. You haven't met our Lady DA yet? Tall, leggy like me? Younger than me? Sexier than me? Bigger hair, bigger boobs?"

As her fury mounted, she'd come up off the rock, whirling around, arms flailing, hands waving. I managed to ground her back onto granite yet again.

I kissed her—anything to calm her down.

"Are you sure you haven't seen Ariadne? You'd like her, Harry. I know you would." A small sigh of defeat escaped her lips. "Hold me, Harry, hold me."

So I did—because I already was.

"You're looking at me like I'm a witch or something, aren't you?

Yes, I told Perry that Tom sent Mallory to dig up as much dirt as she could on him and his Lodge.

"Perry was truly pissed at Tom. Mad as hell. Ready to kill. And that made me happy—real happy." Shit. Jayne, ramping up again.

"I told Perry that Mallory had confronted her uncle, the Honorable Arthur Walker-Doer. Prodded him hard about the old Kipling cover-up. Why he dismissed the murder charge against the cool DA."

Now Jayne had Harry in her sights instead of Perry.

"When you and that fool McCabe investigated Rusty the druggie's murder fifteen years ago, you couldn't pin it on the cool DA because nobody in Kipling, nobody in Ithaca, nobody who was anybody in the whole godforsaken universe wanted the Kipling cauldron to boil over."

That old story. I'd lived it. Lost the woman I'd loved to it. But why mention that now?

My cheek was damp yet again. My handkerchief mopped up Jayne's spittle the best it could, went back to its pocket. Now the pocket was wet, too.

"Hey," I said, "I'm sorry, all that coffee. Gotta whiz. I'll be right back." A man can only absorb so much, you know.

37
AZTEC ANTICS

When I came back from among the trees, Jayne was pacing around our rock. Long, jungle cat strides, ready to pounce. Hands slicing the air like an Aztec priest atop a pyramid, cutting the still-beating heart from his victim. Holding it aloft for the blood-crazed faithful below to behold and egg him on.

"Nobody wanted their piece of the take disturbed." Slice—slice. "And they were all on the take, then and now." Slice. "Perry made sure of *that*," she said. Slice—slice. And slice again.

Jayne, crazy evil, but so damned good-looking, so just plain sexy, you had to watch, had to stare. At least—unlike an Aztec mob—I didn't whoop it up.

"They made sure you failed," Jayne said. "Their pie was not going to be cut into smaller pieces." Sudden laughter, a private joke rattling around in her head? Another mood swing, her eyes fixing on mine. "No more sharing, Harry." Laughter, but no more slicing, thank God.

I smiled, but didn't really get it.

Then a sharp prick, like an ice pick poke to the brain—the photo on Gus's wall. The three of them hanging on to each other. Jayne,

Perry, and Walker-Doer. Maybe that's the sharing Jayne meant. She was talking again.

"Perry found a guy he called the Pilot. Crew cut, tall, slim, never had much to say, all business. He moved drugs for Perry."

Aha, the guy in Stavros's office, leaning against the wall in the shadows. Harry Reno: no longer the Detective in the Dark.

"The Pilot's still here," she said. "When he's not moving product, he sticks close to Perry—even when he's shoving himself up Ariadne's ass." What? I let it ride. Later, maybe.

"Perry brought in another man about the same time. A slick-bald badass. Quiet, but very bad." Jayne's eyes grabbed mine. "Or good, depending on your position." Huh?

"All anyone ever called him was the Dutchman. When Perry had a problem, he gave it to the Dutchman." Jayne's fingers mimed a gun. "Problem solved."

She sat still for a moment, peering into the trees, like she sensed something lurking under the pines. Well, I'd just been in there, taking a leak, and I hadn't seen anything. Still . . . I'd felt a presence, something close by. Maybe someone *was* creeping the trees. But I let it slide. Jayne was babbling again.

"The Dutchman's gone now. At least, I haven't seen him around lately."

Really? Maybe I have. Just not slick-bald anymore. Ponytailed bastard. No need to tell her that. Bet she knows. Lying bitch. Didn't say that, either. No death wish.

A small smile twitched Jayne's mouth. She turned toward me, let her tongue lick lips, flick at teeth. "Perry used me, Harry. And God, how I loved being used."

Don't touch, the brain said. The rest of my body struggling in disagreement.

"You don't need to tell me the details of what Perry had you do. I sorta know how that stuff works, Jayne."

"Do you, Harry? Do you really?" A shake of that soft, frosted hair of hers. "You don't. Really, you don't. Not the things Perry had me do.

The nasty things little Jaynie Painie wanted done. I'll tell you if you like. It'll make you hard."

"Later, babe." I winked. "Later—for sure." I didn't mean it, but I said it nevertheless. Anything to break her spell. Because that was what she was weaving again. But why me and why now?

I stood up, did my own walking and talking act, put a little distance between me and the witch on the rock.

"Tell me who Perry had you seduce, and why he needed them."

The summer breeze stirred her scent; it floated between us. I sucked it in—you would have, too. Then Jayne's eyes widened, snatched mine. Damn woodland Circe. I moved a little closer. No choice.

"No, Harry, I won't tell you any names." Was that what I wanted? Names—

Jayne's tongue flicked at teeth, ran circuit around lips yet again. "But I was good, Harry, really good, back then. Still am, right here, right now." Oh shit. Who and why long forgotten.

We sat, hugged for a while. I might have kissed her. Maybe she kissed me. Maybe hands went here and there, searching—hers and mine. Hard to remember. I nuzzled her ear. A little-girl squeal. Very sexy.

A squirrel chattered. We broke our clinch. Her spell dissipated, blew away.

Jayne sniffled, wiped her nose. She was winding down, her iceberg now only a puddle. I had tried absorbing all that she had told me, but it wasn't easy. I was too damn wet.

"And then Ariadne showed up, and Perry built his Temple of the Labyrinth out in the lake with his casino money," Jayne said.

A flash of blue-gray. Someone under the trees? I ignored it. Only room for Jayne in my head just then.

"Perry did things out there with Ariadne and the others I won't tell you about, because—believe it or not—I am not yet ready to die."

Jayne stood up, stretched, let her breasts strain against her blouse. "Can we go back to Kipling, Harry? Please? Can we? I'm so tired."

As soon as we turned back onto the lake road, Jayne fell asleep.

We'd just about reached Kipling when she stirred, mumbled, "What about *your* story? I told you mine."

I waited her out. She drifted back off, and we coasted on into town. I found Jayne's apartment without any trouble. She still lived where she always had. We shuffled to her door, unlocked it, and went in together.

"Put me to bed, Harry." Her voice soft, a sleepy purr, intimating a bit more than just slumber in store for Harry and Jayne.

"Okay." A little finger tap to her nose. "You need to hit the bathroom first?"

"Oh, Harry. So gallant. Yes, I do."

So she did, and I got the hell out of there, while whatever needed doing in her bathroom got done.

No Jayne anymore, so the little hula girl back on the dash—but no Waikiki wiggles. Sulking because I'd picked Jayne over her. So what? It was only for a couple of hours. Kid just doesn't know how lucky she's got it.

Time to kill before visiting old Walker-Doer's Victorian play land. Time to kill before that butler of his would try his damnedest to make me look stupid again. Time enough to try to corner Kipling's coroner.

The Volvo found a spot to her liking, and I went in to see the good doctor himself.

Fine gold letters on Doc's frosted glass proclaimed who lurked within: Durwood D. Decker, M.D. Beneath his name, smaller gold letters reminded you Doc was also Lake County Coroner—very small gold letters. Not good business to call unwanted attention to the fact that *Oh, I fill out death certificates, too*. Not polite to remind your patients of their impending mortality too forcefully, so, small gold letters.

His waiting room was much like any other doctor's waiting room —full of patients who looked like they'd been there since yesterday and wanted to be somewhere else today.

The receptionist said, "The doctor will be glad to see you when he finishes with his patients." I turned, surveyed the waiting room. Not going to happen anytime soon.

"Look, uh . . . Sandy, all I really want is to see Doc's coroner's notes and his report. For the cabin fire, you know, Mallory Mordred, the crisped corpse."

"Sure," said Sandy the Receptionist. "Just as soon as Dr. Decker comes in today."

I checked my watch—two o'clock. "Do all of these good people," I swung my arm in an all-encompassing arc, "know the good doctor isn't with us today?" No answer.

"Where is Doc Decker?"

"How should I know?" Sandy said. "I'm not married to him."

I could have slammed Doc's door on my way out—broken some of Doc's frosted glass, made a patient or two of his jump up, shout, *What the hell.* But I didn't.

38

VICTORIA'S HOUSE—ROUND TWO

The Volvo sniffed out the lake road once more. From town to the judge's the asphalt ran fairly straight for the most part, curving a little here and there where it skirted cliffs, offering a glimpse of brown sand and equally brown rocks below. Overhead, the sun hung by itself in a cloudless heaven. Out where blue sky kissed silvery lake waters, a greenish line glimmered, like an ancient copper gutter laid down by God to make the waters behave.

Maybe the judge's ponytailed butler would be as complacent today as God's lake. Yeah, right. Good luck with that, Reno.

Twin granite pillars still guarded the judge's entrance. And while I didn't expect the mugs perched on top would have found other employment, it never hurts to verify facts.

But no, they were still up there—frightening the locals, entrancing the occasional tourist with their weirdness. And the driveway still ran between towering oaks. An arrow-straight road for an arrow-straight man. You could believe it if you wanted to. I sure as hell didn't.

The Volvo sailed serenely along the judge's shady drive until a black-assed crow cawed and dropped a load on the windshield. I hit the wipers. All that did was smear crow shit around—sticky paste half obscuring my vision. After a couple of swipes back and forth, the damn fluid ran out. Maybe I could ask the judge's friendly butler to top me up.

Yeah, right—good luck with that one, too.

Like the washer fluid, the oak trees finally petered out, too. The judge's mansion loomed up, still framed by the crescent of evergreens on the hill behind it. I crawled out and climbed the stone steps, just like before. Weren't any more; weren't any less. Just too many. Just like before.

"Ah, Mr. Reno. So good to see you, so very good." Willem inside, imprisoned by etched glass and green wrought iron. He invited me in with a sweep of his hand.

I was supposed to trust the butler—remember? So in I went. I asked him if he had ever considered the slick-bald look.

"Indeed, sir, indeed." Not even a smirk. "This way, Mr. Reno." Well, maybe a small twitch. Just one corner of his mouth. But elusive, like the butler himself.

"If you please, Mr. Reno—quick march." Quick march, my ass, you ponytailed bastard. I thought it. I just didn't say it.

So on we went. And yeah, it was a snappy pace. Maybe the old judge was still pining away for lost yesterdays out in his Norway. Anxious to pound more World's Fair crap into a gumshoe's thick skull.

Nope. We passed the judge's embassy-level dining room with its French doors and the Norwegian trinket beyond, and trudged on.

Eventually Willem said, "My apologies, Mr. Reno," and we started to climb a spiral, wrought-iron stairway—two stories' worth of corkscrewing green metal. Probably the same shit the judge had used to guard the front doors. Thrifty old bastard.

Over his shoulder, Willem said, "Do tread carefully, Mr. Reno. The judge is receiving in the Crow's Nest post meridiem." Whatever the hell that meant.

I quickly realized it meant an acrophobia-inducing Everest ascent to reach the old fart. There had to be an easier way, an elevator somewhere. Or maybe Willem tied the judge into a bosun's chair and hoisted the rotten bastard up to his nest.

And that was the image that stuck. The butler, gray ponytail swinging to and fro, sinewy arms hauling on hemp, as the kindly judge, black robes flapping like crow wings, ascended from his dungeon lair to the uppermost room of Victoria's manse: the Crow's Nest.

Turned out, that wasn't too far north of the truth—the elevator part, that is.

Willem waited at the top of the stairs while I turned the last two corkscrews. At least I wasn't panting. He smiled, twisted the door's shiny brass knob, and announced, "Mr. Harry Reno, Your Honor." Ah, so important a visitor. Still, I looked before I leapt.

The judge's Crow's Nest was the glassed-in observation post atop the stack of turret rooms I'd noticed my first visit. Floor-to-ceiling windows let the old bird survey his kingdom—left, right, and almost all around. Okay, no Thugge assassins or parking lot riffraff lurking inside. Safe enough.

I stepped in and so did Willem. Not going to be a private tête-à-tête, because butler made three. Not good. Willem opening a window, the judge claiming I had jumped.

Then again, if the butler locked me in the Crow's Nest all alone with Walker-Doer, I might just sail on out on my own. Hard to stomach the judge and his pretensions of piety and rectitude—the phony old fraud.

But none of that happened. Willem left the windows alone, and Walker-Doer kept smiling instead of pontificating, and I stayed put.

Also, no wondering if what I detected was flowers, Jayne's perfume, or the effervescence of a ghost, like at the burned-out cabin. No sir, not up in the judge's Crow's Nest.

The only scent encased in glass up there was sour old man.

"Have a seat, my boy," the judge said, so I sat in a captain's chair while the judge sat in its mate, both of us in padded comfort this time.

If the autopsy results had thrown him off his game, he didn't let it show. The teeth in the death's-head face formed a smile along with their lips—a grin like rigor mortis hangs on you, but a smile nonetheless.

"Let us have a drink, Harry, my boy." The judge sported a brown tweed jacket over a blue pinpoint oxford shirt, a yellow bow tie sprouting at his throat. The judge's informal attire.

Willem buttled about at the drinks cart, served, then went to sit by the door.

"A butler who sits instead of stands?" I asked.

Willem smirked, but didn't reply. So I let a sip of gin and tonic slip inside and settled back to listen to what Walker-Doer wanted to say.

"They tell me the young lady who died in the cabin was not my niece, but someone else. Do you know who she was, Harry?" I gave a shoulder shrug for an answer.

The judge let me by with it for now, though his brown trousers, sharply creased, flexed a bit at the knee. Creases sharp as a bayonet's edge, lest mere mortals should conclude the judge sought the informality of comfortable clothes in the good old summertime.

He didn't. Plus, he was droning on again. "The fact the dead girl was not my niece does not, in and of itself, imply my niece is alive, does it, Harry?"

I told him I had to agree with that. His polished brown shoes looked spiffy as hell on the old son of a bitch. Hope they were pinching his feet.

"Nor does it mean she is dead. Correct, Harry?" The judge's didactic recitation—just annoying as hell. The juniper juice took the edge off it a little, though. I'd guzzled gin and tonic almost as good in Hong Kong once. A butler had served it, too. And I'd had more than one.

"Harry," the judge said, "please stay with me on this."

Okay, you old bastard—words in my mind, not in my mouth. Not yet, anyway.

"What it means, Harry, at this particular juncture, is that your employer has found my claim of benefits under the life insurance policy to be without merit." The judge dabbed at a spot of gin and tonic he'd let slip past his mouth and onto his shirt.

"And your company—or if you'll allow, your former employer—has communicated to me I am under no obligation to allow you to investigate the now nonexistent claim." The splotch from his drink acquired a twin. No handkerchief cleanup this time. His focus elsewhere.

"Nor," said the judge, "need I have anything whatsoever to do with you personally—from the company's perspective, you understand." I offered him another shrug. Again he let it slide.

"She has a sweet voice, very British. Clipped, but sweet. Who is she, Harry?" A third shoulder twitch; a third pass from the judge. Harry Reno, on a roll.

"If my niece was not the body found in the cabin when it burned, she must be somewhere else now. That you would not dispute, would you?"

I told him no, couldn't dispute that at all.

"And you are without employment, correct?"

I told him something always turns up.

"And it has, my boy, so it has." The old crow sat up straighter in his captain's chair, his excitement as palpable to him as it was unfathomable to me.

"I shall employ you to find my niece, Mallory Mordred—alive or dead." One hand waved a dismissive apology my way. "I feel somewhat responsible for the whole tragic series of events, indeed I do." The old crow's beak swiveled. "Willem, please give Harry his retainer."

The butler off his seat before the judge had finished saying *please*, his outstretched hand offering a manila envelope.

I ignored the ponytailed nuisance and kept my sights fixed on the old crow. "Why would I want to work for you, Judge? What could you offer me that I would take?

"If you don't mind, would you have Willem show me the way back down and out."

39

THE OLD CROW CACKLES

The old judge smiled, shook his head, told me no, don't go. "Harry, I hope you are not ready to be *down and out* just yet," he said. "I have both wisdom and knowledge to impart."

After that, if I didn't want what he offered, I was free to leave. Or so he promised. "And Willem will most certainly show you the way back down and then out, Harry."

Willem grinning now, too. Gunmetal eyes matching his gray ponytail. Neither quite still, both roving a bit to and fro: judge—shamus—judge . . . well, you get the idea.

"Now, my boy, you asked what could I offer that would induce you to take my coin, convince you to sleuth for a deluded old man." The judge sipped a little more gin.

"The truth, Harry. That's what I offer." His hand a bit shakier, letting more than a drop or two dribble onto his shirt yet again. "The unvarnished, unadulterated truth. What do you say to that?" The judge's handkerchief darted out, blotted at gin droppings dotting his shirt, then shimmied back up his sleeve.

His eyes held mine.

What I wanted to tell the old fraud was that I'd already imbibed the straight goods as served up by Gus the bartender. Already gotten the scoop from Jayne Rask while I sat on a hard rock where the cabin wasn't anymore. And maybe some of what she'd spilled up there might even be the truth—in her mind.

And slimy little Karl, he'd prattled on so convincingly that what he said had, if not the ring of truth, then at least its reverberations. Oh, and Tom Kuster. His Mallory-not-a-phantom bullshit clanged false enough to be fact now, too.

But no mention of any of that in the Crow's Nest. The old judge was right. I wanted to hear his truth. Not that he waited for an answer—of course not.

"Now, Harry, I must confess to you, and in front of Willem here, that it is I who am at fault in this matter. I set the events in motion. I put a bug, so to speak, in my niece's ear. I only wanted her to be a success, Harry."

"Say again, Judge?" He didn't.

"You should not mistake my motives, my boy. I wanted Mallory to make her name in investigative journalism. She deserved the bright lights, the recognition *60 Minutes* stardom brings. So I decided to help her along."

The judge set events in motion? *He* put a bug in her ear? Maybe he ought to talk to Jayne. She'd claimed it was all her fault, her bug. Well, a person does have two ears, but—

"Judge, top of the story, and I'm already having trouble believing you. Help Mallory? Sure. Bring down your Lodge? Topple your bull and goat off their pedestals? I noticed the two of them still out there guarding your entrance."

I stood up.

"Sorry, Judge. I'm not buying what you're selling. Have Butler Boy over there show me down and then out." But no step toward the door. Just needling the old bastard, and he knew it.

"Sit back down, Harry." I did. "I have not finished selling, as you put it. Hear a bit more, won't you?"

His lips pulled back slightly from stained teeth as he spoke, and he seemed more like a skeletal death's head stuck on a rag doll's body than ever. He was trying hard to smile and be friendly, but dying old man stench draped every word with decay.

Still, I told him, "Okay." I'd stay and hear him out.

"The Lodge of the Labyrinth is no mere big boys' sauna club," the judge said. Ouch. "Not at all, Harry. Rather, the Lodge is an amalgam of the state's finest minds, its wealthiest industrialists, the cream of the professions. The Lodge exists to bring wealth and power to this elite—and to do good works, too, of course. But power first, without which nothing is possible."

No use interrupting. Like Gus, Walker-Doer had found his rhythm.

"I stood second to Pericles Stavros as he built his power base, stood second as he grew his drug business. And I stood second as the casino rose beside the lake."

The old crow paused, drumming fingers on the arm of his chair.

"Harry, just as an aside, if you accept my retainer, we shall *nunc pro tunc* all of this—as we say in the law—to the point just before our conversation began. Making it confidential."

His fingers drummed a little harder.

"To protect the two of us. A lawyer-investigator relationship with my niece the client." His death's-head grin shot itself my way again, Maglite bright this time. "Or her estate."

Maybe that was the law. Maybe it wasn't. Didn't really matter. He kept babbling.

"But I broke with Pericles Stavros after his temple rose on that isle of the damned. Appalled by what he does there. For he works *Evil* in his temple, Harry—*Evil*."

In court, Walker-Doer could intone *Evil* in censure, and the jury would nod its agreement while the defendant quaked at his fate. We weren't in court, but I shivered anyway. So what? Anyone would have —spooky old fart.

But it didn't matter what I thought or did. Walker-Doer went on lecturing relentlessly.

"Do you know what goes on, out on that island in the lake, Harry?" I shook a *no* his way. He never noticed.

"Perversion and death. Because those are the twin touchstones of the *Evil* that comprises Pericles Stavros." The judge indicated the wet ring his drink had made on the mahogany table between our chairs. Willem sprang up, wiped it dry, sat again.

"The genius of his temple subterfuge lies in the use of technology. Low-light cameras and sound equipment record the rituals conducted in his Temple of the Labyrinth. The recordings fix the successful aspirants to Pericles like fish nailed to trees, waiting to be filleted."

The old judge might be cultured and erudite, but he was also an old North Woodsman, harsh and practical. Nail fish to trees and gut 'em? Yeah, I'd seen him do that a lot—in his courtroom. I didn't mention it, though.

"Of course the Lodge brother, the aspirant, knows what he has done in the temple, what acts were committed to advance in degree, to increase in power and wealth. But the recording of such acts becomes blackmail in the hands of that evil Greek. Thank you, Willem."

The judge grabbed the butler's proffered drink, sipped, and sailed on.

"But the evil has continued, Harry. Grown, even. More young women, more unexplained deaths and disappearances. And now with Mallory, it must stop."

Walker-Doer paused. He'd been gazing out the windows of his Crow's Nest as he recited the last of his lecture. But with the mention of Mallory, he swung back around until I couldn't escape his skull-face stare—no grinning now.

"Harry, I shall require several things of you in exchange for the knowledge you will doubtlessly glean in the performance of your duty. And in addition to the increase in knowledge, you shall also increase your own wealth. Should you fail, the retainer remains yours to keep."

His rheumy eyes cleared as he drove his lance home.

"Your penalty for failure, however, will be the loss of the knowledge necessary to calm yourself as to your past. Here in Kipling. With Gwen's mother."

The old bastard. The old, black-winged, evil-hating bastard. Gwen's mother and the past. Walker-Doer knew what had happened and why back then. His price the knowledge of his niece's whereabouts, her continued safety, her rescue if I found her in peril—if she were still alive.

A man's pride makes him bargain with the devil at times. Mine did that afternoon in the judge's Crow's Nest. I should have gone home to Ithaca and Penelope and given up on the past, but I didn't. Might have saved some lives. Maybe even some worth saving.

"Deal, you old bastard," I said instead.

Walker-Doer cackled—then again, maybe it was only a laugh. "We shall have coffee in the library, Willem. To celebrate."

40

NORWEGIAN BONFIRE

Willem pressed a button. The wall next to him parted, revealing a small elevator. "Please take the lift, Your Honor. I shall escort Mr. Reno down the iron maiden."

The Old Crow nodded his acquiescence and stepped into the elevator.

As the door slid shut, the butler slipped an admonition inside. "Mind you await us at the bottom, Your Honor. No wandering about." Gotta wonder. Who's in charge? Butler or judge?

Willem opened the door of the Crow's Nest, bowing me down the iron stairs. "Trust, Mr. Reno. But mind your step. Always mind your step."

I minded, but I went first anyway.

The iron stairs vibrated, dancing to the elevator's tune as it descended with its carrion bird cargo. Willem held back, following at a safe distance. Maybe he didn't trust me any more than I trusted him. At the bottom, the judge had obeyed his minder. The elevator door remained shut awaiting our arrival.

"Clear to open, Your Honor," Willem said. The door slid back. And that was the last normal thing I noticed for a while.

The *whomp* and concussion of a detonation pushed Willem into me. He felt hard, not soft. The judge stumbled out of the elevator. We broke our clinch and caught him before he hit the floor.

Another boom rumbled. Ceiling plaster rained down. It sure as hell wasn't thunder. Two somethings somewhere had exploded.

"The safe room, Your Honor. Await my signal." Willem shoved the old crow back into his iron cage, and down the elevator went—to the safe room, I guess. Never made it there myself.

Willem's nimble fingers jabbed numbers on a keypad set in the wall. A door slid open. A small arsenal of lethal weaponry appeared: assault rifles, pistols, shotguns. Ammo.

The butler nabbed an M16 and politely handed it to me. He snatched one for himself. "I should say we are under attack, Mr. Reno."

"No shit, Willem."

"Full auto," he said, and passed me spare clips, stuffing more into his own pockets. "This will be too big a job for your little .38." Damn, so I hadn't snuck the snub nose in under my coat after all. The butler was on to me.

In a few moments we were at the back of the house, standing either side of the doorway to the Judge's embassy-level dining room, the barn with the mirrored walls and French doors.

Make that the former French doors. Shards of glass littered the floor as if a giant hand had banged the Frenchies shut a mite too hard. The splintered mirrors didn't like what was happening, either. Shots peppered the doorframe.

I shoved Willem down and out of harm's way. More rounds dotted the walls beside us. That got us moving again.

Dancing flames lit the room, bright reds and yellows reflected and refracted in mirror shards and broken glass. Yet more bullets dimpled the room.

We crabbed our way over to where the French doors had hung—me hugging the right wall, Willem doing the same on the left.

I peeked around the shattered doors in time to see Norway's uppermost dragons belching real fire and black smoke as they toppled into the furnace below. White-hot heat seared my face.

I ducked back as bullets whizzed.

Willem emptied his clip toward the trees and maybe our unseen intruders. More bullets, more shattered mirrors, more pockmarked walls assured us they were out there somewhere.

The butler dusted himself off. "The Norway is no more, Mr. Reno. I fear the judge shall be devastated." Talk about coolness under fire.

Willem slipped a fresh magazine into his rifle. "To the wall! Covering fire!"

He let loose two short bursts—first left, then right, crouching low and moving rapidly out onto the patio. I didn't hesitate.

I sprayed the low stone wall and the cemetery beside what had been the Norway. I sent a third and final stream toward the pine trees on the hill, and followed Willem's lead, crouching low, cradling the M16 like I'd been taught to do all those years ago, reloading on the run, survival instinct and muscle memory taking over. Ranger training.

Willem circled left. I circled right. We ended up at opposite ends of the patio wall.

Under the trees, a man moved, raising something to his shoulder. I fired a burst his way. He spun around, but whether I had hit him, or he had turned to run, I couldn't be sure. He didn't go down. At least not where I could see.

Coal-black smoke billowed across the lawn, acrid fumes stinging my eyes, bothering my nose. Through the haze a scarlet disc glimmered—the sun wavering above the pines, as if afraid to descend. Well, why not? Sure as hell wished I was anywhere but where I was right now.

Automatic weapons exchanged fire to my left. Willem had found a new friend. The shots stopped as quickly as they had started—hey, not all friendships are meant to last.

A couple of heartbeats, and then the butler signaled me to stand up and fire.

He followed suit, and we went over the wall together. Willem, a nice, sharing sort of chap when it came to danger. A good egg, Penelope would say.

"Move right, Mr. Reno. Clear your side."

Off at the run, crouching and weaving, up the hill—nothing happened. In a few moments we met at the edge of the trees. No bodies under the evergreens, just a flattened trail in the pine straw, as if one man had dragged a second into the woods.

Willem and I moved back to the judge's manse the same way we had departed—dodging and weaving, offering each other covering fire.

And from the shattered French doors, we decimated more pinecones. No reply.

We looked at each other, and the staid English butler—or whatever the hell he really was—grinned and said, "Fun, Harry. Bloody marvelous fun. By the by, mind your hand. You've a nick. Now, to the judge. Follow!"

Nick, hell. I tried stanching the blood dripping from hand to floor with my handkerchief and raced after the butler.

Damn, but he could move fast.

41

RUFFLED FEATHERS

Willem and his gray ponytail led me back through the judge's dining room to the spot at the bottom of the iron stairs where he had sent Walker-Doer down to the safe room. The butler courteously relieved me of my M16 and battle dressed my wound. A man of many talents.

Then he picked up a telephone hanging inside the concealed armory, punched in some numbers, said something like, "Semper ubi, sub ubi." What the shit? And in response, the elevator began to rise toward us.

Willem grinned. I grinned back. What the hell else could I do?

"Latin at school, Mr. Reno?"

"Yeah, Willem. The priests and the brothers tried beating some of their lingo into me. But that was a few years ago. Afraid I'm a little rusty."

"Indeed, Mr. Reno. Do try then to follow me on this. *Semper* means *always*."

"Yeah, I remember that," I admitted. A hard-ass marine had tried beating that into me, too. He'd ended up wishing he hadn't tried so hard.

"And *ubi* means *where*. Would you know *sub* on your own, Mr. Reno?"

"Yeah, Willem. *Sub* means *under*. Like *submarine*."

"Well done, Sir Harry. You have deciphered it. The safe phrase informing the judge order is once more restored." The elevator had almost reached us. I didn't need the judge laughing at my ignorance too.

Words strung together in my head. I blurted them out: "Always where under where—I get it, Willem. Always wear underwear. I was right. You and the judge do still belong to the sauna club for big boys, no girls allowed. Just dumb-ass, little kid shit."

But I was laughing. You would have, too. If you'd had Latin beaten into you.

"Oh, Mr. Reno. Girls are most definitely allowed. Or should we say young women and substitute *required*? But all in good time. All in good order."

The judge's birdcage opened, and the old crow flapped out. "Report, Willem," he cawed.

"Intrusion repulsed, Your Honor. Perimeter secure. The Norway, alas, is no more."

The old judge's teeth clenched, his skinny neck tensed—the muscles standing out along the sides of his throat in stark relief, like the raised trail a mole leaves on a golf course green.

Losing Norway had to be tough on the old bird—family relic and blond goddess. But he rallied quickly. "Coffee in the library, Willem. With a tot of brandy."

Soon the judge and I sat facing each other, our chairs turned a slight angle inward. In the fireplace, Willem had a warming blaze crackling. Even in the good old summertime, a fire felt good, up here in the North Woods. And yeah, I had another drink, even if it was leavened with coffee. Didn't so much want the brandy as need it. Busy afternoon.

"Harry, no doubts now about what we are up against, correct?" The old judge fighting mad. Blasting Norway to smithereens sure had ruffled the old crow's feathers.

"No doubts, Judge," I said. "I think I tagged one of them. Just so you know."

No doubts, except who were the good guys and who were the bad guys. I sure hoped I'd signed on to fight for the right side—if there was a right side.

Walker-Doer nodded, turned to Willem, who stood a proper and respectful butler-distance away, sipping his coffee with nary a slurp. Some servant, huh?

"I note no alarm sounded to call attention to the intruders, Willem." No note of reproach in the judge's voice. He let his rheumy eyes hold the question, though.

"The intruders did not breach the perimeter, Your Honor. Not with their own physical presence. Mr. Reno and I prevented that." A slight nod of the butler's head my way. "They remained in the woods. And yes, I do believe Mr. Reno winged one, Your Honor." Willem inclined his head toward me in recognition and added, "A damn fine shot, Harry. I beg your pardon, Judge." The library no place for such informality, I suppose.

"Then explain the destruction of the Norway, Willem."

"RPGs, Your Honor. Rocket-propelled grenades. Two, I should think. Fuel-air warheads. Hence the near-instantaneous immolation of the Norway."

Walker-Doer's face said, *Please*. So did his voice. "Harry, you have to help me."

Oh no, not the judge, too. At least the old bastard wasn't on his knees with his arms wrapped around my legs, like Lance. Nor choking me like Alice. Not yet, anyway.

"I said deal, Judge, and I meant it. I'll take your coin, but I need your info. And some real help from you. And Willem."

The butler grinned at me for the third or the thousandth time today. What the hell was he up to, grinning at me like that? And always when his boss couldn't see him do it.

"You shall have my help, Harry," the judge said. "A list of contacts—friends and enemies. Mostly enemies, Harry, mostly enemies."

The old bastard sighed over *enemies*—not a wistful sigh, though. More like he meant he still had people to eliminate. Even if they were friends.

I hadn't signed on to be the judge's hired executioner. I told him so.

The judge ignored what I'd said and handed me an envelope. Inside, he said, were the lists. Shit, twenty names, friends and enemies.

"Judge, I'm not sure I agree with you. I wouldn't, for instance, put Gus on the enemies side of the ledger. Or Tom Kuster, either." Well, maybe I would.

Walker-Doer cocked his wizened head to one side and gave me a quizzical perusal.

"Perspective, Harry, perspective. From this angle, you look crooked to me. But I know you are not. Else I would not retain you." A skeletal claw combed at wisps of frail hair.

"So perhaps it is my perspective that is skewed. Perhaps that is why I imagine Tom and Gus consort with the enemy. Or, perhaps, it is your perspective that tilts them this way and that."

I stayed quiet.

"My suggestion is talk to as many on the lists as possible and report back to me soon. But remember, Harry, my lad, above all else, it is Mallory we must protect and save. The destruction of the Temple of the Labyrinth is secondary—though a demise devoutly to be desired."

Why the hell couldn't the old fart just say *Find Mallory*? Why all the fancy Christmas wrapping? Why talk to twenty people and decide if the judge, like Santa Claus, had the naughty and nice lists right? Come on. Santa already knows before he tells the reindeer giddy-up.

Did Walker-Doer just want me too busy talking to the wrong people to find out the truth? Sure didn't figure if Mallory needed saving. And quickly.

As I rose to leave, I asked the judge, "Since it's not Mallory, any idea who the dead woman is, or rather, was?" I knew; did he?

Walker-Doer shook his head. "No, Harry, no. I do not have any idea at all. Perhaps an acquaintance of Mallory's. Perhaps not."

"Do you know if Mallory ran with the tattoo crowd?"

"Certainly not," the judge said.

"Any chance she belonged to the 'I screw, do you' club?"

A harrumph jumped out from between his teeth. "Your investigative technique is most peculiar, most peculiar indeed. I suppose you must ask impertinent questions in your endeavors. But again, no. Most certainly no. Do not, however, abuse the latitude I have allowed you. Willem will show you out now."

The butler led. The PI followed.

He waltzed me all the way to the front doors and their green wrought iron without saying a word. And without any Cheshire cat imitations.

"Do be careful," the butler said. "Kipling's grown quite rough. Too many goons, Sir Harry, too many goons." Damn, echoes of Gus. Why should that surprise me.

His admonition delivered, Willem shut the doors in my face. And probably stood there grinning at me for the fourth or fifth or ten thousandth time today. I'd lost count.

Down the steps I went. My tired ass sank onto the Volvo's tan leather, my good hand turned the key, and off we cruised—with the Volvo's windshield still stained with crow shit. Imagine that. Fucking no-good butler.

42

A SPIKE IN THE DEATH RATE

After all the fun with the judge and his butler, I felt the need to hit the motel for a quick shower and change of clothes, along with a short nap. Then off I sailed to see Gus for a late dinner. And maybe a beer or two or three.

As the Volvo curbed herself in front of the Tam-O'-Shanter, a Kipling PD cruiser pulled in behind me, its siren blip a reminder Kipling cops dogged my every footstep.

Discretion trumping valor, I strolled over, said, "Howdy do," to John the Cop. Most cops, I think, like a pleasant *Howdy do*. John, however, proved the exception.

"Cut the crap, Reno. Get in. We're going for a ride."

John's steely cop stare didn't intimidate me. His hand mimicking a gun pointed at my chest didn't faze me, either. But why fight fate?

"Front or back?" I asked. The cage did not look inviting. Not at all.

He patted the front seat. "Get in, Harry." I'm a sucker for anybody who calls me Harry.

John lit the lights, fired up the siren, and we rocketed down Kipling's main drag, sending cars and pickups running for the sidelines as we headed into the city's poorer reaches.

"You just don't remember me, do you, Harry?"

"Nope." I'd seen him come into *The Pioneer* one morning, seen him at my motel herding cowboys, but that was it. I said I was certain I would have recalled anyone with his combination of personal charm and Indy 500 driving skills.

"Cut the crap, Harry."

So I did and hung on tight, trying to conjure a name from back then, stick it on this cop careening through the night. Started with the *A*'s, then tried the *B*'s, then . . . well, you get the idea.

By the time I'd run through the alphabet down to the *V*'s, John was screeching to a halt in front of a dilapidated flophouse. Some of Kipling's finest were poking around in the alley beside the boarded-up building. An ambulance pulled in behind us.

John headed off to check on his blue brothers. I stayed put.

"Hey, Reno! Over here." John, his hand waving encouragement. "Come on."

Rotten smells were seeping out of the alley into the cruiser. So why not mingle with the garbage outside? I shoved my carcass out and headed his way.

The cops were standing around a blue tarp covering a body next to an overturned garbage can. One cop obligingly pulled the tarp away.

I didn't like what I saw.

She lay on her side, fetal-curled, golden hair floating lifeless in a pool of liquidized crap, a syringe stuck in her arm. Her hustler's miniskirt rode high above her hips, black panties covering a little, but not much, of her rear. My ex-cop eyes continued inventorying the deceased.

A purse lay next to her, its contents distributed across the pavement. Her halter top had given up trying to conceal her breasts. Someone had ripped it from her shoulders.

It lay across her stomach, spent and finished, just like the woman who had put it on—Elke Sorrenson, Kipling's comeliest front desk clerk.

"Who found her?" I asked.

A cop turned, said, "Who the hell are you?"

Before I could fire back, John the Cop did my talking for me. "He's

Harry Reno. He's okay." Wow. Wasn't John just pointing a make-believe gun at my chest five minutes ago?

The cop shrugged, said, "Sorry, Sarge. A neighbor phoned it in. Told dispatch there was a body in the alley again."

John pulled me off to the side a little ways, stepping over puddles left by rain, miniature lakes in which empty cups floated and flattened beer cans graced the asphalt beneath.

I wiped my nose on my sleeve, my handkerchief in the trash back at Queen V's mansion. John glanced at my bandaged paw, didn't say anything. Maybe he didn't need to.

God, but the alley smelled.

Elke Sorrenson dead. That stunk, too. She'd been a cute kid. Sexy as hell. Karl wouldn't be good with this, not at all. Hell, neither was I. She'd jabbed a hot shot and died. Why?

John grabbed my shoulder. Sort of startled me. "Hey . . . Harry. I know she worked at the motel. You okay?" I wasn't, but that got me back to the here and right now.

"Yeah, I'm okay. And now I remember you—John Wetherall." I didn't tell him I'd finally thought to read his name badge. "You weren't a city cop fifteen years ago. Sheriff's deputy, right?" That much I'd remembered on my own.

He nodded. But there was something else. I just couldn't snatch it. It drifted in my head, just out of reach. Like Elke.

"They're ready to bag her. You need another look?" John, softly, for my ears only.

A head shake—No.

They loaded Elke Sorrenson, or what used to be Elke, into the ambulance. Another life zippered. Lights swirled. The ambulance headed out.

Raindrops sprinkled. Then the big drops, plopping hard against trash can lids, smacking asphalt, splashing cop trousers, beating down on cop heads. A private eye getting wet, too.

So the cops in the alley beat a retreat, hurrying toward cruisers, this night's death already fading, washed away by rain and thoughts of spending patrols in wet clothes.

But right now, unlike the rapidly departing gendarmes, I didn't feel the need to wash Elke out of my head. I wanted her to stay there, the reminder I needed to find Mallory quickly. And make damn sure nothing similar befell Gwen—or Brynn.

We walked slowly back to his cruiser, neither of us worrying much about wet clothes. Maybe John had demons rattling around in his head, too.

"Take me back to the Tam," I said. "Okay?"

John Wetherall let me sit up front with him again. This time we eased away from the curb instead of racing toward the Brickyard's checkered flag. And that turned out to be a good thing.

A Kipling Police cruiser slammed to a stop in front of us, skidding sideways until our fenders were kissing. But just a cousinly kiss, no harm done, the excitement short-lived.

Still, Sarge didn't seem all that happy. He flung his door open and stalked over to the other cop. I could have stayed where I was, but I didn't. Getting wet somehow felt right tonight.

John put his hands on the roof of the cruiser and leaned in. I nodded my hello to Lance. Didn't seem the time or the place for my *Howdy do* nonsense.

Before John could say anything, Lance fired fastball questions his sergeant's way: "Who was she?"—"Is she dead?"—"What happened?"—"Where's Gwen?" And again, "Who was she?" Dumb-ass blue ox cop. Boy never would make detective.

John stood there, rain dripping off his hat, waiting for Lance to wind down.

I didn't have that luxury. Or the hat. I had things to do, women to see. I was supposed to pick up Brynn at midnight. And I wasn't about to let her or her mother down. Not after Elke in the alley. No sir.

I rapped knuckles on the cruiser's roof. A *rat-a-tat-tat* louder by far than the rain.

Lance shut up. John eyed me, shook his head, focused back on Lance. "It's not Gwen. The body in the alley was Elke. From out at the motel. Elke and only Elke."

"Sarge, you sure it wasn't Gwen?"

John kept calm, a sergeant's judicious grimace plastering his face—somewhere between you're-an-idiot and you-are-pissing-me-off disgust.

Damn it. I needed John to get me back to the Tam, so I could get something to eat. Girls giggle when my stomach growls. But it can't really be any kind of turn-on. Really it can't.

"I saw her," John was saying. "Reno saw her. It was Elke Sorrenson, Lance. And only Elke in the alley."

"Okay," the big idiot said, and shot away, lights flashing, siren wailing. My mind wandering on its own, Elke-searching. Stomach rumblings masking my real jitters. Who would have given her bad shit? And why?

"You ever been in love, Harry?"

"Huh? What? Oh, yeah. All the time, John. It's my permanent condition." Poor Elke.

"Well, Lance and his obsession with Gwen—it's going to end badly for one of them. Maybe both of them. That's just my professional opinion." John opened his door. "I got a personal one, too." Huh? He slid behind the wheel.

"Hop in. I'll take you to Gus's. And yeah, Harry. I can hear your stomach."

Despite John's promise to ferry me back to the Tam-O'-Shanter, he pulled into a liquor store parking lot along the way instead. A couple of winos got up and shuffled off, clutching paper-bagged bottles to their chests like priests hugging Bibles.

"Let's talk a minute, Harry."

"Yeah, we probably need to."

"Look," John said. "I remember you as a pretty hard-nosed cop back then. Never willing to back off the case or a clue. I don't know why you're here now, except that you work for the insurance company."

No need to brag about working for the old crow instead. Time enough later for that.

"I was a deputy sheriff back then," John said. I nodded. "I'd just made it out of the academy. Been on the job a month or so when all that shit with the DA and Rusty Neel went down."

I did my nodding equine act some more, just like I had for Gus.

"Maybe Gwen's mother mentioned me," John said. Huh? Gwen's mother?

"I don't remember that," I said. "But yeah, I sort of remember you. We got along all right back then. You were new. I was still gung ho." Gwen's mother? Why would she have mentioned John? And if she had, why couldn't I remember it? What the hell.

"If you were trying to learn how to be a cop by watching me, you picked the wrong guy. All I did was get my girl killed and lose my job. Some role model, huh?" John didn't disagree.

So I said, "But you're right, Mac and I had you figured for the only deputy who wasn't in on it—the drugs and the cover-up—when the DA killed Rusty Neel."

"I know, Harry. You're right." Sadness flickered in John's eyes, but his voice was steel. "I didn't help run drugs, didn't protect the marijuana growers. When a job came open with the Kipling PD, I took it."

We sat in the cruiser, our bodies still, eyes on recon, though. I liked who I saw. Guess John did, too.

"The main thing is this—I'm on your side," John said. "There's only a couple of us who are." That many, huh. "So, if I can help, ask. I'm still a reasonably honest cop. And I don't like that Lodge and its temple out in the lake."

I felt the same. I told him so. John nodded.

"I'm worried about Gwen working the casino. I know she likes you, Harry. Maybe she'll listen to you." John's knuckles white on the steering wheel. "She sure as hell won't listen to me."

Why would John Wetherall care so much about Gwen? Was he in love with her, too? I didn't ask. "I'll try, John. And I'd be glad to have a friend here in Kipling."

We bounced out of the parking lot without hitting any winos.

When John dropped me off at the Tam, he said, "Stay loose and in touch."

"You bet," I said. But could I really trust him? At least he didn't wear his hair in a damn ponytail, so he had that much going for him.

The Tam's front door opened. No sirens wailed. I headed for the bar, and Gus handed me a beer. I needed it. Wanted it, too.

43
DINNER WITH GUS—DESSERT WITH TOM

My eyes had seen too much today to let them stare back at themselves in the bar's mirror, so I took my rear to a booth and waited for Gus and dinner. After a bit, he came out of the kitchen with a steak and a salad and a beer—barkeep intuition, I suppose.

"You look rough, friend Harry." Maybe it was my bandaged hand, the patched eyebrow. The slumped shoulders. Maybe the sadness I felt filling my eyes.

"I've had a busy day. And a worse night. Just so you know."

Between bites, I told Gus some of what had happened out at the judge's Victorian fantasy land. No harm in spilling that. Then I told Gus about Elke Sorrenson in the alley tonight. The corners of his mouth turned down and his red-whiskered face hardened.

"Harry, what Stavros is doing up at the casino is bad enough, but what he does out on the lake in that damn temple—that's a special brand of evil." Guess he'd been talking to the judge. "It needs shutting down. He won't stop because we ask him to. He's having too much fun."

"So what do we do?"

"We wait and we think," he said.

"That's it, wait and think?"

"For now, Harry. Unless you have something a wee bit better."

I didn't, so I asked him what he'd heard people saying about it not being Mallory who died in the fire at the cabin.

"Nobody's really surprised." Huh? "There's been some all along who've claimed they've seen her since the fire," Gus said.

People who claimed to have seen Mallory alive? And nobody in Kipling even mentioned it to Harry Reno, the burned-out-cabin shamus?

"What the hell, Gus. It was accepted gospel last trip. Dead. And gonna stay that way. What the earthly hell."

Maybe I should have sat at the bar. Then the mirror could confirm how I felt—stunned and beyond angry, beet-faced and ready to put the hurt on somebody, anybody.

My hand shook off the beer it was holding, balled itself into a fist, came up off the table, cocked and ready, Gus the target. He was nearest, that's all.

And then the fist became a hand again, and the hand held the beer once more, and I drank. No fisticuffs tonight, just dejection ringing my bell for the next round. Some detective you are, Reno. So, what the hell else is new, Harry?

"Let's get you another beer," the bartender said.

Gus waving at his barmaid, holding up one finger, pointing at me, then at the ceiling. Harry's beer on the house. That I could figure out. But a live Mallory and a dead Elke? No, I couldn't solve those conundrums.

Gus ambled off. Then Molly the barmaid appeared with my beer, and I had something else to consider. She smiled, set my beer down. And all of a sudden, I wanted to say something to hurt her, make her cry the tears I couldn't over Elke and her black-pantied ass in the alley. Let Molly know life's hard.

But I couldn't. Instead, I let beer and a white bodice shielding barely contained breasts distract me, just like they were supposed to do—cold beer, hot barmaid.

Still, what about Mallory? What about Elke? "I didn't order another beer," I said.

Sudden hurt in Molly's soft brown eyes. Like I'd snarled, pulled the old Reno-makes-'em-cry routine I felt like doing a moment ago. Maybe I had anyway. Idiot Harry trying to make amends. "But I'm sure glad you got me figured out, Molly." Big smile. Mine, not hers.

Then her face lit up. Maybe because I remembered her name. I smiled, she smiled, and the world was right again, for a moment. The barmaid turned, making sure her short kilt of a skirt swished around her legs and her bottom, just like it was supposed to do.

"Bye, Plain Old Harry." Then off she went to smile at other guys, and I went back to frowning over other women.

Gus finally reappeared, and my green eyes focused a somewhat diminished fury on the fake Scottish bartender.

"What the hell, Gus. The coroner said it was Mallory, the cops said it was her, the assistant fire chief said it was her. And now you say everybody knew it wasn't. What gives?" I sounded hot because I was hot—just not fighting hot anymore.

"Easy, Harry, that's not exactly what I said. Some people claim to have seen her *since* the fire. That night, up at the cabin, it *was* accepted gospel. Mallory Mordred—dead, bagged, zippered." At least he didn't say *like Elke*.

Gus across from me, leaning in close, one hand gripping my wrist, the wrist that was supposed to help its hand propel the beer to my mouth. Or maybe smash my mug into Gus's mug. Happy hour long past for Harry Reno.

"But about a week later," Gus said, "Tom Kuster came in trying to glom a free meal and a beer. He'd made the rounds of the other bars and headed in here before going back to *The Pioneer* to drink himself to sleep. That's what he'd been doing every night since the fire. Trying to drink himself to death, some said."

Gus kept squeezing my wrist, keeping my hand from putting beer to lips.

Why the hell was he frowning at me? What was he, a barkeep who doesn't approve of his customers getting drunk? Gus shook his head, turned me loose. I drained my beer and waved at Molly. One more wouldn't kill me. I'd buy it myself, damn it.

The barkeep was talking again.

"I brought Tom a beer and some food, sat down to make sure he ate. He cut a piece of steak, popped it in his mouth, began to chew and talk, all at the same time—you know how he does. Tom said his sad days were over. He'd upgraded to melancholy. I wasn't exactly sure what the difference was, but he looked happier." Well, good for him.

"So I asked him why the change. He leaned in close, that damn shaggy head of his touching mine, and said, 'It's time to tell. She's alive, Gus. Mallory's alive and safe now.'"

"Have you seen her?" I said. Where the hell was Molly with my beer?

"Tom did," Gus said, answering a different question, one I hadn't asked. I let it ride.

"And you believed him?"

"Yeah, I did, Harry. I still do. Why else would he have said it, if it wasn't true? Unless he'd seen a ghost." Molly set my beer down, started to smile, changed her mind, huffed off.

"Who else has seen Mallory?" Gus shrugged, avoiding my eyes, twisting his bulk around in the booth, checking his bar for haints, maybe.

"There he be in the flesh." Gus's booming publican persona asserting itself full in my ear. Tom Kuster waved, smiled, headed our way, greeting his buddies among Gus's Regulars and Occasionals. A last bite of steak. I'd eaten all of Gus's dinner I could stomach. Maybe I'd like Tom's dessert better.

I stood up and waited for the son of a bitch.

When Tom finally reached us, the bartender stuck out his hand. Tom grabbed it, gave it a quick shake. But when I offered mine, Tom seized it in his big paw and pulled me to him, turning a handshake into a bear hug.

Gus slipped away, shaking his head, chuckling at my plight.

"Harry, I love you, man. I love you," Tom said. "Where you been?"

His words were a little slurred, but Tom's bear hug had strength. And the editor of *The Kipling Pioneer* sure looked better than when I'd seen him this morning. Did he even know Jayne had taken a shot at him? Maybe tried to kill him?

I didn't mention it. I needed him focused on another female tonight. I wanted Tom to conjure up a Mallory mousse for my dessert. I needed something sweet like that tonight, something other than bullets and burning buildings and too-soon-dead girls.

"Sit down, Tom, take a load off. Let's talk, have a beer."

Tom didn't sit, though. He put his hands on his hips, swiveled left, then right, surveying the bar scene. "How about my booth?" Tom pointed toward the bottle green neon restroom sign. "It's comfy back there," he said. "Soft leather. And close to the facilities. Don't worry. Molly knows how to find it. You buying?" I should have known—mooch instead of mousse for dessert.

We sat down across from each other. I grabbed his eyes. He blinked first.

"What, Harry? What are you staring at? You mad about something, man? You said let's talk. How come you're not? And what happened to your hand?"

Before I could answer, Molly appeared with our beers. Laugh lines eddied around Tom's mustache, spreading like ripples from a cane pole bobber just hit by a bluegill. Tom reached out, let a fingertip brush the barmaid's wrist. "Those birds are new, aren't they, Molly?"

"You like them, Tommy?" Molly asked. What the shit. *Tommy?*

Tommy said he did, and she held out her hand so I could see them, too. On the underside of her wrist, a brace of birds flew, black-inked and delicate. I said, "I like them, too." Clever, huh?

Molly curtsied and headed off to push more brews. Time to

remind Tommy why I was here. "I need to talk to Mallory," I said. "Where is she?"

"Molly's over there, Harry. Up by the bar."

"No, *Tommy,* not *Molly.* You heard me—*Mallory.* I have to see her and talk to her. Soon, real soon. Like tonight."

His brow wrinkled as he considered what I'd just said, his foot out in the aisle, waggling gently as he worked his way through to an answer. He picked up his beer, took a slow sip, set it down. "You a friend, Harry? A real friend?" I let him hang a bit. "Well, are you?"

"Yeah, Tom, I am. You know any girls with lip tattoos?" I knew the answer. I wanted to hear it from him, though.

"I'll have to think on that one, Harry."

"Think hard. And quick. Somebody killed Elke Sorrenson tonight." No reaction. "I saw her in an alley, a hot-shot needle jabbed in her arm." Tom's eyes drifted—maybe he already knew Elke was dead. "So I need to see Mallory," I said. "Soon."

His eyes came back, focused on my face. My green peepers bear-hugged his blue pair—a not quite friendly sort of squeeze. He squirmed his way loose. I let him.

"Come see me tomorrow morning, Harry. Early. At the Hash House. We'll have breakfast, talk about . . . her." He was grinning again. "Who told you? Gus?"

I stood up, laid a now-friendly hand on his shoulder. "We'll keep her safe, Tom. You, me, Gus. I'll see you in the morning. I gotta go."

On my way out, I flipped a gunman's salute Gus's way. The old fraud smiled, boomed out, "Haste ye back, friend Harry!"

I would, but not tonight. A bite of Tom's Mallory mousse had satisfied me for now. I headed out to the Volvo and Perry's casino. And Brynn.

44

DIAMOND LAMENT

The night had cleared. No more rain. Good. Let some other gumshoe somewhere else get wet in an alley watching a life get zippered—poor Elke. No more giggling and jiggling.

The Volvo headed toward the neon glow of the casino—its come-hither searchlights piercing the night sky with a shaft of scarlet thrown in for excitement tonight, like Brynn's red highlights. Careful, Reno.

I pulled under the casino's porte cochere. No Sven at the doors. Still home nursing his ear, maybe. I could always hope. The parking valet started my way.

Plain Old Harry floated in the air. Then Brynn herself came bouncing down the steps. No waiting for the valet to open her door. She jumped in on her own.

A nod to the gorilla. "Thanks for nothing, pal." He scratched his ear, tilted his head. I've seen smarter specimens in zoos.

Then Brynn's sobs swung attention from gorilla to girl, while the Volvo meandered across the half-empty parking lot, finally stopping under a pole light.

What the hell was wrong with her? The car, not the girl. Swedish commiseration or Nordic condescension? Maybe just green with envy. Hard to tell. Cranky old Volvo.

Tears streamed down Brynn's cheeks, sparkling like liquid diamonds under the lights. Her hazel eyes pleaded with me to hold her. I did. I kissed her, too—sorry, Penelope. But I only felt sorry later. Sorry I hadn't kissed her sooner.

"What's wrong, sweetheart?" Wow, *sweetheart*. That's good, Reno—real good. Now she knows you care. Some tough-guy shamus you are.

"Oh, Harry, Elke's dead. I don't want to party tonight." Party tonight? I didn't ask. Instead, my fingers wandered her hair, stroked her cheek, flicked slivers of diamonds away.

"We're going back to my motel," I said. "Now don't look at me like that—no party. I promised your mother I'd keep you safe tonight. That's all. Bad stuff seems to be going down in Kipling today. I don't want any of it coming your way."

Brynn turned away, let her eyes roam the parking lot. More diamonds trickled, sparkling in the light from the pole. I let them this time. Then her eyes shifted back to me.

"Let's get out of here, Harry." A swipe of her hand dried her own tears. "I hate this place." She got no argument from me.

On the way back to town, Brynn's mood improved somewhat.

"Harry, I can't think about Elke anymore tonight—I'll just cry. I don't want to cry anymore right now. I'm too sad."

I couldn't argue with that, either.

The Volvo found a twenty-four-hour convenience store. Brynn and I went in. "Get whatever you need for tonight," I said.

She did, but I smacked her hand when she pointed to the condom display behind the front counter—just a playful smack. "I'm not that kind of guy—at least not tonight."

Brynn giggled, "Then I'm not that kinda guy, either." She kissed my cheek. "Tonight, anyway." She laughed, hugged my arm.

I wasn't sure if she really meant for me to buy the condoms or not. So I didn't.

The bucktoothed kid at the cash register mumbled, "Thank you," when I handed over a twenty, seemingly relieved Bonnie and Clyde hadn't pulled out artillery, hadn't said, *Give with the cash, loser.* Hadn't ventilated him with lead when he made change.

I grinned, told him, "Stay loose, goose." No reply. Good enough —tonight.

Brynn giggled, hugged my arm some more. This time she didn't let go. It was awkward, but I got us through the store's front door and back into the Volvo.

"Kiss me, Plain Old Harry," she said, and I did. That made twice. Not that I was keeping count. Too lost in Brynn's luminous eyes for arithmetic tonight—hazel, but tinged with blue, flecked with green slivers. Eyes like a forest, she said—brown earth, green leaves, blue skies.

Yeah, that's what made me kiss Brynn—her two big . . . forest eyes. Really.

With Brynn in the passenger seat and me behind the wheel, the Volvo chauffeured us onward. And just to be safe, earlier I'd stuffed my grass-skirted island babe in the glove box for the night.

The little hula girl hates competition, remember?

"This is it," I said, and helped Brynn out—gallant Sir Harry.

At the door to my room, she tried to kiss me again, but I told her no, gently, ever so gently. I might even have kissed her as I told her no. In we went.

"It ain't much, but it's home."

"Oh, Harry, I love it." Then, very softly, "It's perfect—so are you."

Careful, Reno swirled in my head. Just tuck her in and go see Karl. So I told her I had business with the night clerk, wanted to ask him about Elke. Told her the bathroom was hers. Just get in bed and stay in bed. No wandering around tonight.

She frowned a little, but she hit the bathroom like I said. When she came out, she still had her panties and bra on, thank God. I really did need to talk to Karl.

Brynn said, “I’ll wait up, Plain Old Harry,” and scampered into bed. She twisted a little under the sheets and a black bra sailed out—so convincingly big it had to be hers.

I caught it and laid it on the dresser. Brynn’s laughter filled the room. She blew me a kiss. I had to leave now or I never would.

So I grabbed the doorknob and did some twisting of my own.

She threw me a pout. I sent a kiss back. “Don’t open the door while I’m gone—especially if it’s Lance.” Puzzlement now. Maybe she didn’t know the blue ox like I knew the blue ox.

“When I’m finished with Karl, I’ll knock—quack out a *Donald Duck*.” My nose pinch a fair approximation of Disney’s irascible fowl. “Then let myself in.”

Now she was laughing again.

Go, Reno, go. Sounded almost like Penelope’s voice. Brynn’s laughter followed me outside, bouncing and echoing in my head all the way down the motel sidewalk, all the way to the front desk and Karl.

The lobby doors swished open. Laughter faded—shamus time.

45
GREASY TEARS

I'll say this for the little shit. Karl didn't lock himself away from the world at night like some security-conscience night clerks do. No bell to ring to rent a room here. Then again, maybe Karl still expected somebody to show up tonight. Not the pizza guy, I bet. Or me, either.

"Hi, Karl." My voice filled his small world.

The night clerk jerked, his literary work flew off the counter and landed on the floor, and maybe—just maybe—little Karl wet his pants.

I didn't ask. He didn't say. I didn't bother to look.

Karl glared, until his mail-order hotel hospitality course kicked in and reminded him to smile and say, "Good evening, Mr. Reno. I mean, good morning. Welcome back."

Last trip, Andy Jackson had loosened Karl's tongue, with a ten-dollar assist from the Treasury's Mr. Hamilton. But this time no trading money for knowledge. I just didn't have the inclination. He was going to come clean, or I'd beat it out of him. Elke's death had me riled.

And Reno riled ain't pretty.

I moved toward the counter and stepped on his magazine. I picked it up. *Preteen Hookers.* Ugh. Consistent, though. Back it floated to the floor in pieces.

"You're next," I growled.

Karl made to reach under the counter. Steel-hard fingers caressed his throat. "Listen, you little shit." My steel-barreled .38 poked his ear. "Bring that hand up slowly, very slowly. It better be empty." It was.

My grip moved to his arm, dragging Karl around the counter to a lobby chair. The sort motels buy wholesale: hard, ugly, and splotched, the coffee stains factory-installed.

I kept my gun to his head.

"Sit." He did. Close up, greasy black hair, thin on top.

My eyes roamed the rest of the creep. Serious ring-around-the-collar problem, like the grime a motel bathtub sees after weeks of construction cowboys showering job site dirt away. Pants stained with . . . hell, why ask. The whole package just disgusting.

"Stay put," I said, locking him in place with my patented ear twist, my .38 back in its holster, its civic duty on temporary hold.

I rummaged behind the front counter, curious what Karl had reached for.

Well, well. A little girl's automatic in a box with some big girl panties. Pink, no black. The panties, not the gun. Spoke volumes for Mom and Pops that they let Karl keep toys of that caliber at their front desk.

I dropped the clip, racked the slide. No ammo. Hell, Karl hadn't even been ready for action if any showed up. I dropped the gun in my pocket. I left the panties where they were.

"Gimme the front door key, you little bastard." I locked us in.

"Let's talk. In the laundry room, not out here." Ear twist again. Another yelp. "You wouldn't want anybody to see you cry, now, would you? Let's go."

The laundry room smelled of cut-rate disinfectant and cheaper detergent. Dirty towels rested in carts, waiting for the night clerk's kind ministrations. One cart over in the corner had waited extra long —the towels molded. To hell with Stuart Dillingham III and the company's tight-ass ways. He and I were going to talk. No more cheapie motels for Harry Reno, no sir.

I pushed Karl onto a metal folding chair. He sat like a good German—just following orders. But his dark eyes were leaking, tears running down his face, cascading off his chin, staining his shirt's grimy fabric. Or maybe cleansing it. Hard to tell.

The little man tried wrapping his arms around himself, doing his damnedest to contain his shaking. Wasn't working. Every second or so, an arm darted out from its brother's embrace and a hand swiped at the gush of water pouring from his eyes.

Useless creep. Too many tears, not enough manhood. And my Elke news sure wasn't going to dry his eyes, either.

"Hey, Karl." He raised his head, beady eyes staring, lips trembling. He tried biting his lower lip to make it behave. Didn't work. The lip just quivered its way out of the teeth's grasp.

Was I really such a scary guy? Maybe so. So I got right to it.

"Your girlfriend's dead. The cops found Elke in an alley tonight." I finger-jabbed his shoulder. "Bad heroin spike in her arm." Another poke. "What do you think about that, Karl?"

I expected the news of Elke's demise to complete Karl's transformation from solid to liquid. Instead, Karl turned off the tear faucet. He stopped shaking and stood up without asking permission. Wow. A show of German independence.

Or maybe he already knew about Elke.

"Fuck Sven," Karl said. "Fuck Stavros." His hotelier's impassive calm firming up a bit now, along with his manly vocabulary. "And fuck that fucking Pilot." Repetitive, but right on the mark. "You gotta help me, Mr. Reno. You gotta help me."

Well shit. Karl, another of Kipling's wounded, stumbling blind into traffic on the help-me highway, hoping to bump into yours truly. First Gwen and Lance, then the judge. Oh, and Alice and John the cop and . . . I lost count.

Karl stood there, fists balled, determination spilling from his eyes instead of the liquid misery of a moment ago. "I'm done with their sex games," he said.

Then the old Karl reappeared. The faucet ratcheted the other way, and tears flowed again. He collapsed back onto his chair, cradling his head, shaking as if hurricane waves were buffeting him, knocking him this way, then that.

I waited him out.

When the shaking finally slowed, then stopped, Karl raised his head, said, "I mean it. I'll help you fix Stavros and the others for good. I loved her, Mr. Reno. I loved her!"

Good. Maybe his crybaby act was really over. I needed an angry and determined Karl. That's the guy who would help me nail Stavros.

But whichever one he turned out to be, Crybaby Karl or Karl the Lakeside Avenger, he'd really need a new shirt. Glops of snot had transferred from nose to sleeve. I shuddered. I'd almost stuck my hand in the goo as I gave him a consoling pat.

So yeah, disgusting in every way I could imagine, and in ways I didn't even want to contemplate. His *Preteen Hookers*, remember?

But since I was playing the kind, sensitive sort of shamus tonight, I strolled out to the lobby to get Karl a nice, hot cup of coffee before coaxing info out of him.

Ah, the ever-so-gentle art of persuasion.

46

CRUMMY TIDBITS

A sweet roll to go with Karl's coffee. Just what I needed to bribe him into spilling his secrets. Three on a plate in the lobby. One had mold and one had bite marks and droppings like the mice had been visiting. But the third one looked somewhat okay.

Back in the laundry room, I fed it to Karl along with his coffee, and left the other dainties out in the lobby for whoever or whatever might happen by.

"Okay, Karl." I brushed a crumb off his knee. "You and Elke. Just tell me what's what, and the two of us will put some fresh flesh on your girlfriend's corpse, so to speak."

Kind and gentle, that's me—interrogation's an art form. You gotta paint a picture that grabs their attention. Karl's tears started up again.

"Elke and me, we do . . . we did . . . she . . ." He sniffled, reined in his stuttering, bit hard on the grammar bridle. "Elke and *I* were at the temple Saturday." Chin up now. "I am good at electronics and snooping. Remember, Mr. Reno?"

His tears stopped. On-off, on-off. Odd. Almost like he was playing the part of grieving boyfriend, instead of living it.

"So Saturday afternoon, Elke and I went out to the island, to the Temple of the Labyrinth. We were working a ritual."

"What's a ritual, Karl?" Hot damn. Now we were getting somewhere.

"Well, to move up in the Lodge of the Labyrinth, you must prove yourself, I guess."

"What happens in a ritual, kid? Hurry it up, okay?" Bra-less Brynn. Back in my room.

"I'm not completely sure, Mr. Reno."

"Take a guess." God, this wasn't going to be quick. I kept pushing. My hand made a move for his shoulder. Karl's eyes widened.

"It's sex, Mr. Reno. It's pretty raunchy." Yeah, yeah, yeah. Raunchy to you. Normal to me. The hand back on my knee once more.

"You record this raunchy stuff, right?"

"Yes, that's why I'm here. I mean, there. Oh, and I light the torches, too." Fucking confusing. Dumb little prick.

"Look. Just start at the beginning and stop at the end. Okay?"

"Okay." Karl settled into his story. "We go over first, to set things up."

"Who's we, Karl?"

"The mistress and her handmaidens."

"Then what? And hurry up, will ya." Brynn, the mistress of my dreams. In my bed. And me stuck here. With greasy Karl.

"Later, when it's dark, Mr. S and the Minotaur come over, too. On the yacht."

"Mr. S. That's Pericles Stavros, right, Karl?" He nodded. "The Minotaur, who's that?"

"The Pilot. It used to be the Dutchman." Hmm. Used to be. File that for now.

"And they have the new guys with them. Oh, and Pan. He's on the yacht, too, Harry." Pan? New guys? What the hell. Guess I'd just have to let him let prattle on. Bra-less Brynn would have to wait. Damn. Double-D damn.

"That is when the fun begins," he said, and snickered. "It's dark by then. I wait in the woods until they climb the steps. When everybody passes the first torch, I light it and run ahead to the next one while the new guys are staring at the torch behind them."

Karl was looking at me, like I'd be just as excited as him to light tiki torches in the trees—fat chance. "When they pass the second one, I light that one, too. Then run ahead again. The third one I always light just before they reach it, so it goes off in their eyes."

"And that's the fun, Karl?" If there were a hundred torches, I'd have to kill him. "The fun that's so raunchy? That it, kid?" God damn it. If he didn't speed up, I'd . . . .

Karl's shoulders drooped. His head followed. Guess he thought I was making fun of his storytelling skills. So I tried puffing up his ego to get him back to spilling the temple's trade secrets. And get me back to Brynn.

"Man, Karl. I bet you scare the shit out of these new guys when that third torch flares. They ever wet their pants?" Wonder where I got the idea to ask that?

He shot me his sheepish face, but then he was off and running again.

"That's good, Harry. I bet some of those big shots do. Yeah, I bet they do. When the Minotaur runs up and scares them, just like on Halloween."

"Is that all that happens, Karl? Just a scary walk in the witchy woods? Tell me some more about the raunchy fun. When does that start?" I knew when my fun might start. As soon as I could get Karl through his bullshit and get back to Brynn.

The little man licked his lips, maybe hunting for sweet roll crumbs, maybe thinking about island fun. Whichever, he jumped into his fairy tale again.

"When Mr. S gets them to the temple, Dewey plays his pipe and dances around. He's Pan." Dewey, huh? The guy in the black pickup. The one who tried to kill me and Tom.

"That's when I head around to the side of the temple, Harry. There's a door behind some bushes. I slip inside as quick as I can, because we need to start the ritual. I work the controls.

"I crank the front doors open, and Mrs. Stavros and the girls walk out of the temple onto the, the . . . portico! That's it, the portico." Oh-my-God. Just get on with it, will ya.

"I get to watch them drop their robes. I bet that's when the rich guys do wet their pants, Harry. Oh yeah." Karl giggled. A little, preteen girl giggle.

Hey, maybe Karl was the one who left those black lace panties on my pillow last trip after all. If he had, I bet he didn't need to borrow them. Probably came from that box under the counter in the lobby. Or his dresser drawer.

God, if that's the truth, then my dreams of Gwen and Brynn and Elke are just that—the foolish fantasies of an aging male. My sexual desires bubbling over into the realm of make-believe. Bubbling over, like the brew rising from a witch's cauldron. A mist that catches in your nostrils, snakes inside your brain, makes you think thoughts the witch wants you to think.

But who the hell is the witch? Which one? Gwen or Brynn? Hadn't Brynn just tossed her bra at me? That was witchy. But if it had been Elke, no chance of quizzing her about the black lace panties. No sir. Not now.

I caught Karl scoping me. He had his worried face on.

"You okay, Harry? You look kind of funny."

"Yeah, yeah, yeah. I'm okay." My brain sure as hell hadn't told me to kiss Brynn tonight. Another part of my anatomy had been doing my thinking for me. Time for a Reno brain break.

"You want some more coffee?" I asked.

47
KARL COMES CLEAN

"So these babes drop their clothes." I handed Karl his coffee, took a sip of mine. "What happens next?"

"The Mistress, Mrs. Stavros, does that, too." The little man licked his lips. "She's really something." Oh, hell, a mother fetish. Why wasn't I surprised.

"Then they go inside the temple."

"And after they all go in, what do you do, Karl?"

"They don't all go in. Dewey has to stay outside."

"So who's this Dewey again?"

"He dresses up like Pan. Not Peter Pan, but Pan the Greek goat guy. I didn't know who Pan was until Mr. S explained it to us. You know, the Labyrinth, the Minotaur, King Minos, all that stuff. Helps us play our parts in the ritual, Mr. S says. Helps if we know some Greek myths."

Karl shrugged. He didn't get it. I did. Stavros wanted an educated workforce. Big deal.

"Dewey wears the goat man costume and plays a little pipe. But he can't go inside," Karl said, and paused.

"Okay, I'll bite. Why not?"

"Because Mr. S says Dewey's too horny to be around women, especially naked women. Dewey likes them best when they're dead. Then they can't smell the goat on him. That's what Mr. S said. Pretty funny, huh?" Yeah, chuckle, chuckle.

"What's this Dewey idiot look like, Karl?"

"He's big. And mean. And he's strong, real strong. And he's hairy, Harry."

I hate people punning my name. Just a personal quirk I have.

"Ow—ow. Sorry, Harry. I mean, Mr. Reno. I don't mess with Dewey. And I don't tease him about his drool."

"His drool?"

"Yes. He drools all the time. It's always soaking his shirt."

"Born like that, huh, Karl?"

"No. That is not it at all, Mr. Reno. Dewey killed a man in a knife fight in a bar. But first the man cut Dewey's face, down to his lip. Before he died. That is why Dewey drools."

"Dewey go to jail, Karl? They give him the chair?"

"No, Harry." Karl's puzzled face. "Mr. S is a very good lawyer. Dewey's still here. He played the goat man in the ritual Saturday night. Remember?"

"Oh yeah. You said that, didn't you? I gotta pay better attention." Sarcasm—just words wasted on the night clerk. "Hey, this Dewey clown. He drive a pickup, an old one?"

"Yes, Harry. A black one. Why?"

"Never mind." The giant doofus at the auto glass place. For sure the same guy tried to run us off the road. Pan. "So what goes on inside this temple of yours?" Gotta hurry him along. Shit, Brynn's probably sound asleep by now.

"I don't exactly know," Karl said. "I stay busy in the control room. I just watch gauges and dials. I don't see a lot of what goes on. But sometimes I hear things. Screams, mostly."

Sounded like the little shit was lying to me, so I reminded him he had to tell his Uncle Harry the truth. And, like I said, no Jackson or Hamilton this time. Coercion, physical and pure.

"That hurt, Mr. Reno. I thought you were going be nice, be an okay guy. Now you're being like Mr. Stavros."

Stavros, huh? Little whiner. Pissing me off all the more, so I laid the hurt on him again. Harder.

"Okay, okay, Mr. Reno, I do know what goes on." Karl eager to please now. "Elke told me what they had her do. Mr. S gave her a lot of money to do it, too." Yeah, right. I bet money ain't all Mr. S slipped your girlfriend. But I couldn't verify that with Elke. No sir. Just a silent stiff now, all alone and cold as a frozen fish on a slab in the morgue.

And Brynn. Hot and bra-less and all alone in my room.

"Speed it up, Karl. I don't have all night." A pinch of skin, a twist, just so he knew I really was running late. He yelped.

"You don't have to do that, Mr. Reno. Really you don't."

"Sorry, kid. Just got some bad habits. Leftovers from my cop days. Nothing personal. Now hurry the fuck up. Tell me the rest of it."

When he'd finished, I reminded him not to talk to anybody else about him telling me about all this ritual crap. Could I trust him, though? Hard to say.

Out the lobby doors, back to my room, and the amazingly attractive Brynn. Maybe she was still awake. Probably she wasn't.

48
PARTNERS IN CRIME

"Harry Reno, God bless you!" Alice Vaughn not only seemed glad to see us, she also said she had breakfast ready. Alice ducked back into the kitchen.

I gave Brynn a swat on her rear. "Go help your mom."

Brynn nabbed my arm, gave it a quick squeeze. Electricity coursed through me like current through copper—oh, man. Brynn scampered off to help Alice, and I found my way to Tom Kuster and his favorite booth.

Before I could even say hello, he stuck out his hand. We shook. "Partners in crime, Harry, partners in crime," he whispered.

"Come on, Tom, gimme a break. I need some coffee first." I slid into the booth. "What the hell are you talking about?"

The editor grinned, let it morph into a smirk. Then Brynn materialized with coffee.

She touched the back of my neck, and I sat there, another jolt of electricity shaking my soul. A sorceress for sure, but in a Wendy the Good Little Witch sort of way.

"Here, drink your coffee, Harry." Tom pushed the mug toward me, so I quit watching Brynn gliding back to the kitchen. "Looks like you're right, you do need it this morning."

Focus, Reno, focus. Yesterday—what a day and a night. Maybe today would be calmer. I slurped coffee, no need for table manners with Tom. Plus, we had the place to ourselves. He'd said meet him early, remember?

Thomas Kuster seemed clean and sober, properly pressed and turned out this morning. A green-striped oxford shirt with all the buttons fastened and accounted for; a hint of khakis under the table; brown loafers tapping time to a tune only Tom was hearing. Plus, he was wearing socks. Even his Mark Twain hair was under control.

Had he achieved all this on his own? I'd sure as hell needed some help getting dressed this morning. Well, maybe I hadn't needed the help, strictly speaking, just wanted it.

I forced my thoughts off the girl in the kitchen and back onto the guy in the booth.

"Okay, Tom, I give. Partners in crime. What the hell's that mean?"

"I talked to someone last night. After Gus's. After I got back to the paper."

"Who, Tom?"

"A little bunny, Harry."

God, I wasn't up to this today. I started to let a *Son of a bitch* loose, but he must have read the famous Reno poker face. Too early to trot out intricate clues.

Tom backed off and just told me what he wanted me to know. "Gwen came to see me last night, hopping up and down outside my door, thumping her tail until I stumbled down the stairs and let her in." Gwen, huh?

"Oh man, Harry, do we have some heavy shit to cogitate on." Damn it. Hippie Tom, despite the button-down.

Then Brynn and Alice and food showed up, and my whole world seemed lit by more than just the sun peeking in the Hash House windows.

"Here's breakfast, Plain Old Harry," Brynn said. A plate of ham and scrambled eggs appeared in front of me. Rye toast guarded the plate's perimeter.

"Want something to go with it?" she asked. Yeah I did—her. "Well, do you?" She was holding the something behind her back. I nodded and kept my lust to myself for now.

A jar of homemade grape jelly settled itself on the table. Oh, God, a perfect breakfast. Brynn stuck out her tongue, glided back to the kitchen, her swaying hips rocking my soul.

"Hey, Harry." Huh? Oh yeah, Alice, the mother of those hips. "Don't let your eggs get cold. And don't let my daughter fall in love with you, you old fool."

Alice swatted my head with a menu, headed back to the kitchen. But it was a playful swat. Guess I had Mom's approval. Up to a point.

But when I shoved a forkful of eggs into my mouth, Penelope appeared beside Tom and glared at me. Not really, of course. She was back in Ithaca. At least, I hoped she was.

When I blinked, whatever I'd seen or hadn't seen had vanished.

I gobbled some more eggs and slathered grape jelly on my rye toast. Tom was talking again. Maybe he'd been droning away all along. I hadn't been paying close attention. Penelope's glare somewhat of a distraction. Even more so than Brynn's hips.

"Harry, I said we have to do something, and do it fast. Before he sucks more girls into that sex-crazed ritual of his. I've had it!" Tom fist banged the table—hard.

What the hell? My fork jerked up, splattering yellow on the window beside me. A featherless reminder that chickens lay eggs.

"Shit, Tom. Take it easy. Look at the damn window." I grabbed a handful of paper napkins, tried cleaning the mess up. I only made it worse. Of course I did. I gave up.

"Harry, I mean it. Do you know who killed Elke? Well, do you?" Loud, but nobody turned to stare. We had the place to ourselves, remember?

"No, I don't, not for sure. And quiet down, okay?"

"Well, I know where Elke was Saturday night," Tom said. "And I know what Stavros had her doing. It went wrong, bad wrong. Some damn animal screwed Elke so hard, she died."

I munched toast. That didn't exactly match what Karl had told me. I didn't mention it, though; my mouth was full.

Neither of us said anything. We sat and stared at each other. And kept staring. Finally, I decided to stick a pole into Tom's logjam of a brain and see what floated free.

"How do you know all this?" The detective-in-the-diner in expert interrogation mode.

"Well, I don't know for sure, but somebody in that damn temple Saturday night killed Elke. Or had her killed. I do know that for sure." Tom Kuster, investigative journalist, reeling in a story. Or not.

"Why not just an accidental overdose?" I said. "And why didn't anyone find her until Monday if she died on Saturday?" Plus, she'd looked too damn fresh in the alley to have been kaput for days. But, hey, no need to interweave Tom's yarn with skeins of Truth. Plenty of time later for that.

"She didn't OD," Tom said. "Elke wasn't into drugs. She didn't use." Really? Not what Karl had said. So I pushed the point. Tom still insisted I was wrong.

"I know that for a fact. Elke liked sex, not drugs. Don't look at me like that, Harry. And no, I'm not going to tell you how I know that." His eyes avoided mine, gazed at coffee instead.

"But you're right," he told the java, "I don't know what they did with her until they dumped her in the alley Monday night." His eyes staring at something in the mug only he could see. "I don't know, Harry, I just don't know."

I asked him why he thought her death had something to do with the temple. His head came up, coffee insights left to cool for the moment.

"Because that's where she'd been Saturday, all afternoon and all night. Damn it, I said don't look at me like that. I know because she canceled our date. So I went to find her."

Tom Kuster said *date* like it needed to be in quotation marks. And now Tom didn't have to explain how he knew Elke Sorrenson liked to have sex. He paid her to have it with him. So maybe the streetwalker getup wasn't a plant.

"I can read your mind, Harry, and it's dirty. It's not like she hooked in alleys. She didn't—ever. She was first class. She was doing what she did to earn money for college. Somewhere far away from Kipling. I was helping her pick a good one." Yeah, right.

"Okay," I said instead. "But how do you know all about the ritual on Saturday?"

"Gwen, Harry. Little bunny Gwen. Remember? Thumping her tail outside and inside *The Pioneer* last night."

Oh no. Now I understood his whispered *partners in crime.*

Tom meant Gwen had thumped her tail with him in the biblical sense last night. And since he had seen me pat Brynn on her rear, saw her touch me in return, he assumed Brynn and I were Bible thumpers, too.

Well, I knew what I'd done or hadn't done last night. And so did Brynn. When she'd rolled out of bed this morning, she'd said, "Cover your eyes, Harry," and I had. We hadn't made love, or even anything close. I should have set Tom straight, but I didn't. Male ego, I guess.

Instead, I shook his hand and agreed to be his partner in crime. He and I would avenge Elke's death and protect "our girls" from a similar fate. Tom and Harry—pulling a Samson on Stavros's Temple of the Labyrinth.

I finished my coffee, took a last bite of rye toast. We walked up front, and I tried to pay for breakfast. Alice said, "No, I'll put it on Tom's tab." Then she winked at him.

My God, was he doing her, too?

49

THE CORONER LEAVES US HANGING

We walked outside. Tom stopped, arched his shaggy eyebrows, said, "You're the detective. What do we do now?"

"Let's go see the coroner," I said, "see what he has to say."

Tom said, "Okay," but his mop of white hair was busy skywriting *No use*. So what if he thought grilling the coroner was a waste of time. I didn't.

The cops at the scene had said "accidental overdose" last night. Maybe Doc Decker would just squawk like them and parrot the same line. But Doc's office was around the corner, and I wanted him to say it to my face. Maybe I'd poke my finger into his white coat, shove him around a little. Or a lot.

"Come on, let's go see the coroner," I said again. "It'll be fun. Maybe I can get him to doctor my hand." I waved my bandaged left around.

As Tom and I walked, we plotted our strategy. Tom said hold a powwow with Doc in his office. I said powwow the old bastard in the jaw and then stick a stethoscope up his ass. At least we agreed on the powwow idea.

I was getting worked up and didn't care. Correction—I did care. I was going to enjoy putting the squeeze on Doc Decker. Coroner, my ass. More like Stavros's rubber stamp boy.

My jaw muscles clenched, teeth grinding hard against each other. I know they did. I felt them doing it. I marched shoulder to shoulder with Tom, ready to beat some truth out of an old man. And proud of it.

A light wind brushed our faces. Wispy white clouds, as ephemeral as a corpse's tattered shroud, drifted above us. Sunlight poured out from the end of the street, a yellow orb rising, crowning the trees along the sidewalk with golden halos. Birds chirped, urban squirrels squealed. We kept strolling.

Hot damn. Corpse clouds and all the rest of Mother Nature's shimmering bounty, plus a quack to punch. Yeah, it was gonna be a beautiful day. I could just feel it.

Down the street and around the corner, a Kipling Police Department cruiser sat outside Doc's office, the cruiser's lights swirling, marring the otherwise beautiful morning.

Tom and I ducked under the crime scene tape and walked in the front door without knocking. Helped it was John Wetherall inside. Sarge turned to see who had ignored his yellow fence. "You two don't play by the rules, do you?"

John wasn't angry, just weary. His eyes were holding themselves open, but you could see they didn't have the heart to stay on the job much longer. His shoulders drooping as much as his eyelids, just hanging around until he took them someplace soft. Like home to bed.

In a chair behind the front desk sat a woman in faded purple scrubs, sobbing. She held her face in her hands while her shoulders did their damnedest to hunch together.

Sandy, Doc's receptionist. Upset as hell. And easy to see why.

The coroner had his medical office in an old building that had once been some type of store. Pipes and ductwork bisected the waiting room, disappearing through walls into parts unknown. Old plumbing and heating recycled into modern architecture, I guess. Penny and Sharlett, the girl at the travel agency across from my office, know about that sort of stuff. I don't.

One pipe emerged from an interior wall—crossing the length of the waiting room, neatly dividing the room into equal halves—and disappeared through another wall.

The pipe painted fire engine red, an artsy contrast to the soft pastel of the ceiling—a restful sky blue. Calming, just in case you had to wait for a while to get in to see the good doctor, had to wait to have him listen to your complaints.

But the wait today would be a long one. An eternally long one. Because the blue ceiling and red pipe and Sandy's sobs aside, what really grabbed your attention there in the waiting room was the coroner himself.

Doc Decker hung from his fire-engine-red, thick-as-a-football-lineman's-forearm, artsy overhead pipe—the one bisecting the soft blue of the waiting room ceiling. One of his waiting room chairs lay overturned beneath him.

The noose around his neck looked nice. A tasteful rope necktie, maybe a tad too snug, though. Doc's face sure lacked that peace Death is supposed to bring when it lifts earthly cares from your shoulders and leads you gently into that Good Night.

Instead, Doc's dead eyes bulged, his black tongue protruded. Dr. Durwood D. Decker had slowly strangled to death, fighting his choice all the way, fingers digging into the noose until nails broke and bled.

Good luck on the other side, Doc. I hope you're headed downstairs, all the way down, where it's good and hot, you lying bastard.

I might even have expressed those sentiments out loud. John's head seemed to be nodding in agreement to my maybe not-so-silent reflections.

"Harry Reno." John said my name without enthusiasm. Body number two, and right at the end of his shift. And now he had me to deal with again.

"I don't guess Doc Decker is seeing patients or handing out coroner reports this morning, right, Sarge?"

"Cut the crap, Reno. I'm tired."

"Who found him, John?"

"Who do you think?" He pointed to Sandy, the purple-clad receptionist, the one doing all the sobbing. John took a step toward me, an aggressive step. Maybe he wasn't as tired as he said. Maybe he was mad. Maybe at me. Maybe I really ought to cut the crap.

A lot of possibilities. I picked one and held up my hands in surrender. "Look, John, I had a long night, too. So I'm sorry, okay?"

He backed off. I asked if Doc Decker had left a note.

"Yeah, Reno. He did."

John scrunched his eyes. Then he wrote something down in a little notebook, the kind cops stick in their pockets and take out to write stuff down in. Important stuff, like *Reno's a dumbass*. Nuggets of knowledge you don't want to forget.

His pencil had teeth marks in it—deep teeth marks. The nuns always told me not to chew on my pencil, that I'd end up in Hell because I'd poisoned myself with lead. And, as Sister Scary-As-All-Shit liked to remind me, I'd be down there talking to the Devil, with bad teeth to boot.

Maybe John didn't know how dangerous pencils could be. Maybe he'd gone to public school. I left it alone.

"Any chance you'd tell me what the note says, John?"

"Yeah, Reno, there is a chance, a chance in Hell. Why don't you go there and look for it."

Damn, maybe Sarge did know Sister Scary-As-All-Shit after all. I ignored his suggestion and kept pushing. "Hey, I didn't like what we saw in the alley last night any better than you did. I didn't like it so much that I did a little investigating on my own. Interested?"

"Not now, Reno. Tonight, yeah. But not now. Now get out and hand the lady a Kleenex while you're at it. You, too, Tom."

John turned away and went back to his notebook and chewed-on pencil.

Tom and I did as we'd been told: obedient little puppies with Kleenex stuck to our paws. Hell, I gave Sandy the whole box. She looked like she needed it.

As I reached for the doorknob, John said, "Softly, Reno. Close it softly. We're honoring the dead in here." And then, just as softly as me closing the door, "Gus's at ten thirty tonight, Harry. And bring Tom."

An ambulance cut its siren, pulling to the curb in front of the coroner's, mingling its swirling lights with John's. Gurney time at the circus. We pushed our way through the gathering crowd and headed back to the Volvo.

As we walked along, the morning lake breeze was busy stirring discarded newspapers lying on the bench at a bus stop we passed. The papers fluttered, trying their damnedest to escape their Plexiglas prison. A beer bottle lay next to the bus stop. I stooped and picked up the newspapers and bottle and dropped them in a trash can.

The beer bottle made a nice clanging sound. Tom heard it and turned around.

"What are you doing, Harry?"

"Beautifying Kipling. You mind?" Surly, like John the Cop.

How does something hurt so bad you'd take your own life? Keep the hurt to yourself, permanently. How does something feel so good, you'll do it, knowing you might die? Why drugs, when you're so cute and sexy? And young? Why dangerous sex? And why kill yourself when you've sworn by Hippocrates not to play God? Why?

Why the hell not?

I caught Tom eyeing me. And like that, I decided to put the hurt on him when we hit *The Pioneer*. He knew something and was keeping it to himself. Guess I'd just have to wrap my fingers around his beer-bottle windpipe and squeeze until it popped out and spit in my eye.

In the meantime, I whistled us on down corpse street. "Ramblin' Man," I think it was.

50

TOM'S TUESDAY TRUTH

The editor unlocked the paper's front door and in we went. He reached for the lights.

"No lights, Tom." My gruff, you're-the-current-object-of-my-affections voice. "Lock it." He did it, but seemed puzzled, not understanding the mood swing.

"What gives, Harry?"

"You, Tom. That's what gives. Anybody around?" My voice gravel and grit, growling on its own. "Anybody coming in to work today?"

"No. Just you and me. Jayne took the day off. You know, after, well . . ." Wow, maybe Tom did know she'd pulled a gun on him, tried her damnedest not to kill him while he slept.

"What gives? You're mad, I can tell," he said. "Is it Doc Decker? Elke? Me?"

We locked eyes. Mine fierce. His staring warily out of their skull, flitting here, there. Ready for me, even if they didn't know exactly what I had in mind. Well, neither did I.

I needed and wanted answers. That much I did know. I could push softly or prod roughly. Choices, always choices. I started hard.

"Let's talk Mallory," I said. "I need to see her. Now. Right now."

"Me, too, Harry. Me, too."

"So where is she?"

"I don't know." I took a step toward him—an unfriendly move, the kind a tiger makes toward soon-to-be-devoured prey. "I don't know," Tom said again, sidestepping away. The tiger followed.

"Harry, I mean it. I want to find her, too. I haven't heard from her in a couple of days. That's the truth." Words coming too quickly. Mendacity hovering too close.

I shoved him into a chair.

"Take it easy. We're in this together." Tom glanced up. "Partners in crime. Remember?"

"Are we, Tom? Or are you just jerking me around? You could have told me a week ago Mallory was alive." My fist balled, knuckles white. In front of his face.

"But you didn't," I said. "How come?" Tom's eyes locked on my belt buckle now—trying not to think about the fist, I suppose.

I sat down in the chair across from him, pulled in close, put my hands on his knees, tried a suddenly softer approach. My tiger a purring kitten for now.

"If we are in this together," I said, "if you and I are going to save Mallory, protect Gwen and Brynn, topple the temple, save Christendom, you gotta tell Old Harry what the hell's going on up here in the North Woods." I leaned back, turned loose of his knees.

"Tell me what Stavros is up to, what the judge is up to, which cops I can trust, which ones I can't," I said, and beamed a friendly smile his way. Lots of tiger teeth on display, though.

"Maybe I can figure that last one out on my own. I'm gonna trust John. To hell with the rest of 'em." And to hell with smiling.

"That include Lance, Harry?" A little hitch in his voice.

"Especially Lance. He thinks with his dick. Like you." No purring. Not anymore. Hands back on Tom's knees—squeezing. Eyes wide. His, not mine.

Tom squirmed, couldn't escape, finally leveraged a shrug my way. Good enough. An improvement anyway. I turned loose of his knees.

"You're right, Harry. I do. When it comes to Mallory. Hell, everybody knows I've been her puppy dog, trotting along, collared and leashed and led. From the moment she walked into this office." He stood up, put his hand on his heart. I let him.

"I do confess it, my liege, and do submit myself to your tender mercies."

"Shut the fuck up then," I said. "And sit down." He did.

If he went all Shakespeare on me, I might as well walk out the door, try to find Mallory on my own. Shakespeare Tom had always pissed me off more than Hippie Tom ever could. And I wasn't alone in that judgment.

I fist-bopped Tom's head. He yelped. Oh, it couldn't have hurt much—he had that white mop of Mark Twain hair to cushion his skull. And he'd just said he'd submit himself to my tender mercies, hadn't he? So he couldn't really complain. But he did anyway.

"You don't have to do stuff like that, Harry. I'm on your side, remember?" Honest to God, whining like Karl. Pissing me off.

"Don't say that again. Don't tell me you're on my side." My fingers digging into flesh, squeezing. "I know who is and who isn't." Tom squirming some more—just like Karl.

My tiger hunting again, claws out.

Tom, big as he was, cringed, trying his damnedest to get away from me without getting up. Didn't work. His chair was hard-backed hickory. No give to it. He tipped it over, and himself along with it.

I grabbed the front of his shirt. Yanked him upright. The chair was a sensible piece of furniture. It stayed where it was, out of harm's way.

I jerked Tom close, called him a few choice names. Harry Reno, mad as hell. Because I'd been jerked around too, by everybody I'd met in Kipling. Both now and back then.

And there in *The Pioneer* that morning, it all just boiled over. Like the stew pot on the stove when you go to take a dump while it . . . well, while it stews and boils over.

And I was sick of eating shit stew.

Hard interrogation, not giving a flying fuck who I hurt or what I broke. I stalked into *The Pioneer*'s breakroom, smashing everything in sight—except the coffee maker and its semiprecious glass pot and a couple of mugs. I do have limits.

"Fuckin' A, dude," Tom said, "take a toke once in a while. Mellow out some."

Hokey, but it worked. My anger washed away, cleansed by a chance phrase and the destruction of inanimate objects instead of the quivering editor.

When our laughter subsided, we'd both calmed down—and without any weed. But I'd made my point. And Tom cut out the bullshit about Mallory, too.

"She called me yesterday. We set up a meet for tonight. She needs money. She's scared, Harry. She told me she could feel something closing in on her."

I must have telegraphed disbelief, let my poker face do my talking. Tom shrugged.

"That's what she said. Something—not somebody—stalking her. I asked her what she meant, and she just got mad. Said I didn't love her, said she knew I wanted her dead, and a lot of other crazy shit, too." His hand stirring his hair, conjuring a vision I couldn't see.

"I just let her rant and rage. It didn't last very long, though—not long until sobs replaced sneers." Tom tried smoothing his hair. Didn't work.

"I told her again I loved her and I'd protect her, come hell or high water. Yeah, Harry, I really did say that. Stupid, huh?" Yeah, but I let *stupid* slide.

"So where do we meet her, Tom?"

"You remember where the county road turns off and climbs away from the lake and into the trees?" I didn't, but no need to confess my memory problems to Tom.

"The old roadhouse we used to go to?" Tom said. I let my face say *Oh yeah, that one.*

"Twin Cedars," he said. "Nothing much left now. It burned down. Years ago." An I-remember-when look plastered Tom's face. I nudged him. But gentle like.

"Sorry, Harry. Lots of good times out there. Remember? With Jayne?" I didn't. Probably just as well. "There's an old springhouse," he said. “Behind the restaurant. Back in the trees. We meet there. When we need to.”

“When’s when?” I asked.

A smile began cracking Tom’s face, morphing into a mischievous grin. Something left from breakfast stuck in his teeth. “At the witching hour, Harry. Midnight.”

Now he was ruffling my hair instead of his own. “You sure you wanna tag along tonight? Ghosts still scare you?” I ignored his little jab, let Tom have his fun with my ghosts. I’d been pretty rough on him this morning, so I let it go.

“Sure, I can wait until tonight. Let’s meet at the Tam at ten thirty. You and me.” I didn’t mention John the Cop. No need to spook Tom.

We shook on it, and I headed out the door to see Lake County’s high sheriff. Maybe I’d see how bopping him on the head worked. Hell, you never know unless you try.

51
TUESDAY MORNING PHONE CALLS

As I walked out of *The Pioneer*, the little black minder clipped to my belt chirped. Penelope Phair's number flashed on the pager's screen. Across the street was a pay phone next to a convenience store, so across the street I went. Rule Number One: never keep Penny waiting. Guess that's why she bought me the pager.

I stepped in and pulled the door shut—no outside interference to spoil my call. And nothing did, except my own stupidity. She picked up on the first ring—never a good sign. "A little quicker next time, Reno."

"I thought you liked it slow, Ms. Phair. Long and slow." Dead air. Try again.

"What's up, Penny?"

"I am. Up early and ill. If you must know, if you care—Henry." Oh shit.

"Preggers, Penny?" I tried a lighter approach.

"No, I am not." Well, whatever it was, she didn't sound happy. "And perhaps shortly, I shall never be." Huh? Never be what?

"Ah, Penny, I'm sorry. Just kidding." Oh brother, this was not going well. Not well at all. Did she know Brynn had spent the night in my room? How could she know that?

"Look, Penny, I just let her sleep in my bed. I spent the night in the recliner. Honest." Shit. Why the hell did I say that?

"And who might this *she* be, Mr. Reno? Does this *she* sport a name? Or did you forget to inquire?" What the hell was wrong with her this morning? Better question—what the hell was wrong with me.

"It was Brynn," I said, "Alice's daughter. You know. She works up at the casino. I went to pick her up because the other girl died." I wasn't making sense. I knew it. Penny had me spooked over this preggers crap. And she wasn't letting up, either.

"Died before she could experience you," she said. "How tragic. Hopefully, Binty Brynn made up the deficit." Binty?

"Penny, what's wrong?"

"You are what is wrong, Reno." Well, nothing new there.

"Penny, I just, I just . . . I like Brynn, I, ah, I mean, I really, really like her, I mean, she's just a nice kid, I mean . . ." This wasn't helping. I couldn't stop babbling.

"Just a nice kid," I said again.

"Indeed, Reno. *A nice kid*. So now you bed goats." She hung up. Damn British bitch. Dumb-ass detective. I didn't call her back.

When I'd left *The Pioneer*, my intention had been to stroll over and engage Lake County's high sheriff in some cheerful conversation about what a lousy job he did wearing that shiny gold star he kept pinned to his chest.

Instead, my pager had talked me into calling Penelope. But now, after that confusing conversation, I was in no frame of mind to cross swords with Kipling's version of the Sheriff of Nottingham.

I opened the phone booth door and breathed in the scent of motor lorry fumes. Motor lorry fumes? Hell, that's Penelope Phair speak, her damn British English. And what the hell did her *Binty Brynn* mean? Screw Penelope.

I pulled the door shut again and dialed Mac McCabe's direct number down in the state capital and listened as the ringing began. I needed my old boss to be in. Iron Mac had to help me with Kipling.

A growl replaced the ringing in my ear. "Speak."

"Mac, it's Harry."

"Bad timing. Can't talk. Fucking meeting." Iron Mac's speech pattern on the telephone consists of short phrases punctuated by obscenities—same as when he isn't on the phone.

"Mac, wait. I gotta talk to you about Kipling and Stavros. Some bad shit's going down up here. I need help."

"No can do."

"You mean not now, or not ever?"

Mac broke his telephone rule and bent my ear for, oh, thirty seconds. That's long on the phone for Mac. It didn't exactly help.

"Forget it, Harry, it's Kipling. Stavros—green light—running guns—tech stuff—CIA—asshole DEA—bulletproof—blind eye. Nobody fucking cares. Not about drugs, not about dead girls. No direct help. Answer what I can. Find out what I can. No promise on-ground support. Remember: Stavros—bulletproof—motherfucker."

Then a sea change; his words slowed. "Come down to Ithaca, Harry. The boat. Friday night–Saturday. We'll talk." He'd softened, his brusque speech almost caring now.

"And Harry, bring Penny along, too. Friday, six o'clock. And be kind to her. Remember, she needs you." Penny needs me? Now what the hell did that mean?

Mac hung up without saying good-bye—like always.

A final call to make—let Walker-Doer know Harry Reno was alive and Elke Sorrenson was dead. I sucked deep air, cleared my mind, dialed.

"Judge Walker-Doer's residence," Willem said.

"It's me, you phony Dutchman. Reno." The *Dutchman* sobriquet a shot in the dark, something I'd picked up on while interrogating Karl.

"Ah, Mr. Reno. So good to hear your voice," Willem said. "So very good."

"Well? What are you gonna do about it?"

"About what, sir?"

"Me calling you a phony Dutchman."

"As you wish, sir," the butler said. Like Penny, no fun poking the butler this morning.

"Look, Willem, I need to talk to your boss. Is the judge there?"

"He is, Mr. Reno, but alas, he reposes indisposed. Too much recent excitement. Surely you recall that to which I refer." Bet that gray ponytail of his was busy swinging while he played his telephone games with me.

"Well, you'll have to do then, Willem." The son of a bitch probably had a shit-eating grin on his face, too. "I've run across a couple of leads that might be promising," I said. "Tell your boss I might even find his niece for him." The briefest of dead air.

"That would be welcomed news indeed, Mr. Reno."

"Cut the *Mr. Reno* bullshit, Willem. At least when it's just the two of us. I'll be Harry and you be Willem. Or Dutch, or Billy. Okay?" The butler at full pause this time.

"I think not Dutch, as you put it. Or Billy. Willem suits."

"Sure you're English, Willem?" No pause this time—not at all.

"In a manner of speaking, Harry. In a manner of speaking." With a guy like the butler, it was hard to tell exactly where he was or what he meant at any given moment. Or even who he was.

"Okay, Willem it is then. Hey, Willem, you ever get a night off? The judge ever let you roam on your own?"

"At times, Harry. Indeed."

"You wanna go for a ghost run tonight? Ride shotgun in case it's a setup? Ride along in case we gotta play Ghostbusters? Bring along one of those big ray guns like you and I played with yesterday?"

"I believe I might persuade the judge to allow me this evening for my own amusement. When and where?" he said.

"Ten thirty. Tonight. At the Tam-O'-Shanter. You know, Gus's place." Maybe I heard him snicker—maybe not.

"I know it well, Harry. Indeed I do."

"Just you, me, and Tom Kuster. And a cop. A good cop. You like good cops, don't you, Willem? They don't scare you, do they?" Dead air. I filled it.

"Tom's gonna take us all on a ghost run up to Twin Cedars. I just think I'd like some company. You know, I scare kinda easy, don't I, Willem?"

"As you say, sir." That snicker again. Or maybe just Willem sucking some air.

"But might I be allowed a comment," he said. "You handle yourself with a gun like you've killed before." Yeah, well, so do you.

"See ya tonight, ya hardheaded bastard," Willem said, and not in his English, oh-so-proper butler voice, either. Then he hung up.

Where had that last bit of tough guy shtick come from? What the hell was up with the butler? I quit scratching my head and tried my neck—no better luck. I gave up.

The Volvo ferried me out to where the cabin used to sit. I spent the rest of the day there thinking things through, mooning over Brynn, drinking some beer. Pissing in the trees. Might have been a lot of beer. I forget.

But the little hula girl remembered. She always does. Plastic heifer.

52
A TUESDAY NIGHT SING-ALONG

"Laddie, 'tis a trouble collector you be, for certain." A late-night hamburger and fries appeared, along with a fresh beer. I turned in the booth, looked up at Gus. A fake Scottish barkeep, but Gus himself genuine. I was in too deep with him now—no doubts allowed.

"Hey, you big moose, I'm off duty. Where's *my* beer? Where's *my* burger?" John put a hand on Gus's arm and squeezed. If Gus felt it, he didn't let it show. John slid into the booth.

"What are you staring at?" I grouched.

"Not much, I guess. Just never seen a real live mope before." Mope, huh? Didn't sound like a compliment, even though John smiled when he said it. So I took a swing at him.

John leaned back—quick like. My right missed like I wanted it to—by an inch. Just boys being boys. But that left me still wondering what the hell a mope was.

The Tam's front door banged open and banged shut. Tom Kuster lurched across the almost empty barroom, then towered over the booth—swaying.

"Clan Tam bunched all together," he said. "One lightning strike and all honesty in town would fritter away, become but ethereal nothingness." What the hell had he been smoking?

Tom put a paw on Gus's head and rubbed for all he was worth. The barkeep brushed him off with a flick of his hand.

Tom took a step back, held up his hands, palms out, said, "Accept ye my capitulation, oh Chief of Clan Tam." It was going to be a long, fuzzy night if Tom kept that act going.

"Apology accepted, Thomas Kuster," Gus said. "Another bit of help for friend Harry the Mope tonight, are ye?" Funny, real funny.

"Aye, Angus, that I am." Tom straightened his stoop, slowed his swaying. "And for your information, friend Harry, mopery has honest antecedents. But it is not a compliment, dear sir. Shakespeare himself trotted it out in *Henry V . . .*" And that's as far as Gus allowed him to go.

"Sit down, shut up." He shoved Tom down beside me. "Molly—beer," Gus said. Was Tom Kuster my third friend here tonight? I had doubts more real than imagined.

"Tom, we still good for Mallory at midnight?" I asked.

"I'm not sure, Harry." My fist came down fast and hard. The table jumped—beer spilled—heads swiveled.

"What the hell, Tom." My words close and hard in his ear. "You said Mallory at midnight, and it damn well better be true. Because if it isn't . . ." My voice low—menacing.

I fist-banged the table again. More liquid gold sluicing across brown wood. My eyes narrowed, lips twitching, bull snorts escaping my nostrils.

"What the hell, Kuster. What the earthly hell."

Tom looked away, put his shaggy Mark Twain head down, and just stared at his beer. He was pissing me off and he knew it.

Maybe Mallory wasn't really alive after all. Maybe Clan Tam was going to take me out in the witchy woods and plant me in a hole in the ground. Maybe that's what you do with mopes. I drained the beer in front of me on the off chance it might be my last.

Random thoughts ricocheting around in my skull. Probably not a good idea to have spent the afternoon getting the far side of half-drunk. John and Gus watching me, trying to gauge how high I'd blow. Tom with his white-haired head still buried in his arms.

I tried resurrecting the camaraderie I'd just buried. "You said midnight. Now you tell us you can't remember. The hell with it, Tom." But it was my happy, the-hell-with-it voice. "Maybe she's out there now, loping around in the cedars, getting needles in her socks, throwing one hell of a hissy fit because nobody's there to kiss her hello."

John snorted.

"Hey," I said. "What sort of half-ass dating service you running, Kuster?" It had started out funny, but I lost the laughter at the end. I reached across the booth, grabbed Tom's nose, gave it a twist—but not Reno hard. Just Harry hard.

Still, Tom yelped. Out of the corner of my eye, Gus shaking his head, telling me, *Stop*.

I let go of Tom's nose.

"Easy . . . Harry . . . take it . . . easy." Tom breathing hard, in and out, little bursts.

"The hell with it," I said. "Let's load and go. Who's in on this?"

Nobody met my eye, nobody said *I'm in*. Nobody said anything at all. And where the hell was that ponytailed butler? Willem had told me he was in for a ghost run. Nowhere to be seen now.

"Figures, just fucking figures." Me again—nobody else talking, remember? Hot as hell, fists hard balls of danger down at the ends of quivering arms. I wanted to kill something. I settled for draining Tom's untouched beer. "The hell with it. I'll go by myself."

I tried bolting the booth. Gus pushed me back down. I kept trying to stand. I couldn't—Gus, the Highland Hercules. So I sat, but not quietly. "Now what the hell do we do?"

"Easy, Harry, easy." This time John sang the chorus instead of Tom.

Then Gus chimed in with the next verse. "We're all going with you, Harry. No worries there. And we're going now. I'm pissed at Tom, too." Gus's eyes grabbed mine. "You keep looking around," the bartender said. "You expecting somebody else? Willem, maybe?"

"What about you?" I said. "You expecting him? Well, are you

—*Angus?*" I tried pushing him away. Might as well have been shoving a Sherman tank.

"No, Harry." Gus brushed the tip of my nose with his finger. I got the message. Could have been his fist. Those arms of his, remember? How they make two of mine? Harry Reno, back under control, sort of.

"Four's plenty," I said. "Let's roll." A calmer shamus, just not a happier one.

"Guns, Harry?" Gus again. "Are we going armed? Some of us? None of us? Big guns, little guns—ray guns? You decide. You're the one getting edgy tonight."

"Maybe we all ought to carry except Harry." John the Cop chiming in.

"Nuts to all of you." But I laughed as I said it. "I've got mine. Any of you can bring whatever cannons you want." Up beside the booth now. "I'm rolling." A step toward the door.

"If you're frightened, stay here," I said. "I'll tell you a ghost story to the scare the panther piss out of you when I get back."

I winked at Molly and headed out. She smiled back. Probably afraid not to. My two trusted friends plus Tom trooped after me.

Finally, Harry's world rotating correctly, instead of careening out of control. Maybe.

53
GHOSTS IN THE CEDARS

The Volvo headed out the lake road. John behind the wheel, the little hula girl dancing on the dash, wiggling her disapproval. After a while, we turned away from Great Cold Lake and began the climb into the ever-present cedars and pines. Plenty of ghostly birches, too. While we drifted along through the woods, ground fog crept out of the trees and blanketed the road.

John slowed, and, as if by magic, the skeletal remains of the restaurant materialized. If it had been a church, it would have been tolling midnight—perfect timing.

We pulled off into the old parking lot. Fog; nothing but thick, white fog. I climbed out, walked back to the Volvo's trunk. John and Gus followed; Tom didn't. He stood gazing vacantly off into the white nothingness enveloping us.

"He'd better not have brought us up here on a snipe hunt," I said.

Funny, huh? You know, snipe hunt, just kid stuff, here in the fog with loaded guns. No? Well, guess you had to be there. Whatever, splintered the tension. Tom wandered over.

"What's in the trunk?" He picked up the shotgun. "You gonna shoot somebody tonight, Gus? Buckshot their brains?"

"Aye, and ye would do the deed ahead of all, Thomas Kuster. Gimme that blunderbuss." But Gus grinned when he said it, and Tom grinned back. The gun changed hands. Camaraderie—North Woods style.

John said, "No guns tonight, boys. Too foggy." Reality check. I didn't like it, but he was right. We'd come up here to find Mallory, not kill her. Or ourselves.

"You said midnight. It's midnight," I said. "Where is she?" Tom shrugged. "What's that mean?" God, but the man was perfecting pissing me off.

And where the hell was that ponytailed butler? Why hadn't he shown? Was he lurking out there in the fog, too? Waiting for some mope to appear? What the hell was a mope, anyway? And what the hell was Penny's problem? Why Mac's *Be nice to her* bullshit?

Stale beer thoughts, not important. Concentrate—Mallory.

John looked to Tom, said, "Assuming she's here, how do we find her in this mess?"

"Oh, it'll be all right," Tom said. "I'll find her. Here chick, chick, chick." With that, Tom plowed into the fog soup and was gone.

I rounded on Gus. "Did he have a bottle with him in the car? Is that how you kept him quiet on the ride? Well?"

"Easy, laddie. Just a nip now and then from a wee half-pint of Scotch. No harm. He'll find her. He always does." What the hell.

"You've been up here before, haven't you? You and Tom. Damn it, Gus. That's how she's gotten what she needs." I wheeled on John. "What about you? You in on this, too?"

"No." Emphatic. I let it go.

"Blink the lights three times, Harry," Gus said. "That's the safe signal."

I said something nasty, then made the Volvo wink like he'd asked—nothing. "So where the hell is she, Gus?"

"It's different every time. Sometimes she's in the woods, sometimes she's hiding in the restaurant. Sometimes she's near the springhouse, like Tom said." Gus laid a Highland paw on my shoulder. "And

I've had her just appear beside me, too. Like magic, Harry. Damn spooky."

"Let's do something," John said. "I'll circle the perimeter." His finger traced the tree line we couldn't see. "Check the springhouse as I go, look for Tom. Maybe Mallory will be where he is. Gus, you stay here by the Volvo, keep blinking the lights. Blow the horn if she shows. Harry, you check the restaurant. See if they got any donuts." Cop humor.

Gus offered us a drink from Tom's Scotch. I took a good pull and drained it. Pissed off, remember? "None left for us, laddie," Gus said. John shrugged and moved off into the fog.

I groped my way toward the ruins that used to be Twin Cedars, the poshest restaurant in the woods Kipling ever did see. If only I could see it tonight.

As I picked my way across the old parking lot, the outline of what was left of the restaurant began to materialize out of the fog. Chimneys stuck up at the corners like a castle's towers. The broken roof line formed the battlements. The restaurant's twin doors—hanging by a hinge apiece next to desiccated cedar trees—stood fog duty as the gate to the castle itself.

I stumbled inside. No roof, no stars, no moon—no nothing. Just drifting whiteness all around. Damn, but I felt woozy.

Then I bumped into her.

I recognized Mallory from her pictures. Red hair, pale skin, but glowing with an ethereal, otherworldly beauty the pictures had failed to convey. She'd chosen a cloak to protect herself against the chill and damp of the fog.

I backed off a bit. Startled. Mallory let her cloak drift apart. Oh my god.

Never seen a redheaded woman naked in a fog before—not a live one, not a dead one, not a ghostly one. Never seen one since. But I sure saw one then.

At least I think I did. My head was swimming. What the hell had been in that half-pint? Still, if I was going to start finding naked women in fogs, this sure seemed the right one to start with.

I couldn't tear my eyes away.

Red hair cascaded over her shoulders. Her eyes were scarlet daggers. Crimson nipples tipped her breasts. When my eyes wandered below the navel, well, she was red there, too. And all of her encased in a milky white softness that might or might not have been skin.

No wonder old Tom Kuster fell for Mallory, and fell hard. No wonder he did anything she asked. No wonder at all.

The fog swirled; so did my head. Funny, but I'd felt fine on the way up. A little buzzed maybe, a tad mad—but fine. Felt good when we got here, too. But not now.

Only I remembered all of that later. Right then and there, confronting the redheaded, naked apparition, all I could do was say "Hey." Yeah, Harry Reno, tough-guy PI, Lance's man of the world, could only squeak out, "Hey." At least I didn't call her babe.

Mallory reached out a hand—beckoning me to follow her out of the restaurant—and slipped away into the fog, clutching her cloak about herself as she scurried away.

I followed. Of course I did. Breaststroking in fog soup. Trying to catch up. Two, three, or forty more steps—don't know, wasn't counting—then I tripped, hit the ground hard. With my head.

Something woke me. A scream, an owl screech, who the hell knows. I stumbled upright and headed off into the white soup to find the naked redhead. You would have too.

A spectral shape came gliding toward me out of the all-enveloping whiteness. Not a redhead, though. A female with frosted blond hair, wearing a leopard-print cowl and cape, floated out from behind a tree. Or were the leopard spots maybe blood splatters?

I wanted to look away, but her breasts—straining at the confining cloak, threatening to burst forth—pulled me in. She showed me bare leg up to her thigh. Her pointed nose and chin seemed more sexy than witchlike. But something akin to a blackened bullet hole in her forehead pretty much spoiled the whole effect.

Whatever mental gymnastics my brain was performing, it was an unrehearsed routine.

"Who are you?" I said. Why I asked, I don't know. Just seemed the polite thing to do. I knew damn well who she was supposed to be.

"Jayne? That you?" My voice thick, like I'd imbibed maple syrup instead of Scotch. With a sweep of my hand, I invited her to sit with me on a rock. She accepted.

I ran my finger along her bare leg. Then the world slowed its whirl, and I heard what Jayne was saying. "Harry, you must be ready to wreak my revenge."

"Ah . . . what revenge, Jayne? And on who? Or is it whom?"

"Harry Reno, you idiot. You'll know my killer. You'll know why he killed me."

I had to have seemed puzzled. Doesn't a person have to be dead to haunt you? That's what I'd always thought. But the Jayne ghost talked like her death hadn't even happened yet. Maybe she wasn't even dead, wasn't a ghost. I definitely should have skipped the Scotch—too late for that now.

I do remember saying, "Huh?"

Jayne's ghost eyes flashed. Not like they did in life, not all periwinkle blue and inviting. But instead with the blue-tinged whiteness of a dead-of-winter full moon.

Then her wraithlike fist slammed into me hard, as if it was clutching a ten-dollar roll of Washingtons. The silver sort as opposed to the greenback variety. Down I went.

My hip struck a root while my shoulder glanced off a pebble the size of Britain's Rock of Gibraltar. I stayed put. Dazed and, yeah, scared shitless, eyes shut. Weren't girl ghosts supposed to be like Casper's Wendy? Soft and friendly? Like Brynn? Didn't you have to be dead to be a ghost? Like Elke?

When I finally had the nerve to do it, I opened my eyes and glanced around. No Jayne. So I tried sitting up by rolling over on my good side first. That hurt, too. I may have passed out. I don't know. I really wasn't paying attention anymore.

I came to with Gus shaking my shoulder, his voice loud in my ear: "Here's the wee lad himself, John. Alive and well."

Gus pulled me upright, whispered, "Don't trust Tom Kuster, Harry.

I think he spiked the Scotch." Gus put his arm around me, holding me steady. "Anything strange happen to you, Harry?" Gus was staring straight at me now. "It sure did to us." I wonder if he saw what I saw?

"We got a body to call in," Gus was saying. "A twice-dead body." He hugged me tighter, as if he feared I'd morph into fog. "We found Mallory. Only this time, she's really dead."

54
THE LADY DA

Out of the shower—shaved and dressed—and somewhat recovered from my night in the cedars. But still trying to absorb reality. Mallory Mordred, truly and finally dead.

We'd stayed until they bagged the body, and a detective had asked us some desultory questions. Probably helped having John Wetherall there. Besides, nobody—except maybe Tom—seemed to care Mallory was kaput. The cops said they'd let the Walker-Doer know. Maybe he'd care.

But that was last night. Or early this morning, I suppose. Head still a bit woozy.

And now I needed to call Penny and tell her I'd found Mallory—sort of. Then I wanted to hit the Hash House, have my rye toast, and tell Brynn all about last night. Oh, and call—

A knock on my motel door. Change of plans?

"Open up, Reno. Police!" My eye at the peephole—dark. Someone outside thumbing it. Could be anybody. I tried stalling.

"Say that again?" Where the hell was my gun? "Who's there?"

"Two seconds and we take the door down, shamus," the voice outside said. "And you with it. One . . ."

I bowed to the inevitable, opened the door, said, "Howdy do."

The two sheriff's deputies weren't amused. One braced me, frisked me for weapons. The other made a protective sweep of the premises, as they say.

"Sleeping alone last night, huh, Reno?" The tone definitely wasn't friendly. Plus, like Lance, he kept me pinned to the wall.

The other deputy said, "The DA wants to see you, Reno. Now."

"Tell her to call my secretary. Make an appointment. Unless you got a warrant. I got other plans today." Didn't work.

Been through it before. Knew the routine. Pulled my head in low as they shoved me into the cruiser's cage. The headache I had from last night was enough. It didn't need company.

And then we were off, headed downtown. On the plus side, they hadn't cuffed me—not yet, anyway.

The ride to the DA's office passed in silence—strange. Cops usually want you to talk. So they ask innocuous questions, cloak their interrogation with the guise of friendly chatter until you begin to tip over and spill the goods. But no questions for Harry Reno. None at all.

The perp walk to meet the Lady DA—Perry's hot-blooded wife, Karl's lust mother—started at the sheriff's sally port. In a steel door, down a gray corridor, through another steel door, and finally a pause at a portal of the normal wood-and-glass sort.

Black letters on the door's frosted pane spelled out DISTRICT ATTORNEY'S OFFICE. Below that, red letters shouted ARIADNE STAVROS LAKE COUNTY DISTRICT ATTORNEY. Just in case you didn't already know who you were there to see. Or is it whom?

But a nice touch, either way—bruise black to go with blood red. And the sheriff and the DA keeping house together. How convenient.

In we went.

A waiting room and a receptionist sitting behind glass, waiting to admit you to the Holy of Holies. Hard-backed chairs to wait in, while you waited. And that was it. Not even an *Architectural Digest* to peruse.

Authentic Spartan. Bet Leonidas and his three hundred would feel right at home.

Then the crone behind the glass crooked her finger, the two sheriff's boys jumped to it, and in I went to see the Lady DA.

She was leaning against the edge of her desk, long legs crossed in front of her, long arms crossed, too, cradling her breasts. Those arms of hers certainly had a big job to do. Maybe they could use some help.

Mrs. Pericles Stavros—Ariadne to friends like me, she said—held out her hand, took mine in hers, squeezing ever so lightly. "Harry," she cooed, "I'm so sorry to drag you out of bed this morning. After the just awful night you must have had."

More cooing, more squeezing.

She said this was her only open slot today and she just wanted to meet me and see how my investigation was going and what about the poor dead girl and the horrible revelation it wasn't Mallory who died in the fire but now Mallory was dead and could I possibly do lunch so we could talk and would the two handsome deputies please leave the two of us alone and she'd call when she was through with Plain Old Harry.

And that's how it all came out—in a deep-throated, Lauren Bacall, coaxing rush, sexy as hell. Maybe she thought I was Bogey.

The deputies got out like the good little boys they weren't, and Ariadne Stavros asked me to sit beside her on the office's leather couch. Come to think of it, I guess it was her leather couch, too. Whichever, that's where she put me. And like the deputies, I did what she asked.

Some tough shamus, huh?

Her words kept flowing, and all you could do was drown in them. Not all witches need bubbly cauldrons and arcane incantations to work their magic. No sir, they sure don't. And a flounce of that silver-streaked black hair—her hand running through it—didn't hurt, either.

Neither did the view down her blouse. No bra in evidence. How 'bout that?

I even tried to watch her performance without being seduced. Didn't work. Instead, I let her soft throaty voice and violet eyes draw me in. Maybe the color came from contacts, maybe it was nature's own, maybe I didn't really care.

The Lady DA wasn't like the two deputies. She did have questions for Harry. Lots of questions. But the Lady DA sunk her claws into Harry's hide ever so gently. And she didn't have to scratch very hard. She just made sure Harry couldn't help himself.

Sometimes even I hate Harry Reno.

A half smile played at the corners of her lips as she talked, lips painted a slightly sharper shade of plum, just a shade or so deeper than her violet eyes—the seducing eyes that sat either side of her perfectly straight and beautiful nose. A fainter mauve caressed her eyelids while her lavender blouse worked overtime to keep her free-floating breasts barely contained.

I didn't want to think about what was underneath her black skirt, but I did. Maybe black lace panties. With little red bows. Maybe no panties at all.

And Ariadne really did call me *Plain Old Harry*. Kipling was a place peopled by witches, I was sure of it that morning. And I didn't give a damn if it was.

"Harry, Plain Old Harry." She was cooing again. "That's what the girls like to call you, isn't it?"

I left that one alone. So she knew about Brynn and Gwen, so what. I could handle her, I was sure I could. I'd met plenty of district attorneys. Tough girls, timid guys—sometimes the other way around. Some of them smart, some of them stupid. But this morning didn't match any of my prior encounters, didn't fit into a pattern I could discern and analyze.

I know now that Ariadne was casting a spell. But what the hell, most women, if they half try, can do that. But Ariadne drew her magic from a deeper, more ancient source. Something more complex than a *Cosmo* "How to Bewitch Your Man" article.

I had fun on the couch with Ariadne until a fly landed on my nose, so to speak, and her spell evaporated like fall frost at the touch of the morning sun.

I sat up, wiped my mouth with the back of my hand, told her, "No.

Stop it." Then I said, "What are you doing to find Mallory's killer, find out who strangled Lacie Doyle?"

Ariadne didn't like being told no. Didn't approve of being asked to behave. Didn't like being questioned about her murder investigations. Maybe I shouldn't have said, "Go ahead, say something snarly, bitch." But I did.

So she bit me.

In the twitch of an eye, she transformed herself from cuddling kitten into harrowing harpy, and all without so much as sliding away from me. Instead, she simply sank her teeth into my shoulder and bit hard—hard enough to draw blood.

And it all happened right there on that soft leather couch of hers, both the cooing and the bloodletting. Only now her voice wasn't soft anymore, didn't purr when she called for her deputies—when she said, "Get in here, boys!"

I stood up, raised my hands, put them on top of my head. I could have taken a poke at her boys as they came in, could have grabbed Ariadne, tried to bluff my way out of her vixen DA den. But I didn't; no death wish. Instead, I let the two deputies pull my hands down, put the bracelets on.

"Tighter," she said, and the bigger ape made sure the cuffs bit hard—just like Ariadne herself. "Book him, George." She spat out *George* as hard as she spat out *book him*. She'd gotten herself all worked up just because Plain Old Harry wouldn't play her game.

"What's the charge, ma'am?"

"Mopery, George. Mopery on a leather couch, with intent to be a creep. That'll do for a start." Maybe Ariadne and Tom Kuster studied Shakespeare together. I don't know. I never asked.

No resistance as her two goons hustled me out, but they held on tight, just to make sure.

First stop the property desk. A bored deputy relieved me of just about everything but my pants. The holding cell a steel cage that let prowling jailers watch you do whatever it was you wanted to do—cry, vomit, piss in the pot by the drain. A high window, steel bunk beds bolted to a concrete floor. A passed-out stumblebum busy sawing North Woods logs. Kipling's drunk tank.

I wasn't surprised to be there. I'd expected to end up right where I was at some point this trip. I've seen lots of drunk tanks over the years, from both sides of the steel bars. I sat on the bed and waited for stage two of the DA's interrogation—waited for the tough stuff to start.

It never happened.

After a couple of hours, a tall deputy in a crisp brown uniform strode up to the cell door, unlocked it, and told me I was being released. The crisp deputy marched me to the property desk—his uniform sporting nary a wrinkle as he walked. I signed the proper forms, and the bored deputy behind the cage shoved my earthly possessions back at me.

But not all the stuff I needed for a day by myself in Kipling. Both my guns were still asleep back in my motel room. The deputies hadn't let me take my toys with me to see their Lady DA. I felt sort of naked.

Plus, my shirt had blood on it. And purple lipstick.

But that aside, what a nice place the sheriff ran. A first-class, top-of-the-line hoosegow. Still, I wanted the hell out of Dodge before the mood in the jail changed, before the Lady DA put the bite on Harry Reno again.

So I tugged on my jacket, and out the door I went. But not too quickly. That would have been unseemly. But quick enough.

55
HARBOR DOUBTS

As I stepped out of the sheriff's jailhouse paradise and into sunshine, I scanned for a pay phone. There, across the street. I made my call, but no answer. Not even the recording. Where was Penny when I needed her? Mad as hell at two women now.

Try Walker-Doer next? No way. If he didn't know his niece was finally dead by now, then the hell with him. He could keep his blood money. I hadn't cashed his check and never would.

But hey, if I did make the call, the butler might answer. I could chew him a new one. Willem on my shit list this morning, too. I don't like being stood up. I can stand it. I just don't like it. Either way, no call.

Walls closing in on me out here in the sunshine in the phone booth. A need to walk, let my head clear a little. Plus, no choice. No wheels. The Volvo snoozing back at the motel, too.

Deputies coming out of the sheriff's office, cop-staring this way and that. Maybe turning me loose had been rethought. I didn't wait around to find out. I didn't wave good-bye, either.

My feet took a cross street, headed toward Kipling's waterfront.

Maybe some cabbies were hanging around there, whiling the afternoon away with the canoes.

So down to the sea and ships I went—on foot.

I surveyed the lake from the harbor wall, trying not to breathe too deeply. Lots of dead fish, floaters like me. Ore boats and grain ships should be out there cruising the waters, but I couldn't spot any—just empty horizon. Lake traffic wasn't what it had been fifteen years ago.

But then again, neither was anything else—not since Gwen's mom. And now Elke. And Mallory and Lacie Doyle. All dead.

Brain jab. No chance yet to sit down with Gwen and work through our shared Kipling problem. Well, I could. If everybody else would get the hell out of the way and just leave the two of us alone. And quit dying. For a minute—or an hour—or a night.

Stop it, Reno, stop it. So I tried to.

Didn't work. Doubts about the whole reason I was in Kipling swirled and eddied in my head, while harbor stink assaulted my nose.

What really had happened to Gwen's mother all those years ago? Had the crazy broad really killed her? Or had someone else killed the two of them? Had Jayne been speaking truth to lies? Did it really matter anymore?

I sat on the wall, let my feet dangle over water. Tried unscrambling my thoughts.

No matter how hard I tried, no matter whose black lace panties I conjured up—only confused images of Brynn and Harry, Gwen and her dead mother, Elke and Karl, Walker-Doer and Willem, Tom and Jayne, Stavros and his sharp-tooth wife, their bull man and his goat buddy, and their damn temple out on that island in the lake kept whirling in my head.

And Mallory Mordred and Lacie Doyle, flotsam and jetsam bobbing along.

Fog ghosts floating before my eyes. My brain would try to grab a cottony handful, only to have the bewilderment dance away, because it wasn't really there. Because like last night, all that went on in Kipling was only a figment of my imagined reality, just a brain fever you can't take two aspirins for and call Doc Decker in the morning. Because Doc isn't taking calls right now, he's too busy swinging.

This was getting me nowhere. To hell with Kipling. Go home to Penelope. Now. Need a cab for that. No luck. Maybe I could at least find some coffee.

Off I trudged, putting one foot in front of the other as mechanically as a soldier marching off to the front. Only my confused brain had decided to quick march to the rear, elected to abandon my quest for the truth.

But my feet wouldn't pick up the pace, even though my nose hated the smells it was inhaling. Maybe the three of them—mind, nose, and feet—weren't talking to each other. Wouldn't be the first time.

Waterfront beer joints gave way to tonier establishments. Places where young, short-skirted secretaries perched on bar stools, delicately pecking at their lunches while they dissected bosses and boyfriends.

Where their older versions sat on tired haunches at tables, sipping white wine, nibbling chicken salad, recounting their weekend affairs to the approval of their wearied and jealous girlfriends. The ones with nothing with which to regale their still-desirable tablemates.

I hate restaurants like that.

Then I realized I knew one of those still-desirable women. Sitting in a black wrought-iron chair under a big green-and-white-striped umbrella at a posh sidewalk café was Jayne—by herself. Maybe she'd give me a ride back to the motel.

She wore a white sundress that showed off her tan and the sun freckles spangled across her chest. Her reengineered breasts helped the dress look good, really good. A gold necklace with a single white pearl dangled down between the breasts, just in case you needed an excuse to stare, or to start a conversation.

I didn't need an excuse, but I took a good look anyway. And started a conversation.

"I need a ride," I said. She didn't look up.

I kept staring down at the pearl. "Back to the motel," I said. Still nothing. Something softer, perhaps. "Hello, Jayne. You're looking beautiful today—alive, vibrant. I love your pearl."

"Well hello, Harry. I didn't see you standing there."

She was wearing her hair back and off her face, a thin tortoiseshell headband keeping the frosted locks in place, holding the years at bay. I skipped telling her that. I expect she already knew it. That's why she was wearing it that way.

Jayne was holding a Bloody Mary, dabbing her lips with a white linen napkin as she said hello. A white-jacketed waiter appeared—like I said, the tonier end of the harbor. I told him I was joining the lady and I'd have what she was having.

Jayne smiled up at me, patted the chair beside her. "Sit, Cheetah, sit." So I sat.

"I'm leaving Kipling, Jayne. Leaving today—now. If you'll give me a ride."

"Does it have to be right now, Harry?"

"Yes, it does."

"Well then, you shouldn't have ordered a drink, now, should you?" Laugh lines crinkled her eyes but not her makeup.

Damn it, off my game today—screwy, sharp-toothed Lady DA. "Then I guess I'll have some lunch with you, too."

Jayne smiled and that's when I noticed a bruise on her forehead, faint under her makeup, but a bruise nonetheless. I opened my mouth, then let it shut. Maybe I knew the answer. Maybe I didn't. Either way, why ask. I had lunch to decide on.

"What's good?" I asked.

"Try the turkey, cucumber spread, and bacon sandwich, Harry. You'll love it. It's called You Turkey, Me Jane. Perfect for us, don't you think?"

I smiled and asked the hovering waiter to bring me one, then said, "Been waiting long, Jayne?"

"All my life, Mr. Reno." I knew what she meant. Did she?

"That's awfully nice of you, Ms. Rask." She smiled. Maybe she did know what she meant. Jayne, screwier even than that nutty Lady DA. *Watch yourself* floated between my ears.

"Harry, let's go for a walk after we eat, just the two of us, down by the lake and over to the park. Like old times. Can we?"

My green eyes grabbed her blues, held them while I said, "Sure." After a moment, Jayne blinked.

"Why don't you want to look at my boobs, Harry? That's where most men stare." A kittenish smile. "Probably because my hips are getting a little wide."

Before I could disagree, the waiter brought our lunch, and we both asked for another Bloody Mary at the same time. Jayne giggled; Cheetah laughed. The waiter smiled his tip smile, chuckled appreciatively, and hustled off to the bar to cement his gratuity.

Quickly, because I'd caught him scoping out more than just Jayne's pearl dangling there.

We finished our lunch, and I sprang for the tab. Off we strolled, Jayne hugging my arm. She had a citrus scent on today. Very nice. Very inviting.

"Thank you," she said. "And Harry, please don't think of leaving Kipling just yet. All your answers are here. I'll help you find them. Really I will."

Wow. All my answers? Why here, why now? Had she been stalking me? Seen me wandering around, slinking in and out of phone booths, sniffing harbor breezes? Then caught a table here where I couldn't miss her? Or was this just a chance encounter? I doubted all my choices.

Jayne planted a quick kiss, skipped ahead along the sidewalk, twirling around slowly while I caught up. "Are they really too big, Harry? My hips, I mean?"

She linked my arm with hers again, snuggled in closer as she made her play for me to stay. And it sure as hell wasn't those hips cuddling my arm. I could feel the pearl and her other two ornaments. I just couldn't see them right now.

"You don't want to leave Kipling without finally boiling those old ghosts out of your skull, do you, Harry?" She had me there.

"What happened to your shirt?" Jayne finger-tapped the Lady DA's lipstick smear.

I smiled, shook my head, said, "Nothing important."

Jayne kept her cheek glued to my shoulder. Made it hard to walk, but we managed. I felt a tear escape and melt on my sleeve. Or maybe it was just a drop of her sweat. Either way, the other strollers we passed smiled at two people in love or looked away, their prudishness on display for all to see.

I slipped my arm around Jayne's waist, told her I still loved her.

"Go to hell, Harry. Stop it, or I'll call Penelope." She laughed; I laughed. We both knew she wouldn't. She never had. On we strolled.

56

FOREST TALES

Jayne stayed on my arm until we walked into the park and stopped at a bench. We sat, watched clouds float by, her periwinkle eyes all adrift, mine slightly unfocused as well. A Bloody Mary or two, or three too many, perhaps the problem.

"Touch me, Harry. I don't care where. Just touch me. Let me know I'm real."

I pinched her nipple—discreetly, but hard. Something Jayne had always liked. All she said was "Thanks."

I waited, but *Thanks* was it, her eyes focused on her feet now. Or on the past, or on the park's asphalt path. I couldn't tell.

"Harry, I know why Perry wanted Mallory dead." So that's why we're here.

"She figured it out. Mallory was smart. And beautiful." Jayne spat out *beautiful* like a kid spitting out asparagus—because it tastes bad.

"Smart how, Jayne?" I let *beautiful* ride. "What did Mallory figure out?"

"She didn't really figure it out. I led her to it. Showed her where to search, where to dig, who to talk to." Jayne's finger flicked at a tear.

"I guess I knew the truth all along. I was just afraid to bring it up. I always thought, well, maybe he'd take me back." Who? Tom? Perry? I didn't ask.

Jayne sighed, her blue eyes wandering away from the detective beside her to the white clouds overhead. Then the eyes closed, stayed that way. Perhaps something inside had caught her attention. I gave her a moment or two, then—

"Jayne, do you remember telling me this? Up there at the cabin?" No more pinching. I was trying out Harry's famous massage technique instead. Seemed more appropriate to the moment.

Jayne's peepers opened. I kept at the rubbing.

"Oh, I guess I did tell you, didn't I? Sorry." She pushed my hand away, gently, though.

"It's okay, Jayne. Why don't you start at the beginning. The real beginning. Start there and work forward." I let my hand drift back to where it'd been.

"I don't even remember the beginning." Her hand atop mine now. "Really I don't."

I considered that a moment, then said, "Why don't you tell me about the photo in Gus's bar, the one of you and Stavros. And Walker-Doer, before he got so old."

The blank look on her face a puppy's stare, trusting and eager but uncomprehending.

"I don't know the picture you mean, Harry. Gus has a wall full of them. It's been a while since I've been in there." Her hand back in her lap, clasping its mate. Mine resting on my knee.

"It's a photo of you and Walker-Doer and Stavros," I said. "Twenty years ago, maybe. Summertime. You're in the middle. Walker-Doer and Stavros each have an arm around your waist, like they're trying to make sure the other guy doesn't get you.

"Everybody's smiling, though, like the tug-of-war is just a joke." I squeezed her knee. "That jog anything?"

Jayne smiled. Maybe she'd liked being tugged on. Or having hands knead knees. "I guess that's close enough to the beginning for you, Harry. But I don't think you're going to like what I tell you." Her smile gone now.

"Are you sure you want to know? It might change memories of Gwen's mother." Her hairband came off. Jayne's hand fussed with frosted locks. The hairband glided back into place.

"Oh hell, Harry, no might about it—it will. Are you strong enough for that?" Guess she'd found her focal point, her periwinkle eyes bright dots.

But what about me? Was I strong enough, she'd asked. Strong enough for what? Gwen's mother had hinted at things back then, told me she had a not-too-distant past I wouldn't like. But when the naked woman beside you says that, you just tell her it doesn't matter. And you tell her that because it's the truth, at least right then. But now? Not so sure.

Still, I said, "Yeah, I can take it." Wrong again, Reno.

"Perry and Artie and *moi*. They were hugging me because that's what we did back then. They shared me, Harry. Sometimes one at a time, sometimes two at a time. I did whatever they wanted. And sometimes I surprised them with what I wanted done, what I was willing to ask them to do to me."

I might have blushed. No mirror around. So only a maybe.

"Don't look at me like that, Harry. It was a sixties vibe, for God's sake."

"It's okay, Jayne. I'm not judging." Her eyes said I was. Maybe so. I had Gwen's mom on my mind, remember?

"They were fun to be with. Lots of money to spend. On *moi*," she said. Yeah, lots of money. Jayne always liked that.

"But then things started to get a little too kinky, even for Jaynie Painie. That's what they called me back then, because I loved being hurt—I liked your boob pinch just now, Harry. Did I say thank you?"

She ran her tongue over her teeth. Oh God, why me? Why now? Why not?

"So they introduced me to cocaine, white snow, and then there wasn't anything I wouldn't do. We filmed a lot of it, Harry. I guess that stuff is still out there somewhere. Maybe old Walker-Doer still has some of the films." Snarl.

"Maybe the judge and that butler of his sit around and watch home movies from the good old days and jerk each other off." Roar.

Jayne wasn't soft anymore. Ramping herself up, getting loud. I put an arm around her, pressed a finger to her lips. "That's all right, babe, it's all right. It was a long time ago. Like you said, the sixties."

She cried again for a bit. I helped her dry her tears, and her story started up again—softer.

"Perry decided that it would be fun to have an initiation rite, a sex ritual, to confirm his new Lodge brothers. But not at that temple out in the lake. That came later. After *Ariadne* showed up." Whoa, snarling again.

How 'bout that? Imagine another female not liking our Lady DA.

"Perry's dad had built a maze inside his Lodge of the Labyrinth, in the basement—you know, the old building downtown. He put up some plaster columns to make it look like a Greek temple. Lots of twists and turns and spooky stuff everywhere. But after Ari died, Perry added something special—something really twisted." Her smile said she liked really twisted.

"What he had built for me—oh, Harry, God forgive me, but I loved what he had me do in that cow contraption of his. I just loved it." Really? Then why the tears?

I pulled her up off the bench, leading her away from the lakefront and onto a path that wound deep into the park's woods. Away from little kids and families and park bench widows. Jayne not smiling anymore. Bawling instead, crying her eyes out, ice melt everywhere, just like before, up at the cabin. Leading her away from the easily offended.

Harry Reno, the sensitive-to-a-fault gumshoe. Damn female mood swings.

57

COW TALES

After a bit of a stroll, we found another bench. This one wooden like before, but the path bare dirt now. I sat her down, finished drying her tears, yet again. I was beginning to get pretty good at it.

"Harry, it was fun." A sniffle. "I guess I'm ashamed to say it . . . No, I'm not, damn it." No tears anymore. "It *was* fun. I was young, I was beautiful, and I loved it. It made me feel powerful, in charge, all these horny old guys lusting after me.

"Hell, half of them never lasted long enough to get it inside me. Looks alone, Harry. My looks alone."

Yeah, and you still got 'em. I thought it. I just didn't trot it out. Safer that way.

"Strapped into Perry's contraption. They just came right then and there when they saw me lashed and buckled inside that cow skeleton, naked and ready for them. My bare ass, my boobs hanging down. Strapped there, facedown—writhing around."

Yeah, I bet they did.

"But I wore out my welcome. I got hooked on the coke. Turned unreliable, they said. Perry and Artie were kind, though. They made sure I dried out, made sure I got off what they'd fed me for so long. Buyer's remorse, I called it.

"Been easier to have killed me. Kinder, maybe. Look at me now, Harry. Look at me now." Tears came, but stopped just as quickly. A swipe of her hand—all gone. Crazy bitch.

"So when I dried out, when I came back, started working at the paper, I'd been replaced. The ritual had gone on without me. That's what the cow contraption was for, Perry's ritual. Artie and Perry had found a new girl." Jayne's hands holding both of mine.

"Gwen's mother, Harry. She became their new cowgirl." My heart stopped; started up again, ragged, skipping. "I'm sorry, Harry." Yeah, me too.

But I let it go for now. I had a job to do. For Gwen's mom. Not the cowgirl, but the one I had loved. Back then. By the lake. Here in this park.

We sat, still holding hands, communing over lost souls, perhaps. Finally, Jayne's eyes said she hadn't spilled everything yet.

So I pressed her gently—hard for Reno to do gentle, takes real effort. But Harry pulled it off there on that bench, deep in the park's greenwood. And I found the answers I'd avoided for so long. The reasons Gwen's mother died. The who and the why.

If I could believe what Jayne was spilling, that is.

"Oh, Harry, I might as well tell it all. I'm a dead woman no matter what. Perry and Artie, they had to replace Gwen's mother when she told them she wanted out. The crazy woman, your final proof, your star witness. The woman you and Gwen's mother went to interview that last day. The one who . . . who died.

"That's who Perry and Artie had replaced Gwen's mother with. When she'd taken all she could. In the rituals. In the cow."

My stomach tried doing a flip, a Tarzan swinging on the vines flip, a chasing Jane through the trees flip.

Then my grip on today slipped and I saw myself and Gwen's mother on the porch of the trailer. The crazy woman inside, waiting. Gwen's mother going in without me. The AC humming. The radio playing. The shots.

Then I was back in the park.

"That's who took her place when she said she wanted out." Jayne talking again; me listening.

"That's how they knew each other. Gwen's mother got her the part, convinced Perry and Artie she'd be the perfect replacement. And I think that's why they both died.

"The crazy woman blamed Gwen's mother for hooking her up inside that damn cow. So she shot Gwen's mother and then killed herself. I don't think it happened the other way, Harry—if that helps."

Now I had the why and maybe the how. Time for Harry's other big question.

"Who's Gwen's father, Jayne? Perry? Walker-Doer? One of the faceless labyrinth crowd?" My hand hard on her arm. "Who, Jayne?"

Wrong approach and I knew it. But I couldn't stop. I'd taken a hell of a blow. Gwen's mother strapped in that cow contraption, naked, screwing, loving it. Up to a point anyway.

Jayne pulled free. Or maybe I pushed her away. I don't remember.

"Let's go, Harry. You're getting tiresome. I want to go home now." I trotted out my rubbing act again. I might have pinched her—hard, then soft.

"Hey. You Jayne, me Cheetah. Remember?" We kissed.

"Yes, I remember. That was fun, wasn't it? I think I was in love with you. For a little while, anyway." This time she kissed me. Not all mood swings have to be bad, you know.

We stayed clasped together while I whispered my question again, "Who's Gwen's father, Jayne?" Harry's voice: soft; needy. "I'll be okay with whoever it is. I promise."

"Oh, Harry, I have to pee." Jayne's trademark shyness suddenly on display. Imagine, a woman who loved to fuck while strapped inside a fake cow carcass shyly asking if she could go pee. She even took a finger, touched a red nail to a white tooth.

I would have done anything for her right then—or to her. All she had to do was ask. My emotions not mine to control.

But we only walked on down the woodland path and found the old park pavilion in the clearing. A Ranger recon to make sure no stumblebums or raccoons were lurking inside.

"Sure you don't want to go back inside and watch me pee, Harry?"

"You go ahead," I said, "I'll watch the trees instead."

She laughed, flounced her skirt, smiling as she slid inside. They still hadn't soundproofed the place, so I walked back out into the clearing.

She wasn't in there long.

"Yuck, Harry. You could have wiped the seat for me." Jayne, just playful.

I smiled, told her I guess that I should have, not very gallant of me, not very thoughtful—or something close to that. I was fighting her magic, and she knew it.

"Now I don't want to go home, Harry. I just had to pee. Let's walk, find a cozy spot. Away from all these prying eyes." What eyes?

She flounced her skirt a little higher this time. Black lace panties? Maybe. Black for sure.

Jayne reached out, took my hand. We followed a path that led away from the pavilion and deeper into the trees. She kept holding my hand in hers, squeezing it ever so lightly as we walked, tickling my palm. Her magic flowing, stirring my insides.

I let it, damn it. I just let it. A witch's spells can be like that. Hard to resist, especially if you don't want to.

Above us, the sky was beginning to shade toward late afternoon, the sun settling into the trees. We found a flat rock—like Kipling's enchantresses, always lots of those around.

We sat, and I fired off more questions.

And while I did all that—there in the woods that afternoon—I ignored the prickly feeling skimming across my scalp, dismissed the vague idea of being watched, discounted my general feeling of impending danger.

Shouldn't have, but I did.

58

FULL DISCLOSURE

"You said Mallory knew something, Jayne. Something important enough for Perry to want her dead. What?" I waited. Nothing, so I tried again—softly, with a kiss or two or three.

"No prying eyes here," I said. "No ears except mine and this rock's. You said Mallory knew something about Stavros and what happened back then. What was it?"

Jayne turned, glanced up at the trees—the sunlight now thin, diffuse—and began to hurry her tale. Staring down at her hands, she said, "I told Mallory the why of Gwen's mother's death, Harry. Why the crazy woman killed her, why Perry needed the crazy woman dead."

She twined her long fingers together, each crimson thumbnail absently scratching the hand of its mate as she spoke. "But I fed Mallory more than just that, Harry. A whole lot more—and maybe some of it wasn't exactly true." Well, hell.

"What did you tell her?"

"I don't know if they were lies. I only know it might have happened the way I said it did." Jayne turned her head away, tear slivers sparkling in the sunlight filtering through the trees.

"What did you tell her?" I said again, still friendly. For now, anyhow.

"I told Mallory the crazy woman knew Perry put pressure on the cool DA to kill Rusty Neel, the drug dealer. And the crazy woman knew how Perry did it. I think Gwen's mom knew that, too." If Gwen's mother knew, why didn't she just tell me? Oh, the cowgirl gig. That's why.

"Damn it, Jayne. You're getting me confused. I thought the cool DA was the one trying to horn in on the Lodge's drug schemes, not Rusty the Druggie."

Was Jayne lying? Hard to catch a tell—her eyes stayed focused on the forest floor.

"Poor Old Harry. You and Mac thought Rusty was small time. Uh-uh. Rusty had connections. Way down south—in Dixieland." She touched my ear, ran a red-painted nail down my cheek. I shivered. Anyone would have.

"Rusty's murder was part of a three-way drug war in Kipling. Perry, Rusty, the cool DA," Jayne said. She wasn't making a lot of sense, and I'd lived it, investigated it, thought we'd cracked it wide open back then.

I said as much.

"Yeah, Harry. Whatever. You just missed the Perry connection."

Mac and I knew we'd missed something. That's why I went to interview the crazy broad with Gwen's mother.

"Tell me what I missed, Jayne." Simple, direct. Out it all came. But was it true?

"The cool DA taught a law class up at the college," she said. "You remember it? It's closed now. I bet it never figured into your investigation. You and Mac missed that, too, Harry. A nice college full of pretty coeds. Coeds who signed up for the cool DA's criminal law class in droves. Horny droves.

"Rusty Neel took classes up there, too. You couldn't miss him, driving around town in that red sports car of his, top down, that lion cub riding beside him—if he could keep a lion satisfied, think what he could do for your loins. I mean mine, Harry, not yours."

Her laugh, not mine—my thoughts drifting. My eyes on back then.

"Are you getting tired of me, Harry?" Jayne trailed red nails across the top of my hand, made sure she still had my attention—all my attention. Now she did.

Then I noticed the pearl dangling between her naked breasts. She'd unbuttoned her blouse, while I was busy not paying attention. And where the hell had her bra gone? Oh, the restroom in the pavilion. That's where. Harry Reno, the pinecone gumshoe, back on his game, paying attention. Sort of.

Jayne was babbling again.

"Perry had one girl in particular he knew he could use to drive a wedge between the cool DA and Rusty. A Greek girl. At the college.

"He had her come on to Rusty. Easy enough. Rusty was good-looking. Had plenty of pot. Liked girls, not boys. And the girl Perry used was a knockout. She just oozed sex."

Takes one to know one. Kept that to myself, though. Instead, my fingers flicked at the pearl, tweaked her bare nipples. Jayne smiled, cupped her hand over mine, kissed me, then went on with her tale.

"Perry made sure the Greek girl hooked up with the cool DA, too. Not hard there, either. The cool DA chased skirts, smoked pot. No secrets there, Harry. You and Mac detected that much, I suppose."

I offered her a shoulder shrug. Why give away what we hadn't known?

"There was a fight in the college parking lot—Rusty and the cool DA—over the Greek girl. Then she picked the cool DA over Rusty, because of the fight. Because Perry told her to."

"Why didn't Rusty get charged?" I asked.

"Because the cool DA started it," Jayne said. "Threw the first punch. All the witnesses agreed on that." Yeah, I'd missed that. Mac, too. If it really happened. Could have, but did it?

"Then the Greek girl convinced the cool DA that Rusty was out to kill him."

"You help with any of that, Jayne?" She ignored me. It was her tale and that's all she was hearing.

"Rusty went out of town, had the crazy woman watch his lion cub.

Well, the lion cub got out. The crazy woman let him loose. She had to," Jayne said.

"Why?"

"The cool DA had something on the crazy woman," Jayne said. "Something Perry had that Greek bitch give the cool DA, so he could force the crazy woman to let the lion cub out."

Greek bitch? Thought she was just some hot college chick.

"The sheriff fielded the complaints," Jayne said. "Rusty's lion was loose, in the park, scaring people. The sheriff called the district attorney's office. The cool DA said, 'Just shoot the damn cat.'

"So the deputies did, and dumped the body back at Rusty's farmhouse. It laid there in the heat for a couple of weeks until Rusty came back from down south. Crows, vultures. Must have been gross, Harry. Just gross." Jayne shuddered.

"We knew about the lion," I said. "That's the point Mac and I used to start our investigation. After Rusty came home, found his lion dead, he went to the sheriff's office, threatened everybody. Hit a deputy, said he was going to kill the cool DA.

"And then a couple of nights later, somebody blew Rusty's shit away. In his own driveway. And the cool DA said, 'So what? Drug deal gone wrong.'"

A glimpse of blue, or maybe something blue-green. In the trees. Then it was gone. Like the clues I'd missed all those years ago.

"That's when Mac and I were sent in to investigate. That's when Walker-Doer was brought in to prosecute. But you're right, Jayne. We didn't know the why behind the dead lion."

Jayne's periwinkle eyes flashed, lit from within with power, not laughter. She was enjoying leading Harry around, showing off what she had known all along, parading the clues Harry had missed. Letting him know he wasn't really all that sharp.

"Rusty's threat scared the cool DA," Jayne said. "Scared him because Perry's Greek bitch told him she knew Rusty was going to kill him. And soon."

Jayne's tongue peeked out from between her teeth, licked lips, darted back inside and started forming words again.

"She used her Greek body to convince the cool DA he had to kill Rusty first. Used it to get the cool DA's brother to do the actual killing. She had quite a body, Harry. Still does."

My mouth opened—nothing. It shut on its own.

"So that's how Perry got the cool DA to get his brother to kill Rusty Neel. How 'bout that, Harry?"

Yeah, how 'bout that. Damn. My mind was reeling.

Fifteen years ago we hadn't been able to figure out a simple murder-for-sex plot. And because of that, my pride led me to take Gwen's mother with me to interview the crazy broad. To let her see her ace detective in action. My goddamned fucking pride.

All that got me was the death of the cop I loved back then. And I wasn't doing much better now: Elke dead; Mallory dead; maybe the coroner was my fault, too.

Dizzy thoughts swarming. Fingers scratching at eons of rock. Enough. I inched back to the forest and Jayne. She'd started talking again while I was busy clawing granite.

59

A ROCKY RESOLUTION

"So I told Mallory that Ariadne, our Lady DA, was the mastermind behind the murder of Rusty the lion-loving drug dealer all those years ago," Jayne said.

"You did what? Wait a minute. Who? Ariadne? Stavros's wife? That's your Greek bitch? Back then and right now?" Harry Reno, still the detective in the dark.

Jayne cackled—no laughing anymore. "Some PI you are, Harry Reno." A fierce blue light poured from her eyes.

"Quit messing with me, Jayne. You're talking about Ariadne—the Lady DA—the fucking Mistress of the Labyrinth, the temple, whatever. Right?" My hand in the air, ready to slap—punch—hurt her. Why, I had no idea.

"Stop it, Harry." Jayne scared; sexy all but forgotten. "Please stop." My hand found hers. We sat beside each other, quiet for a bit. Maybe I was as crazy as she was.

"That wasn't her name back then, but it was her. I'm sure of it," Jayne said. "At least I think I am." Her fingers wandered through her hair; the tortoiseshell headband came off and back on. Her citrus scent floated between us.

"Yes. It was her then, and it's her now." Jayne ramping up. "After the cool DA left town and died, the Greek girl came back with a law degree and became Ariadne Stavros. Perry paid for it. I hate her, Harry. I do—I do—I do." Cobra spittle spotted my shirt.

"Yeah, I get it." Who don't you hate? I didn't bother asking. But was Ariadne really these two different women? Or was it all just a fantasy Jayne concocted to set up Mallory?

"What happened?" I asked. "With Mallory?"

"Mallory said she would write a story that would bring them all down, all at once. She told Tom all about it, too. And she might have done it, except Perry got wind of it. Somebody must have put a bug in his ear." Lot of bugs in Kipling. Lot of ears, too.

"Then Perry scared her so bad with the murder attempt at the cabin that she went into hiding. You know the rest," Jayne said.

"Who else did you tell this to?"

"Only Artie." Jayne tried out a little-girl pout, let red lips suck a red-tipped finger. Wasn't working. Not even with the bra-less look.

"What the hell, Jayne. Who the hell didn't you tell?" I screamed, fists clenched, ready to hurt her.

"So what if I told Walker-Doer? I had to tell. Had to, Harry." Her words spilling out fast now, her breath gasping, uneven. "I should have told you. I know that now." Jayne tried opening those periwinkle chambers to her soul, tried drawing me in.

Good luck with that, bitch. She kept trying anyway.

"I don't know who killed Mallory last night," she said. "Or had her killed, I mean. Doesn't matter. She's dead now, right?" Wrong time for her little-girl smile.

I said it sure as hell did matter.

"Well, she's stabbed in the back and gone now. That's all that matters," Jayne said. "Fucking little granola bitch. Stabbed in the back. Serves her right."

Stabbed in the back? Ariadne had told me the cops weren't released a cause of death yet. So Jayne must have killed Mallory, if she knew she'd been stabbed. I picked up a rock.

"I ought to bash your goddamn head in." Danger radiating from me—palpable.

Jayne started to touch me, drew back, realized her peril, hugged herself tight, fearing what I was threatening to do.

"You no-good bitch." The rock over my head, hard in my hand.

Jayne's mouth opening slightly, lips miming, *No, Harry. Please don't. Please don't kill me.* Her blouse floated open, making it hard to miss that pearl and her other two ornaments.

She cupped her breasts, blew a soft witch kiss up at me. The rock started down. Slowly.

Maybe I was wrong, reading too much into what she'd said. Maybe a sheriff's boy had rolled over this morning, said, *Stabbed in the back, Ms. Rask. That's how Mallory died. Oh, and you sure are good in the sack, Ms. Rask.*

Anyhow, her spell worked, if that's what it was. I threw the rock as far as I could into the trees, and sat down beside her.

Jayne said, "Kiss me, Harry," and I did. She knew me better than I knew myself.

We sat awhile with me holding her until her sobs subsided. I wasn't happy with myself and I sure as hell wasn't happy with her.

Did she stab Mallory? If not, how did she know how Mallory died? Or did she just make it up? Here in the woods. All of it. Including the cow shit. No way to tell. Not right now.

And what she had said so far about Stavros and the cool DA and Ariadne didn't make a whole lot of sense, didn't really tell me a complete story. Yeah, Ariadne Stavros was one hell of a sexy bitch. But the rest of it? I didn't know then, and I still don't. Not for sure anyway. Nobody left to ask.

"Finish your story, Jayne."

"Sorry, Harry. It all just gushed out, didn't it?"

All the while Jayne and I sat there on that rock—or danced around it—my Ranger instincts still floated at the edge of my consciousness.

A little while ago, down the path that led back to the pavilion, I'd caught a quick flash of color. Just a glimmer, but enough to alert me that maybe someone had decided to tail us. And just now. Was that the same blue-green? Not sure.

I reached for my gun—shit. Back in my motel room. Again a glimpse of blue-green, a man amidst the trees?

"Time for Jayne and Cheetah to make their way out of the jungle," I said, my shamus sense finally shoving us up and off the rock.

It happened so fast, I can only recall it now as if a home movie were clicking by in slow motion—one frame, then another, and another—just my own personal Zapruder flick.

Harry and Jayne stand up—Jayne takes a step away—looks right at Harry—smiles.

"I killed Mallory in the woods last night," she says.

The tortoiseshell headband off and back on—hair all neat and in place again.

"I stabbed her and killed her and I'm glad I did," Jayne says.

Then her left eye twitches—just a little periwinkle blink.

She's looking over Harry's shoulder.

Jayne's skull explodes.

A piece grazes Harry's cheek.

Brains and gore spray, speckling Harry with red dots and red blobs.

Then Harry hears the shot that did all of that.

Surprise on Harry's face along with the gore.

He hits the ground. On top of Jayne.

The ground around them red-wet.

Harry rolls off. Cradles what's left of Jayne.

He touches the crimson pearl on her chest. Then looks at his finger.

Finger red-tipped by blood pumped out by Jayne's now-silent heart.

Harry smooths her skirt.

At least that's what I remember—what I play over and over in my head every night. I sat there on the ground beside our rock and waited for a second shot to take me out. Didn't happen. And that was the end of my afternoon walk in the woods with the bewitching Ms. Rask. It was also the end of Jayne.

60

MOTEL MUSINGS—MORNING ACHES

Maybe John found us first. Don't know for sure. Never got around to asking. Medics checked me out, cleared me. One tried cleaning some of Jayne's gore away.

I remember brushing his hand aside, telling him, "Thank you, I'm just fine," but I wasn't. A detective took my statement anyway.

John loaded me into his cruiser—let me sit up front—stopped, bought me beer. A lot of beer. Dropped me off at the motel.

In my room, Harry and Reno took drunk—trying to figure out the whole bloody mess, but with only limited success.

Who killed Jayne? Who did Jayne kill? Or was it whom? Whom gave a shit. The beer flowed and Harry tried to out-drink Reno. Didn't work.

I was in bad shape. That I could get out of the recliner and walk to the sink for yet another beer staggered me. But so did the beer. I'd drunk a lot of them.

The little .38 rested on the table next to my beer. So far, I'd managed to keep the bottle mostly in my hand and the gun mostly on the table. Suicide? Thought about it. Just a trigger pull and then a short flight up or down—God's grace or the Devil's pitchfork.

"Yeah," I said, "you really are having a bad night, Reno. And you deserve it."

I shook my head, drank some more beer, said, "No, I don't, Harry. I don't deserve this any more than Jayne deserved her head exploding. That ruined both our days."

I stumbled to the bathroom, hit the shower. The hot water sobered me a little, rinsed some blackness from my soul. I toweled off, put on shorts and a T-shirt, and popped another beer. No use staying sober forever.

But why kill only Jayne? Why not me, too? No idea, so I moved on. The shooter—who? No firm idea, but I had a list of possibilities looping around.

Tom Kuster. Why not. If Jayne had stabbed Mallory, killed her in the cedar woods, that would give Tom reason to shoot Jayne. But why not just blow her brains out when she came to work? And a shot at that distance, in fading light? By a drunk? No, not the Tom I knew.

Willem the butler hovered in my head, there in the recliner. A professional hit man? Yeah, no doubts about that. A butler and a hit man. But why would he kill Jayne? *Dunno,* said the beer.

The hit reeked of professionalism, though. No beer doubts about that. Timed for a spot that left us far from help, far from prying eyes, alone and naked in the clearing with only a rock for cover. Perry's Pilot. Mr. Crew Cut. There was a professional.

And that's who my beer-soaked brain fixed on there in the motel room that night after Jayne had joined the body bag brigade.

Until the too-many beers slugged Harry and Reno, and down they both went.

I woke up the next morning to a headache. So I drank water, swallowed aspirins, munched stale crackers. Hit the shower again. Headache cured, sort of. It was a ritual I'd performed too often not to believe in it. It would work. If not right now, then eventually.

Outside, a cool breeze greeted me. Windows down, rolling as far as the motel office. Inside to see Karl. The little shit actually grinned when he saw me.

"Hello, Harry. How's it going? I just made some coffee. Want some?"

"Yeah, I do. Good coffee. Not the shit you stir with your dick." His smile evaporated. His *Harry* faded, too.

"Mr. Reno, please don't talk that way. I thought we were buddies."

"Don't whine. It pisses me off."

"Very well, Mr. Reno. It's just, well, I remembered something about Elke, about that night, and, well, I guess I just didn't think to tell you about it before now." The little shit smiled like that piece of news would renew our friendship.

I took steps to disabuse him of the idea.

Karl tried to shrink away. I grabbed him by the throat, frog-marched him backwards into the laundry room, and asked him what gives, holding out on a buddy.

When he didn't answer, I parked his ass in a folding chair. "Stay put," I said. He did.

I found a chair for myself, sat, rested my arms on the back of it, stared into Karl's beady eyes. His right one then his left one stared back at me for a moment, then both jerked away.

When Karl raised his head again, an obsequious hotelier's smile plastered his face, but the eyes wouldn't play along. Fear was busy dancing a jitterbug, with Doubt for a partner. Karl sure didn't like it when I put the hurt on him.

"Listen, you little shit, I'm not gonna be your friend for long if you don't tell me what you know when you know it. I don't need to hear about it later—understand?" He nodded his head. What the hell else could he do? "So what is it you forgot to tell me?"

"Elke wasn't working the ritual alone that night, Mr. Reno."

"Okay. And . . ."

"I never told you who the other girl was—you know, the other girl in the ritual, Mr. Reno."

I forked his nose between my knuckles, twisted my prize a bit, and listened in silence as Karl yelped. Yelped because it hurt, and yelped because he was too afraid not to yelp.

"It was Gwen, Mr. Reno. Gwen was the other handmaiden. Please don't hurt me."

"Sure thing, Karl, and call me Harry now, won't you?"

Karl stared, ashen-faced, Doubt jitterbugging with Fear once more. Then he decided I was friendly again and said, "All right."

"So why is that suddenly important?"

"I think they're going to use Gwen in the next ritual," he said. "And Brynn, too, Harry."

His *Harry* was still a shade tentative, but he was brightening up now that I'd stopped tweaking his nose.

"I think they're going to kill them both. No, I'm sure of it, Harry. They *are* going to kill them both. The next ritual is going to be a Final Ritual." Hard swallow. Mine, not his.

"When, Karl?"

"Saturday night. And Mr. S himself told me that this time it was a Final Ritual. Very important. Mr. Stavros himself told me that." Karl, self-inflating again.

"This Saturday?" I asked the little weasel.

"No. Mr. S himself told me a week from this coming Saturday. He said it would be a Final Ritual. That's what Mr. S himself informed me of, Harry."

Sounded rehearsed. I let it slide. Right into the deep black pit I'd used for all the other intel I'd gathered but couldn't fathom.

"And you're good with helping me make it Stavros's last Final Ritual?" I asked.

"Yes, Harry. I shall assist you in bringing his evil to an end. By myself, if need be. I loved Elke." Yeah, yeah, yeah. You'll get over it. Maybe.

"Okay, sounds good," I said. The little beady dots he used for eyes held my green peepers while he stuck out his paw to seal the deal.

We shook, and I told him, "See you soon, son," and left him to finish whatever it was he had been up to before I strolled in.

I couldn't trust those two dancing dots of his though; much less the sneaky brain peeking out through them. But right now, his offer to help was all I had.

I climbed into the Volvo, told her, “Sniff out some breakfast,” and off we rolled. Damn, but the little hula girl seemed unsettled this morning—maybe she was hungover hungry, too.

61
HARRY'S ENLIGHTENMENT

As I walked into the Hash House, I detected bacon frying, coffee brewing. And something burning.

"Damn it, Sam. You cremated the toast again." Alice's fury the screech of a freight train jumping the tracks. Her bony shoulders poking her head through the kitchen door while she chewed on her cook. God alone knew what it sounded like to poor Sam back there in the confines of the kitchen.

No chance to ask him, though. The diner's proprietress flung her foul mood my way. "You filthy swine." Maybe she meant the pork in the kitchen.

"Hi, Alice. Glad to see you, too."

"Like hell you're glad to see me." She gathered her anger, shoved it full in my face. I retreated toward the nearest booth. Alice stomped after me.

"And if you are, you soon won't be. Why in God's name didn't you pick the girls up last night?" Alice hammered Formica. "What was so god-awful important you left them up there at that perverted casino?"

Her hands clenched shut, popped open—then repeated their routine.

"Go ahead, Harry Reno. Tell me one of your man-made lies. Go on, you filthy, stinking swine." Well hell, she did mean me and not the bacon.

"I didn't show because I was with Jayne Rask when somebody killed her. That's where I was, Alice." I can do angry, too.

"I had to talk to the cops. They took me back to the motel. I wasn't in any shape to drive, no shape to do anything but sit in my room." I skipped the part about getting drunk. No use upsetting Alice even more.

It worked. She calmed down. Me, too.

"Sorry, Harry. I heard about Jayne. I didn't know you were with her. That's awful. But it's no excuse." Oh God, here we go again, I thought, but I thought wrong. Alice stayed calm.

"When you didn't show, Brynn said Sven gave her a ride home." Hands tucking hair back into place. Hers, not mine.

"I guess it wasn't as bad as I'm making it out to be. Brynn's home—in bed, asleep." One hand smoothing apron creases, the other hand clutching her order pad. "Sven was taking Gwen to her apartment, but he brought Brynn straight home first."

"What about Gwen? Was she still with him?" I asked.

Alice's hands on the table now, narrow body leaning in. "Yeah, she was." Eyes downcast, scanning for table crumbs, her kitchen towel wiping at something only she could see.

"You saw her?" I asked.

"No, but Brynn told me not to worry." Her eyes found mine, held them like the rest of Alice used to hold the rest of me—back then. After Gwen's mom. "They were just going to Gwen's apartment," Alice said.

"*They* being Sven and Gwen?" I asked. Pronouns, confusers of honest tales.

Before Alice could answer, the bells on the Hash House's door tinkled, and Lance strode in—all six foot six of him. He headed over, said, "Hi, Alice," stuck out a paw for me to shake.

"Breakfast before or after your shift, Officer?" With Lance, best to keep the questions simple. A hand ran across his cop-short bristle of hair. Maybe I shouldn't have given him choices. A spark of enlightenment flared in his eyes.

"Before, Harry. Just coming on. Alice makes sure I'm . . . what do you call it, Alice? Oh yeah, fueled up for the day." Pride lit his face. Perhaps because he'd remembered something so complicated. Poor dumb blue ox cop. Then Alice ruined his morning and, eventually, his life.

"Hey, dumbass. She was out with Sven last night. How'd you let that happen?"

"What? Who was, Alice? Who was with Sven last night?" Lance, genuinely puzzled.

"Gwen, you idiot. Sven took Gwen home from the casino last night. When Harry didn't bother to show up." Oh shit.

Lance's upper lip began twitching uncontrollably, then a tic squinted an eye. His neck turned red and his face followed suit. "Where's she at?" Lance clenched the giant hams that doubled as his fists.

"Try her apartment, you stupid fool." Lemonade Alice, never sugar-coating the truth.

The ox cop's giant frame shook, he spit on the floor, said, "Screw it," and stormed away. The Hash House's bells tinkled as merrily at his exit as they had at his entrance.

I swung onto Alice.

"He's liable to kill her. Or Sven. Or both of them. Is that what you want?"

No waiting for her answer. I didn't give a damn about Sven or Lance. I did about Gwen. I was up and out of the Hash House and running after Lance.

"Easy, big guy." My hand found his shoulder, tried slowing him down. "Let's talk."

"Fuck off, Reno." He brushed the hand away, opened his cruiser door. I slammed it shut.

"You trying to die, too?" Down I went, and stayed down. Damn ham-fisted blue ox cop.

When I finally raised my head to give it a shake, Lance and his cruiser had disappeared, the siren's wail already faint. I let my jaw move a little on its own. Still worked—not broken, just sore. But not as sore as the rest of me was with Alice. I headed back into the Hash House.

"What the hell did you do that for, Alice?"

"I don't know, Harry. I just don't know." She put her head down on the table, let tears dampen Formica.

Sam the cook stood in the kitchen door, drying his hands with a towel. A flick of his brown head indicated I should join him. So I did.

"She'll be all right, Harry. Just flip the Closed sign on the front door. I already called John. He's on his way to Gwen's."

"Why call John?" Something in Sam's eyes, a furtive glimmer, made me ask. But no, that wasn't right, not furtive. Something else.

"You don't know, do you, Harry?"

"You're right, Sam. I don't know what I don't know. So enlighten me." Pity. Maybe that's what I saw in Sam's eyes.

"John's Gwen's, well … he's . . ."

"What, Sam? Spit it out. What is he?"

"John's her father, Harry. Gwen's father. Always has been."

I must have sat down, because that's where I was when my brain started working again. On a stool at the diner's counter, sitting down. With Sam standing behind the counter, pushing a mug of coffee my way.

"What the hell," I heard myself say. "What the earthly hell."

"I guess we all just thought you knew. That he'd told you, or Gwen told you, or her mom did, you know, back then. Or you just figured it out on your own. You being a detective and all. Sorry." No sarcasm in Sam's voice, only concern mixing with contrition.

Sam the Hash House cook, the only for-sure honest man I'd met in Kipling. He hadn't known that I hadn't known.

We both stared at the counter for a bit while I sipped coffee. Finally, Sam spoke.

"How about I drive you over to Gwen's apartment. John won't let Lance hurt her." Sam the Hash House cook, a good and decent man.

A glance over at Alice. Crying, shoulders shaking, head wobbling back and forth in the cradle of her arms. So damn pitiful I dumped my anger back inside and stood up.

"Thanks, Sam. You take care of Alice. Just tell me where Gwen lives."

62

FATHER JOHN

The Volvo didn't know the way, and despite Sam's directions, I managed to get us lost.

The little hula girl thought it was funny, though. So I shoved her grass-skirted rear into the glove box. Could have sworn I heard her say *What the shit, Big Kahuna?* But might just have been my imagination. Tart-tongued little bitch.

After some serious backtracking, I made the right turn instead of the wrong turn, and we ended up at Gwen's apartment just as a city cop and one of the sheriff's posse led Lance out in cuffs. The big ox didn't seem happy, and neither did anyone else.

I parked at the curb and walked a little fast toward the apartments —a little too fast.

"Whoa there, pally. Police investigation. No civilians." God, but I hate *pally*.

"Sergeant Wetherall called me in," I said, and started toward the apartment.

The cop didn't fall for it. "Another step and you're under arrest."

I stopped, smiled, said, "Okay." Not the time to test the officer's patience; he didn't have it with him today.

Behind him, John was helping Gwen down the steps of her apartment building. Who I didn't see was Scandinavian Sven, the casino's Indian doorman.

Next to the apartment stood an ambulance, with its rear doors open and a gurney ready to be loaded. The gurney had a body on it—a live one, because the corpse that wasn't raised a hand and waved feebly at Gwen.

And she waved back between sobs—Father John glaring like he could kill them both, Gwen on the steps and Sven on the gurney. John held Gwen tight, steered her away from the ambulance and toward his patrol car. He saw me, nodded his head.

The officer said, "Halt." I kept going. I needed to hold her, too.

A hand grabbed my shoulder, started spinning me around. I let it, then hooked the hand's ankle and dumped the cop ass-first onto the blacktop.

Then I had one arm around Gwen and the other around John, hugging them both. Father John pulled himself free, guiding us toward his cruiser, shaking off his blue brother's attempt to arrest my progress.

I sat in back with Gwen. She put her head on my shoulder, sobbing, while I tried to hold her, my mouth mumbling inane ramblings like, "It'll be okay, sweetheart. I'm sure it'll all be okay."

Same words I'd said to her mother, while I'd tried to wipe the blood from her shattered face, all those years ago. John got us out of there fast.

When I finally pulled my mug out of Gwen's hair, I saw a fence topped with razor wire. The Kipling PD's cops-only lot. John herded us inside.

For a sergeant, he had a nice setup. Instead of a desk in the squad room, John had a true office: walls, a door, chairs to sit in, awards and pictures on the walls. His office looked a hell of a lot better than mine back in Ithaca. Big deal.

"Harry, I'm going to get us all some coffee. Why don't you and

Gwen just stay put. I'll be right back. You hungry, honey?" Gwen shook her head. I kept a smart-ass *Yes dear* to myself, and John headed off.

"He's your dad, isn't he, Gwen?" More crying. Smooth, Reno, real smooth. I handed her some tissues and waited for Father John to return.

A cup of coffee, a donut, and more tissues worked to dam Gwen's tear river, but it wouldn't last. She'd probably be bawling and mewing over Sven for the rest of the day, unless she was sleeping. Then she'd probably be dreaming about him. Scandinavian Indian, my ass.

"If Harry said something, I'm sure he didn't mean to upset you, honey. Right, Plain Old Harry?" John shot a hard stare my way. So he knew my nickname, so what.

"Gwen, I'm sorry," I said.

"It's okay, Harry." Her hand on my hand. "Really it is."

God, but she was beautiful that morning. Golden hair frolicked when she moved her head to look at me or John, and even the harsh florescent lights in her father's cop shop couldn't wash the glow from her skin.

But when I snapped to John instead, I just couldn't grasp it all. John's daughter. John the Cop. Sergeant Wetherall. Gwen's mother's man. Back then, before me. But after Stavros and Walker-Doer, and that damnable cow contraption. Did John know about the cow? Should I mention it? No. Definitely no. Not here. Not now. No cow. Still . . . .

I couldn't stay calm, so I didn't.

"Why didn't somebody tell me? How come you came to me for answers about your mom? Why not just ask him?" I pointed to John.

Gwen said, "Oh, Harry," and tears spurted again.

John stood up, gave her a fatherly kiss, clamped my arm in that steel vise of his. "Harry and I are going for more coffee." He leaned over, put the Kleenex box in her lap. "We'll be right back, honey. I love you."

John marched me down the hall to an empty interrogation room. In we went. I sat—he stood—I waited.

"You idiot," he said.

"Yeah, I hear that a lot."

"Must be a reason, Reno. Must be a reason."

"Yeah, there is," I said. "So what is it? Why did everybody but me know? Why everybody but Harry? Why, John?"

"Because you're too dumb to see the obvious, Reno. That's why. Back then and right now. That honest enough for you? Direct enough?" John had his arms folded across his chest, his mouth a tight line, lips barely opening as he spit out his words.

"I'm still lost, John. Help me out." Maybe it was my plaintive puss. Maybe it was John's innate goodness. Maybe it was just Kipling.

John told me what I didn't know. How he and Gwen's mom met, fell for each other. Why it didn't stay love for her, why they didn't stay together.

Then he told me how few or how many knew her backstory.

He finished up with, "I still loved her. She just didn't love me. And she'd met you. I stepped back, and you stepped in. Sometimes it's just like that, Harry. Sometimes it is."

John Wetherall, Kipling's decent man number two.

That morning, there in the Kipling Police Department interrogation room, John said, "What do you think? We stop Stavros, right? And shut down that damn temple." Neither of us told the other one no.

63

COFFEE WITH THE LADY DA

John and Gwen stayed put at the PD. Another cop ran me back to the Volvo. I headed toward Mickey D Land and more coffee. But first, I had a call to make.

The phone booth smelled like last night's wino had mistaken it for a urinal. I left the door open while I dialed the judge's number. Willem answered.

"We need to talk. Where the hell were you the other night?"

"Then by all means let us do so, Mr. Reno."

"The old crow's there with you, isn't he, Willem? He knows Mallory's dead, right? Jayne too?"

"Indeed, sir."

"How about I cruise by now?" That way I could at least grill butler boy and his boss about what Jayne Rask had said before her head exploded. Dead air. The butler's hand covering the mouthpiece while he consulted with his boss, no doubt.

"The judge will receive you at five, Mr. Reno. Do be prompt." *Click.* I'm a big boy. Things like that don't piss me off. Not much, anyway.

"Fuck it, Jayne can wait," I said, and kicked the phone booth door. Yeah, I felt all better now. Ponytailed bastard.

Back in the Volvo and headed toward coffee again.

As I stood in line inside the Golden Arches, "Harry Reno" floated softly in the air as equally soft fingers brushed my neck.

At least I didn't spill my coffee. But only because the tired-looking woman behind the counter hadn't entrusted me with any yet. I glanced over my shoulder to see who found me so irresistible. Oh, hell no.

Violet eyes, silver streaks in black hair, red lips slightly parted, revealing glistening-sharp teeth. A pointed tip of a tongue flicking out and back in, lizard-like. Fortunately, the lips weren't purple today.

And all of what was below that flicking tongue and those biting teeth was sheathed in a tight-fitting dress that bulged out and drew in at all the right places. High heels put her red smoochers and white biters and violet peepers even with my own equipment.

I flinched—I shuddered—I just couldn't help it.

"Hello, Plain Old Harry," the Lady DA said, her purring soft. "What a coincidence, you here, me here. Let's have coffee. My treat."

I tried saying *No*, but then I found myself in a booth with coffee and Ariadne—with her hand on my leg. Man, but the Lady DA worked fast.

"You get around, Harry. You seem to be right where the action is. Why haven't you been back to see poor lonely me?"

The Lady DA's black hair fell across her face, along with its silver frosting. Her lips in a pout, her hand working its way up my leg. I couldn't scrunch into the booth any farther, so I gave up and let her work another of her spells.

"Harry, you and I don't need to be enemies. Not here in Kipling. No Penny in Kipling, Plain Old Harry. No Penelope at all."

Her breath hot on my cheek, her hand rubbing closer and closer. Any moment now, she'd slip under the table, unzip my pants, and do what girls do under tables for twenty bucks. That's how heavy the Lady DA's come-on was.

But she didn't. What she did do, what she did say, unzipped me as much as if she had. "Perry wants you to go sailing with him today." Her lips kissed her finger; her finger pressed the kiss to my lips. " And I want you to go, too."

Visions of Ariadne in a black two-piece, or maybe just bikini bottoms, swirled in my head. I almost blurted out *All right.* But I didn't. Not yet, anyway.

"You going to be on board, too, Mrs. Stavros?"

"Harry, why so formal? So distant, so hostile?" Her hand gave up rubbing my leg and went right for it. What the hell was wrong with her?

I pushed her hand away as gently as I could. Didn't work.

"Okay. Ariadne, then. Why would I go sailing on Perry's boat? Even if you were on it—naked. Too easy to drop Plain Old Harry over the side."

I nabbed her hand, held it tight, made it behave. "Accidental drowning. Too bad, so sad. No, I think I'll keep my feet and the rest of me dry. No dice, Mrs. Stavros."

I turned loose of her hand.

And that should have been the end of it, but it didn't work out that way. Oh no, it sure didn't. Her hand was back again, working overtime.

"I'll stay here in Kipling, in my office," she purred. "That way you won't have to worry about evil old Ariadne making the mean men throw poor little Harry in the drink to drown."

Sounded more like *in the dwink to dwond.* Stupid, huh? Sexy as hell if you were the one in the booth with the Lady DA, though. And I was.

And as she said all that, Ariadne gave up stroking my leg and began teasing my ear and my neck. Nobody in the restaurant was paying the slightest attention to us. Maybe they were used to seeing their district attorney pick up guys in booths. Maybe just too polite to stare.

I don't know now and I sure as hell wasn't thinking about any of that right then. I was, however, still interested in staying alive.

"Same objection, Mrs. Stavros, whether you're on board or not. Harry overboard. End of Perry's problem. End of Harry. No thanks."

Once again, that should have settled the question of me sailing with Perry, since as I told Ariadne I wouldn't go, I was pushing my hip against hers, not quite shoving her out of the booth, but moving her along that way.

But it didn't settle anything at all. She just shoved back. And being the gentleman shamus I am, I let her.

"Perry has a business proposition to trot out, Harry. Something important for you to consider." Purring again, flicking fingers up and down my zipper. I forgot to say stop.

"He'd like a yes, but if you say no, Perry won't make you walk the plank. He won't be happy, but he won't be mad enough to kill you—I swear." A quick kiss to cement her promise.

So I said yes. "And you don't have to sequester yourself in your office."

"Oh goody, Harry. One o'clock. At the dock by the casino. Maybe Perry will show you my island. It's a fun place. I know you'd like it. But I'm so sorry, I have to be in court." Damn.

And with that, she honest to God licked my ear, her tongue darting and snaking as she cupped my chin with her hand. Then a kiss on the lips and she slithered out the door.

I took a sip of coffee, tried to figure out what had just happened. Unlike the gumshoe in the booth, the coffee was cold. I gave up and threw understanding away, along with the cup.

But at least I knew enough to take the little hula girl out of the glove box, restore her to her rightful place on the dash.

Anything to take my mind off the Lady DA.

64
GORILLA REPARTEE

At a quarter to one, the Volvo found herself a quiet spot under a tree and settled down in the shade for a nap. The tree where she'd stopped sat on the perimeter of the dock's parking lot. No yellow-lined spaces for muddy pickups with sagging boat trailers. Either you knew where to park or you didn't. Either you had a yacht in the water or you didn't.

I scored two didn'ts.

A tasteful iron fence, pointy and black, surrounded the parking lot, more for appearance than security. But enough protection so the little hula girl should feel safe. I left her on the dash and got out to stroll around.

Four very expensive toys rocked gently in their slips, held captive by mooring lines. No doubts about which one was Perry's. The biggest of the four sported ARIADNE in alternating red and black capitals across its stern. Then again, maybe it was hers, not his.

So, in the water sat Ariadne's yacht. Out in the lake sat Ariadne's island. On the island sat Ariadne's . . . Well, you get the idea. I was here to see the yacht, the lake, the island. And maybe Ariadne's labyrinth of a temple.

Why, I had no idea. Maybe the Stavros pair wanted to impress me, show me their grandeur that wasn't Greece. More likely, what they had in mind was intimidation.

Whichever, it sure was a perfect day to go sailing. Clouds skimmed across a cobalt blue heaven. Warm sunlight caressed my neck. A breeze, soft as a baby's cheek, snuggled and cuddled my face. And the slow, rhythmic slap of the waves promised a gentle time out on the lake today.

I sat on a bench and waited for Pericles Stavros.

At least I shook off my doze before Stavros had a chance to decide between waking me up or putting me to bed permanently—feet crunching across gravel woke me.

"Hello, shamus."

"Howdy do, sleazebag," I said and stood up, glancing around.

One of the Stavros gorilla tribe was shuffling around just off the path, knuckles almost brushing the ground. The clown in the red velvet chair, the one who'd been guarding the entrance to Perry's casino office.

He had a shotgun over his shoulder and his other hand gripped a gym bag with the handle of a tennis racket sticking out. Cans of balls in there, too. Trapshooting today out on the lake, maybe? With tennis balls instead of clay pigeons?

"Hey, King Kong. You giving tennis lessons today?" I asked, all friendly like.

"Watch your mouth, smart guy. The Boss don't like smart guys," the gorilla said.

"Undoubtedly why you're sailing with us today, Mr. Kong," I replied.

Stavros laughed; so did King Kong. Hell, you'd laugh too, if Perry signed your paycheck. But the gorilla bared his teeth as he chuckled.

"You always let him talk to your guests like that, Perry boy?"

"No, Harry. Only you. And only when Sven's not around to do it instead." Stavros reached over, patted King Kong's shoulder—no Sven today. No surprise there.

"This guy doesn't like it when somebody makes fun of him,

though" Stavros said. "Makes him mad. So be careful. The rest of us are harmless enough."

"I guess he stays mad a lot then, huh?" I said.

"Yeah, he does." Stavros grinned at me. "Try to be nicer to him. He's a good guy in a fight. Sometimes."

Okay. King Kong, one of the thugs in the Tam-O'-Shanter parking lot on a recent Sunday night. Now my face was wearing a smile, too. And my eyebrow didn't even seem to mind.

The rest of the boat party began crunching into view.

A guy about my height—gray hair cropped short—watching our exchange. His swim trunks were red and faded, his T-shirt black and faded and sleeveless—lean legs and arms corded with muscle poking out of his outfit. Scuffed boat shoes looking as if they really had seen sea duty, not just a sartorial affectation sported by a wannabe sailor.

A slight smile played across his face, pulling a corner of his mouth upward a bit, as if this whole exercise in tough-guy posturing merely amused him.

And in case we weren't up to the job of keeping him happy, he had a babe on each arm—ready, willing, and busty enough to make sure he stayed happy. Perry's Pilot, Mr. Crew Cut.

I shot a wink his way; a grin ricocheted back. What was it with guys grinning at me here in Kipling? I smiled back, just to be friendly.

Then my smile erased itself. The girl standing behind Crew Cut and his two dates. Tall, long-haired, blond, her white bikini straining to contain her top and her bottom—and both halves of the swimsuit failing miserably at their assigned tasks.

Gwen waved, tilted her head slightly, shrugged her shoulders as if to say . . . Hell, I don't know what she was trying to tell me. Guess she decided not to stay indoors mewling over Sven. Maybe the day wasn't going to be so perfect after all.

"Hey, shamus," Stavros said. "My wife says you're hard to figure when it comes to women. So I brought three along for us to play with. So nobody can complain they're lonely. Pick one." I shook a *no* his way.

Stavros walked over to Gwen, scrunched her rear, said, "Go keep

Reno happy." Gwen flashed a lopsided smile and linked her arm in mine. Her arm felt soft. My face felt hard.

"What about me, Boss?" the gorilla said. "There's only three girls and four of us. Five if you count Karl. But I don't think he likes girls. Right, Boss?"

Wow, the gorilla could count. Amazing. I told him so. The gorilla wasn't amused.

"No broads for you, King," Stavros said. "You can play wampum with your willie. When we ain't looking. We'll take care of the broads." The gorilla laughed. Paycheck funny, I guess.

"Let's get out on the lake—today," Stavros said. "Where's that little greasy creep Karl?"

"He's got ice chest duty, Boss," the gorilla said. "I told him to hurry, too."

"Well, go help him, King Kong," Stavros said, and laughed.

I tried hurrying him along, too. "Hey, Knuckle Dragger. Watch out hauling the cooler. Don't scrape those hairy hands of yours on the dock. You might get a splinter."

King Kong rounded on me, one fist balled, the other hand filled with a bait knife. Maybe not so tame after all.

"Don't call me names. Don't say stuff like that. I don't like it."

"Sorry, King. How about I get you a banana?"

That sent the gorilla over the edge. I blocked his wild swing and then sat him down hard on the dock. Just like I had in the Tam's parking lot. I took his knife away, too.

Crew Cut laughed, and Stavros muttered something about having to hire better help. The gorilla sat on his butt, rubbing his chin. Oh yeah, and he tried steely-eyed glaring, too. Like he wanted to kill me.

Stavros said, "Get your sorry monkey ass up. Go find Karl and the ice."

And miracles of miracles, he did it without complaint. Even with a *sure thing, Boss* smile. Maybe he was tame after all. Paycheck tame.

65
SWIM LESSONS

Once King Kong and Karl stowed the ice, the yacht and the party got under way. The gorilla took the wheel, Karl passed out beers, Stavros put his arm around the ginger-haired hooker, Crew Cut tried out the brunette.

And I sat in the stern with the semi-virtuous Gwen and her stuffed to the gills canvas tote.

The rush of the wind and the slap of the waves made it hard to hear your neighbor. The throbbing twin Mercs didn't help, either. So I leaned in close, and Gwen rested her head on my shoulder, let her breasts cuddle my arm. Hell of a thin bikini.

"What are you doing here on Stavros's boat? He's a thug, Gwen."

She pulled away, her face flashing hurt and a pout all at once. And no more boobs warming my arm.

"He's okay, Harry. He's nice to me. And I thought you'd be glad to see me. After the mess this morning." More hurt; more pouting. More hard nipples threatening to burst thin white fabric asunder. No wonder Father John worried about his daughter. No wonder at all.

"Look, the casino's a fun place. I get that," I said. "But it's not a good place. I don't like you working there."

"Now you sound just like Dad. Or Lance. And I hate him. Lance, not Dad." Gwen thrust her shoulders back for emphasis, her bikini top stretching, but still holding—thank God.

"I know I haven't been around to see you much," I said. "Except this morning. I'm sorry. It's just, I keep running into dead bodies."

Silence. Only waves slapping, twin Mercs throbbing, gulls screeching, and Gwen's frosty stare—which had a voice all its own. I tried a different tack.

"So where's Brynn today? How come she's not out here with us?" Wrong course.

"You'd rather have her here, wouldn't you? Instead of me. I knew it. I just effing knew it." Gwen brushed hair out of her face and started to cry.

So I hugged her close, whispered, "No, I only want to be with you."

She sighed, said, "Kiss me, Plain Old Harry," and I did. But I kept it light, Penelope. I swear I did, John. You know I did, Brynn. Sometimes I have to do distasteful things. When I'm working a case. Gwen's mother had understood that. So I know all of you would understand, too.

If only I did.

I kissed her again—just a lip brush. She smiled, tried gazing soulfully up into my face. What she saw I don't know. What I saw I did know. Her pupils weren't the least bit seaworthy.

"Did you take something, Gwen? Something for the cruise?"

"Oh, that. Perry gave me a little pill. He said I'd have more fun." She slipped a pair of sunglasses on. "We're having fun, aren't we? Without Brynn? Kiss me again, Plain Old Harry."

I did, but I wasn't having fun.

The gorilla sailed us out onto the lake, and Karl came by with beer. I took one, just to be polite. Gwen said, "No thanks," so I took hers, too. Never any harm in being too polite.

The sun felt good, the breeze blew worries away, and Gwen snuggled in closer and dozed awhile. Gave me a chance to try and figure out what Stavros was up to. And to drink my two beers.

After a bit, King Kong cut the throttles. The yacht slowed until we were just rocking in the gentle swell. The gorilla dropped anchor, and the girls did the same with their bikini tops. They all knew the drill, including Gwen. Not good. Really not good.

Stavros said, "Don't burn those titties," and motioned for me and Crew Cut to follow him below. So I did, after I checked out one of the other deck ornaments.

The ginger-haired hooker had perched herself on the padded platform aft of the cabin. She smiled, wiggled out of her bikini bottoms, and crooked a finger my way.

Like any of us, my virtue has limits when reality intrudes. But my reality right then was Stavros and his crew-cut Pilot. So look was all I did.

Down below, we sat around a tasteful teak table. I grabbed a coaster for my beer. So did Crew Cut. Stavros just plunked his beer down hard on the wood, amber brew wildcatting its way out of the can's service entrance. He pushed his coaster aside and started in on me.

"I like you, Reno," he said.

I told him I liked me, too.

"Your tough-guy act, that's good, too."

I politely informed my host it wasn't an act, rather my everyday jacket. And I felt comfortable wearing it whatever the company or the setting.

"How you treated my wife," he said, "well, that was okay, too. Ariadne needs that every once in a while." Which of the whiles? The bite or the coffee? I didn't ask.

Stavros belched, guzzled beer, belched again. "You're an odd guy, Reno. A small-time, cheap-ass PI. But you strut like you got steel balls and the world by its fucking tail."

I agreed with him on all he had said.

"So why mess in my shit? Every time you dip your cheapie shoes in the water around here, some broad ends up dead." Stavros finger-ticked the bodies off, one digit at a time.

"Look, Reno. Three of 'em. Elke in the alley—Mallory in the woods—Jayne in the park. Four, if you count Gwen's mother." That hurt. And yeah, she did count. More than all the others.

"And if you add in that crazy dame in the trailer, five." Stavros waggled four fingers and a thumb at me. "Plus that red-haired hooker in the cabin." The middle finger on his other hand shot up. "Six," Stavros said. His grin ear-to-ear.

For whatever reason, I was staying reasonably calm. Why, I had no idea.

"You couldn't figure that out back then, you can't get it through that concrete cranium of yours today. How come, Reno?"

A fair question, I admitted. So I simply informed Pericles that not knowing the truth, not understanding the whys and wherefores of our earthly existence, caused me sleepless nights. Therefore, I quested after the dragon to slay it and attain peace, if not also understanding.

He snorted at my little soliloquy. "Lay off the fucking smart-guy talk. I read Shakespeare. And older stuff. Latin and Greek. I'm a scholar of more than just the fucking law." Stavros puffing up, just like little Karl. "I move within the elite of society, yet I carry within me the savage past of my ancestors. Not that classical Greek shit, but the gods eating their own kids and enjoying the taste of the meat." He smiled. I didn't smile back.

"I just try to make it relevant in our modern-day, too-straitlaced world. And so far, I don't seem able to interest you in following the same path. Why the fuck not?"

I told him I admired his ability to be both earthy in his use of the copulation verb, and to be able to fool courtrooms full of people with his phony eloquence and manners.

"What about it, Reno? So you don't scare off. Every man has his price. What's it gonna cost for you to play my game? You wanna be my security chief? Run the drunks out of my casino? Make a shitload of money? Bang all the broads you want?"

Bet Ariadne made him say all of that. Probably bit him—just to be sure he remembered to offer me the make-believe job. Harry's poker face telegraphed Reno's answer.

Stavros didn't like it. So he leaned on me harder.

"Hey, I made sure that daughter of Alice's got a job at the casino, along with her buddy topside. So I'm a nice guy," Stavros said. "And I like your girls. All your girls."

Arms and smile spread wide. Stavros's bonhomie as phony as the bought-in-Kipling Hawaiian shirt he had on.

"That bimbo topside you're snuggling with—she's cute snatch, Reno—like her mom was." I stood up, fists balled. "So's that broad you sleep with back in Ithaca. Wouldn't want anything bad to happen to either of them." A wink.

I took a step nearer the smirking winker.

Now Crew Cut was standing, too. The yacht rocked gently. Stavros sat at the table, pleased as hell with his taunting.

"Go fuck yourself," I said. The fists stayed clenched, ready.

Stavros levered his bulk out of his chair—slowly, one pound at a time. "The judge must be paying you well, Harry, to take shit like that off of me." Still smiling—him, not me.

"Just joking, that's all," Stavros said, and play-punched my shoulder. "Come on, I'll show you my island. Hey, I need another beer."

The three of us went topside into dazzling sunshine bouncing off topless deck ornaments.

Karl was bent over, rummaging in the beer cooler. He straightened up, handed his boss a brew along with a smile.

Stavros took a sip, laughed. "Time for you to learn how to swim, little man. Gotta know how to swim if you're gonna crew on my boat." Karl's smile sidled away.

King Kong stepped behind Karl, Stavros nodded, and the gorilla tossed the little man overboard. Everyone laughed, except for me and Gwen. She was asleep in the sun—maybe burning her titties—and I just didn't think it was funny.

And neither did little Karl. "I can't swim. I'm gonna drown."

"Hey, Harry. Karl can't swim," Stavros said. "But he can't crew for me if he can't even dog paddle. So I'm giving Karl his first swim lesson." Stavros leaned over the rail. "How you doing, Karl?"

Laughter from everybody but me and my girl. Gwen stirred a little, tried opening her eyes. "Too bright," she murmured. Maybe she should buy bigger sunglasses. If they made such things.

"I'm gonna drown." Karl's plea ended in *gulp* instead of help as he swallowed sturgeon spit.

I snatched an orange life jacket and tossed it to Karl.

"If I do decide to sign on as your security chief, I'm sure you'd want me to show initiative. Right, Boss Man?"

Stavros stopped laughing, so everyone else followed suit. Then he grinned, and so did everyone else—except Karl. He was too busy trying to wiggle into the life jacket.

"Sure, Reno. Good job. Hey, King Kong. Let's circle the island. Show Reno the sights. We'll pick up Karl on the way back. Don't run over him."

Stavros leaned over the side again and waved at Karl, told him to practice his backstroke. We left the little man floating his worries away.

Then, finally, the hard sell. Stavros's arm around my shoulder, walking me away from the others, his voice low and slow.

"I could just put you over the side. Let you go for a swim. All alone. Someplace way out in the middle of nowhere. Like right over there." He pointed at water as distant from shore as the earth from the moon. No fake smiles now. Just tough-guy strutting. Still, kind of amusing.

"Too much to drink. Said he'd swim back," Stavros said. "Couldn't stop him. Over he went and down he went. Without any lead in him." Not very original, not very scary.

Stavros kept selling the hard line.

"Dear Penelope—Dear Gwen—Dear Brynn—So sorry—Love, Perry —P.S. See the three of you bitches again. Real soon—naked, maybe dead."

His eyes, my eyes, locked in tandem. My hand slow to his head, touching the white streak in his black pompadour. "Who the hell does your hair, Fatty?" He snorted. I walked away.

Eventually, even Pericles Stavros tired of showing off Ariadne's island, and we cruised back and picked up Karl. Really didn't see any improvement in his swimming skills. He was just drifting in the water, miserable and blue-lip cold.

King Kong headed us back to the dock. We never got to try blasting away at the gorilla's tennis balls. Or setting foot on Ariadne's island. Oh well.

I drank some more beer, cuddled with Gwen, tried figuring out why Stavros felt such a need to scare me. No luck.

Because something else had grabbed ahold of my head. Images I'd been suppressing. The island. That hard mound of pines and rocks. The one I sat on the beach and stared at. As the sun went down. The woman I loved next to me. The woman I'd let die.

And now instead of her beside me, I had my arm around the little kid I'd pushed on a swing in the park all those long years ago. Her daughter. All grown up.

At least Gwen put her top back on before we docked.

66

VICTORIA'S HOUSE—ROUND THREE

The Volvo still sat under her tree in the parking lot. I loaded Gwen into the front seat and got us the hell away from Stavros and his idea of a good time. Maybe I should have put the little hula girl in the glove box first. She and Gwen were bitch-glaring each other.

The Volvo cruised back to town, and we dropped Gwen at her apartment. I checked the time and decided to head out for my five o'clock with Walker-Doer and Willem.

The judge's gates stood open. The Volvo sailed on in, heading down that long, bone-white driveway leading the unsuspecting straight into the all-enfolding embrace of the old crow's wings and the tender mercies of his counterfeit butler. The unsuspecting. But not me. I'd visited before. Remember?

Like the driveway, Lincoln's steps were still there, too. I climbed them two at a time and rang the judge's bell. Round Three. The front doors opened, and there stood Willem.

"So where the hell were you the other night?" I said. "You know, when we went on that ghost run."

"Precisely where you would have desired me to be, Sir Harry."

I believed him. What choice did I have? We headed off in search of the judge. Willem led. Sir Harry followed.

The butler and his gray ponytail stopped at the library. No Crow's Nest today, thank God. Willem rapped his knuckles daintily on the closed door. A little too daintily. No answer. In we went —unbidden.

We crossed the polished wood and stepped onto the rug in front of the fireplace. A fire crackled. The judge still cold, I guess, in the good ole summertime. The red wing chair and its black cousin still hunkered down on the leopard skin. Just like last time. The judge snoozing in the red one.

Willem placed a hand on the old boy's shoulder. Really, more like two fingers. And that's all he needed to do. The old crow's eyes popped open, his head swiveled upwards, and the judge said, "Hello, Harry."

"Hello, Judge," I said, and sat down in the black chair—unbidden.

A glance at Willem, an indication I was going to reach inside my coat for something. He nodded his assent, and I pulled out an envelope, held it out for the judge.

Willem nabbed it instead. Damn, but the butler was quick. "I believe Mr. Reno desires to return his retainer, Your Honor. Unearned, as he probably imagines it."

"Harry, my boy. You have earned every penny of it," the judge said. "Well, almost. We still have a little unfinished business with that temple and its priest, don't we?" A chuckle of sorts slipped out from between his yellowed teeth.

The old crow almost giddy, instead of grief-stricken. He'd hired me to find and protect his niece, and it had turned into a classic Reno fuckup. Niece missing until she fished up dead.

So old Walker-Doer should have been mad as hell at me. Only his death's-head grin said the opposite. Maybe he was easy to read after all. The old boy was just a cold-hearted bastard who wanted his enemies dead. And now one of them was. Hell, maybe more than one. Mallory and his old tug-of-war pal, Jaynie Painie. Two ghosts gone a-glimmering for good now.

While all this was looping through my brain, Willem had slipped out, and now he came back, carrying the drinks tray.

"Put them on the table and sit with us, Willem," the judge said. "Yours is the position around which the plot must now pivot. We must all agree upon that, Harry. We must." Huh?

"Judge, I got to admit you've lost me. I waltz in here and try to return your retainer because I didn't earn it. Because somebody killed Mallory while I stumbled through the cedars. But instead of demanding your money back, plus interest, you're practically congratulating me on a job well done."

A swallow of gin and tonic trickled down my throat.

"Then this ponytailed character of yours brings the drinks, and you invite him to sit with us, not as a servant, not as an equal, but as the central character in whatever it is he's cooked up. "I know he's the bartender. Is he your chef, too?"

The old crow cackled and something approximating mirth escaped through his beak. "Oh, Harry, my lad. Dear Harry." The judge's grin ear-to-ear now. Still not a warm sort of smile—nothing you could toast marshmallows with.

"I admit it, Judge. You hired a bozo to investigate this whole mess. Maybe that's what you wanted from the start. A dumb-ass private eye who had his mind focused on other stuff, on other women. One who didn't really give a damn whether he found your niece or not."

I pressed on.

"But this beef-brained Sherlock somehow figured out he was being used. And not just by the guy paying his tab, but by every damn person he came in contact with up here in Kipling."

"Bravo, Harry. Bravo." One skeletal claw smacking against its mate. "You have solved it. The riddle of Kipling. Everyone does indeed use everyone else. Keeps us honest, Harry."

"Well, that's just great, Judge. Just great. It is great, isn't it—Billy?" Bogart stare Willem's way. Then a repeat tough-guy performance for the old crow there in his scarlet nest.

"He doesn't like it if I call him Billy. Does he ever let you call him Billy? Or Dutch? Well, does he, Judge?"

"Harry." This time the *Harry* came from Willem. And his *Harry* crept into our little tiff catlike, on soft paws.

"We are friends here, Sir Harry," the butler said. "One and all. United in purpose. United in allegiance. And we do not stand alone. More are with us. Together we will pull down this evil temple, pull it down upon the head of Pericles Stavros—if only metaphorically."

Metaphorically, huh? Maybe the meaning would come to me in a minute. Maybe look it up later. Maybe just slurp gin and tonic for now. Try to keep from looking stupid.

"But make no mistake, Sir Harry. Down the temple must come, and down it shall come."

Yeah, yeah, yeah. Willem did seem serious as a heart attack, though —figuratively speaking. There, I had it—*figuratively-metaphorically*. Good old gin and tonic. Better than my OED any day.

Walker-Doer nodded his head, said, "It was your idea from the start, Willem. Let it be all yours at the end. Tell Harry."

So the butler did.

67

THE BUTLER'S TALE

"Harry, I was what you would call a high muckety-muck in Perry's sacred Lodge. I was not, thank God, the Grand High Pooh-Bah. Just a nabob, if you will." Oh, shit. This was going to be awful. I didn't say it, I just thought it. Still—

"I don't mean to interrupt you, Willem, but is this going to be a long tale? Can we maybe have another round, before you really get into it?"

"An excellent request," the butler said. "Judge?"

The old crow nodded, held up a finger. "You may keep mine coming, Willem. But light on the gin, long on the tonic."

"And yours, Sir Harry?" the butler said. Damn if he wasn't grinning at me again. And now the judge sat there watching him do it.

"Make mine match yours, Billy."

"As you wish, Sir Harry."

Willem wasn't gone long. The drinks came back, along with a bowl of corn nuts. Who the hell eats corn nuts, I almost asked. No need. An old crow, of course. Crows like corn. Then how come the old crow wasn't sipping Old Crow? Maybe the judge wasn't a whiskey man. Whatever, the corn nuts were tasty—homemade. And while the old crow's refill stayed gin and tonic, mine and the butler's had morphed into a good old summertime Tom Collins apiece. Willem, man of unlimited talents.

"Harry, I really was what you would call a high muckety-muck in Perry's sacred Lodge."

Oh God, he really wasn't going to let up. He'd said it once already. Bet if I interrupted him to tell him that, he'd just start back over at the beginning a third time—so I didn't. I swallowed a slug of Tom instead. And a bit of Collins, too. Willem bore on.

"As high muckety-muck, I have played the part of Minotaur in the rituals over the years—the chap who shags the Mistress of the Labyrinth, as it were." Well, hell, that's why he grins so much.

"As Minotaur, I participated in all Rituals, both First Rites and Finals. Until I took exception to the ritual murder aspect. And the filming thereof."

Ritual murder? Filming it? Huh—oh, I get it. Karl's nonsense. I didn't say any of that. I guess I didn't have to. Me and my damn poker face.

"You appear shocked, Sir Harry," Willem said.

"Yeah, yeah, yeah. Whatever. Ritual murder, huh? You mean something Satanic? Human sacrifice? A Black Mass or something?"

"No, Harry, my boy," the judge said. "Something far older than any perversion of Catholic rites. Something predating our ideas of Satan. Mythic truths from antiquity." The judge slurped the last of his drink. "Please enlighten Harry, won't you, Willem?"

"Of course, Your Honor," the butler said. And man, did he ever. The Dutchman was quite the storyteller.

"Whilst the rituals remained sex only," Willem said, "I participated willingly. And so did all involved. The new inductees into the cult of the Mistress of the Labyrinth, her handmaidens, the priest, the guides, Pan, and of course the mistress herself. All willing, all glad they were a part of something ancient and greater than themselves."

Willem glanced away from the low fire slumbering in the grate and winked at me. If he'd just let me in on some inside joke, well, I'd missed it. He poked the logs, steepled his fingers, and continued his tale.

"The videotaping served as blackmail if an aspirant—remember, that is the term for a new inductee—went astray. The tapes served as a way to bring wanderers back into the fold.

"Of course, sometimes wanderers strayed too far from the flock. Such wanderings were discouraged. Terminated. With extreme prejudice, as the movie phrase goes."

Movies, huh? Don't know anything about that. But I'll give Willem this much. His *extreme prejudice* was as prosaic as a president on tape ordering a hit on another head of state. No emotion in the butler's voice, just the necessity of the act bleeding through.

"Gradually, however, Pericles Stavros and his wife, Ariadne, began to introduce elements into the rituals that raised concerns. A shift occurred, Sir Harry. The Final Rituals assumed an additional purpose. One neither I nor the judge approved of.

"So I ceased to play the part of Minotaur. Indeed, I ceased to play any part at all." The butler's head swiveled a degree or three toward the red chair. "I believe that precipitated the fatal break. Would not you agree, Your Honor?"

"Yes, Willem. It happened exactly as you say. You omit, however, the fact of the Pilot assuming your role as Minotaur."

"I did not omit, Your Honor. I simply have not reached that point in our narrative."

"Oh. Of course, Willem. Of course." My God, I'd never seen the old crow so docile. He'd be eating corn nuts out of his butler's hand next. Who the hell was this Willem, anyway?

"As the judge points out, the Pilot assumed my role in the rituals. And, increasingly, my role in the Stavros organization. Until I had nothing left to do but to play the butler, so to speak. And so I have. Even unto this day, Sir Harry."

"Okay. I'll bite," I said. "What did the Stavros pair do to piss you off, Willem?"

"They began to slay the handmaidens as part of their Final Rituals, and to sell the videos. Snuff films, I believe you Americans style them."

And when he glanced sideways at me this time, Willem didn't grin, didn't wink. The look on his face made me glad he was on my side. At least, I hoped he was on my side. I still wasn't completely sure. But I hoped so. Of that, I was sure—completely sure.

"So that's what drove you out into the wilderness. Right?"

"Indeed, Sir Harry. Cast out into the Wilderness, as you so eloquently phrase it." Only Willem's *wilderness* had a capital *W*. Guess he wandered in an even bleaker landscape than I'd imagined.

I didn't want to, but I had to ask. "Tell me how this ritual shit works, Willem."

"Would you like a detailed explanation, Sir Harry?"

"Not really. Unless you think I need it."

"Perhaps not." He considered this for a beat or two, then rolled on.

"We, the procession that is, assemble on the beach under flaring torches. Thence to the island on the Stavros yacht—the one you sailed on today." No secret there. But gotta wonder how much you know about the yacht's deck ornaments, Willem. Probably plenty.

"Pericles plays the part of the priest. Care to know what he wears?"

"No," I said.

"The role of Pan is played by Dewey. He wears—"

"Yeah, yeah, yeah. He's the goat man. Get on with it, will you."

"You've met the Pilot—the Minotaur on ritual nights. His costume is mostly himself, except for the bull mask," Willem said.

"Yeah, but it probably musses his hair."

"A delicate touch, Sir Harry. Delicate indeed."

"Okay, so Crew Cut plays the bull now," I said. "Who else goes along for the party?"

"Aspirants, those wishing to delve further into the arcane mysteries of the Temple of the Labyrinth. Usually two, Sir Harry. Aspirants, not mysteries. They wear—"

"Skip that part," I said.

"Very well. As you wish. The guides—guards if you will—accompany them. Clothed appropriately . . ." Willem paused, gazed at the fire a moment. "In black and red," he said quickly, and grinned.

Damn, the butler had slipped some description in on me anyway—and I knew to watch him. Double damn.

"After proper invocations, the procession passes into the woods on the island and wends its way up the hill to the temple. Karl's job is to light torches."

"Yeah, Willem, he's told me all about it. I know the broads get naked, too."

"Oh, Sir Harry. Surely you desire me to describe that?"

"No, maybe I'll see it for myself."

"Indeed." Willem rose, freshened my drink and his, and then returned to his tale. The judge was sound asleep, snoring.

"Once inside, the merriment increases. Strange noises, weird lights, the Minotaur running about helter-skelter. Solemn oaths sworn, potions consumed, women ravished." A grin lit the butler's face once more. "Descriptions, Sir Harry?"

"No," I said.

"Here I must beg to differ. The couches—the ritual platforms upon which the handmaidens recline—are important. We may perhaps need rescue Gwen and Brynn from their ravishing softness."

"Okay." So I'd have to listen to it. Didn't mean I had to like it.

"The couches are *X*-shaped, each handmaiden spread-eagled thereon. These couches—and the handmaidens themselves—may be positioned hydraulically, as in a dentist's chair, for ease of access. So an aspirant need only stroll up to penetrate a handmaiden at the most agreeable height. So she is drilled most precisely. Up, down, then in and out, in and out, over and over until exhaustion sets in, so to speak."

I stood up, pointed a finger at the butler. "Enough, Willem." I sat back down, point made. Or so I thought.

"At the end of the in-and-out fun, each aspirant must make a choice—plunge a ritual dagger into the young woman he has just penetrated with his . . ."

"Yeah, I get it. The broad he just nailed," I said.

Willem fixed his eyes on mine—his voice cold now, like the steel in his eyes. "Your description of *just nailed* would fit Gwen, perhaps Brynn, too," he said.

I came out of my chair, fist cocked, rage reddening my soul. "You fucking fake limey bastard." Willem threw his drink in my face. And that was the end of it. He was right. I needed to hear this. I said so.

"We must work together, not against one another," the butler said. Willem handed me a towel. Maybe he'd had it up his sleeve.

"Yeah, I know. I said I was sorry." Ponytailed bastard would have just laid me out. I knew it. He knew it.

The butler scooped up the drinks tray and the wet towel, and headed out the library door.

68

RITUAL REVELATIONS

Willem returned with java instead of gin. But just for two. The old crow had slept through my little fit and didn't require a change of pace. The judge snored; we pressed on.

"So what happens at that point, Willem—the point of the dagger, that is."

"The girl dies or she doesn't." Well, no shit. I tried again.

"A little more detail, Willem, if you please." The smallest of smiles twitched the butler's mouth.

"If it is not a Final Ritual, the girl never dies." Willem stopped. "Unless an accident ensues or good cause arises." Elke. Maybe he meant Elke.

"Okay, I give," I said. "Fill it all in, if that's what you have to do." Oh, that made him happy, that damn grin of his ear-to-ear. "But keep it short, okay?"

"If it is not a Final Ritual, Sir Harry, if it is in fact but First Rites, and the aspirant does not stab his handmaiden, he is congratulated on completing the ritual. And that is as far as he goes in the Lodge of the Labyrinth. He remains a member, but his usefulness is denoted by a metaphorical asterisk, so to speak. One that precludes advancement. Or added wealth."

Willem, just keeping it short. And that grin of his just staying plastered where it was.

"If, however," he said, "the young lady is indeed stabbed, then it is revealed that a prank has been perpetrated. The aspirant has only pierced a sheep's stomach filled with theatrical blood. The handmaiden has slipped off her couch—Ariadne prefers *altar*—before the aspirant drives home his blade. Gory, but harmless. And the aspirant moves on up in the Lodge."

Willem's gray eyes gunmetal-hard again. "A Final Ritual ends differently, though. The handmaiden does die. Unless the aspirant balks at the deed."

"Did you maybe leave something out, Willem?" I waited—nothing.

Ponytailed abomination. I said it to his face. Just tired of saying *bastard*. He took it well and started back up again.

"You did ask for a limited narration, Sir Harry. Remember?"

"Damn it. Go ahead. Tell me the details. All of them. Okay?"

"As you wish. In a Final Ritual—unlike a First Rite—the handmaiden is restrained on her couch. She cannot simply roll off and survive. And, the aspirant is inside her as he makes his choice. Not so in his previous ritual encounter.

"One hand clutches the upraised dagger, his other hand rests on her heaving middle—no sheep's stomach in a Final. If the aspirant chooses to slit her open, she dies.

"If the deed is not performed, she dies soon enough. Whilst the aspirant soon crosses the River Styx as well."

"And that's what you used to do—play Charon, help ferry them across."

"My compliments, Sir Harry. Hades's ferryman indeed. Your words, however, not mine." I noticed he didn't say no. I knew he was a killer. So what. We'd need one for this business.

"How do you keep the, what . . . aspirants from seeing what's going on?" I asked.

"The aspirants wear a helmet whose visor obscures their vision so they cannot see. Not in either version of a ritual. Until in a Final, the helm's visor is raised, and the aspirant sees his victim cuffed to the couch. A conscious choice, as it were, to step over the moral line and do murder," the butler said. Okay, the Reno poker face understood it now.

"What about the girls—can they see what's happening?"

"Yes."

I thought a moment, then said, "They must catch on that something's different, right, Willem? In a Final. Getting strapped down wasn't a part of the deal before."

"Indeed, Sir Harry."

"So?"

"So Ariadne tells them not to worry. Just part of the Final's fun. A gag ball muffles any eventual protests. The more they writhe, the more aroused all become. And the handmaidens only experience final fun once, remember? Whether they survive or die."

So the Lady DA tells the girls not to worry. And they buy it. Imagine that. Maybe she lets them snort a bit of incentive first.

"In either eventuality, the mistress wishes this to be a permanent dismissal for the beauties in her pageant," the butler said.

At least my dismissal had only involved a bite and a temporary jail cell. Nothing too permanent. Not yet, anyway. Bet the Lady DA had something in mind, though. Kinky bitch.

"How do they get rid of the bodies?" I asked. "Now that you're out of it."

"The ones who are not sacrificed upon the altar become like Elke in the alley. Karl burns the other young maidens—the holy hecatombs the aspirants do stab—at the crematorium out by the lake. Dewey assists him."

I'd had enough. I told him so.

"No," he said. "The Minotaur and the mistress. You must know their functions, also."

"Okay, I give. What do the Pilot and Ariadne do?"

"He fucks her," Willem said.

I knew the answer. Still, I asked, "How?"

"Do you know King Minos and the legend of his Labyrinth? The artifice of Daedalus that helped conceive the Minotaur?" Willem asked.

"Been a while," I said.

"Well then, Sir Harry. Do read up when the chance presents itself. But for our purposes now, the Mistress of the Labyrinth is strapped inside a surrogate bovine—a skeletal cow. Strapped in and suspended facedown, naked, for ease of access, as it were."

So that's where Perry the Priest got his cow idea. Greek myth. And that's where Gwen's mother had been. In Perry's cow.

Willem's face was easy to read now. No longer playing the part of Minotaur, but still longing for the *ease of access* gig. The Pilot doing the mistress now, not Willem. And Dutch didn't like that much.

"She is quite delicious, Sir Harry. Quite delicious." Yeah, I knew something about that myself. Sort of embarrassing—both times.

"Okay, what's their function, besides fucking?" I asked.

"They saturate the temple with their lust," the butler said. End of story. Thank God.

The fire in the grate had roared itself into ashes while the butler spun his tale of bulls and goats, mistresses and maidens, marble temples and torch-lit woods.

"So where does that leave us, Willem? What do we do now—wait, I know. We bring down the temple. Just metaphorically, of course. But how do you propose to do it? Metaphorically speaking."

"An inside job, Sir Harry. I may be wandering in the Wilderness, but I am still needed at times," the butler said. "And we shall manufacture one such occasion. You and I, and certain others of our allies. And here is how we shall accomplish it."

The explanation took a while. I had questions; he had answers. He had questions; I had answers. The judge, thank God, kept silent—still dozing. He'd swallowed a lot of gin for an old crow. The butler and I had switched to coffee, remember?

I didn't like any of it. I told him so.

"So much so, it makes a difference joining together to bring down the temple, to save Brynn and Gwen?" Willem asked.

I guess it didn't.

So we shook on it. I still didn't like it. Just not so much that I was willing to pull a Pontius Pilate and wash my hands of it.

The old crow stirred, opened his rheumy eyes, said, "Metaphorically, Harry, my lad, only metaphorically." Well, shit, maybe he'd been awake all along.

Willem walked with me to the judge's front doors. Walked, not led. I commented on the change.

"Partners in crime, Sir Harry," he said. "Perhaps bring Tom along to our upcoming conference at the Tam—keeping enemies close, as it were. He has reconciled himself to Jayne's demise rather quickly, I believe. And John Wetherall, bring him also. A good man. Good indeed." I didn't and couldn't disagree.

"Now hie thee hence to Ithaca." He grinned when he said it. Of course he did. "And whilst there, please do tell Iron Mac that Dutch said hello."

And with that, Willem shut the doors in my face yet again. What the hell? So the butler knew my old boss. I'd have figured it out eventually—maybe.

The judge's gates still stood open, but I didn't cruise on through. Instead, I stopped, craned my head out, took a closer gander at the two guys atop their pillars.

The bull man still puffed out his chest and glared. The goat man leered and played his panpipe, just like before. Comical stuff to a casual visitor, to someone just driving by on the way to somewhere else. Two odd-looking statutes, perched up there at the whim of the eccentric owner of whatever lay beyond the gate. Only whimsy, that's all.

Harry Reno knew better now, though. Knew what those two did when they weren't at home. I'm no prude, but what went on out on the island in the lake, well—what went on wasn't nice. It had to stop.

And I had to be the one to stop it. With a little help from my friends. If I had any.

69

HARRY'S THURSDAY NIGHT DILEMMA

After all the corn nuts and coffee, I needed steak and wanted beer. So the Volvo took me to the Tam, and Gus fed me. Between bites, I filled him in on the meeting with the butler and his judge. But I left out Willem's Sir Harry nonsense.

Gus asked me if I had any plans for tonight. Before I could answer, the phone rang down at the end of the bar, and he answered it.

"Harry. It's Brynn. Says she wants you."

When the bartender finally quit chuckling, he handed me the phone, and I said, "Hi, babe." Brynn's whispered response drifted into my ear on a sultry breeze that set me quaking and reaching for beer.

But the brew hitched in my throat as she said, "You don't need to pick me up tonight. I bought a car, a Mustang. I can drive myself home." Phantom hands socking my gut. "But can I come by the motel? I'm getting off early." Hot damn.

"Sure," I said. Even made the word sound like I was back under control. I wasn't. Only now anticipation instead of the old one-two punch roiling my world.

"Good. Mom said it's okay," she said, and hung up.

Brynn's *good* had had one hell of a sexy purr to it. Bet Alice didn't okay that. So what? At least the phantom hands drifted away.

"Gotta go, Gus," I said. "Headed back to Ithaca in the morning. I'll be back sometime next week. Then we'll make our plans."

"I know. And dinner's on the house tonight, Sir Harry." Hmm, maybe the bartender had talked to the butler already. Trading Tom Collins insights, no doubt.

Back in my room, I tidied up the bachelor pad the best I could. Brynn and the Perplexed PI were getting to be old hands at this. All those midnight rendezvous up at the casino. We'd realized right off that—well, we'd danced all around it is what we'd done so far.

We both knew we had to boogie one way or the other eventually. Heat up or cool down. And sooner rather than later.

A car pulled up. A door shut. I checked the peephole. Made sure it was Brynn and just Brynn and opened the door.

She sat on the bed. I sat in the recliner. We talked.

She told me how she didn't really like working at the casino, but Gwen seemed to love it. And the other stuff that went with it. The island temple gigs and cruising on the lake.

"Gwen's done two of those things, Harry. She calls them First Rites. Out on the island. She said they're fun. And Mr. Stavros gives you a lot of money to do them."

Brynn's hair kept falling across her face. I tried brushing it out of the way for her. Teeth snapped at my hand. But only playfully.

"She told me it wasn't much different than backseat screwing—you know, like in high school," Brynn said. "Just with older guys. Classier, though. The boat, the yacht, I mean. And that Greek stuff." A flick of her head, a snort of disgust. Seemed Brynn didn't agree with her friend Gwen's idea of a good time. Well, neither did I.

"Gwen wants me to be in a ritual with her. Real soon. I guess because Elke's dead. I don't want to, Harry. Gwen might like that stuff, but I don't." Oh God, those forest eyes, shinning virtuously bright, shoulders thrust back, daring the world to disagree.

Well, hell. Here was a beautiful young woman ready to quit the sordid life before she really got started, maybe even ready for something with Plain Old Harry. And I was about to foul it all up because Harry Reno, shamus-by-the-lake, had a special part he needed her to play.

My dilemma—was I asking her to do this for me, or for herself, or for Gwen? I knew the answer. I just didn't like it.

So I told her about the plan to topple the Temple of the Labyrinth and why it was important, how it could save Gwen and a lot of other girls. I told her about the snuff films. Thank God, I had to explain what a snuff film was. She'd had no idea.

I didn't tell Brynn the whole plan, just what we needed her to do.

"No need to tell Gwen anything," I said. It sounded as if Gwen would know what to do without being told. Just get naked and hope Harry keeps you alive. Simple. That was the plan. For both girls.

"I'll do it," Brynn said. She stood up and smiled. My conscience ticked over. I ignored it.

"That means you're going to have to see me naked, Harry. I wouldn't want you to forget what you're supposed to do to topple that old temple, just because you'd be seeing me naked."

She pulled her top up and off. My God. My conscience. At least she was wearing a bra.

"Brynn, not tonight." She threw a major pout my way. My hand running through her hair, soothing girl, stirring detective.

"Let's wait," I said. "Until after the island." My fingers tracing the outline of her barely contained breasts. "I won't let them touch you. And Stavros won't be able to do this anymore after we're through with him." Something finally clicked. I stepped back, made my fingers stop their fantasizing.

"And now that I've seen some of what I'll see on the island," I trotted out a Harry-size smile, "I won't fall over dead." Like hell I wouldn't. Her hazel eyes were big, too.

I kissed her. Lightly. On the top of her head. Her breasts brushed my chest. Her pout was gone. She was laughing again as she hugged me.

"I think I understand," Brynn said. "You're sweet." Sweet I might be, but I sure didn't understand why I was telling her not tonight.

Then again, when I'd kissed her, I'd caught a glimpse of Penelope standing there. Not really, of course, but my brain put her there. I'd blinked, and Penny had disappeared from my sight, but not from my head.

To make up for Brynn's disappointment, I said we'd still spend the night together. I told her the bed was hers. The recliner was mine. But first, some TV. More pouting. But that's how we did it. Or rather, how we didn't do it again.

But she left her blouse off. I'm not perfect, but I do work at it. I covered the girl and her bra with a blanket and settled in to watch whatever she wanted and needed to watch.

I woke up early with last night's decision haunting me—the insistent refrain from that new cop reality show Brynn liked still swirling in my brain. What would I do when they came for me? And who exactly would *they* be?

I had no answers. All I knew for sure was I had promised Mac I'd go sailing with him and bring Penny on Friday after work. And be kind to her, too.

But that had been a while ago. Right now, with Brynn in the bed, sailing with Penny sure didn't seem like something I wanted to do.

Other thoughts snapped in my mind.

Two dead women: Mallory and Jayne. And before that, Elke in the alley. And Lacie Doyle—the I-Screw-Do-U chick, crisped in the cabin. They all counted for something. And before all of them, my star witness in the trailer. And Gwen's mom. No way to put a price on her death.

And now this live woman still asleep here in my room. Couldn't let anything like that happen to her. I just couldn't. What the hell. I'd told Iron Mac I'd be in Ithaca. Our plan needed his help. Harry and Penny would just have to worry about themselves. We had before.

I left Brynn a note. *Sorry about the nightmare. Sure didn't mean to scare you. I just get them sometimes. Nothing to worry about— Hey! Gotta go sleuth. Back in a few days. Watch yourself. Stay safe. I love you.*

Or something equally eloquent. Hard to remember. I slipped outside and drove away.

70
SATURDAY NIGHT CASINO SCHEMES

Pericles Stavros wiped his mouth with his napkin and belched. "You want any of this?" he asked the Pilot.

"No."

"Hey—you. Get this shit out of here. I'm full." The gorilla by the door jumped to clear Perry's dinner from his desk. "Tell Sven to get in here. And then you stay gone. Got it?"

"Sure thing, Boss."

Perry shook his head as Sven limped in. "Some tough guy you are, you heap big Injun. Scalp 'um any Lances lately?"

"That's offensive, even for you, Papa P," the Pilot said, a half smile flexing one corner of his mouth.

"Good, I like being offensive. You mind, Sven, you care if I make fun of you? Call you Injun?"

"No, Boss. It's okay."

"Sure it's okay. Everything I do is okay. You got that?" Perry swung his eyes toward the Pilot. No answer—just a mocking half smile.

"Let's make some plans," Perry said. "Hey Injun. Think you can limp along on a Final Ritual a week from tonight? You gonna be all better next Saturday night?" Perry tweaked Sven's ear, jostled his cast.

The doorman tried out his tough-guy face. Didn't work. He winced; Perry grinned.

"Reno's a softy, right, Injun? But that Lance—he sure the hell did a number on you. You wanna sue him?" Perry's laughter filled his office, echoing wall to wall.

"I can still do it, Boss. I'm okay."

"The hell you are. Your arm's in a cast and your face . . ." Perry let it go at that. "So you're out next Saturday night. No ritual for you, Tonto."

"I know I'm a mess, Boss. But I wanna kill that son of a bitch Lance." Sven touched what he called his ear. "And Reno, too. Lemme help next Saturday."

"Your trigger finger still work?" the Pilot asked.

Sven pointed, mimed shooting a gun. "It works."

"Good. Then start keeping an eye on the casino for us again," the Pilot said. "Watch the doors while we deal with Reno. Just don't let all the money leak out." Sven didn't look happy.

"And let Karl drive you home next Friday night," the Pilot said. "Understand?"

"But I got a date Friday—" Sven said, but the rest of his words sank back inside. "Yeah, that works." The Pilot's scowl one hell of a motivator.

The Pilot turned to Perry. "How about we get back to planning, now that you've filled that gas bag of yours." One day, Perry thought, one day. But not tonight.

"We already showed Reno the island," the Pilot said. "Now all I need is him on it. Get him there and he won't come off alive. Think you can manage that, Papa P?"

"You watch your goddamn mouth, tough guy. I'm the boss, not you."

"If you say so, Papa, if you say so."

Perry belched again. "Fucking stomach. I talked to the Dutchman. He'll take part if we need him, but he won't play the Minotaur—not for a Final, he won't."

"Works for me, but we don't need him," the Pilot said.

"We need him there if we're going to kill him," Perry said.

The Pilot shrugged.

"Karl, he'll help Reno get on the island. That work for you?" Perry asked. "Or are you gonna gripe about that too?"

"You get Reno on the island, and I'll kill him. But not just Reno. Karl has to go, too. And the two girls. And this crop of aspirants. You okay with that?" The Pilot's eyes held Perry's. "Killing them all?"

Perry nodded—*Yes,* the nod said.

The Pilot smiled. "So leave all that to me. I'll make the plans, do your killing. You just remind Ariadne who'll be bull-balling her, come next Saturday night—Pericles."

The Pilot hit the door, his laughter echoing down the hallway.

71
HARRY'S KIPLING-ITHACA-KIPLING ODYSSEY

I rolled back toward Kipling after my time down in Ithaca with a sour taste in my mouth. One I'd put there myself. My encounter with the frosty Ms. Phair kept looping in my head like an old-time *News of the World* black-and-white movie trailer: *Harry the Heel Still on the Loose.*

At first, sailing with Mac hadn't been as bad as I had expected. Penny wasn't pregnant. But she sensed right off that something between Brynn and me had changed, that it wasn't just a harmless flirtation anymore. Penny's good, remember?

So I tried reminding Penny that Brynn was only a young girl who I liked. Probably shouldn't have said *young*. Maybe should have used *whom*. Probably shouldn't have said anything at all.

Penny called her Binty Brynn again, her way of mocking the woman I hadn't slept with, I guess. Wasn't sure, so I'd asked Penny what *binty* meant. Big mistake.

"A whore, Mr. Reno. Do you comprehend that bit of the Queen's English? Well, do you, you bloody awful man?"

I told her she was wrong, Brynn wasn't a whore. Or anything even close to a whore. That just made everything worse.

"So it's shagging the Queen Mother herself, now, are you, Mr.

Reno? My, but how you have risen in this sordid world of ours."

Penelope had stomped to the stern of Mac's cabin cruiser. I went and stood in the bow. The gray storm clouds that dogged me the entire way down to Ithaca kept it up while Penny and I fought and fenced with each other outside in the rain, while Iron Mac stayed dry up there on the bridge, smoking his cigar.

Penny wouldn't go below and towel off until we had things right between us. That's what she said. And she held to that position. So we both got soaked.

Mac finally intervened and made us kiss and make up and dry off. At least the drying-off part was for real. On the plus side, Mac had offered to help me with the temple problem, sort of.

"Bring me hard evidence—I'll bring hard law." But I'd heard that speech before. As usual, Iron Mac was short on words and specifics.

"Been watching—long time—afar and up close," he said. Whatever the hell that meant.

After all of that fun, I had a case of my own that kept me busy the first part of the week. I traced a daughter for a worried mother and a somewhat concerned father. I found the girl. Nobody died. Sir Harry the Heel, detective knight-errant nonpareil.

And so now here I was Thursday about noon wheeling back into Kipling—the little hula girl oblivious to Harry's dilemma. She'd swayed her hips all the way down to Ithaca. Bounced happily while I traced the girl. And wiggled her ersatz grass skirt furiously the whole way back to Kipling. Ah, sweet plastic bliss.

The Volvo pulled up in front of the Tam-O'-Shanter, and I went in to see Gus.

"Laddie—about time. How was Ithaca? You want a beer?"

"Want and need, Gus. Sometimes they're one and the same. A ham and cheese on rye would help, too." Gus's short-order cook in the kitchen must have heard my squawk.

He stuck his head out, waved, said, "I gotcha covered, Harry. Good to see ya again."

"Chips," I called after him. "And I don't want seedless rye." Guy's always in a hurry.

Molly appeared with a Moon Girl. I smiled; she smiled. Hot barmaid. Cold beer. We let it go at that. When Gus brought out my food, he watched while I ate.

"You okay, Harry?" he finally asked.

I laughed—a sour-sounding cackle. "Let's talk about something other than my love life. If that's okay with you."

"What did Mac say? Any help for us there?" Yeah, Mac had told me he and Gus knew each other. And not just from back when. Didn't take Mac many words to say it, either.

"If we find hard evidence, he'll bring hard law," I said. "We're on our own, Gus. Just so you know."

I stared at him; he stared back. I took a bite of my sandwich, felt a caraway seed lodge between my teeth. Gus kept staring. I kept chewing. It hurt. But I'd asked for it, hadn't I.

"Then let's do it," Gus said. "You and me. And whoever else we can drag along."

"Then get 'em together," I said. "Let's make it Perry's final Final Ritual." A swig of beer cleared my seeded rye logjam. Life can be like that: sometimes good stuff hurts. Then it doesn't.

"I'll put the word out," Gus said. "John, Willem—who else, Harry? Oh, Lance is out of the pokey. Not a cop anymore, either. You want Lance here tonight?"

"No."

"You sound sure," Gus said.

"I am. We need brains tonight, not oxen. We can let Lance loose to paint the town with testosterone later. I bet he'll choose vivid colors, like puke green, blood red."

We laughed. It wasn't a joke, but we laughed anyhow.

"What do you think, Gus?"

"You're right about Lance. Puke green. That's good. A weak link for sure." He wiped his face with his bar towel. "Drinks too much." Maybe he meant me, too. "I'll gather the clan," Gus said. "What about Tom?"

Willem had said bring him. I wasn't so sure.

"No? I agree," Gus said. "About closing time? That all right?"

"That's okay with me. No Tom; no Lance."

"Try to stay out of trouble, laddie. It seems to find you and cling to you." I shrugged—words seemed inadequate.

"Soon it'll be time to wash the years away." Angus MacGregor, the bartending philosopher. He went to lend Molly a hand with the lunch crowd.

I finished the sandwich, scarfed the rest of the chips, left the beer half drunk, headed out the door. The Volvo was still there, so I let her take me to the motel. I wanted to talk to Karl. I ended up talking to Pops instead.

72
MRS. BURLINGTON

"Karl ist nicht here, Herr Reno. He works not until tonight." Pops beamed as he told me this. Why, I had no idea.

"So where is he?" I asked.

"He studies to become the, ah . . . funeral man. The one who works the, the . . ." Pops was struggling. Finally German and English collided, and he spit out *crematorium*. Nice. You know Pops had to be proud. Little Karl, following in his father's Nazi boot steps, learning how to work the ovens. Didn't know that for sure. Still . . . sure seemed a possibility.

I tried again. "So where is he? I got something he's been looking for." I had self-respect in mind, but I didn't tell his old man that.

"I will make sure he receives it, Herr Reno."

"No. I need to see Karl in person—like now." My kindly face must have done the trick.

Pops shined up, said Karl was working at the Chapel by the Lake Mortuary and Crematorium. Wow.

So I told Pops, *"Auf Wiedersehen,"* and went to find Karl.

The drive out to the crematorium wound along the lake shore, up on the cliff road. Trees crowded the landward side of the asphalt, while visions of Gwen and Brynn bikini-danced on the sand below.

Good thing the state put guardrails on the cliff side. The Volvo kept drifting.

I told the little hula girl to tell the car to pay attention to the road. I was too busy babe detecting. Maybe I heard her say, *Surf's up, Big Kahuna. Dive in. Sure you don't wanna dip your board? Dance the dirty tiki-tiki with those bikini bimbos?*

Then again, maybe the little hula girl hadn't said a word. Maybe those were my thoughts. But she does love messing with me—just for the island fun of it.

Either way, I glued my green eyes to the asphalt. No more drifting.

The Chapel by the Lake Mortuary and Crematorium sat in a spot where the road dipped down from the cliffs again. The white-pillared main building obviously housed the funeral parlor viewing rooms and those intimate offices wherein slick salesmen guilt you into buying Uncle Ed the best coffin, the most elaborate service you can't afford and that Uncle Ed most certainly doesn't need or even care about anymore.

I hate funeral homes. Right up there with casinos. I walked inside. Hey, it can't always be fun being Harry Reno.

A pleasant-enough-looking fellow decked out in standard grieving attire greeted me—pleasant enough if you discounted his corpse-like grin and cold-as-a-dead-fish handshake. His smile faded when I told him I was looking for Karl, and not for a cardboard box and a hole in the ground for Uncle Ed.

"Ah, young Master Karl. I should imagine him with Mrs. Burlington. At our crematorium." He pointed toward a small brick building. "No civilians allowed inside," he warned.

I thanked the walking cadaver and got the hell out of there.

The burn house sat down by the lake. A concrete road connected it and the main building. The concrete ran on and ended at steps that led out to a small dock. My feet steered the rest of me toward the crematorium.

The little man came out just as I walked up. Like usual, Karl cringed first and then tried a smile on, pretending he was happy to see me.

"Harry, what are you doing here? I mean, how are you?"

The smile couldn't conceal the wariness in his voice. Maybe the little shit had been doing something he shouldn't have, there in the burn house with Mrs. Burlington.

"Get back in there," I said, and shoved him. Karl's smile faded.

"You can't go in there, Mr. Reno. It's not allowed."

"I need some answers, and I don't want your boss to see me beat them out of you. Might give him ideas how he ought to treat you." I shoved him again. "Go on. Get."

He shrank back into the building. I followed and closed the door behind us.

"God, Karl, what is this place?" I knew the answer. Mrs. Burlington over there on the trolley, the sled you go coasting downhill on into the flames. And Mrs. Burlington sure was ready for the oven. Both naked and dead. Just wanted to hear Karl say it.

"It's where we cremate people."

"And you do that? All by your little elf self?"

"Well, sometimes," Karl said. "I'm still in training." Then the smug light clicked on. "I am currently charged with ensuring that the combustion system has a proper supply of propane. I am quite knowledgeable concerning such matters."

I reached for his ear—just reached, didn't touch. The smug light blinked off.

"Good, Karl, real good. Maybe we can have a cookout sometime soon. I'll let you fire up the grill. How 'bout that?"

Karl's face collapsed from smile to sullen, like I'd opened the valve on his self-esteem and it was hissing out, dissipating. He tried grasping a handful before it evaporated altogether.

"I am also engaged in the study of mortuary science." His chin lifted. "I intend to become Kipling's preeminent mortician." Not that bullshit again.

"Yeah, yeah, yeah," I said. "And I'm gonna turn into Peter Pan and fly off to Neverland and fuck Wendy." He didn't seem to appreciate my humor. Maybe I'd hurt his feelings. So what.

"Hey Karl, I think what you really do out here—the real reason they let you work the furnace room—is that this is how they get rid of the bodies after the Final Rituals. The girls who get snuffed at the end. You know, killed, kaput. Dead."

Little Karl shot a deer-frozen-in-the-headlights stare my way.

"I think you and your buddy Dewey load the bodies on a boat, down in that sea cave, or whatever Stavros calls it, there on the island. Then you and Dewey bring the bodies over at night and crisp 'em. Up the stack. No urn needed. Am I right?" No answer.

I shoved him. Hard. "Well, am I?" Karl had his I'm-scared mask on. Good.

"But that didn't happen with Elke, did it? No flames after the snuff. Because there wasn't any snuff that night. Because Elke and Gwen weren't in any Final Ritual, were they?" Karl nodded his agreement. Too scared to open his mouth. "Just a regular ritual, the kind where nobody dies," I said.

Karl kept nodding.

"So Elke bought it because she really did get a hot shot in her arm. Bad heroin or whatever. Right?" God, but I hated squeezing answers out of the little man. Why couldn't he just open up and tell the truth?

"You got her that stuff because she begged you to. Maybe did something for you so you would. Come on, you little shit. Say it."

This time he bucked up a bit, proved he wasn't totally spineless. "No, Mr. Reno. No. I loved Elke. She didn't have to do anything for me . . . unless she wanted to. I brought her drugs because I loved her." Oh, brother. I thought only mothers did that.

"But she didn't reciprocate, did she?" I said.

Karl's face and his mouth both said, "Huh?" So I tried again, simpler this time. "Elke, she didn't feel the same way about you that you felt about her." Now he got it.

"So you bought her the antifreeze she craved that night, hoping she'd fall in love with you for a bit, and it all went wrong. Who gave you the stuff, Karl? The hot shot that killed the girl you loved. Who, Karl?"

The little man broke down, put his head in his hands, began crying —real tears, not the crocodile species. He sobbed and shook, and I let him. When it was over, I started in on him again, but a little gentler.

"Who, Karl? Tell Uncle Harry." Uncle Harry's the softer sort —Reno's not.

"Sven," Karl said. "That's who always gets what she needs. Needed." Sniff. "I already told you that. You hurt me then, too. It's the truth." Pathetic little twerp.

Karl tried backing away. I followed. He bumped into Mrs. Burlington on the burn sled.

"Yeah, you told me. There at the motel." I doubled a fist under his nose. "I just don't think you told me all of it." The fist stayed balled down at the end of its arm, ready to punctuate my info request. I took a step back, though. Gave little Karl some room to breathe on his own again.

"So that night you needed something. Elke needed something. Did you tell Sven who it was for?" I took a step back toward him and Mrs. Burlington. Back into the red zone.

"Well, did you, Karl?" My fist in his face, ready to clock in for work. Karl flinched, bumped against the burn sled again. Ended up sitting in Mrs. Burlington's lap—the naked and dead Mrs. Burlington.

He was back on his feet pretty quick. Can't say I blamed him.

"Sven got it from the Pilot," Karl said. "Sven gave it to me. I gave it to Elke. There at the motel. She'd said we'd do something, if I got her some stuff, said she'd wear that outfit I liked."

Aha, her hooker getup. My fist relaxed, became less threatening.

"She shot up, got this funny look on her face and then . . . she was dead. I didn't know what to do." Karl's sobs loud again, not soft like lake waters lapping at docks. Not soft at all.

Karl plunked down on the cremation sled beside Mrs. Burlington, one hand absently smoothing her soon-to-be-crispy hair.

"So, what did you do, Karl?" I leered at him. "There in the motel room. With Elke. After she was kaput." Just trying to get his mind out of sob mode. That's all.

"That's Dewey stuff, Harry." He jerked his hand away from Mrs. Burlington, stood up. "I don't do that," he said. Really? Wow.

"I didn't know what to do. I called Sven. He said he'd be right over."

"And did Sven come right over?"

"Yes, Harry."

"Anybody come with him?"

"The Pilot," Karl said. Like pulling teeth. If he didn't cooperate a little better, he'd be toothless soon.

"Tell me what happened in the motel room with you and Sven and the Pilot and Elke."

"I asked Sven what was wrong with that stuff he gave me. He just shrugged."

"What happened next?" Karl was telling it like he remembered it—image by image—but God, it was wearing on me. I had already guessed how it worked out.

"He laughed at me, Harry. The Pilot laughed at me." Bingo. Got that right.

"Did the Pilot, did Sven, did either of them say anything?"

"The Pilot told me, 'Tough luck, little man.' I took a swing at him." Right again.

"How bad did you hurt him, Karl?"

"I missed." He hung his head, closed his eyes. Guess it wasn't a pleasant memory.

"Hey," I said, loud, in his ear. Eyes open now. "What if you and I could get back at the Pilot. Fix Sven. Fix Stavros, too? What if we made sure they paid for what they did to Elke? Would you help me do that?"

"Even Mrs. Stavros?" he asked. "Fix the mistress, too?" God, like talking to a child.

"Yeah, her, too." So much for his mother fetish.

"Yes, Harry. Yes," he said. "How?"

73

KARL'S FIERY CONVERSION

I needed Karl on our side. Without him, John and I would be on the outside looking in, while Willem tried going it alone inside the temple. I needed in, so I could grab the snuff videos. Karl had told me that Stavros kept all his ritual videos in a vault in the temple. That meant the masters of the snuff films—the Final Rituals—were there, too. At least that's how Mac and I figured it.

The tapes would put Perry and crew away for good. Might put Karl away, also. I still wasn't sure how he'd feel about that. Maybe I ought to ask him. Maybe I would, but not just yet. Get him on board first.

So I told him some of our temple plans, told him how he could help.

"I'll do it, Harry. I will. I hate him. He always had his paws on Elke."

He who? The Pilot, Sven, Stavros? Probably all three, probably all at once. Poor kid—Elke, not Karl. "And I bet she hated it, right, Karl?" The little man's eyes searched the ground. No answers there.

Hey, maybe not *poor Elke*. Maybe Elke liked that sort of stuff. Like Jayne—like Gwen's mother . . . Stop it, Reno, just fucking stop it. "What about Gwen? Does Sven paw her, too?"

"He tries, Harry. I don't think she lets him do much. He sees her naked at the rituals. He sees that. We all do."

I swallowed a giant lump of a swallow. I'd seen some of her naked, too. So what. It's my job. It's not me. Yeah, right. Reno's not much good when it comes to convincing Harry.

I let failure ride for now. "You going to work up at the casino anytime soon, Karl?"

"Tomorrow night," he said. "Friday." Idiot. Like I didn't know what today was.

"Sven's out of the hospital. Have you seen him?"

"No, but I heard that, too. I think he's going back on the front doors. Up at the casino, Harry." Complete idiot.

"Yeah, Karl. I know where the front doors are."

"Sorry." Squint-eyed, expecting me to hurt him again. Well, let him keep thinking it.

"What if you told Sven you'd pick him up Friday—take him to work. Run him back home afterwards. You know, his arm and ear and all. Think he'd go for it?"

"Yes, I know he would. Mr. Stavros already told me I'd need to do that," Karl said.

Now why would Stavros say that? Or, more particularly, why would he tell Karl to do it? Why not one of the gorilla tribe?

"Why'd he ask you? You ever drive Sven around before?" Karl's eyes found the floor. "You little weasel. What the hell's going on?"

I made a grab for his shoulder. Karl jerked sideways, fell over a gas line, hit the floor. I stomped his ankle.

He stopped wiggling, managed to say, "Ow. That hurts."

"It's supposed to, kid." I lifted my shoe, let it rest on concrete instead. "Just so you know. It's supposed to."

Then I asked him again if driving Sven around was normal procedure.

"No, it isn't, Mr. Reno. It's just that sometimes Sven has too much to drink. And Mr. S says to take him home. So I do, especially now that he's hurt. That's all, Mr. Reno—really."

His lie rolled out of his mouth and lay there waiting for me to pick it up and fling it back in his teeth—like a carp you hook easy but don't really want. You could toss it back into the water, but it's not worth it. You might just catch it again. So you leave it on the bank, and let it die on its own. Like Karl's little lie.

"Look, kid, you happy about Mr. S giving you a swimming lesson?" I had him back up and sitting in a chair, resting his ankle.

"No, Harry. It . . . it scared the shit out of me. Really. I did something in the water I shouldn't have." Oh-my-God. The poor lake trout. "I think he'd been happy if I'd drowned." Hell, wouldn't we all.

"Yeah, but then who'd run the video stuff," I said. "Sven?"

"No, he doesn't know how to do that, Harry. He's not that smart." Karl actually puffed out his chest when he said *smart*. Poor useless little wimp. "Mr. S needs me. I do not know why he threw me in the lake. Maybe to scare you?" Hmm, useless, but not completely stupid.

"How about Elke, Karl? You happy about what Mr. S and his pals did to her? You like that, buddy?" The little man started crying again.

"Well, do you?" I touched his shoulder—soothingly, didn't put the hurt on him. Didn't need to. "You with us, Karl?"

He wiped at his nose. Then he stood and stuck out his hand. I shook it. I had to. Something gooey stuck to my fingers.

"I am with you, Harry Reno—Fire and Blood, Body and Soul—unto the End." The little shit actually executed a formal bow as he made his pitch. *Fire and blood? Body and soul? Unto the end?* What the hell?

Maybe his dad said goofy shit like that—Pops, Kipling's very own little big man Nazi.

All I wanted his twerp son to do was let me and John sneak inside the goddamn temple. None of this fire and blood and unto the end crap. The hell with that. So I let it go.

Instead, I told Karl what I needed him to do with Sven, and how I needed it to go down and where. I told him it wouldn't hurt much, but it had to look legit. So it might hurt a little.

He winced, said, "Okay," and swallowed the frog croaking in his throat.

"You're sure Sven's going to be part of the procession?" I asked. "Lance didn't hurt him too bad?"

"Mr. S himself told me Sven would be a guide Saturday night," Karl said.

I took him at his word, even if it was a lie, and we made plans to get John and me across to the island after we snatched Sven. Our hostage-taking hustle had a decent chance, but I sure as hell had doubts about Karl.

I said, "Hang loose," and we left it at that.

The Volvo headed back toward Kipling, away from Karl and his oven obsession. Mortician, my ass. The little shit just liked burning stuff. Especially naked women.

And maybe that's why Karl was grinning as I left.

74

MISSING BABES—FOUND FRIENDS

I spent the rest of Thursday chasing my tail. I missed Gwen here and I missed Brynn there. Then I missed Brynn here and Gwen there. That kind of day. Why it put me in the mood to call Penny, I don't know. But it did. I had the Volvo find me a phone booth.

"Mr. Durlingham's office," said a voice I didn't recognize.

"Don't you mean *Dillingham*? And where's the fair Ms. Phair, Stu's official secretary? And who the hell are you, by the way?"

"I don't think she works here no more," said the decidedly non-British English speaker. "Hey, who are you? Cussing me like that? And what the hell do you want?"

"Definitely not you, babe. Put me through to Stu. Chop-chop. Like right now."

And miracle of all miracles, she did as I asked. Probably the only thing she'd do right and fast all day. I almost felt sorry for Stu—almost. But more importantly, where was Penny?

"Stuart Dillingham The Third here." All caps—same old Stu.

"Harry Reno himself here. Where's Penny? You didn't fire her, did you? Because if you did, I'll twist that chucklehead of yours right off your scrawny-ass neck."

Stu should have hung up. He didn't.

"Why, thank you, Reno. So nice to hear your cultured voice once again. Ms. Phair did most assuredly not quit, as you phrase it. She remains domiciled at her townhouse this day—ill, she advised me. But, my good man, I must inquire, whatever caused your brain to insert such nonsense into your always impious speech just now?" Stu: The Pompous Ass Supreme.

"I got the idea from that idiot who answered your phone. That's where I got it."

I hung up on Stu; dialed Penny's home number. The line dead, not even the answering machine. Odd, damn odd.

I tried Mac McCabe.

"Not available," his secretary said. So I told her to have him call me at the Tam and started to give her the number.

"He has it," she said, and hung up.

Puzzlement stared back at me from the phone booth's Plexiglas wall—the hell with all of them. Concentrate on important stuff. Stomach rumblings roiled my gut. Digestive juices complaining about no work to do. I'd forgotten about eating while lurching after girls. I slammed my way out of Ma Bell's coffin.

Maybe the Volvo heard my stomach rumblings. I don't know. Not for sure. But we ended up back at the Tam-O'-Shanter. Maybe the little hula girl suggested it to the green love of my life. Sometimes the little hula girl's like that, telling others where to go—island shrew.

I strolled into the Tam. No Gus. I found my way to the bar and sat and waited. I sensed him before I saw him—his whiskers blowing in the ceiling fan breeze, the scent of red Scottish heather mingling with stale beer.

A hand on my shoulder, then Gus himself in the mirror. I swiveled on my stool and tilted my head until I could see his red-whiskered face. He winked at me. A damn Willem-wink. Son of a bitch.

"It's all right, Sir Harry. We're all in, all together now."

"What the hell does that mean, Gus? Where's Penny? Where's Mac? What about Brynn and Gwen? You got 'em hid out back or something?" I sounded hot because I was hot.

Gus held up his hands, palms out, placating.

"They're okay, Harry. Mac called a little while ago. He and Penny are researching something, so she called in sick and took her phone off the hook. That's all. Researching something to help us. And Brynn and Gwen took a day off, too. They went shopping."

What the shit. What the earthly shit. Did everybody know what was going on but me? Everybody but the detective? Probably.

It wasn't too many ticks before five, so Gus sat a Moon Girl in front of me, and I drank. While I sipped, I checked out the moon witch up there on her sign. Never too early, never too late—huh, babe?

Gus put a cheeseburger and fries and a blob of coleslaw in front of me, and I ate. After I peppered the slaw. Always pepper the slaw. Another Moon Girl appeared, and I drank her, too.

I felt almost human again. I told Gus that. He said, "Aye, I dinnea ken otherwise."

"The hell with you, you old fraud." But I laughed when I said it.

He said, "Okay," and kept grinning at me like his name really was Willem. I headed for Gus's back room and crashed. Cot time.

Gus woke me sometime before closing and repeated the feeding routine: beer, food, beer. But he kept it light. The food and the beer. At least I felt ready for whatever was coming my way.

"You needed sleep, Harry. So I let you."

"Thanks. Now what?" I'd given up trying to figure out today on my own.

"An early closing and a special meeting afterwards. Old friends, remember?" Gus left it at that and ambled off to help Molly with the Thursday-evening crowd.

The crowd—such as it wasn't—thinned early. We closed up without running any Occasionals or Regulars or anyone else out prematurely. I shut the front door.

Gus said, "Go ahead and lock it, Harry. John and Willem know the secret knock." Secret, huh? Maybe they'd teach it to me. I went to take a leak, and when I came back, there they were. Already inside. Damn.

John sat next to me in the booth by the Tam's restrooms, the one favored by Tom Kuster. But no Tom tonight. Not after the debacle up at Twin Cedars.

Across from us, Willem and Gus were snuggling and making out. Not really, but they did act, well, if not exactly like childhood sweethearts, then like two guys who knew each other pretty well. No surprise there.

Gus asked, "It's not going to be only the four of us against the evil Bull and Goat Empire, is it, Harry?"

I damn well knew the old fraud had talked to Mac, so I said, "You tell me. And then tell them," and pointed to John and Willem. No need. They already knew. Iron Mac's tentacles snaking afar and up close, I suppose.

So I told them about my chat with Karl out at his crematorium playhouse on the shores of Great Cold Lake. "Karl says he's with us. He's mad about what they did to Elke." I leaned back in the booth, tried letting leather and brew soothe my worries for a moment—didn't work. "He'll do what we tell him. I just don't trust him."

Willem asked *Why* with his eyes. So I answered him.

"I don't know, Dutch. You tell me." So he did.

"Karl is emotionally unstable, Sir Harry. Prone to rash decisions. But capable too of covert planning. He has peepholes all over your motel."

I told Willem I had already explored that subject with the night clerk.

"Well then," the butler said, "we may most certainly use him, but Karl may have his own agenda. He will not be aiding us solely because he likes and admires you, Sir Harry."

"Yeah, I sort of figured that out on my own, Willem."

John hadn't said a word tonight. He'd nodded hello, but that had been it. So I prodded him a little. Always good to know what a cop's thinking. "What about you?" I said. "How do you feel about Karl?"

John the Cop—Gwen's dad—set his beer down, wiped his mouth.

"Not good, Harry. If he's helping because you hurt him, he'll crumble on us at some point. Like when we need him the most." Heads nodded. "Or he'll double-cross us *and* Stavros," John said. "Karl didn't decide to help us all on his own, you know."

"Yeah, I know." I wasn't happy. Neither were they. Karl was a weak link—one I'd forged all by myself.

"Better idea, laddies?" Gus this time. We shook our heads. "Then Karl it be. But let us plan as if Highland treachery were afoot."

75
WAR COUNCIL

The four of us drank some more beer, munched pretzels. In between mouthfuls, we set about planning the destruction of Pericles and Ariadne Stavros's Temple of the Labyrinth, along with their porno empire, too.

Since they just couldn't leave the babes well enough alone, we were going to help them along the road to recovery. After Saturday's Final Ritual, Perry and Ariadne would just have to make do with doing each other—until they both went to jail.

The plan was to kidnap Sven late tomorrow night, creating a hole in the entourage necessary for a Final Ritual. Stavros would have to turn to Willem to fill the gap in Saturday night's procession. And Willem filled us in on why.

"A Final Ritual," he said, "contains aspects too exquisite to entrust to the uninitiated."

Then he enumerated those exquisite aspects in detail for us. John and I shook our heads in disgust. Gus nodded knowingly—too knowingly. His bar, Stavros's money, remember?

Willem kept lecturing.

"Stavros dare not plug the breech entirely with—how do you

denominate them, Sir Harry, gorillas? If Sven has gone missing, he must call on me. You"—a sweep of his hand took in the three of us —"may trust me on this salient point. I know whereof I speak."

Yeah, I guess a retired Minotaur would.

"In a plain-vanilla ritual—as you Yanks might term a First Rite—no one dies," Willem reminded us. "But a Final Ritual concludes with the snuffing out of the life of a beautiful handmaiden or two."

Willem swept us with those cold gray eyes of his. "Gentlemen," the butler said, "we must not allow that to happen. Agreed?"

Nobody disagreed—motion carried.

"With Sven out of the way and guarded by Tom, with Lance as muscle, I shall be our inside man—in the procession and within the sacred temple—guarding the damsels." Willem grinned at me when he said *damsels*.

"It's shit," I said. I couldn't look at John. I already knew how he felt. He just didn't have anything better to offer, either.

Willem shrugged, and we left it at that.

Gus said, "I'll bring Tom and Lance up to speed. They're with us on this. Rest assured."

Yeah, Tom and Lance. A real dynamic duo, be a great comfort to me in my old age, if I lived past Saturday night. But they were all we had. We'd use them—no choice.

"I'll come ashore," Gus said, "a wee bit later Saturday night. After you," Gus nodded at Willem, "and the rest of the procession enter the temple. I'll make sure no one escapes on Perry's yacht."

"And if you might additionally neutralize any lurking goat men or gorillas, that would be of benefit." Willem this time. "We only ask. We need not insist upon it, Angus."

John finally livened up. "We'll need camo—face paint, clothes. We'll need to hide in the woods—all day Saturday. Watch the temple from the trees. Cold rations, no beer. You okay with that, Harry? No beer?" He punched my arm. But only playful like.

I grinned, said I was. We were all beginning to grin, catching whatever had infected Willem. This had to work. And without Brynn or Gwen getting hurt.

The war council broke up. A decent plan, one that offered a solution to our problems. But would it really work?

Maybe, maybe not.

76
SVEN IN TIME-OUT

The Friday-night crowd at the Tam-O'-Shanter hadn't had a chance to get raucous yet. And that was okay by me. I'd spent all day in a nearby town gathering supplies for our island adventure. Now I was back in Kipling and thirstier than a camel crossing Sinai.

"Laddie," Gus boomed. I found a bar stool, and a Moon Girl appeared in front of me—cap off, ready for a kiss. So I put my lips to her slender body and drank. And drank.

"Gimme another." I hate shopping.

I downed that one, too, stood up, used my pants leg to wipe the beer's cold sweat from my palm, and hit the restroom. Then back to the bar, the need in my eyes the same as the thirst in my throat.

"Whoa, Harry." I didn't like the barkeep's advice, but I took it and slowed down on the suds. Even ate a bite or two of whatever his grill guy sent my way. Sort of tasty.

About a quarter after eleven, John and Lance came into the bar, with Tom in tow. As they walked in, the last three customers shuffled out.

John crooked a finger at me, and out the door we went, too. Gus would make sure Lance and Tom knew what needed doing tonight.

John, being a cop, picked a spot where we could watch the Wigwam Casino's entrance undetected. He parked the pickup under the pine trees, and I scoped the casino's front doors through his binoculars.

Our plan was for Karl to drive Sven home. We'd follow, Karl would feign car trouble, stop, and we'd snatch Sven. Some intricate scheme, huh? Foolproof, right?

Karl never showed. Instead, Sven came out arm in arm with Gwen. The two of them as close as a couple can be and still be upright. They kissed and hugged and hunched their way across the parking lot to Gwen's car. Definitely not her mother's daughter tonight—not the mother I had known and loved. But then again, I'd never seen her mom's cowgirl act.

Gwen opened the passenger door, and Sven got in. Gwen slipped behind the wheel. I'd watched her all the way across the casino parking lot. I didn't like what I saw. Not at all. If she was sober, I was Moses. And I wasn't. And not just because all I had in my hands was a pair of binoculars instead of two finger-of-God-engraved stone tablets.

John fired up the truck as I narrated the action. We eased away from under the trees and headed down the road toward the spot we'd picked to ambush Sven and Karl. Only now it was going to be Sven and Gwen. And Gwen wouldn't know to stall the car there.

John didn't say anything. He didn't need to. His clenched teeth and tight jaws told the story all on their own.

"I'll force her off the road," I said. No answer.

"I'll be careful she doesn't get hurt." Still no answer.

"We just block Gwen's car in, pull him out, and get the hell out of there, right?" Nothing.

"We only use pepper spray if Sven doesn't go quietly, okay?" Silence.

"We don't say a word. You ought to be good with that. With masks and black clothes, Gwen won't know who we are, right?" He wouldn't even look at me.

"What the hell's wrong, John?" He finally turned his head an inch my way.

"We're in my truck, Harry. She'll know who snatched Sven." Well, shit.

I did some quick thinking. John wasn't up to it. Even Harry Reno could see that, even in the dark. "Then we follow them. Can you keep back enough so she doesn't see us but so we don't lose them? You up to it? You want me to drive? Answer me, damn it."

"I'll do it, Reno. Just shut up, will you."

John tailed them back to Kipling. Gwen managed to keep it in her lane, and so did her father. She pulled into a low-rent apartment complex's parking lot. Sven and Gwen both got out and walked to the door of a first-floor apartment—in they went. We waited. At last the lights came on and stayed on.

John kept up a low and slow chant: "I'll kill the bastard, I'll kill the bastard." Sounded a lot like Lance. No point disagreeing. I felt the same way. After a couple of minutes, Gwen came back out and drove away.

"Maybe she's headed home," I said.

"Could be," John said. "Or a beer run."

"Let's grab him," we both said, and pulled on our ski masks.

I reached the apartment door first—at a dead run—and kept on going right through the door. A cheap-ass apartment with a cheap-ass door. And a cheaper-ass lock. Perfect fit for a lowlife like Sven. In we went.

"What the fuck!" The casino doorman sat on the pot, his blond Mohawk all abristle, his pants around his ankles, his one good hand trying desperately to wipe the crap off his ass.

Father John yanked him off the toilet, and I doused him with pepper spray. Sven started howling. I sprayed him again, and he quieted down. We dragged him into the living room.

John cuffed him, and I gagged him—just to be polite to the neighbors. Didn't want Sven waking them up. We pulled up his pants and frog-marched him between us to the truck and got the hell out of there.

Turned out to be a perfect place for our amended snatch-and-grab. Sleazeball neighbors in places like Sven's don't call the cops. Too much chance they'll get locked up, too. Always a bench warrant or two or three floating around pond scum who live in places like Sven's.

The truck's cab a bit crowded. Three on a pickup's bench seat is always too many, unless one's female and reasonably attractive, and Sven was neither. Plus, he smelled bad.

John headed toward the safe house where Tom and Lance were waiting to babysit our captive Scandinavian Indian.

When the three of us got there, that's where the doorman went—into time-out. But first, Lance changed Sven's diaper. Figuratively speaking, of course. I couldn't watch. It wasn't pretty. Sven cried a lot, poor baby.

Then John and I went to find Karl, so he could float us over to the island to begin the destruction of everything Stavros. But, unlike Lance changing the doorman's diaper, only a metaphorical ruination planned.

You do remember the old crow's admonition, don't you?

77
SATURDAY LAKE EXCURSIONS

"Mr. Stavros is going to perform a Final Ritual Saturday night, Harry. One where the handmaidens die. He's going to use Gwen and Brynn."

Karl had told me that at the crematorium. Then he'd agreed to help me topple the temple: "I am with you, Harry Reno. Fire and Blood, Body and Soul—unto the End."

I know now what he meant. I didn't then. I surely didn't.

John and I had snatched Sven early Saturday morning, not too many ticks after midnight. Tom and Lance were supposed to hold him captive while Stavros scrambled to find a replacement for his Final Ritual.

Saturday about noon, Stavros settled on Willem—imagine that. Sven stayed in time-out.

But I didn't know that then, either. John, Karl, and I had gone to the island early on Saturday after grabbing Sven—in the small hours well before morning light—in a boat, the sort that's hard to see, hard to hear out on open water.

I started to ask Karl why Gwen was the one who drove Sven home Friday night, but I didn't. We went ashore. Karl showed us the temple's side door.

"I'll open this as soon as the mistress and the handmaidens get naked on the porch. You and Sergeant Wetherall come down the hill and get inside. Nobody will be looking this way. Not with the girls naked . . ." Karl caught John's murder-one face, gave *naked* a rest.

"You've already fucked us over once," John said, "not driving Sven home. If this goes wrong, we'll assume you snitched. We'll kill you. Do I have to make it any plainer for you, Karl?"

"No, sir." Karl's eyes said he believed what John promised. And we would have killed him. Murder wasn't in our hearts that night, but it hovered close by, ready to pounce.

The little man headed back to shore in the boat—Gus waiting there for Karl to return. Gus hadn't wanted to go out on the water, said he would stay on the beach. "To take the Lowland air, laddies," whatever the hell that meant.

Gus also said he'd keep an eye on Karl until time for the little slimeball's part in the ritual. That I did understand.

John and I stayed out of sight in the pine woods. No fire, no tent, no beer—just cold rations and camouflage. We rested and checked our guns, let some desultory talk wander between us.

"I resigned yesterday, Harry. Not a cop anymore." I didn't jump up and run around in circles. Still—

"Why?" I asked.

"You were a cop once. You know if a cop grabs something he's not supposed to, commits an illegal search, violates some slug's rights, the prosecutor doesn't get to use that one piece of evidence that puts the shit bird away for good."

John paused. Sucked air. Blew it out. Started talking again.

"And that's what would happen if I were still a cop, and we grabbed the snuff tapes. Me being involved would poison the whole damn case. No convictions. I didn't want that to happen, so I quit, for good, for Gwen."

Not the time or the place to dispute his legal analysis. Nor his motivation. So I only said, "Thanks."

John flashed a tight smile—no grinning tonight, our situation too grim for that. "Maybe you could use a sidekick, be a two-man detective agency. After this," he said.

Not a bad idea. I told him as much. We left it at that.

John kept watch first; I slept. Then we switched. Morning came, and we both watched and waited. In the afternoon we moved closer to the lake. Finally, Ariadne boarded the yacht.

"I see her, Harry. Gwen and Brynn are with her."

John passed the binoculars, and I saw what he saw. Ariadne, the Mistress of the Labyrinth, and her handmaidens, Gwen and Brynn. And little Karl. The crew-cut Pilot brought them over to the island. They docked at the foot of the stone steps.

Ariadne led the way off the yacht, Gwen next, then Brynn. Karl brought up the rear, all those beautiful bodies swaying in front of him as the women climbed the stone stairway. The little shit probably had a hard-on. I would have, if the circumstances were different. But they weren't, so I didn't.

The Pilot didn't stay to watch them climb. He turned Perry's yacht about and headed for shore. John and I moved out, back through the woods toward the temple.

We watched from the trees as the women and Karl wended their way up the hill and entered the temple through the same side door we would use. Idiot Karl actually swiveled this way then that, scanning the woods, searching for us. The women ignored him, like always.

Later, as darkness descended, the ritual procession assembled over at the dock, down from the casino. We could see torches flare, see shapes moving in the deepening twilight.

We couldn't see who boarded the yacht. We'd expected that—too dark by then. But we knew who should be in the procession, who should play what part, if Willem was to be believed. And if he wasn't to be believed, we were dead men. No illusions about that.

Willem had said, "Pericles plays the role of priest in his amateur theatricals. The lead, if you will. But only if you discount his wife, Ariadne, the Mistress of the Labyrinth. Really her show, what?"

Willem, the fake Englishman, the fake butler—the real what?

The priest led the procession onto his yacht. He went topside along with one of his gorillas while the other one headed aft. The topside gorilla put his paws on the wheel and the throttles. I couldn't see him do that, of course—too dark, too far away. But I'd seen a gorilla at the helm before, so why not tonight.

But little Karl hadn't mentioned the possibility of an extra gorilla. Neither had Willem, or Dutch, or Billy. One more goon than we had counted on for tonight. I said as much to John.

"So what, Reno." Maybe John would make a good partner. We spoke the same language.

The rest of the procession had made its way onto the boat and settled in. Perry's yacht began to sail away from the dock and head toward the island again.

As the yacht drew near, we could make out the Minotaur pawing around on deck, scraping his hoofs on the teak. Music from a flute floated on the breeze, growing louder as the yacht approached. The goat man playing his panpipe while he skipped about in the wake of the Minotaur, now dodging away from the bull man, now drawing nearer.

John said, "That's Dewey, all right. I've put the cuffs on him a time or two. It's him."

Along the yacht's aft railing sat four figures: the two aspirants with their two guides. Since Sven was tied up tonight, one of the guides should have a gray ponytail—too dark to be certain, though.

The goat man jumped onto the island's dock, pulled the yacht in, made her fast to the pilings. Dewey, old Pan himself.

The Minotaur vaulted the gunwales as his buddy was tying off, and raced up the flight of stone steps cut into the living rock of the island. He bolted into the pine woods and disappeared from sight.

"You think he's coming after us?" John asked.

"If it's that crew-cut Pilot under all that getup, I hope so," I said.

After he tied off the boat, Pan piped the procession ashore in grand style, prancing and playing as if he were the focus of the night's festivities. Maybe he thought he was. I never got the chance to ask him.

The procession formed up on the dock and began the ascent of the steps. Pan kept piping, and Perry—with solemn and priestly tread—led the others up.

The aspirants had passed onto the dock single file, and that was how they went up the stone steps. Behind them, the guides—the tame gorilla and the one I assumed was Willem—followed. Single file. There really wasn't any other way to go up the steps, but they all made it seem like a dignified, conscious choice, especially in the face of the wild-animal antics of the goat man. Dignified, like what they were about to do had true meaning.

John and I crept farther back into the trees and waited and watched.

78
MOONLIGHT PROCESSIONAL

The procession took its time traipsing through the woods. Since we knew how it worked, it soon wasn't hard to pick out Karl lighting the torches. When a torch flared, the whole damn bunch ground to a halt. Then the Minotaur would come racing out of the woods, jumping out onto the path, scaring the bejesus out of the two aspirants.

When the procession finally reached the clearing in front of the temple, John and I had a perfect view of the scene. A full moon had risen above the trees, bathing the procession in its pitiless white light.

"Let's kill them now, Harry. You take out Stavros. I'll shoot the Pilot."

"And how do we get away with it, John? How's that get us the evidence we need?"

John could have said, *It doesn't. So what?* If he had, I might have pulled the trigger. He didn't, so we went back to watching. What a show.

As the Minotaur ran through and around the procession there in front of the Temple of the Labyrinth, he would raise his loincloth with one hand and shake his dingus at them with his other. And man, did Crew Cut have a lot to shake. Maybe it was fake. Probably it wasn't.

At least he wasn't snorting and pawing at us, though. The Minotaur and his loincloth did nothing for Plain Old Harry.

The priest started spouting some mumbo jumbo. Perry's voice carried well, and we could hear his pleas to his *mistress,* along with some other bullshit. Just fucking nonsense. But I guess that was the whole idea of it. The fucking part. No lovemaking happening tonight. No sir. Couples would be coupling, yeah, but no lovemaking.

At least that's what I'd been told.

More goofiness poured from the priest's mouth, while Pan hopped around blowing his pipe. Dewey made a good goat man. He had hairy and ugly nailed, along with big and strong.

But his Pan act had a sinister cast, an evil all too evident in his prancing and piping. I wouldn't have wanted to be drawn into his idea of a good time, into his vision of wine-laced lust. No sir, I sure wouldn't.

Pan suddenly stopped his cavorting and fell silent. The temple doors opened, and the mistress and her two handmaidens glided out onto the portico, the tension, the expectation palpable, even up the hillside in the trees.

The Minotaur pawed the ground and snorted, flapping his loincloth, shaking his dingus at the mistress. I couldn't see if Ariadne was smiling, but I bet she was. Kinky bitch.

John, however, wasn't enjoying the show. Neither was I. We knew too well how this extravaganza would end if our plan fell apart.

John had tensed when Gwen and Brynn and their mistress appeared. As the three women let their ceremonial robes fall away, revealing the beauty beneath, I grabbed his arm. His bicep didn't give in my grip, not even a little.

"I'm okay, Harry. For now." I let go.

John's eyes stayed fixed on the women, though, as if a phantom hand had pounded rivets through his head into the tree behind him—bolting his eyeballs onto the scene below. I put a hand on his arm again. He shook it off. Again I let him.

Karl had said, "Head for the side door when the women get naked.

All the guys will be looking at the women. They won't be able to think about anything else."

The little man had that much right. If only you could quit staring at those beautiful babes.

I eventually remembered what he'd said to do, and John and I got moving. We quick-timed it to the door, and Karl let us in. Little shit was snickering.

Later—after it was all over—I remembered John saying as we reached the door, "Smells like rotten eggs." And I'd said, "So what."

Standard pardner speak for us, so we went on in and followed the little man along the narrow passage to his control room.

Karl's part in a ritual consisted of working the levers and knobs and buttons and wheels that operated all the temple's bells and whistles. A touch of a button here, a lever pushed up instead of down, a wheel spun this way or that, and doors opened and shut, lights blinked on and off. Twist a knob, punch a button, fog gushed forth, music went on and off. Screams scraped your ears. Very mysterious, very scary.

Grade-school haunted house crap. But if you have naked women leading the way, three stunningly beautiful naked women, you really don't mind.

And while all this lust drips off you inside the Temple of the Labyrinth—eddying across stone floors like sea waves breaking on hot sand—video cameras and hidden microphones catch the action. Blackmail to bind you to the mistress and her priest; porno profits for Perry's Lodge.

A sweet deal, unless you happen to be a handmaiden. Then not so sweet, if the ritual is a final one. Snuff city, then.

But our plan made sure this Final Ritual never got that far. A carefully plotted hostage-taking scheme to topple the Temple of the Labyrinth. With Willem, John, and myself inside, we planned to take over the night's party.

Karl would keep the temple doors shut. Gus would come over in his boat, climb the stone stairway, and deal with Dewey and whoever else on the outside, while the three of us inside put an end to Perry's perversions. Host and hostess held at gunpoint, the others happy to comply with whatever armed men said to do, so they could stay alive.

The three of us agreed the Pilot and the gorilla probably wouldn't go along with the change in plan. But saving the girls and getting the keys to Perry's video vault, that was our goal. If we had to shoot, we would, and claim they shot first. John had a couple of throwdowns with him, just in case. And I had Jayne's little .22. She'd never asked for it back, and now she didn't need it anymore. No sir, she surely didn't.

Our plan wasn't great, but it had sounded good enough over beers at the Tam. It might even have worked. Only we never had the chance to give it a try.

As John and I peered over Karl's shoulders at the video screens there in the control room, all hell broke loose outside before the priest and his procession could even start up the steps and into the temple.

"Shit," John said—a perfect analysis. I had nothing to add.

79
A LESS THAN METAPHORICAL OUTCOME

On Karl's video screens, we watched Sven run screaming into the midst of the halted procession, waving one arm over his head. His other arm, the one in the cast, the one Lance had broken, dangled at Sven's side, flopping as he ran. Sort of on its own, though, out of control.

Sven didn't stop to chat. He ran straight up the steps, grabbed a naked Gwen with his good arm, and headed into the Temple of the Labyrinth with her.

Perry must have laid out prime money for his audio/visual system. We could have been standing on the temple porch ourselves. Maybe we should have been.

"Lance, no," we heard, and saw Gwen scream as Sven hustled her inside. That's when we saw Lance himself sprinting up the path and into the temple clearing, shotgun at port arms, pounding after Sven.

The gorilla guide stepped into Lance's path. Lance blew him apart, pumped another shell, and kept right on toward the temple steps.

One of the aspirants moved. Now he was between Lance and the temple. Maybe he was only trying to get out of the way.

Lance blasted him too, barreling his way forward over the toppling corpse and on up the temple steps.

I blinked, and on the monitor Lance reached the portico, pushed Ariadne clear of the doors, and disappeared into the temple after Sven and Gwen.

"I'll kill you both," he screamed.

The microphones picked up Lance's voice just fine. I didn't doubt him. The ex-cop sounded crazed enough to keep on killing, now that he'd started.

John moaned—a low, animal sound—said, "Let go of me, damn it. Let go," and broke away from the grip I had on him.

I should have stopped him, grabbed him again, but I didn't. Instead I said, "Be careful." Great advice, huh?

John ran into the labyrinth to find Gwen. Karl snickered.

"Don't screw this up, little man," I said. Karl laughed in my face and ran out of the control room, too. I let it ride, given the circumstances.

I ran down the passageway and out the side door, the little man's laughter ringing behind me—a falsetto keening bouncing off stone walls, echoing in my ears. Behind me—inside the temple—a shotgun blast reverberated.

"Gotta save Brynn," I kept repeating to no one in particular, just trying to remind myself what I needed to do—in case I forgot.

I do remember wondering what Karl had to laugh about when the whole place smelled like someone had used a skunk to consecrate the sacred temple precincts. Seemed sacrilegious for Karl to be laughing in the midst of such a god-awful stink.

My mind was wandering on its own, but my feet kept me on track, propelling me toward Brynn's screams.

I rounded the front corner of the temple and what I saw was this.

Two men lying in front of the steps—a few yards apart—their blood soaking the ground. Neither worth more than a quick glance. A shotgun blast up close does a number on a guy. It surely does.

A woman's screams—a pivot left.

Up on the temple portico, Ariadne trying to squeeze herself through the temple doors as Karl inside laughed and cranked them shut. Brynn naked and shaking. Frozen in place on the portico. Half of

Ariadne's naked self was in, her other naked half still outside the temple—an arm clawing the doors, and its attendant leg adding a kick or two to the effort.

Her head wasn't visible, though. She'd shoved that inside her temple. But it was Ariadne, all right. I knew her voice. When she'd bitten my shoulder in her office, there on the couch, she'd shrieked for her deputies—a shrill cry of command.

She was doing it again. "Open the fucking doors, you little shit."

At least Ariadne and I agreed on one thing. Karl was indeed a little shit, a double-crossing little shit.

Plus, Ariadne didn't seem happy that Karl was busy closing the place up for the night with just him and Sven and Gwen, and Gwen's dad, inside. Oh, and Lance, too—the shotgun again, blasting away inside the Temple of the Labyrinth. Not good, really not good.

Despite the sounds of mayhem in her temple, the Mistress of the Labyrinth still wanted in. Remember, some of her had made it, some of her hadn't.

Maybe that's why she was screaming. "Open the fucking doors, you moron. Turn it the other way." Somehow, I think Karl knew which way he wanted to turn whatever it was he was turning.

"Open the fucking doors," the mistress said again. No variety—still shrill, though.

Dewey threw his stupid flute away, ran up the steps, calling out, "Mistress, Dewey save you," or something equally childish. The big goat shoved his hands between the doors and tried his best to pull them apart.

And it almost worked; he had the strength. The doors started to part. He strained and shoved—knots of muscle and tendon bulged and rippled in the bright moonlight, but the doors wouldn't open just yet.

Ariadne kept screaming. Dewey kept shoving.

Off to the side, the Pilot stood with his hands on his head, his bull mask on the ground—Willem the reason. "Good evening to you, Sir Harry," he said. Willem, not the Pilot.

The butler held a gun to the back of the Pilot's head, blue-green tiger camo peeking out from beneath Willem's ceremonial red robe.

His other hand hovered near the bull man's back, no doubt ready to execute one of his cute martial arts routines. Or perhaps just ready to ice the Pilot the old-fashioned way.

"Be careful," I said. More sage Reno advice. At least the Minotaur wasn't waving his dingus around right now. The two of them moved off down the trail and into the woods. Why, I had no idea.

I faced the temple again. Ariadne hadn't let up. Brynn was still there too, rocking from side to side, hugging herself. Naked and scared.

Perry stood at the bottom of the steps, unable to move, just standing there fat and stupid-looking in his purple priest robe, watching his wife and Dewey struggling at the temple doors.

Behind him lay his dead gorilla. In front of Perry was Lance's second target—the aspirant's blood soaking into the dirt, a slippery, treacherous goo. The other aspirant, the one Lance hadn't bothered to blow apart, must have hightailed it when the fun started. Probably some intuitive desire to stay alive.

I stepped around the blood puddle, shoved Stavros, said, "Get out of here."

He didn't move. Maybe he'd caught some buckshot, too. I never asked him; he never told me. I kicked him in the ass. Said, "Move it, Fatty. Now." He did.

I took the steps two at a time, reached the porch, and scooped up Brynn's gown. I shoved it at her, said, "Put it on."

God, but it smelled up there on the temple portico, like that consecrating skunk had stepped in rotten eggs and tracked them all over the porch while he sprayed. At least I wasn't inside anymore—had to smell far fouler in there.

My brain reminded the rest of me that this wasn't at all like we'd planned it.

Ariadne was still flailing around and screaming. Maybe her ankle hurt—with Dewey's help, she'd managed to get all of herself except that final foot inside. Now her hoof was stuck fast between the temple doors.

I didn't ask her about it. Seemed like the place, but the timing wasn't right.

Dewey was still trying to pry the temple doors apart, save his precious mistress, push her in or pull her out. I didn't stop to chat with him, either.

Brynn had her robe back on. She stood there shivering, hugging herself and the robe, eyes wide. "Harry," she said. That was all she could manage. So she said it again, "Harry."

It was enough. "Come on," I said. I grabbed her arm, and down the steps we went and into the woods—just fast and far enough. Brynn stumbled. I caught her.

"Harry," she said one last time as I hugged her.

Then life turned orange and yellow, and red-rimmed, too—as if the sun had chosen to rise there in the forest, forgetting it lived far away, in outer space. The blast howled—we howled. Pines and birches and larches bent with the howling—so did we.

80
AN UNDISCLOSED MORNING

But now, all that's like a supernova exploding in the void—noiseless—and I'm back in our motel bathroom once more staring at a newspaper headline for the tenth or the two hundredth time:

NINE DEAD IN ISLAND EXPLOSION — PROPANE LEAK SUSPECTED

Reno's foul-up. Irrefutable proof of it right there on our bathroom floor. Black, above-the-fold headlines in Monday's newspaper. Was the temple fiasco just two days ago? Hell, call it three. It's Tuesday morning now, even if the sun itself isn't up just yet. Hard to keep it all straight—explosions and shotgun blasts seem to both compress and elongate time.

The newshounds didn't get it quite right, of course. They never do. Only seven died in the explosion. Two took shotgun blasts before the fireball painted the green woods yellow and orange, made Ariadne's white temple all red-rimmed, its cold marble and cement shattered by exploding propane.

And perhaps Lance and his shotgun killed again inside the temple before the propane blew—no way to tell, not anymore. Nothing left.

Still, there in the newspaper, the essence of truth set out for public consumption: nine dead. I couldn't argue with that. Plus Tom and Jayne and Mallory, and Elke and Lacie Doyle—and Gwen's mom, a hurt so deep I still can't say her name.

Fifteen dead. Not bad, Reno. The lucky double seven plus one. Thanks, Harry.

I wadded the newspaper into a ball, arm muscles quivering with the effort. Then, with exquisite care, I placed the crumpled sphere in the trash under the sink for the maid in the morning. The placing took as much from me as did the crumpling. Trying to keep your world from flying apart does require effort. It surely does.

I eased my way out of the bathroom, waited for my eyes to adjust to the darkened room. I didn't want to stub a toe, crack a shin—didn't want to holler profanities and wake her. I needed and wanted her to sleep for as long as she wanted and needed to do so.

I didn't get back into bed. Instead, I parked myself in the chair over in the corner and propped my feet up on the ottoman.

No cheap-ass, half-broken recliner here. No secondhand junk that Karl's Pops had fished out of some other motel's Dumpster and used to furnish his hot-sheets palace. Not here, no sir. Everything first class—except Harry the Heel Reno. Fifteen dead. Film at eleven.

Brynn stirred, a shaft of pale sunlight piercing the curtains where they met, flickering across her face on the pillow. The sun had come up while I sat in the dark remembering things I'd rather have left forgotten.

I walked across the room, stroked her hair, touched her cheek, said, "Good morning, sweetheart," and kissed her lips. "Time to go see Mac."

Mac had said, "Undisclosed location. Safe. Stay here. Debriefing." Mac doesn't waste words. No point. He'd found us after the Temple of the Labyrinth fiasco. When Gus brought us back from the island, there he was.

And now on Tuesday morning, some of us were at that undisclosed location—government speak, just a motel really, but far enough away from what had happened on the island.

But not everyone who stood in front of the temple that night was here with us. Nor anyone who had been inside when the sun burst amidst the trees.

We sat in Mac's motel room. Brynn, me, Gus. No Willem, no Billy, no Dutch.

Iron Mac said, "No need," and lit a cigar. We sat. Debriefing. Listening. Talking.

Mac spoke like that. Staccato. Laconic. No wasted words, no flowery speeches, no convoluted thoughts trotted out to cloak what had happened at the temple. No need.

"Searched temple. Ruins. No survivors." Mac's delivery spare. "Searched woods. Island. Perry, alive. Pilot, alive. Both aspirants, dead." Cigar smoke clung to Mac like it had to your favorite uncle—a comfort rather than an annoyance when you were young.

But still, the aspirant who ran away, also dead. So sixteen slaughtered—not fifteen. Even better. Good job, Reno, you sour bastard. Thanks, Harry.

Mac fired more short bursts. "Tom Kuster—dead. Lance. Fight over Gwen. Sven escaped."

Yeah, I'd thought it might end that way at some point. Like whenever Sir Lancelot found out Thomas Kuster had been humping his lady love. And deciding Sven had to die, too.

"Walker-Doer. Heart attack—dead." How 'bout that. The judge. Up to seventeen now. A cloud from Mac's cigar drifted. "Ritual tapes—evidence—gone." Mac swiveled his chair, stared hard at me when he said *gone*.

I spread my hands, palms open, a what-the-hell-was-I-supposed-to-have-done gesture. The comfort of his cigar smoke wafted away.

Iron Mac pressed on. "Propane—explosion. Karl, Dewey, Ariadne—dead." A glance at Gus. "Guard on yacht—dead."

The Highland barkeep shrugged. I had as much as told Gus, kill anyone left on the yacht. I let his silent equivocation speak for me.

Good riddance to the judge, too. And Doc Decker. And our star witness, all those long years ago.

Who cares what the final tally is. Did any of it even matter?

Mac talking again. "John, Gwen—dead." Maybe Mac expected me to shrug them off, too. I didn't, because I couldn't. I stayed quiet, though. For now.

"Evidence gone," Mac said again. "No case. No prosecution—Reno." Mac left his *Reno* hanging, an unspoken accusation twisting in his metaphoric word tornado. All this just another of Reno's foul-ups. But they weren't all mine, damn it. Not this time.

I said, "Jayne killed Mallory in the cedars at the restaurant."

Mac said, "Not relevant."

A flash of blue-green suddenly in my brain. The park. The trees. Jayne's blood on the rock. Red spatters on me. Blue-green camo again at the temple beneath a red robe. Willem had killed Jayne in the park. The butler did it, not the Pilot. Harry and Reno enlightened at last.

I stood up, fists clenched. "I think you set all this up with Walker-Doer. You both wanted Stavros dead, and the two of you tried to use me to work it."

"Not relevant—leave it alone." Iron Mac, soothing his congregation.

"Like hell I will," I said. Mac stood up. I swung; he blocked.

Gus bear-hugging my body, pinning my arms. "It's not quite what you think, laddie." Gus's words in my ear—not loud, but not a whisper, either.

"Harry, please." Brynn, beside me. "Please stop." So I did, and she stepped aside.

Mac said, "Ends justify means." His hand on my shoulder, his eyes holding mine. "Not your code of honor, Harry. Mine."

Gus released me, said, "The best laid schemes o' mice an' men gang aft agley."

"Damn it, man," I said. "Speak English."

"The best laid schemes of mice and men often go awry," Gus said. "Sometimes it just turns to shit, Harry." Gus, the ersatz Scottish philosopher, remember?

Mac said, "Karl. Miscalculation. Mine. Not yours. No shame. No dishonor. Not for you." His hand on my shoulder still. "Let it go, Harry. I have—for now." So I did.

"Where do we go from here, Mac? What do we do? I hope you have answers. I don't."

"Home, Harry," Mac said, and his hand stopped caressing my shoulder, found my hand instead, shook it. Maybe he wasn't pissed after all. Maybe it was all his fault.

"Take Brynn back to Alice. Stavros won't bother them. He and I talked," Mac said.

Another long speech for Mac. His voice soft now, his staccato delivery washed away by emotion. Rare in Mac. Hard to discern. But it was there.

"Gus, keep watch. Kipling," Mac said, and sat down. Maybe he was as worn out as I was.

"No more casino," Mac said, swiveling his chair, fixing his eyes on Brynn. Mac's gray, like Willem's, hers hazel and red from crying. Where the hell had Mac found this chair that swiveled? A small desk over in the corner, minus its chair. Wow, some sharp-eyed shamus you are, Reno.

"No more casino, Brynn—ever." A twice-repeated command. A genuine rarity, for Mac.

She nodded a soft yes, mastered the trembling that was her lower lip, then managed, "I know, Mac, I know—I'm sorry, so very sorry."

I wanted to kiss her, hug her, hold her, comfort her. Just normal male urges that morning there in Mac's first-class, undisclosed motel.

Then Brynn began to cry, and I did what I had wanted to do.

"You did what Harry told you to do, Brynn," Mac said. "No shame in that. He almost had it right."

Wow—a year's worth of words. *Almost had it right* my ass. You could have helped a little more. Stepped in a little sooner. I didn't say any of that. No use. Not now. Maybe not ever.

"Harry." Brynn this time. "You did try." She pushed a wayward strand of her hair back where it belonged. "What matters is you tried."

Red-streaked black fell across her face again. She left it there. "Even if it didn't work out, you tried."

Silvery diamonds leaked from blue-flecked hazel—no green today, none at all. "And I love you for that," she said. "Poor Gwen."

Yeah, Gwen as dead as her mother; Brynn alive; the only final tally I could be sure of.

"Take her home, Harry." Mac again. "Say your good-byes. Then get the hell back to Ithaca." No need for Iron Mac to add—*And back to Penelope*. Her name echoed in the room without it ever being spoken.

Brynn wiped at a last tear—said, "It's time, Plain Old Harry. Time to go. Back to Kipling."

I dropped Brynn off at the Hash House, said, "See ya later, alligator," as she slipped out and shut the Volvo's door. She stuck her head back through the open window, reached in, took my hand in hers, said, "After while, crocodile. Just don't make this a forever good-bye, Harry."

She pulled her head away, then her hand followed, and all of the girl was outside.

And just as quick, her head popped back in, and Brynn said, "That nightmare, back at the motel. When you scared me so. You thought I was someone else. You called me a name, a woman's name." I didn't answer her—I couldn't.

"Did you think I was Gwen's mother? Was it her name you were trying to say? Was that it, Harry?" Reno gave her Harry's best smile, and with a silently mouthed *I love you,* I let the Volvo pull away and head out for Ithaca and Penelope.

And for once, the little hula girl kept her comments to herself. Wise choice.

81
A BLACK LACE PANTIES SOLUTION —SORT OF

I never did find out whose black lace panties were on my pillow in my motel room that morning in Kipling so long ago. I saw plenty of women wearing black panties: Elke in the alley; Brynn in my motel room; Gwen when she tried to play the part of her mother for me one afternoon in the Volvo; Jayne on the way to the woods and her death; and even Mrs. Stavros when she wanted and needed to seduce Harry Reno, PI, right there in her Lady DA den.

But here's the rub. Lots of women, lots of black panties—some satin, some plain old cotton, some with lace, some without. But no black lace panties with little red bows, little red bows that when you pull on them, well, the panties just fall away.

I never saw black lace panties like I saw on my pillow there in Karl's motel again—not with little red bows, not in Kipling, anyway. Oh well.

On the way back to Ithaca, I stopped at a Chinese restaurant to grab a bite to eat. Its hopeful proprietor had named his place Number One

Great Wall. Catchy. The red neon sign out front flashed BUFFET—GOOD, so in I went.

The sign didn't lie. Decent food and decent service coupled with "authentic" decor. Had to ask for a fortune cookie after I'd finished my Kung Pao chicken, though—only blip with the service. When the waiter brought it, I poured the last of the tea into my cup and broke open the cookie.

You know I'm a big believer in fortune-cookie fortunes—the wisdom of the ages nestled in a sometimes-crunchy cookie. An ancient and honorable people, the Chinese. Confucius, Taoism, all that stuff and more. But mostly, the fortunes I find, or that find me, just seem to fit.

The one in my cookie that afternoon said,

DARKNESS CANNOT DRIVE OUT DARKNESS
ONLY BRIGHT SUNLIGHTS DO THAT!

After I ate my cookie and its moral message, I drank the last of my tea and chased it with what was left of my water. Somewhere in a Chinese fortune-cookie factory, some dude's job is to watch Harry Reno, then send him a message. I'm convinced of it, sort of.

Anyway, the fortune-cookie dude really nailed this one. Bright light sure as hell had driven away darkness there in the trees on the temple island. Just wasn't so sure it had been my good fortune for that to have happened.

I left my usual 20 percent tip on the table—my way of encouraging the help to strive for that elusive dream, perfect service. Then I paid my bill at the register up front and got the hell out of there.

Behind the Chinese joint I spotted a shopping mall lurking around, waiting to snare a customer or two. On one corner, right out front, sat a store I'd never heard of. Victoria's Secret. What a window display it had. It just drew me in, you know? The old judge's Victorian mansion, the bras in the motel parking lot, the bras in my motel room, the alluring mannequins in the windows, the secrets inside.

Plus, I'd lost the damn black lace panties somewhere on my travels between Kipling and Ithaca. So I never had a chance to ask Penny to model them. In I went. Wow, what a store.

I walked up to a salesclerk. A stunning, redheaded salesclerk. High cheekbones, narrow aquiline nose, soft brown eyes staring steadily out of a tanned face devoid of the usual redhead's freckles. Staring eyeball to eyeball with me. A natural tall, no high heels. I know. I checked.

Her body lean, but feminine without a doubt, as ready for a set of tennis as a roll in the hay. If you had any hay. I didn't. But I sure as hell thought about trying to find some.

But instead I said, "Do you have black lace panties with little red bows on them? Little red bows that when you pull on them, well, the panties just fall off?"

She smiled and said she did. I asked to see them.

She said, "No."

I asked why not? And the salesclerk told me why not—she was wearing them.

Well, being a smooth and cool private investigator, I didn't let that end my interrogation of the redheaded salesclerk. I asked if she had any for sale.

She said, "Not in your size, sir."

The smile she used when she said all that was quirky. She was definitely messing with my head. They taught the strangest sales techniques to the clerks there in this new store, Victoria's Secret.

Or maybe I just caught one who was quirky all on her own—no training bra needed.

I said the black lace panties weren't for me, but for my girlfriend. The clerk asked what size. She matched Penny close enough, except in the chest, but the panties weren't going there. Her waist and hips were just what they should be, like Penny's. Maybe a half-inch difference. But you'd have to be surveying pretty intently to peg that missing half inch. And I was.

So just to be sure, I said, "What size do you wear?"

She didn't bat an eyelash, didn't lose any mascara. "Size four."

I said, "Give me a pair then, but they have to have the little red bows." She wrapped them up and rang them up and handed me my change.

While I was busy stuffing greenbacks back in my wallet, the redheaded salesclerk said, "Would you like your receipt?" All prim and proper like.

My head was down, my thoughts turning around, so I gave her a shamus-gruff, "Yeah."

"Yes, thank you. I'd like my receipt," floated out above my down-bent head, her voice still all prim and proper. Just correcting my old gruff *Yeah*. It startled me.

I looked up into the brown eyes of the redheaded salesclerk—not green like mine, but entrancing nonetheless—and saw she was laughing at me.

So I mimicked her proper intonation, "Yes, thank you. I'd like my receipt." We both laughed, and I said, "I am trainable, you see."

"Maybe we can explore that sometime," she offered.

"Maybe we can," I said, and we left it at that. For right then, anyway. The store's location as well as the salesclerk's name acid-etched on my brain—just so you know.

When Penny opened Victoria's secret package, she glared at me, said, "You shagged Binty Brynn, didn't you?" and threw the panties in my face.

I said, "Huh?" Muffled, though, by the mouthful of panties.

"Translation, Reno. You fucked the whore. That Yank enough for you?" Her chestnut hair would have snarled too, if it could have. What the hell?

"No, Penny; no, I didn't." My hands wadded the panties into a black knot.

"I don't believe you any more than you believe yourself, Reno." My chest tightened. I hate proving negatives.

"But Penny, I didn't." Pretty lame, right? I knew it, yet I said it without hesitation. Big mistake.

"Do not say hello if you see me. Do not ask how I am doing. And do not, really do not, hope to be with me anytime soon. I shall be busy. In other words, Mr. Reno, bugger off."

That I understood. No translation needed.

At the door I turned, felt my head tilt, my lips about to say, *Are you sure?* But nothing came out. The door opened; the door shut. I was outside.

I stumbled down her steps, walked away from her condo, then turned and started back. Stavros's jab in his casino office—way back at the start of this fiasco—had fired in my brain.

Stavros had said, "Tell Penelope I asked about her, hope to see her soon."

I'd sure as hell wondered at the time what that greasy Greek was getting at. Maybe now was the time to ask her. Throw a metaphoric punch of my own her way.

"The hell with it," I heard someone say. Probably was me. Maybe all the women I know really are witches. I didn't go back.

The black lace panties ended up in the first trash can I passed. Wadded up with other discarded dreams. Well, at least that ought to make the little hula girl happy.

You know how that island bimbo hates competition.

EPILOGUE

The yacht rode at anchor in the secluded cove, rocking gently in the lake swell. Granite cliffs rose sheer from the water, capped by pines and aspens, their greens dark against the late-summer sky. Out over the lake, an eagle cruised thermal currents, hunting the cold waters.

Down on the yacht—aft of the cabin—two men stood next to a padded platform on which lay a woman. All three were naked. The slimmer of the two men, the one with the crew cut, moved onto the platform and quickly entered the woman. The heavier man walked to the woman's head. She smiled, brushed chestnut hair from her eyes, reached out, and took him into her mouth. His black pompadour rocked in motion with her sucking.

The Pilot and Perry, just enjoying themselves.

In the trees up on the cliff, a shadow man clad in blue-green camo watched the action below—prone, his rifle nestled on a small log. While he waited for the two men to finish, he sighted his gun. First on the crew cut, then on the white streak in the fat man's hair.

The men and the woman climaxed together. The first shot took out the man with the crew cut, red mist painting the naked, long-legged woman in gore.

The second shot easier. The fat man froze as the first man died. Then the white streak in his hair disappeared along with the rest of his head. His fat body toppled and lay still on the deck of his yacht, the teak now double red-splattered and slick.

Much easier, the shadow man thought, than shooting Jayne in the park's woods—his payback for her stabbing the young woman he had sworn to protect.

And the chestnut-haired woman below was alive. Screaming, "Bloody hell." But alive. He hadn't wanted to hurt her, and he hadn't. Not physically. She'd probably remember today for a while, but she was alive. Iron Mac had wanted it that way.

The shadow man, slick bald once more, no ponytail swaying in lake breezes, kept his eyes fixed on the yacht. The woman was sitting up now, drying her tears, glancing around. Good, so very good.

This was the way she'd been told it would work out. And she'd agreed to it, hadn't she?

Up in the sky, the eagle soared, riding the thermals, ignoring the shots, then dived into cold water, snatched a fish, and headed back to the nest.

The shadow man saluted the eagle, and executed a butler-proper bow to the dead men and the live woman on the yacht below. Then, like the eagle departing above, Iron Mac's Dutch Uncle headed back to his own nest—far from Kipling and the miseries it engendered.

ACKNOWLEDGMENTS

Without editors writers would be at sea and drifting. At least I was. Thanks to Reid and Ed, retired English mavens, for helping me pare and focus the initial scribbling I called a novel. What great names for editors, right?

And once I thought I'd finished writing my novel, Christina and Amy were gentle and professional editors who showed me how much better I could make it. Thanks to the four of you. Any remaining blips are mine alone.

My beta readers hung with me through the years as I cast new and improved versions before their wondering eyes. "Why'd you change that?" "That's not right." "Why don't you...." I paid attention to all their comments. Thanks Barb, Denise, Christelle, and especially Becky.

I also owe thanks to a host of other readers who agreed to read the novel as it evolved. Thanks for tackling what I now know was still a work in progress.

Back when I first started on my writer's journey, I had David

Nunnally, my brother-in-law and friend since third grade, spurring me on. He read and loved everything I wrote. Thanks old friend, I wish you could have been here with your Kindle to enjoy this book along with the rest of us.

Finally and most importantly, I had the support and encouragement of my wife who made sure I had time to write. Plus she gave me cool T-shirts. One proclaimed me Author, another featured the little hula girl, and my favorite: an incredible shirt sporting the first pages of the book you just finished. As Harry would say, Thanks, babe!

ABOUT THE AUTHOR

LEIGH ERBE was a criminal court prosecutor for eleven years. Since leaving the prosecutor's office, Leigh has represented children and families involved in child abuse and neglect cases. And now he writes.

Made in United States
Orlando, FL
06 June 2023

33866421R00238